Patdove:

PASSION'S SWEET ASSAULT

"You can't hire a crew. Don't you know what would happen?" Jack demanded. "What happens when that 'tough crew' of yours gets lonely for some female companionship and decides to take its pleasure with you?"

Gasping in shock that he would even suggest such a thing to a lady, Maggie retorted, "They wouldn't dare!"

"They wouldn't dare!" he mimicked. "That's your favorite expression, isn't it? Well, I'll tell you something, there are a lot of things in this world that men would dare, and this is one of them."

Maggie's breath and heart stopped as Jack's hands clasped her arms and hauled her up against him, and when his lips closed over hers, she thought for a moment that she might faint.

The feeling passed quickly, however, as his initial assault softened, and the mouth that had seemed so intent on punishing her began to move against hers with tormenting gentleness.

Maggie found that her own hands had crept up from their instinctive position of defense to grasp his lapels, and now were moving on to encircle his neck and bury themselves in that thick, dark hair. She could smell the smoke on his skin, taste it on his lips.

Maggie had ceased to think. Instead she had become a woman, a woman with no name, no past and no future— only a present that was fearfully dominated by the physical presence of one man. . . .

TEXAS VIXEN
Victoria Thompson

ZEBRA BOOKS
KENSINGTON PUBLISHING CORP.

ZEBRA BOOKS

are published by

Kensington Publishing Corp.
475 Park Avenue South
New York, NY 10016

First printing: May 1986

Printed in the United States of America

To my daughters, Lisa and Ellen, two very special Texans.

Chapter I

"I reckon she's here," the tall, blond man at the bar commented, sipping down the last of his beer.

His darker companion glanced out the open saloon doors at the stage that was rattling past on its way into town. "So it would appear," Jack Sinclair replied with a resigned sigh. He couldn't help but feel a little sorry for the poor girl, coming home to such a mess, but then, again, there was nothing he could do about it either. Some things just had to be. Jack lifted his eyebrows in silent inquiry at his friend. "Aren't you going to meet her?" he asked.

The blond man shrugged. "In a minute," he said. "Give 'em a chance to get stopped."

Jack nodded his head in understanding. The Swede felt even sorrier for the girl than Jack did, and he wasn't looking forward to meeting her or telling her what he would have to tell her.

Another minute passed, and the sounds from the street told them the stage had stopped and was unloading. "You'd better go," Jack prodded.

The Swede glanced up in some surprise. "Ain't you coming?"

Jack shook his head. "She's got enough problems without me. I'll come out to the ranch in a day or two to meet her."

The Swede's pale blue eyes narrowed. "Tomorrow?" he prompted.

Jack gave another sigh of resignation. "All right, tomorrow," he agreed. He wasn't looking forward to meeting the girl any more than Swede was. "Now get out there before she gets frightened."

Still the Swede did not move. "Ain't you even curious what she looks like?" he asked skeptically, knowing Jack's legendary interest in women.

Jack gave a delicate shudder. "I've seen enough ranchers' daughters. I can wait until tomorrow."

Swede shrugged again. "Suit yourself," he mumbled, trudging reluctantly out the door.

The stage had rattled into Bitterroot late on that spring afternoon, and before the dust had settled Maggie Colson was out the door and on the street, searching for a familiar face, someone who could tell her about her father. The town, she noticed irrelevantly, had changed little in the three years she had been away. She saw a new building here and there, but was struck with how much smaller the place seemed, how much grayer, as if the town had shrunk and faded under the relentless Texas sun. So intent was she on her impressions that she completely overlooked the tall, gangly man who had approached the stage.

"Miss Maggie?" he inquired after clearing his throat.

Maggie looked up into a homely face burned brick red by the sun and topped by a shock of straw-colored hair. It was the kind of face, she knew, that would never tan, no matter how many hours it spent in the sun, but would simply burn red, peel, and burn again. It seemed to be in the midst of that process now. Pale blue eyes full of sympathy and concern looked out of that face, and Maggie's heart contracted in response to the kindness she saw mirrored there. "Yes," she replied, her voice barely steady.

"I'm Swede Sorensen," the man said. "I'm your father's foreman, the one who sent the telegram."

Maggie vaguely recalled the unfamiliar name on the telegram. "My father, is he . . ." She hardly knew what to ask, fearing any answer he might give.

"He's just the same, can't move, can't talk," Swede told her, the kindness of his eyes echoing in his voice as he tried to soften the blow for her, "but he's still alive."

"Thank God," Maggie breathed, blinking back tears, almost weak with relief that her prayers had been answered. "Will you take me to him?"

Swede nodded, reminding Maggie that western men rarely wasted words, and he set about the task of collecting her luggage and loading it onto a wagon he had brought from the ranch.

The two spoke little on the ride out, Maggie lost in her thoughts and Swede respecting her silence. Maggie had been away almost three years, she reminded herself as they rode, three long, lonely years during which she had yearned for the sight of the wide blue sky stretched over the rolling prairies, a hawk circling lazily into an incredibly silent afternoon, a herd of cattle grazing peacefully on a hillside.

Of course, she hadn't wanted to leave in the first place, had argued and cried and pouted and begged, but her father had been adamant. Cal Colson's daughter would have the same advantages that her mother had had, and that had been that.

Margarite Colson, Maggie's mother, had been a cultured, beautiful woman when Cal had plucked her from her Georgia home and dragged her to the plains of Texas. Had he known that doing so would cause her death, had he suspected that so fragile a flower could never survive life on the rugged frontier, perhaps he would not have married her, perhaps he would have resisted the temptationt to make her his own, but perhaps not. In any case, he had done it, and he was too selfish to want to trade the few years they had had

9

together for a memory of the woman he had loved living out her years with someone else. No, he had never regretted his choice. Few men were lucky enough even to know a woman like Margarite, and she had been his, completely his, for however brief a time.

And then there was Maggie, the fruit of their great love. Little Margarite, with her mother's laughing hazel eyes and dancing auburn curls, to brighten his days and to recall the good times whenever he entertained regrets. Little Maggie, who would grow up to be a lady, a fine lady like her mother, if Cal Colson had anything to say about it, and so, when she had turned fifteen, he had shipped her off to her mother's people back in Georgia.

Of course, Uncle Edward and Aunt Judith had not particularly wanted her, especially Aunt Judith. Judith could not be bothered with the countrified offspring of a sister-in-law she had never met, so she, in turn, had shipped Maggie off to Miss Finley's School for Young Ladies in Atlanta, assuring Cal that it was just the place for Maggie to learn the social graces. That had turned out for the best, in any case, since Maggie detested the holidays at her uncle's house and the rather marked attentions paid her by her Cousin Gregory.

Maggie had hated it all at first, even the school, hated the lessons and the constraints and the rules and the enforced manners, but gradually she had grown used to it, almost forgetting what it was like to ride across the Texas plains, stretched out across a half-wild mustang pony with the wind lashing at her face. Almost forgotten, but not quite, so that when the telegram had come, that horrible piece of paper telling her that her father had had a stroke and needed her, she had been on the next train west, all thoughts of parties and beaus and social graces wiped completely from her mind.

In the days that followed, Maggie had slept little, first on the seemingly endless train ride, and then on the jolting stagecoach, worrying about her father, trying to imagine the huge, strong man she remembered weak and ill, and praying that he would, at least, still be alive when she arrived.

Suddenly remembering the man who rode beside her, Maggie began to wonder what had happened to the man who had been her father's foreman for as long as she could remember. "Whatever happened to Deke Perkins?" she asked, grateful for a topic that would take her mind off her father.

The blond man cleared his throat in what she was coming to realize was a characteristic gesture. "He . . . he was getting on in years. The job got to be too much for him and he retired."

Maggie tried to judge how old Deke would have been. He had always seemed quite old to her, but then, she had been little more than a child herself. She started to ask her companion for more details, but one look at his set jaw reminded her that he wasn't much of a talker. Getting information from him would be like pulling teeth, and right now she did not feel up to the effort, so she let the matter rest. Only later would she recall her curiosity about the matter and wonder what on earth it was that had gotten to be "too much" for Deke Perkins.

It might have seemed to Maggie that the town of Bitterroot had shrunk, but still it was no closer to the Colson ranch, and it took the better part of two hours for the silent foreman and his anxious passenger to reach their destination. The ranch, like the town, had changed little. The well-kept outbuildings still sat at precise right angles forming a miniature plaza in the center of the vast, otherwise empty valley, although, sitting there in the waning afternoon sun, they, too, seemed somehow smaller, all except for the house. No, Maggie decided as the wagon pulled up by the front steps, the house had not changed a bit. It still looked massive, perched as it was on a small hill overlooking the length of the valley, its gray fieldstone winking back the sun's rays, just as she remembered.

Swede helped her down, and she allowed herself a moment to take it all in, the vastness of the valley, the solidity of the house, and then slowly, almost reverently, she mounted the stairs to the porch and crossed to the huge front door. The screen door creaked in protest when she pulled it open and stepped inside the cavernous front room. Facing her was the eight-foot-high fireplace that she remembered so well, made of the same fieldstone as the house, fieldstones that Maggie knew for a fact her father had dug out piece by piece, by hand, in order to get just the right stones. Ten feet over her head hung the enormous center beam of the house, darkened now with age and years of smoky fires, but still as firm and strong and secure as the day her father had placed it there. All around her the adobe walls stood, pale and firm and unmovable, welcoming her into the cool depths of the place in which she had been created. She was home.

Behind her Maggie heard the clump of booted feet and she knew that Swede was coming in with her bags. She also knew that he would take her to her father now, and suddenly the one thing that she had been traveling for days to do seemed like the last thing in the world she wanted to do, as if by refusing to see her father she could somehow negate what had happened to him.

"Miss Maggie?" he asked tentatively, as if sensing her reluctance.

Once again Maggie raised her eyes to the massive center beam. Some things, she reflected, never change. Long after Daddy was gone, the things he had built would stand. And she must stand, too, as strong as the man who had made her, a monument to his strength. Drawing courage from that thought, she squared her shoulders. "Where is he, Mr. Sorensen?" she asked, her voice firm.

Swede nodded, as if giving his approval to her resolution. "It's just 'Swede,' ma'am. No 'mister.'" He motioned to the long corridor that led to the only two bedrooms in the house, hers and her father's.

Taking one last deep breath for courage, Maggie forced her feet to carry her across the front room and into the hallway and at last to the familiar door that stood slightly ajar in anticipation of her arrival.

The room was dim, windows shuttered against the setting sun, and for a moment she could not see clearly. Blinking, she tried to focus as she approached the huge four-poster bed that dominated the room. "Daddy?" she whispered uncertainly to the shrunken figure who lay there. Slowly, the almost transparent eyelids lifted to reveal the dark brown eyes that belonged to her father. They gazed at her steadily for a long moment, recognition gradually dawning in them, and then they filled with tears. Maggie's tears mingled with them as she took one withered hand in both of hers and pressed it to her cheek. "Oh, Daddy," she cried, wondering how this could have happened to a man so vigorous, so alive as her father had been.

It had happened, she came to understand as she thought back, still cradling that fragile hand in her own, over a period of time. She now remembered letters that had come further and further apart and had said less and less, until finally, no letters had come at all. How long had it been? Maggie had been too caught up in her frivolous pursuits to even remember, but now she realized that her father had been sick for a long time, a very long time to look now so frail and ghostly. Why had no one told her? Why had no one sent for her?

Without asking the question aloud, she knew the answer, knowing her father. He would have forbidden it, would have refused to cut short her education, to drag her away from the pleasures he imagined she enjoyed in Atlanta. He would have believed her letters, her glowing reports of how much fun she was having, and would never have dreamed that she could possibly miss the rolling plains or the vast emptiness or the endless canopy of blue Texas sky. Only now, now that her father was helpless to protest, could Swede have sent for her.

"What does the doctor say?" she asked Swede later when her father had finally drifted off to sleep, the tears still wet on his cheeks.

The silent foreman had led her back through the now dark house to the dining room where a cold meal had been laid out for her in solitary splendor on the gigantic table. "Not much," he told her apologetically as he watched her pick at the food in front of her. "Don't expect he'll get much better, and don't know how he's lasted this long. Maybe now you're here, he'll . . ." Swede let his voice trail off, and Maggie did not even try to guess if the sentence should have ended with "get better" or "die."

While pretending to eat, Maggie studied her father's new foreman. For the first time she considered how odd it was that her father had chosen a perfect stranger to replace Deke when he had a dozen men right here who were qualified and who had worked at the ranch for years. Yet, studying him now, remembering his gentle concern for her, she judged that Swede Sorensen had certain qualities that made him different from other men, qualities her father must have recognized, and suddenly Maggie was glad to have this particular man to lean on. He would be her friend, and she would need his strength in the days ahead.

That night, in her own bed, in her own room, which some thoughtful male had readied for her, Maggie tried to think, to plan for what must be done. She had a ranch to run now, and whether or not her father survived this illness, she would be the one in charge for a long time to come. Swede was evidently a good manager, if the condition of the ranch buildings was any indication, but some things only an owner could decide, and now she was that owner. She knew she should make some decisions right away, but her weary body betrayed her, and instead she slipped into the healing sleep of total exhaustion.

Most of the men had already left the ranch for the day's work when Maggie finally made her way to breakfast, but a small, wiry cowboy of indeterminate age greeted her and introduced himself as Wiley.

"I been taking care of Mr. Colson since he got sick, miss," he told her, "and I do the cooking, too."

Maggie smiled her appreciation. "Well, now that I'm home, you won't have to look after my father anymore. It must have been quite a burden for you."

"Oh, no, ma'am. I didn't mind at all. Mr. Colson's not much trouble. He just mostly sleeps or lays there staring at the ceiling. . . ." Wiley let his voice trail off, sensing from Maggie's strained expression that this was not good news.

"Yes, well, I really appreciate all you've done," she managed to say.

"You hungry, miss?" Wiley asked hopefully, to change the subject.

She was and gratefully accepted the meal he set before her. After sampling it, however, Maggie could only hope that his care of her father had been better than his cooking. She distracted herself by wondering about the fact that another new man had been added to the ranch staff.

When she had eaten, Wiley instructed her in the few things she needed to know to take over his sickroom duties, and Maggie spent the next hour feeding her father an astonishingly small amount of food and telling him humorous tales about her years at school while trying to ignore the way his eyes devoured her and the almost desperate expression hidden in their brown depths.

When at last he dropped off to sleep, Maggie went back to her room, and carefully closing the door so that no one would hear, she threw herself on her bed and wept, sobbing out her grief at losing the man who had once been her father. He was so frail, so helpless now that it fairly broke her heart to look at him, to see that hungry look in his eyes and know how much he had missed her, how much he had needed her,

15

and to remember how long she had been away. If only she had been home, perhaps he would not have gotten sick at all. At least he would not have gotten so bad. She would have seen to that, would have insisted he see a doctor, take care of himself, rest more, or whatever it took to prevent something like this from happening. Devastated by her grief and guilt, Maggie cried until her tears were gone, her body drained of all emotion, and then the truth she had recognized last night came back to her.

Sitting up, she scrubbed the tears from her face with the back of her hand, recalling her resolution of the night before. Her father's illness was a horrible thing, to be sure, but some things were more important than her private grief or even her father's life. She still had the ranch and all it stood for, the thing her father had worked so hard to build, his legacy to her. It required someone strong, not a sobbing, grief-stricken child to run it, and run it she would. She was Cal Colson's daughter, was she not? No longer the carefree girl she had been just days ago, she was now a woman with responsibilities, and she would not let self-pity hamper her again. She had grieved, and now she would fight. If she could not heal her father, she would at least make his remaining days as comfortable and as pleasant as she could, and she would preserve all that had belonged to him and never, never would he, or anyone else, see her cry.

Splashing water on her face from the pitcher in her room, Maggie reached for a towel that she suddenly noticed wasn't exactly clean. Looking around more closely than she had the previous night, she saw a layer of dust on the furniture and the floors and a rather large cobweb hanging in one corner of the ceiling. Curious now, she went back through the house, down the hall from her room to the huge living room. Everything was neat and just as it should be but, closer examination showed that the whole house was in need of a thorough cleaning. Seizing on this task as something to take her mind off her father, Maggie hurried back to her room and rummaged in the trunk she still had not had time to unpack for a certain faded gingham dress, the one thing she owned that housework would not harm. Finding it at last, she cast one long, regretful look at the lovely gowns still folded so neatly, and carefully closed the trunk lid. Someday, perhaps, she would have a chance to wear them again, but she had no use for such things now, she decided, quickly stripping off the stylish frock she had chosen that morning and slipping into the much older one. The fit was a little snug across the bosom, she noticed with a smile of satisfaction, but it would suit her purpose admirably. Tying a rag around her head to protect her hair and another at her waist to serve as an apron, she set out for the kitchen where she found all the cleaning supplies she would need.

Several hours later, after only a brief pause for feeding her father his noon meal and grabbing a quick meal herself, Maggie was putting the finishing touches on the front room when she heard a horse clatter up into the ranch yard. Assuming it was one of the ranch hands, she lovingly gave one last buff with her lemon-scented cloth to the gleaming oak gun rack her father had carved and then glanced out the front window with only mild curiosity. What she saw froze her in her tracks.

Never would Maggie have guessed that a man on horseback could present such a picture of elegance, but she could think of no other word to describe the scene before her. The horse alone was magnificent. A glorious black stallion at least sixteen hands high, with white stockings and a white blaze on his proud face, trotted briskly past the window. Obviously, the beast had a mind and will of its own and would as quickly have disposed of any weak-spirited rider as he would have shaken off a pesky fly, but the man who rode him today would have permitted no such nonsense. He sat the saddle tall and straight with an air of authority that was unmistakable. Maggie had known riding men all her life, men who spent more hours of their life on

17

horseback than off, and she could see that this man was born to the saddle.

Still, he did not ride like a working man, but rather like a man who rides for the love of it, or who rides to survey all that is his. Yes, that was it, Maggie decided. He rode in as if he owned the place. Smiling at the thought, she was startled a bit to see Swede come out of the bunkhouse to greet the visitor. She had thought Swede would be out working with the rest of the men, and it seemed odd that he was here, and without her knowing it, but before she could solve that riddle, the sight of the stranger dismounting diverted her thoughts. In one fluid motion, he left the saddle, deftly catching the stallion's halter to prevent the beast from lashing back with his teeth in protest at having been mastered.

Too far away to actually hear, Maggie imagined from the way the rider threw back his head that he laughed triumphantly at the stallion's attempted rebellion. Swede was coming forward now, carefully avoiding the horse to shake hands with the rider. The man was tall, as tall as Swede, which was very tall indeed, and far heavier. Of course, Swede was almost skinny. The stranger was a fine figure of a man, broad-shouldered, narrow-hipped, and long-legged, as a fine rider should be. He was wearing a black dress suit that fit him too well to have come ready-made, and a snowy white shirt with a black string tie at the neck. Someone very capable did his laundry, Maggie decided. A black Stetson shaded his face so she could not make out his features, but she could see a clean-shaven chin and a very rakish black mustache.

The two men conversed for a moment, and Maggie saw Swede gesture toward the house. When the stranger's gaze followed the direction indicated, Maggie jumped guiltily back from the window lest they see her spying, but from her new vantage point she was still able to observe the stranger turning his stallion over to Swede and moving toward the front door. Her stomach did a sickening flip as she realized the man was coming right toward her. He was probably some friend of her father's, come to visit him. And her!

Instinctively, her hand went to smooth her hair and encountered the rag she had earlier tied around her head. With a groan, she tore it off and blindly began to make what repairs she could without benefit of brush or mirror. And her dress! Why had she chosen today to wear the ugliest dress she owned, one that didn't even fit? she demanded of herself as she nervously fingered the front buttons to make sure she was still decent.

She should really go change, clean herself up a bit, but she could already hear him coming up the front steps, and if she ran back to her room there would be no one to answer the door, and he would call Swede who would come looking for her, and then she would have to explain . . . oh, it was such a muddle! If only she had known! Well, face it, she told herself sternly, if you had known there was a man like that within a hundred miles, you would have burned this dress. Smiling at that thought, Maggie stepped to the door to greet her visitor.

He had paused before the screen door to remove his Stetson before knocking, and Maggie had an opportunity to observe him, knowing that the combination of the screen door's being between them and the fact that he had just come onto the shaded porch from the bright sunlit yard made her all but invisible to him. He was even better looking than she could have wished, somehow even taller and more imposing up close than he had been at a distance. The carefully combed hair on his head matched his mustache and was as black as an Indian's, as were the eyes that were squinting in an attempt to make her out through the wire mesh.

"Miss Colson?" he asked, and Maggie's heart skittered in her chest at the warm resonance in his voice.

"Yes," Maggie answered, trying not to sound as breathless as she felt.

19

"How do you do? I'm Jack Sinclair. We're . . . ah . . . neighbors, in a way, and I thought I'd come over to welcome you home," he said. He had a southern accent, but not the harsh Texas drawl or even the lazy Georgia slur she was used to. The sound was soothing, as if the edges had been worn off all his words to make them easier on the ear. "And to offer my services, should you need anything at this difficult time," he added. The raffish mustache lifted at the ends as his mouth formed a beguiling smile that almost made Maggie forget to breathe. Fortunately, it did not make her forget her manners.

"Pleased to meet you, Mr. Sinclair," she said, smiling back, although judging from the way he was tipping his head from one side to the other, he still could not quite make her out. "Won't you come in?" She pushed open the door far enough for one very well-kept hand to grasp it and then stepped back, ostensibly to allow him to enter, but as he did, she found herself moving back farther than was strictly necessary, as if to make room for his presence, which seemed to fill the enormous room in a way his physical body only attempted to.

He was still squinting, and Maggie knew his eyes had not yet adjusted to the dim interior light, so she allowed herself to study him in these last few seconds. He was older than she had at first thought, she realized with a slight pang. Close to thirty, if she was any judge, and suddenly she felt very young and gauche. His hair definitely was as black as an Indian's, deep, shiny black, like a raven's wing, but that face betrayed no mixed blood. Quite the contrary, his features were actually aristocratic, a broad, high forehead, smooth, sculptured cheeks and jaw, and a rather patrician nose, or at least it would have been except for a slight bump that gave proof of its having once been broken. Then there were those eyes, as black as night, so dark she could not even see the pupils, and framed by lashes and brows as dark and thick as his raven's wing hair.

By now Maggie had become aware that she was staring, quite rudely, and she might have been embarrassed had she not suddenly realized that Jack Sinclair was staring right back, and not trying to hide the fact at all. In fact, his dark eyes had grown quite round, and the fine, firm lips under that very attractive mustache had opened into a rather large O when his sculpted jaw had dropped. He was staring, all right, and did not seem to be so much pleased as astounded by what he saw. With dismay, Maggie remembered her shabby appearance, and she nervously ran her fingers down her buttons once more and then reached to smooth the front of her skirt, only to encounter the rag-apron she had forgotten to remove. With a small disgruntled cry, she jerked it free of its knot and hastily laid it on the table beside her where she had earlier discarded her head cloth.

"You must excuse my appearance," she told him, as coolly as she could manage. "I was housecleaning, you see, and I wasn't expecting company, and . . ." Her voice trailed off as he continued to stare, not so much condemingly as something else Maggie could not name. He almost seemed shocked, although why her shabby dress should have shocked him, she could not imagine. It wasn't that bad, and she had been cleaning house, after all. "May I take your hat?" she asked after a moment of strained silence in which he continued to regard her with that same stunned expression.

"What? Oh, yes, of course," he replied at last, seeming to pull himself back to conversation with an effort and handing her the large Stetson.

It had taken quite an effort for Jack to pull himself back. If he had had to choose a word to describe his reaction to Miss Maggie Colson, it would have been "thunderstruck." Never in his thirty-one years had he been so surprised. Oh, he had expected a young girl. He had been hearing about Maggie Colson for over a year now, ever since he had come to Bitterroot. He knew she was eighteen, that she had been to finishing school in Atlanta, that people around here thought a lot of her, but never in his wildest dreams had he expected her to look like this. How on God's green earth had ugly old Cal Colson sired such a beauty?

Well, strictly speaking, she was not a beauty, he mentally corrected himself, although all the raw material was there. Those auburn curls that she had tried so hard to tame into a sedate bun, but which even now were engaged in a winning battle to be free, those eyes that had been brownish when he had first looked at them but which, by the time she had taken his hat, had turned a striking shade of green, and that figure . . . Jack almost sighed aloud as he watched the way Maggie's skirts swayed around those gently rounded hips as she walked to the coat rack by the door, and the way those pert young breasts lifted when she reached to put his hat on a peg.

The dress was unfortunate, he had to agree, but it was delightfully tight in just the right places. The only thing that kept her from true beauty, he decided when she turned back to face him, was that chin. That tiny, pointed, determined chin. She had gotten that from her old man, and the rest must have come from her mother, a woman old Colson must have had to bind and gag to get her to allow him near her.

Not that it made any difference what she looked like, Jack reminded himself. He still had a job to do, and Maggie Colson's being pretty didn't change a thing. But why couldn't she have been like all the other ranchers' daughters he had met, with their brown faces and red hands and big hips and yellow teeth? It would have made everything so simple. The thought made Jack frown.

Maggie had thought that if he was still staring with such a shocked look on his face when she turned back around that she would burst into tears or something equally humiliating, but when she did turn around, he was scowling at her instead. Fortunately, that made her a little angry, and that made her a little calmer. "Won't you sit down?" she asked,

22

eternally grateful for the little social niceties that made awkward moments like this bearable.

Jack's expression lightened at the invitation. So far he had behaved like a complete boor. What must she think of him? He had better mend his fences and fast. "Thank you," he said as he took one of the large chairs by the fireplace, which some creative soul had fashioned entirely out of Texas Longhorns. Leaning back, he surveyed the room with approval. "I have always liked this room, but I can see that it has always lacked a woman's touch . . . until now." Jack punctuated his last words with a warm smile and a meaningful look at Maggie who had perched on the chair opposite him, an exact duplicate of the one in which he sat.

Looking around for herself, Maggie privately wondered what he had found to admire in the decidedly masculine room. True, the dimensions suited him, as they had her father when he had been in his prime, and the great fireplace was impressive in its own way. A bearskin rug stretched across the floor between them, and several round braided rugs left over from her mother's reign were scattered here and there to cover large sections of the smooth plank floor. Maybe he liked the bright Indian blankets that adorned several walls or the fine, Italian-made settee that looked so out of place among the horned chairs and the homemade cabinets. Or maybe he was just making conversation.

Before Maggie could decide, he added, "I've always admired this house, too. It's built to last." Allowing his gaze to roam the room and rest on the huge beam over their heads, he murmured thoughtfully, "It will be here long after you and I are gone."

Maggie watched in amazement as he surveyed the room once more, recognizing the unmistakable sincerity of his words. Equally amazing was the way his thoughts matched her own. She felt something warm and new uncurling inside of her, a feeling she had never experienced, a feeling of kinship.

23

Jack let his gaze come back to rest on her face, intending to make some inconsequential remark, but her eyes had turned another color now, still green but paler, and while he was trying to name it, another awkward silence fell.

Maggie folded her hands primly in her lap and straightened her back, conscious that he was staring again. Frantically, she tried to think of something to say. What would Miss Finley tell her to say? The weather seemed too trivial even to consider. Oh, yes, it was coming back to her now. Discuss something of mutual interest. What had he said about their being neighbors? "Did you say we were neighbors, Mr. Sinclair?" she asked, unspeakably grateful, for the first time in her life, for Miss Finley.

"Neighbors? Oh, yes, neighbors. I guess we are," he replied absently, still studying those greenish eyes.

"Exactly where do you live, Mr. Sinclair?" Maggie asked a little irritably. If she were going to all the trouble of making conversation, the least he could do was help.

Now those eyes were decidedly green, and he realized with a small sense of triumph that they turned green, really green, when she was irritated, as she was with him right now, and for good cause. He really had to get ahold of himself. He leaned back against the smooth cowhide and crossed his right ankle over his left knee. "I live at the old Simpson place," he told her helpfully.

Maggie could not help but notice that instead of cowboy boots he wore riding boots, hand-tooled riding boots of shiny black leather that bore only the lightest film of dust, probably acquired on the ride over. He had polished his boots before coming to call. Extraordinary behavior in a country where a man polished his boots only for a wedding, and only if the wedding happened to be his own. Had he said the old Simpson place? Maggie visualized the small cabin the Simpsons had occupied and tried to picture Jack Sinclair, a man who polished his boots and wore tailor-made suits, living there. It was difficult. "The Simpson place? But where do the Simpsons live now?" No one had told her they had moved.

Jack made a vague gesture with one large hand, a hand that had done very little physical labor, Maggie noticed. "Somewhere else, I suppose. They weren't doing too well here and had decided to move on. I was fortunate enough to be able to buy them out."

Maggie frowned thoughtfully. The Simpsons had never ever done well, never in the eighteen years she had known them. They had squatted on a small corner of the valley, land her father had thought too worthless to claim, and had set up what Cal Colson contemptuously called a "three-cow operation." It was common knowledge that they lived off Colson strays, as did the half-dozen other small ranchers who had settled on the edges of Colson's valley.

Jack saw the frown and decided he had better tell her the rest, before she found out from someone else, although why it should matter how she found out, he could not imagine. "I bought out several of your other neighbors, too. I guess it was a bad year, and Simpson gave them all the idea to move on," he told her casually.

"Who all left?" she asked, growing more amazed by the minute.

"Peters, Gaines, Hollings, Wilkins, and Snider," he said, naming every other rancher in the valley.

Maggie's eyes grew wide. Something had happened, that much she knew, to drive those people away, something that had nothing to do with hard times or bad years or any other simple explanation. Could Jack Sinclair have been the driving force? Seeing him now, sitting so casually in her parlor, looking for all the world like a perfect gentleman, she found it hard to believe he had had anything to do with it. Perhaps he had just come along and taken the opportunity to pick up some land cheap. Not that the land he had acquired was worth anything at any price, not with Cal Colson controlling the best grazing land and all the dependable water.

"How is your father doing?" he asked. He could see the

25

way her thoughts were running, and for some obscure reason he wanted to stop them.

Mention of her father had the desired effect of wiping all other thoughts from her mind. "He's about the same, at least that is what Swede tells me." Jack saw the way her hands twisted in her lap, betraying her concern, and he almost felt guilty for reminding her of her troubles. "Would you like to see him?" she asked perfunctorily.

Later Maggie would recall his curious reaction to that question. Jack shifted uneasily in his chair and smiled his most charming smile, although it never quite reached those black eyes. "I doubt that a visit from me would cheer Cal up any. Besides, I came to visit with you, so let's not bother him. He needs his rest."

Now Maggie really did not know what to say, and so she sat, watching him watching her for what seemed a long time. Those deep, dark eyes were studying her, trying to read her thoughts. She was sure of that, but could not imagine any reason why he would want to read her thoughts, or what good it would do him if he could. She had never seen a white man with eyes that dark. Or hair that dark, either, for that matter. It was curly, too, or at least it would be if he let it grow a little longer. Already it had a tendency to wave around his ears and across his forehead. She wondered if it felt as soft as it looked.

"My great-grandmother was a gypsy," he said, breaking the thoughtful silence.

Maggie blinked in surprise. What an outrageous thing to say. "What did you say?" she asked to cover her confusion.

He grinned knowingly. "I said, my great-grandmother was a gypsy. You were wondering about my coloring, weren't you?" he accused gently.

"Oh, no, I . . ." she began to protest, but seeing his very dark eyebrows lift skeptically, she corrected herself. "Yes, I was, I confess. You must think me very rude." In her best finishing-school manner, she gave him a repentant smile and shyly lowered her eyes, the color coming quite naturally to her cheeks. Hopefully, he thought her very beguiling.

He did, and he thought her remarkably clever, too. Where on earth had she learned that little trick, and did she know that when she was embarrassed her eyes turned almost brown? And how could anyone look so appealing with a smudge of dirt across her cheek?

"But since I'm being rude," she continued when it seemed he would not respond, "did you say she was a *gypsy?*" Her lowered eyes rose tentatively, eyelashes fluttering ever so slightly, a playful smile teasing the corners of her mouth. She had practiced all this in front of a mirror, but had never tried it on a living man. She only hoped she did not look like a fool.

Good, God! She's flirting with me, he realized with a slight shock. Flirting and doing a good job of it, too, if his increased heart rate was any indication. How long since he had indulged in such a harmless pastime? Too long, he decided, as he uncrossed his legs and leaned forward, resting his elbows on his knees.

"Yes, a gypsy," he explained, with enthusiasm engendered by her obvious interest. "You see, long ago, back in England, my great-grandfather fell in love with a gypsy girl. When she . . . ah . . . conceived their child," he prudently did not pause when he noticed her crimson blush, "he wanted to marry her, but his family would not hear of it. He was a gentleman, an eldest son and all that. No gypsy's child could inherit the Sinclairs' lands. So my great-grandfather married her anyway. The gypsies married them, I think. In any case, when his family found out, he was disinherited and disowned. Not that he cared by that time, I suppose. Since he was not suited to join the gypsy life any more than she was suited to become a lady, they came to the New World to seek their fortune. And found it here, too, I might add."

"What a romantic story," Maggie exclaimed before she could stop herself, lost for a moment in the dark glitter of his

27

eyes. "I mean, it's very interesting," she corrected, primly, lowering her gaze modestly and toying with the material of her skirt for a moment before looking back up with luminous eyes to assure him, "But you didn't have to explain anything, you know. It's really none of my business."

Did she have any idea what those eyes were doing to him? "I know; it really wasn't any of your business," he repeated with mock sternness in an attempt to bring another blush to her cheeks. He was successful. "I rarely do explain," he added.

Maggie considered his last remark. It held some secret meaning, she was certain, but what that might be, she had no idea, and it was too difficult to reason things out with those black eyes watching every move she made and every thought that went through her head. "Would you like a cup of coffee?" she asked suddenly. Miss Finley to the rescue again.

Jack sat up straight, running two long fingers over his mustache to hide a smile. Did she think she could get away that easily? "I would love a cup of coffee, but only if you allow me to go with you to the kitchen while you make it," he told her, a hint of challenge in his voice that said he suspected her of trying to get away from him and was daring her to try it.

Maggie thought this over for a moment. He could not possibly want to go to the kitchen. That meant that he must simply want to go with her, wherever she went. The thought was very flattering. And a little disconcerting. And probably not true, she chastised herself. He was probably just teasing her. He probably thought she was a child, and she would probably be wise to let him think that. No, not probably. She would certainly be wise to let him think that, but somehow the prospect displeased her. For reasons she did not care to examine, she wanted Jack Sinclair to think of her as a woman.

"Well, of course, if you want to," she told him, tilting her head beguilingly and flashing him her most dazzling smile, just in case he thought she was afraid of him. She rose and began to glide gracefully from the room. "Right this way," she threw back over her shoulder encouragingly when Jack failed to move. Miss Finley would be so proud!

Obediently, Jack rose to follow her, marveling at how she could be so blushingly coy one moment, so honestly disconcerted the next, and such a teasing little minx the next. As they went from the huge parlor into the equally huge dining room, Jack could not help but notice once again how gracefully she moved, and he began to imagine long, slender legs under that swaying skirt, and round, white buttocks that tapered into a tiny waist, and a smooth, slim back. It was a very interesting picture.

Maggie was painfully conscious that he was right behind her as she moved through the rooms. She kept trying to remember all that she had ever learned about the way a lady carries herself, and she tried to imagine she held a book on her head, and tried to keep her chin up and shoulders back, and tried not to swing her hips too much (or too little!), and almost forgot where she was going in the process.

Amazingly, they made it out the side door, across the covered dog-trot and into the kitchen without major incident. Maggie was only grateful that she had not fallen down or slammed a door in his face or otherwise made a fool of herself, and she saw with mingled gratitude and relief that Wiley had left a pot of coffee on the stove.

It would be strong enough to walk by itself by now, but that was the way every man she knew liked it, or at least every man she knew in Texas. There was no telling about Jack Sinclair, though. What if he liked his coffee weak and watered down, like her Uncle Edward and her Cousin Gregory? Not that it mattered. He would drink what she gave him. If he'd let her come to the kitchen alone, she might have made him a fresh pot. It would have kept her away from him that much longer. But now she was concerned with getting this job over with as soon as possible. It seemed impossible to keep her wits about her for dealing with Mr. Sinclair and making coffee at the same time.

The kitchen had suffered from the same casual standards of cleanliness as the rest of the house, and Maggie felt obliged to explain. "You'll have to excuse the room. I'm afraid I haven't made it out here to clean yet," she said as she cleared some dirty dishes from the kitchen table.

"This house has long needed a woman's touch," Jack commented blandly as he took a seat in one of the kitchen chairs. "How long have you been away?"

"Three years," Maggie told him, finding a dishrag with which to wipe the table. Jack sat back to observe the way her uncorseted figure jiggled as she scrubbed at the dried food on the table top. "How long have you been here?" she asked, straightening from her task.

It took Jack a moment to remember just how long he had been there. "A little over a year," he recalled. "They say that the gypsy blood comes out once in each generation. I am proof of that, it seems," he added.

"It's funny Daddy never mentioned you in any of his letters," she said, almost to herself. That was *very* funny. Of course, now that she thought of it, she had not received many letters in the last year. Perhaps by the time Jack had come, her father had been too ill to meet him or at least too ill to bother mentioning a total stranger to her in his letters. Shrugging off the puzzle, she asked, "Do you take sugar or cream in your coffee?"

Once again Jack's eyebrows lifted as he looked around the wreck of a kitchen. "Do you really think you'd find either sugar or cream around here?" he asked with mild amusement.

Maggie almost groaned at her stupidity. Miss Finley again. Asking someone about sugar and cream was something you did in the drawing room at Aunt Judith's

30

plantation house. On a western ranch the only sweetener was molasses, and the thought that someone might actually milk one of the thousands of cows roaming the vast plains just for a little cream was absurd. Maggie managed a sheepish grin. "I think I can safely offer you a cup, at least," she offered.

"Coffee in a cup would be just fine," he assured her with a mock solemnity that made her smile.

With slightly renewed confidence at his teasing, Maggie found a dry rag to use as a potholder and reached across to the back of the big cast iron stove to where Wiley had put the enameled coffee pot to keep its contents warm. The pot was more full than she expected when she tried to lift it, and maybe that caused the rag she was using to shift or maybe she had been a little careless. In any case, the tip of her right ring finger came in contact with the very warm handle of the pot. With a little cry of pain, Maggie released the pot, which fortunately did not spill, but landed with an alarming clatter on its broad bottom, the rag still wrapped around the handle. Instinctively, she put her injured finger in her mouth.

Jack was on his feet in an instant. "What happened?" he demanded, but seeing her finger stuck in her mouth like that, he figured it out for himself. "Is it bad?" he asked, more concerned than he would have believed possible.

Maggie shook her head, her finger still in her mouth, feeling like a little fool, and very much afraid that she might cry from the indignity of it all. She looked up into two black pools of concern and then she really did want to cry, because concern was the last emotion she wanted to read in those eyes. The thought was a little shocking, even more so when she realized how very close he was standing. He was so close that she could see, even though he had shaved, where each of those individual whiskers was trying to grow back, and she could quite clearly smell the Bay Rum he had used after his shave and the cigars he must smoke when not in the presence of a lady.

Looking down, Jack was very much aware of how tiny she

31

seemed, how fragile, and, with that finger between her lips, how very young. Too young for the likes of you, he told himself, but he must not have been listening.

"Let me see," he commanded gently, enclosing her delicate hand in his two much larger ones and pulling her finger free of its confinement. He watched, mesmerized, as the full pink lips parted every so slightly and the fingertip slipped out, wet and glistening with her essence. He could smell the sweetness of her breath mingled with the fragrance of lilacs and the unmistakable scent of woman. Trying valiantly to ignore the heady sensation, he turned her small white hand to view the damage, and saw one tiny red blotch on the end of one very dainty finger. He lifted it to his lips.

Maggie's heart had been beating a frantic tattoo against her ribs from the moment his hand had first touched hers, but when she saw him raise her hand and knew instantly what he intended, that traitorous heart had stopped beating altogether. When his lips, so warm and firm, touched the spot that now burned for an entirely new reason, her equally traitorous lungs released a sigh that sounded horribly close to a moan.

Mr. Sinclair made a funny growling sound deep in his throat, and tightening his grip, pressed his lips into her palm. She felt the faint brush of his mustache, the heat from his breath, the moist touch of his mouth, and instinctively her fingers curved to caress the smoothly shaven cheek. Closing her eyes, she savored the wonderous feeling of lethargy that swept over her, turning her bones to jelly and starting a strange new ache somewhere deep inside. Quite of their own accord, her lips moved, forming the one sweet word that had filled her very being. "Jack."

The sound of her own voice surprised her, shattering the languorous mood. Her eyes flew open, and she was shocked to see a virtual stranger kissing her hand in what she could only suppose to be a perfectly scandalous manner. She snatched her hand back, cradling it to her bosom with its

32

mate, as much to hold in the tingling sensation wrought by his kiss as to protect it, and tried to glare at the impertinent Mr. Sinclair.

Her effort fell sadly short, and instead Jack saw a very shocked and confused young woman whose large eyes had turned emerald green with the intensity of her emotions. Had she really breathed his name? Perhaps he had only imagined it, so overwhelmed had he been by her touch. It seemed impossible that he could have been aroused so quickly by so young and innocent a girl and by the mere touch of her hand. But he had, and he had wanted to kiss far more than her palm. He still did, he realized, as his gaze dropped to that sweet little mouth. Quickly he took a step backward, protecting himself from her very potent presence with a little space, and then twisted his mouth into a wry grin. "My mammy always used to put butter on burns, but I don't suppose you have any butter here, either," he said, his voice only slightly husky.

Still a little breathless from his possession of her hand, Maggie could only shake her head, not bothering to decide if yes or no were the correct answer to his nonquestion.

"Well," Jack said, with forced enthusiasm, "maybe lard would do the trick, hmmm?" Looking around, he found the lard can standing on the worktable nearby. "There it is," he added unnecessarily, since Maggie's gaze had followed his and she had already started moving toward it. Making a quick decision not to try to help her, Jack stood back, sliding his hands into his pockets in case he might be tempted.

Maggie was barely conscious of her actions as she rubbed her finger across the surface of the cool, smooth lard, and she hoped she had anointed the correct finger. Oddly, she no longer felt the burn at all, only the kisses, and she wondered quite irrelevantly why hand-kissing had gone out of style. Mr. Sinclair's brief touch had caused sensations she had never imagined even when other beaus had planted full-fledged busses on her mouth.

33

Aware that she had not spoken since her unfortunate outburst, Maggie forced a nervous little laugh. "I guess maybe you'd better pour the coffee," she suggested.

Jack frowned. Now that he had put a little distance between them, he was thinking more clearly, and he was thinking that he had better put even more distance between himself and Maggie Colson, at least until he had time to reassess the situation in light of the fact that he found her more than a little attractive. Damn! That certainly changed all his carefully made plans. It shouldn't have, he admitted, but it did, nevertheless.

Pulling a very fine gold watch out of his vest pocket, he opened it with a flick of his wrist and pretended to be astounded at the time. "I'm very much afraid I don't have time for coffee, after all. I just remembered an appointment in town, and I'm afraid I'm late already."

Struggling between disappointment that she was losing him before she had time to analyze her feelings toward him and relief at the prospect of being alone to do so, Maggie murmured a polite protest, something Miss Finley had taught her, no doubt, although she did not even bother to listen to what she was saying. He seemed in an all-fired hurry to leave, she noticed with irritation as she followed him back through the house to the main room, almost running in an attempt to keep up with him. He did not even wait for her to fetch his hat for him, but plucked it from the peg himself. For a moment she thought he might simply bolt out the door without even saying good-bye, but he apparently had second thoughts about that and pulled up short just before making his final escape.

Feeling more than a little foolish, Jack stopped at the screen door and turned to face his little tormentor. Of course, she could not know that she was tormenting him, and from the puzzled expression on her face, he realized she did not have any idea why he was making such a precipitous exit, or what a good thing it was for her and her virtue that he was. Taking a deep breath, he called up his reserves of practiced charm and turned on an impersonal but devastating smile. "Thank you very much for a very pleasant visit, Miss Maggie. It has been a pleasure meeting you."

Maggie frowned slightly. Was this the same man who had kissed her hand with such passion—yes, there was no other word for it—just a few moments ago? Surely, he could not have been as affected by it as she had been, or he could not look so cool right now. Valiantly trying to match his tone, she answered in her best finishing school manner. "Thank you for coming, sir. I will tell my father that you called."

Inexplicably, Jack scowled. "Yes, I suppose you'll have to, won't you?" he murmured to no one in particular, and then as if collecting himself, he added more heartily, "Good day, Miss Maggie," and was gone.

Maggie stood stupidly staring after him, watching as his easy gait took him to the barn where Swede, as if awaiting his arrival, instantly produced the stallion. The two men exchanged a few words, and then Jack swung lithely into the saddle and rode away, pausing just once, for only an instant, to cast one last look at the ranch house before disappearing in a cloud of dust. He was not, Maggie noted, even heading toward town. So much for his polite excuses.

The sound of booted feet broke her revery, and Swede's lanky form came bounding up the front steps. He stopped short when he saw her still standing at the door, and pulled off his hat. "Anything wrong, Miss Maggie?" he asked warily through the screen.

Realizing that she certainly did not want Swede to think so, she smiled reassuringly. "Of course not. I just had a very nice visit with Mr. Sinclair." Then, recalling how the two men had talked in the yard, she asked, "Do you know him well?"

Swede hesitated a moment, as if trying to decide what was best to answer, and then said carefully, "Pretty well, I . . ."

An ungodly groan interrupted him. Gasping in surprise,

Maggie spun around, seeking the source of the sound, and then it came again. Her father! Running, her heart pounding in apprehension, she raced to his room, Swede close on her heels. Seeking out the sick man in the room's dimness, she found her father lying just as she had left him, except that his useless hands were jerking restlessly on the bedclothes and his eyes were wide and wild. Thinking he must be in pain, Maggie grabbed the bottle of laudanum the doctor had left and swiftly mixed him a draught, but when she tried to force it to his mouth, he turned away, still making that horrible, frightening, groaning sound. Helplessly, she looked to Swede, who seemed unperturbed by the invalid's agonies.

Swede did not notice her look. Instead he was watching Colson, and the rancher turned his frantic gaze to the foreman. A silent message seemed to pass between them, a question that Swede answered aloud. "Yeah, he was here," he said.

Colson's restless thrashing ceased and the wildness died in his eyes, to be replaced by cold fury. Maggie watched the change, wide-eyed. Rarely had she seen that look in her father's eyes, and when she had, someone had suffered and suffered greatly. She looked to Swede for an explanation, but he was still watching her father, receiving another message. At last he looked at her. "Come into the other room, Miss Maggie. I got something to tell you."

Once again that hideous sound escaped her father's throat, an awful, guttural, primal moan, but this time she recognized it as a primitive form of communication. He was protesting.

Swede sighed resignedly. "All right, I'll tell her here. I just don't think you need to hear it. It'll just get you all worked up . . . all right, all right," he conceded when the thrashing threatened to start again, but for a minute he did not say anything, swallowing several times instead.

"What is it, Swede? What does he want me to know? Is it something about Mr. Sinclair?" Maggie asked anxiously, noticing the way her father's clawlike hands tightened at the mention of the name. Still, she was unable to understand her father's violent reaction to the man. He was a perfect gentleman . . . well, maybe not perfect, exactly, but close, much closer than most men out here came. It just did not make sense.

Swede took a deep breath and let it out with a sigh. "See, Miss Maggie, Jack Sinclair come to the valley about a year ago." That much Jack had told her himself. "About that time some of the smaller ranchers around here started pulling up stakes, heading out. Sinclair, he bought them out." Sinclair had told her that, too, and she remembered how she had wondered about it at the time. Seeing the suspicion in Maggie's eyes, he hastened to explain, "Didn't nobody ever accuse him of anything underhanded. Oh, there was some trouble, all right, but it started long before he got here. He probably just took advantage of the situation." Swede winced slightly as her father grunted his disagreement.

"Anyhow, he tried to convince Mr. Colson that there was room for more than one big ranch in this valley. One day, he come over and they had a row. Not a fistfight," he hurriedly explained, seeing Maggie's reaction, "just a good old-fashioned argument . . . and Mr. Colson, he . . . well, that was when he got took real bad, had a spell. Doc called it a stroke, and that's what put him in this bed." Swede let his narrow shoulders droop, obviously worn out from making such an uncharacteristically long speech, but Maggie did not notice.

Instead, all she could see was her father, as vigorous and healthy as she remembered him, being laid low by the likes of Jack Sinclair. Her small hands closed into fists as she recalled his reluctance to visit her father, his dismay over her statement that she would tell him of the visit. Of course, he had no wish to be remembered to Cal Colson, although she would imagine a man like Sinclair might get some perverse satisfaction out of tormenting an enemy that way. Why had he come at all, then? The answer was painfully obvious. He wanted to look her over, possibly get on her good side, knowing that her father could not speak, would probably never be able to tell her of Sinclair's treachery. He had wanted to charm her, knowing that her father could not live forever, and assuming that a green, young girl would easily fall in with his plans to divide up the valley.

Divide up the valley? Never! Never would she allow a square foot of it to fall into any but Colson hands. Not as long as there was breath in her body. She would preserve and protect the land that was her birthright. How could he ever have thought otherwise? He had not known her, of course. That would account for it. Never would he think that a mere girl could stand up against him, not when he had felled the mighty Colson. Well, she would show him she was a Colson, too. Kiss her hand, would he? She would make him rue the day he had laid a finger on her.

Looking down into her father's ruined face, she promised him quietly that she would protect their land and that Sinclair would never, ever get a particle of it. So intent was she on watching the rage in her father's eyes fade into a look of satisfied contentment and pride, that she failed to notice Swede's disturbed frown, nor would she have understood it if she had.

Later that night, when Maggie had settled into her bed and put out the light, she could not help but relive Jack Sinclair's visit in its entirety. She had behaved like a silly schoolgirl, no doubt about it. Nearly swooning when a man touched her hand! It had been like something out of a dime novel. No wonder Sinclair had thought he could trick her. He could not trick her now, however. She knew him for what he was, a man who had used threats and probably violence to drive off the small ranchers who had lived in the valley for years just so he could get a toehold here. Then he had tried the same tactics on her father. She smiled grimly at what would have happened to Sinclair if her father had not had a stroke. He had destroyed men for far less than trying to take over his valley.

Maggie was not so vain that she imagined herself capable of destroying Sinclair, but she could prevent him from destroying her. It was that simple. She was in the superior position. She had the Colson name, the Colson power behind her. She had Swede and her men, fighting men, if she knew anything about her father and his hiring practices. If Sinclair wanted a fight, she would give him one. Not that she suspected Sinclair of wanting to start a range war. He hardly seemed the type to soil his hands with anything so nasty. No, he was more the bully type, throwing his weight around to frighten those who were easily frightened, but a man who would back off when faced with a real fight. Obviously, he had not reckoned with the fact that every one of the Colsons were fighters.

On that thought, Maggie drifted off to sleep, to dreams of beating Jack Sinclair in some sort of wrestling match. She was winning, she knew she was, even though his hands were on her, all over her, touching places where he had no right to touch; but she was winning, she had him down, down until he kissed her hand, and then for some silly reason, she surrendered. For some equally silly reason, she did not mind at all.

Chapter II

The days that followed passed in a blur of caring for her father and cleaning the years of accumulated grime from the rooms of her beloved home. Usually she took her meals at odd hours or with her father in his room, but the first time she joined the men in the dining room, she was surprised to see not one familiar face around the huge table. Swede had introduced her to all of them with a degree of awkwardness excessive even for the awkward foreman, as if he felt a little guilty, or perhaps personally responsible, for the fact that she knew none of them.

They were a typical crew, Maggie judged, weatherbeaten and seasoned, as real rangemen should have been, but she could not help but notice that they all wore sidearms. She had wanted a fighting crew, she had to acknowledge, but seeing men who were supposedly going out to work cattle carrying an extra seven pounds or more of steel strapped to their hips seemed a little excessive. It was almost as if they were inviting trouble.

Later she confronted Swede for an explanation. "What happened to all the men my father used to have working here?" she demanded.

Swede's ears turned a fiery shade of red and he shifted uncomfortably. "They left, Miss Maggie, or else got killed," he told her unhelpfully.

"Killed!" Maggie gasped. "How did they get killed?" Cowboys occasionally got killed, she knew, in accidents or stampedes, but she could only remember one such incident in her lifetime on the ranch.

Again Swede shifted uneasily from one foot to the other. "I told you, there was some trouble here awhile back."

Maggie almost stamped her foot in frustration. What did she have to do to get an explanation from this man? "What kind of trouble?" she asked with exaggerated patience.

"Squatters."

Maggie frowned. Squatters? No one had mentioned anything about squatters to her, ever. It was something every cattleman dreaded, the poor sodbuster who came seeking free land and set up a homestead on open grazing land. Most cattlemen, like the Indians before them, did not believe in owning land. You owned cattle, the land was free. A man used all the land he could hold, and if he was the strongest, he held all the best. Cal Colson had always held the best. He had, she remembered, filed a claim on the land the house and ranch buildings stood on, so he owned it outright. The rest of the valley, with its knee-high grass and its clear, flowing streams was his only by the right of might, so legally, anyone could come in and file a claim, pay a small fee, and own it.

Legal or not, it was the worst thing that could happen to a cattleman, because the farmer invariably fenced in his water, cutting off the thirsty cattle from their only means of survival. Cows were such creatures of habit and were so stupid that they would stand at a fence and bawl until they died of thirst before they would go looking somewhere else for water. Then the farmer would plow up the grass, digging out the roots that had taken centuries to grow, and plant crops that were bound to fail because it never rained enough or else it rained too much all at once. When the crops died, the terrible Texas wind would carry off all the soil that the grass had held so tightly, and the ground would be good for nothing. The grass would never come back once that happened, and the land could never be used for cattle or farming or anything again.

"Squatters came to the valley?" Maggie asked, unable to believe it could have happened without her knowledge.

"Yes'm, about two years ago. That was before my time, but there was a fight. It was bad," Swede told her, finally volunteering some useful information.

"But Daddy drove them off?" Maggie said. That much was obvious. Otherwise, they would have still been here.

"Don't mean they won't be back," Swede warned. "Folks see that grass, they think anything'll grow here."

"Someone must have sent them," Maggie guessed. "I mean, farmers don't just pull up stakes and go someplace unless someone has convinced them it's better than where they are. Who was it, Swede?" Maggie thought she knew. In fact, she was certain. It was just the sort of thing a man like Jack Sinclair would do. He would be the middleman, buy up mortgages, foreclose after a few bad crops, and sell the land again, until he got tired of it or people got wise to him and he had to leave town in the dead of night, but with his fortune made.

"Don't know, miss. Never did figure it out. He kept pretty much in the background at the time," Swede said, not a sign that he might be lying to protect someone.

"It was Sinclair, wasn't it?" Maggie insisted.

Swede seemed genuinely surprised. "Oh, no, ma'am. He wasn't even here then."

Maggie nodded knowingly. "That figures. That's why no one ever pinned it on him. Now he's come along and laid claim to all he could easily get of the valley, driving out the weakest, until all he had left was my father."

Swede scowled. "You're wrong, Miss Maggie. Jack, he'd never do a thing like that. He's a cattleman, through and through. Hates nestors, same as you."

Maggie almost snorted in a very unladylike fashion at the

42

thought of Jack Sinclair as a cattleman. Those hands had never done a day's work of any kind. What right had he to call himself a cattleman just because he might own a few dozen cows? She did not remember until much later that Swede had called him "Jack," as if he knew him well.

"Tomorrow's Sunday," Swede said, apropos of nothing.

"Is it?" Maggie asked absently, her mind still on the evil Jack Sinclair.

"What I mean, the circuit rider's gonna be in town. I was wondering if you'd like to go to church." The town shared a minister with several others. so church services were only held every few weeks.

Maggie considered this. Going to church meant so much more than just worshipping God. It was a social event, the one time, except for weddings and funerals and other festivities, when people could get together for a visit, to see each other and gossip and exchange news. Maggie had not seen those people in three years. And she would not see many of them now, she reminded herself sternly, as she remembered how Sinclair had run off all of her nearest neighbors. But the people from town would be there, and those from the ranches to the south and west of town, those not in the valley, those not coveted by Jack Sinclair, at least not yet. "Yes, I'd like very much to go, but my father . . ."

"Wiley can look after him for the day," Swede said, and so it was settled.

Maggie could have driven the buggy herself that morning, but Swede insisted on doing it. He said it looked better, or at least that was what Maggie thought he mumbled as he helped her up to the buggy seat. Now that they were actually going, she had to agree. She probably would have felt a little foolish trying to drive while wearing her Sunday best.

It wasn't the best dress she owned, of course. Her wardrobe was full of clothes that were much too fancy or fragile for western life, but today she had chosen a gown of gold taffeta that hugged her neck and wrists modestly, while

43

still managing to reveal her womanly curves. Tiny pearl buttons marched down the bodice and disappeared into an elaborate drape that swooped into a fashionably large bustle. Maggie knew just how to move in a bustle, too, having spent hours and hours at Miss Finley's practicing that very thing. It was an art, Miss F. had said, to walk so that the bustle swayed gently without appearing to wag. A lady never attempted to appear provocative, of course, but it certainly didn't hurt to draw a little attention to what a nice figure one had. Even Miss Finley agreed with that.

The golden dress sang out crisply whenever Maggie moved, making her feel very elegant, and she was not ignorant of the fact that the glistening gold of the gown reflected the golden highlights in her auburn hair. Having added a perky little excuse for a bonnet that was not much more than a collection of feathers and ribbon set at a jaunty angle on her piled-up curls, she had expected a small reaction from the enigmatic Swede, since he was, after all, a man. Unfortunately, she got nothing except his muttered insistence on driving her to church.

Undaunted, Maggie determined to ignore him and enjoy the ride. She had not paid much attention to her surroundings the day she had arrived in Bitterroot, and so now she took advantage of her freedom by savoring the vast, open plains that spread around her. Her valley, she decided, was magnificent. The grass had just greened up for spring, and as soon as they had a good rain the bluebonnets would bloom, covering the earth with a sweet indigo carpet.

And the sky. Maggie tried to remember why she had never noticed the sky back East. Surely they had the same sky. It hung over all the earth, just like this, didn't it? No, she admitted. The sky did not hang just like this anywhere else in creation, stretching from kingdom come to kingdom come and arching up to glory. This morning not a cloud marred its radiance, and Maggie allowed its beauty to soak into her.

Too soon they were in Bitterroot itself, and once again

Maggie looked around at what was at once familiar and yet changed, recalling only that on her first day back she had thought the town smaller than she remembered.

Now she noticed as they drove down the main street that a few of the businesses had changed hands over the years, and that Mr. Alexander had added on to the Merchantile. At the end of the street someone named S.J. Kincaid had built an office, although the sign gave no hint as to what kind of business was done there. The schoolhouse looked very much the same as Maggie remembered it from the time she had gone there as a child. Miss Milligan, her former teacher, would be married by now, she guessed, and some other young person would have taken over teaching the school.

This morning the school was a church, if use could sanctify a building in that way, because it was the only building in town with enough seating for a large crowd, aside from the saloon. She was early, and she could see people mingling around in the schoolyard, clusters of gossipy women and smoking men and children racing in and out among their elders' legs in frantic pursuit.

Maggie was extremely conscious that almost all conversation ceased when her buggy pulled up to the gate, and she might have felt ill at ease at causing such a reaction had not the very same Miss Milligan she had just been thinking of called out her name and came rushing over just as Swede assisted her to the ground. The taller woman whisked her into a quick hug, welcoming her home with ecstatic utterances that Maggie could not understand, because by the time Miss Milligan had released her, the rest of the women in the yard had arrived to take their turn at joyously welcoming her home. How many people expressed their distress at her father's illness and their gladness at her return, Maggie lost count, but she now felt truly home, back among familiar faces, faces of those who cared for her.

Maggie was pulled into a group of women who all seemed to be talking at once and asking her questions that they did not give her time to answer. At some point Maggie obtained the information that Miss Milligan, who was just beginning to show a pregnancy, was now Mrs. James, having married one of the sons of the rancher by the same name who lived just south of town. She also learned of other marriages, a few deaths, and many births, and was introduced to the new circuit riding preacher, Reverend Graves, who promised to visit her father as soon as he could.

The clanging of the school bell interrupted the renewing of acquaintances, and those in the yard filed boisterously into the building. Maggie found herself seated in a front row between Miss Milligan, now Mrs. James, and Mr. James's younger brother, whom she remembered only too well from her school days. Reverend Graves gave her a formal welcome from the pulpit (or lectern, as it was during the week), and made her feel quite like a returning heroine. The service began with a familiar hymn, and so caught up was she in the treasured familiarity of the scene, she barely noticed the slight disturbance in the back when some latecomers were seated.

When the service was over, Maggie was again assailed, this time with invitations to Sunday dinner or to come for a visit on this day or that day. Maggie did not feel that she could promise any visits at all, and apologetically explained that she could not leave her father, but she asked her friends instead to visit her at the ranch.

During a momentary lull, Maggie allowed her eyes to scan the crowd of people still loitering in the schoolyard and, as if her eyes were a magnet drawn to steel, her gaze found a tall, masculine figure whose black head rose several inches above those of the men clustered about him. He was smiling, she could see, and shaking hands as if he were a politician running for office. Once he threw back his head and laughed as Maggie remembered seeing him do once before, at some remark someone made. Then, as if sensing her eyes upon him, he looked up suddenly and their gazes locked. He

46

smiled, an entirely new smile, different from the one he had for the men, a smile that sent Maggie's heart racing in her chest. It took a moment, but Maggie managed to remind herself that this man was her enemy, the man who had ruined her father, and she set her lips into a prim line and turned politely back to the matron who was telling her about a new grandchild, without giving him a sign of recognition.

He had known she was there, known it the moment he had entered the schoolhouse, even before he had seen her. It was only logical to assume that she would come to church, of course, but he had instantly sensed her presence, his eyes finding her auburn head and its ridiculous bonnet almost instinctively. In a way, he was glad that he had been late for church. It gave him time to get used to her presence. It would never do for her to suspect that he found the mere sight of her unsettling.

He had been a little surprised at that himself, as a matter of fact. He thought that he had straightened himself out on that score. If he found her attractive, there was no reason in the world why he should not indulge himself with her company. Well, maybe there were one or two reasons, but none she needed to know about. Seeing her socially should not upset his plans, and might, in fact, help them along. If she trusted him . . . but why had she turned her head just now as if she did not know him? Was she being coy? Jack smiled to himself. Maybe she was just nearsighted and hadn't recognized him. Well, he could get closer. That would be no hardship at all.

A few moments later Maggie was conscious of a small flurry behind her, a slight ripple of movement, a change in the focus of the crowd, and when the tiny hairs on the back of her neck stood to attention, she realized that Jack Sinclair had joined their little group. Without turning, she could picture how he would have approached the ladies, oozing charm and smiling winningly at the gullible females who seemed only too willing to be charmed and won. Simpering

47

giggles answered his deep-voiced compliments, and even before she could make out his exact words, she knew they were compliments. That was stock and trade for a shyster like Jack Sinclair. Thank heaven she was now immune to such tactics.

"Oh, Maggie, there's someone you must meet," Miss Milligan/Mrs. James was whispering in her ear. "He's the town's most eligible bachelor, you know, and I do mean eligible," she giggled. It was unseemly for a grown woman to giggle, Maggie decided. Steeling herself, Maggie turned obediently around, her face carefully expressionless.

Even so, she was unprepared for the impact seeing him again had on her senses. He seemed to have grown taller in the time since she had last seen him, and broader, and more handsome, too, she admitted reluctantly. Memory had been imperfect in that respect. He was dressed in a dark blue suit today, but it fit him just as well as the black one had, emphasizing his broad shoulders and lean waist almost indecently. The black one suited his character far better, though, Maggie thought acidly, black for Black Jack. Apparently, other women were just as susceptible to his charm as she had been at first, judging from the reception he was getting. And judging from the way he was watching her, he expected the same reception from her.

"Maggie, I'd like you to meet Jack Sinclair," Mrs. James was saying. "He's a newcomer, but he's made himself very welcome here, I can tell you." I'll just bet, Maggie thought. "Mr. Sinclair, Maggie Colson, Cal Colson's daughter," Mrs. James concluded.

Jack was removing his hat and sketching a small bow in her direction. "Miss Colson and I have met," he said pleasantly, his smile fading slightly as his black eyes searched her unresponsive face.

The whole thing was just perfect, Maggie thought. Could not have been more perfect if she had planned it, especially the witnesses. To cut him was one thing, but to cut him in public, well, that was a masterstroke. Cal Colson had always dealt in master strokes. Schooling her face to betray nothing, Maggie nodded slightly. "Yes, we've met," she agreed blandly. "In fact, you might even say I know Mr. Sinclair too well . . . or at least well enough to wonder that he dares to show his face in a church."

Mrs. James gave a slight gasp. "Maggie, whatever do you mean?" she asked weakly.

Maggie gave Sinclair the haughty look she had practiced so often in front of the mirror, delighted that his charming smile had slid into an ugly scowl. The crowd around them had fallen into deadly silence, hanging on her every word. "But I guess it is just Christian charity to allow him here. Jesus himself sought out the company of *thieves.*"

This time it seemed that everyone in the crowd gasped, but Maggie barely noticed. Her attention was on Sinclair's face, which had gone a dull red even as his mustache curved into a mocking grin. "Are you calling me a thief, Miss Colson?" he asked with surprising mildness, but Maggie was not fooled. He was furious. Strangely, that knowledge failed to frighten her, but rather made her bolder.

"If taking another man's land is still considered stealing in the state of Texas, then yes, I am, Mr. Sinclair. Of course, if you have not yet succeeded, then I suppose you are only guilty of coveting, but that's still one of the commandments, isn't it?" Maggie knew she should have left then, turned on her heel and flounced off. It was the perfect exit line, but something in Jack's expression held her there. He was still grinning that awful grin, but his eyes were glittering like glass, reflecting the anger she knew he held in check only with the greatest effort, but when he spoke, his voice was still mild and even faintly caressing.

"Oh, that," he said, nodding as if he only just now understood to what she was referring, and then he grinned for real, a wicked, taunting smirk. "I was afraid you were going to accuse me of stealing your heart."

This time it was Maggie who gasped as the crowd broke into a nervous chuckle. How dare he? How dare he tease her when she had just called him the scoundrel that he was to his face? Her cheeks flaming, she opened her mouth to reply to his preposterous remark, but finding her mind had gone blank in her fury, she snapped it shut again. Uttering an impotent huff, she finally did turn on her heel and flounce away.

Hastily searching the schoolyard, she spotted her foreman lingering outside the fence. "Swede," she called, her voice wavering slightly, "we'd best be going now." She saw the blond head nod and the lanky form separate from a cluster of cowboys and lope toward her.

Maggie was trembling from reaction when Swede handed her into the buggy, painfully aware of the sympathetic murmur that had arisen to comfort Sinclair for her unspeakable rudeness. They would condemn her for her actions, of that she was certain, especially considering Jack's surprising response to her accusations. The only thing she could hope for was that some would criticize her to her face so she could explain her motives. Apparently, not everyone knew just what Jack Sinclair was. It was time the people in Bitterroot learned just what kind of a viper they were harboring.

Behind her, standing exactly where she had left him, but with the taunting look gone from his face, was Jack Sinclair. In spite of his mild response to Maggie's stinging accusations, he was experiencing a tidal wave of rage that he was having quite a time controlling. As angry as he was, it would not do to let people know it. They would suspect, of course, that his pride would be injured by such an attack, but he had defused some of that suspicion with his teasing reply.

What he could never reveal was that that cheeky little spitfire had tweaked far more than his pride this Sunday morning. Jack was vaguely aware that someone was addressing him, apologizing for Maggie's behavior, excusing her on the grounds that she had been away or her father was sick or some such nonsense, and he was accepting it, mechanically nodding his head politely and assuring everyone that he understood completely—while all the time he did understand completely, but had no intention of excusing her.

Mentally he cursed the Colson foreman. It had to have been Swede. No one else had the guts to tell her what had happened, and Colson didn't have the ability, so it had to have been the Swede. He could have told her the *whole* story. If she had heard the whole story, she never would have acted like that. It was ironic how concerned he was now about what she thought of him. Originally, he had intended either to charm or bully Miss Colson into going along with him and it hadn't mattered much which technique he used, but that had been before he had met her.

Meeting her had changed everything. When he had discovered what a delectable little piece she was, he had decided to win her over. It hadn't been a snap decision. When he had fled her house after that first meeting, he had not even been certain that it would be wise to see her again, but some thought on the matter showed him how foolish it would be to deny himself the company of the only desirable woman in a hundred miles. She needed him, too. She might not know it, but she did—or at least she would, very soon. It was only right to put himself at her disposal, and Jack had admitted to himself quite honestly that he wouldn't mind a bit if she were very, very grateful to him. He had not had to make a decision that would be so favorable to her. He could have decided to use force to get his way, but he hadn't, and that was why her accusations today had stung far more than they would have had he chosen to scorn her feelings. Well, she would pay for this, he vowed, clenching his hands into fists as he excused himself from the ladies and made his way to his horse.

As if sensing his mood, the stallion tried to back off as he

51

approached, but Jack jerked the halter, forcing the beast's head down, and he meekly allowed the master to mount, knowing that he could avenge himself another day. Today the man was in too foul a mood.

Maggie, on the other hand, was feeling much better now that she was away from Jack's disturbing presence. Replaying the scene in her mind, she realized that even though Sinclair had turned the tables on her, she had still succeeded in humiliating him in front of his neighbors. It was a small victory, to be sure, compared to what he had done to her father, but it was a start. The battle lines would be drawn now, and the prospect of a fight made Maggie Colson's blood run faster in her veins. That he would retaliate she had no doubt, and she would have been disappointed if he had not, but women had weapons that men did not, and men were necessarily limited in what they might do to a woman. Of that much Maggie was certain. So involved was she in her own thoughts that she did not notice the puzzled looks Swede kept flashing her. At last he spoke.

"You have a problem with Mr. Sinclair?" he asked.

Maggie turned innocent eyes to her foreman. "Whatever makes you think that?" she asked guilelessly.

Swede scowled. He had a sister, and he'd seen that phony innocent look bfore. "Something about how he looked like he could chew nails when you walked away from him, I reckon." Swede fixed his pale blue eyes on her until she turned guiltily away.

But Maggie's guilty feelings lasted only a moment. "Did he really look like that?" she inquired after a moment, unable to keep the delight from her voice.

"Well," Swede drawled in disgust, "if he looked at me like that, I'd go for my gun. What'd you say?"

"I called him a thief, right to his face," she told him triumphantly, but at Swede's horrified look, she hastened to defend herself. "It's the truth! He did try to steal our land. Did you expect me to ignore that, to be polite to the man who put my father in that bed?" she demanded.

Swede squirmed a bit on the seat. "That ain't the strict truth, Miss Maggie," he began.

"Whose side are you on, Swede?" Maggie angrily inquired. "The way I remember it, a man owes loyalty to the brand he rides for. Have you forgotten that you still ride for the CMC?"

She could feel the anger emanating from the long body next to her, but Swede betrayed nothing. Only his red ears told her she had struck a nerve, and rightly so. He should not have had to be reminded where his loyalty lay. "I reckon I know who I ride for, ma'am," he said tightly.

"You may have to do more than remember, Swede," Maggie warned.

Swede's blond head swiveled in surprise. "You expecting a fight?"

Maggie smiled smugly. "I won't run from one if it comes to that. I won't let Jack Sinclair steal the CMC, no matter what I have to do to stop him."

Swede muttered something Maggie did not catch, but when she asked him, he simply grunted, "Nothing," and they finished the ride home in silence, Maggie planning how else she could put Jack Sinclair in his place, and Swede silently contemplating how to keep peace in the valley.

Maggie's life settled into a routine of caring for her father, and so it was several weeks before she realized that none of the people who had promised to visit her had come. She had been expecting Mrs. James to come the very next day, and had eagerly anticipated reviling Jack Sinclair to her, but she had not come, and neither had anyone else. Whenever she had a few moments to herself, Maggie wondered about it, but she rarely had a few moments to herself, and so she never managed to find a satisfactory explanation.

She met with Swede every morning to discuss the

workings of the ranch. To her relief, Swede treated has as if she had a right to know what was going on and at least pretended to consider her suggestions. He might very well have been one of those men who thought women didn't have good sense, but he seemed to respect her and was, at any rate, too polite to indicate in any way whether he valued her opinions or not.

She wondered idly why he had never married, although he was not really that old, probably no older than Sinclair, who wasn't married either and who was far better looking. Of course, a lot of men in the West did not marry simply because there weren't enough women to go around, and Swede wasn't the kind of man to attract women the way Sinclair did. She would be far better off with a steady man like Swede, or so she tried to convince herself, but she could not quite manage it. It seemed that every time Swede touched her, which he did occasionally and quite impersonally, she could not help but remember how it had felt when Sinclair had touched her. Try as she would, she could work up no excitement at the prospect of being kissed by Swede or any other man at the ranch, but instead found her dreams haunted by a tall, dark man whose lips burned like fire wherever they touched, and they touched the strangest places. It was very discouraging to a woman bent on revenge.

"It's the first of the month," Swede announced one morning when she had been home a little more than three weeks. The first of the month was payday for the ranch hands, and that would occasion a visit to town so the men could squander their hard-earned money in the saloon and maybe even pay a visit to one of the women who kept a house nearby. It was also the time to make a trip to town for supplies. In the old days, Maggie had always made the trip with her father, and she thought with yearning how much she would give to be able to go back to those carefree days. "You want to go to town?" he asked, interrupting her revery.

"My father . . ." she started to object, but once again

54

Swede told her that Wiley could take care of her father for one day, and so she allowed him to convince her to go.

The streets of Bitterroot were bustling with the most traffic they ever experienced. The staff of all the area ranches had come in for the monthly celebration, and boisterous cowboys rode pell mell down the street, whooping and shouting and oblivious to the dirty looks and curses thrown after them by the more sedate citizens, who rode in wagons or buggies.

Perched high on the seat of the spring wagon, Maggie could see it all, and the smile that curved her lips was half nostalgia and half present enjoyment. She did not even mind the dust which, raised by the churning of hundreds of hooves, coated everything and which she felt certain would soon obliterate the striking emerald green of the dress she had worn.

She had worn that particular dress for a special reason. It was a little formal for a visit to town, but it was the one thing she owned that she felt completely comfortable in, knowing that it fit to prefection without making her feel like she had been trussed like a Christmas turkey. It was difficult enough to wear her corsets with no one to help her tighten the laces. She had to tighten them herself before putting the cursed thing on, and then hold her breath while she latched the metal clasps that ran down the front of the thing. It was an uncertain process at best, and so she never bothered with it when she was at home. Going to town, however, demanded a certian measure of propriety, and only a young girl—or a trollop—appeared in public unfettered. Since Maggie had prided herself on being neither, she had chosen a dress that did not require unpleasantly tight lacing, but which still made her feel pretty enough to give her the confidence she needed for a possible confrontation with Jack Sinclair.

Maggie had given considerable thought to the matter, and she was positive that he would be in town today. It was too good an opportunity to miss, given his propensity for politicking. Yes, he would be there, with bells on, if she knew anything about Jack Sinclair, and she would be there, too. And never the twain shall meet, or something like that, she decided. They would have to meet, of course, but when they did, she would freeze him out with all the fury of a Texas Blue Norther. Just see if she didn't. Maggie allowed her eyes to scan the crowds of people assembled on the wooden sidewalks, feeling a certain growing excitement at the prospect.

Swede found a vacant spot in front of the Mercantile in which to park the wagon, and she told him to go enjoy himself while she attended to her shopping. He seemed a little reluctant to leave her alone, but she assured him that she did not want to follow her all over town when he could be having a good time, so he finally agreed to leave her after deciding on a time to meet her back at the wagon.

First Maggie went to the bank. She had looked over the ledger books that her father had kept with but little attention to accuracy, and she wanted to reassure herself that the ranch had sufficient working capital. Swede had been very vague on the matter on the few occasions when she had asked about it, and she could only assume that he knew as little as she did.

The banker was Judge Harris, her father's oldest friend. He had, she assumed, once actually been a judge, although he had never been involved with the law as long as she had known him. Maybe now that she was older she would question him about that sometime, she decided as she entered the bank. A pimply-faced young teller whom she did not know obviously recognized her and told her to go on in to Judge Harris's office.

The judge looked up absently when he heard her enter and then rose quickly, his wrinkled face folding into a pleased grin. He was not much taller than her own five feet, four inches, and was almost as round as he was tall. His face bore the marks of cares and concerns that Maggie could only

56

imagine, and his pewter-gray hair gave him an air of wisdom. He was, without doubt, the man to go to with a problem, as Maggie knew well. No self-respecting problem would dare defy his solution, and his air of confidence gave the impression that he knew it only too well.

"Maggie, my darlin', it's good to see you again," he told her with genuine pleasure, coming around his desk to take her hands in welcome. He had greeted her in the schoolyard the morning she had attended church, and only now did she realize how odd it was that he had not come out to the ranch to pay his respects to her and her father. He placed a fatherly kiss on her upturned cheek and seated her in one of the straightbacked chairs that faced his desk. Taking his own seat again, he studied her with pride. "You've grown into a lovely young woman, Maggie. Cal must be proud of you." His smile faded and the crinkled face grew solemn. "He'd tell you, if he could. I'm sure of that."

Maggie blinked back the tears that sprang to her eyes, lowering her gaze to where her hands clenched in her lap for a moment while she regained her composure. She would not cry. She would not. "Thank you, judge," she said at last with a brave smile.

A moment of awkward silence passed before the judge thought to ask, "What brings you to a dusty old bank on a beautiful day like this?"

Recovering completely at the mention of business, Maggie straightened her shoulders and replied, "I wanted to check on my account, judge. I can't seem to make heads or tails out of the the books at the ranch." Her expectant smile froze on her lips as the judge frowned and looked away and began to shuffle some papers across his desk. After a few moments, she prompted him. "Judge?"

"The news isn't good, Maggie," he warned, turning sympathetic eyes back to her. Very gently he told her what the balance of her account was.

Maggie gasped. "That can't be right!" The amount he

had named was not small, by any means, but still would barely cover the expenses of a large operation like the CMC for more than a few months. "Check the books!" she demanded. "I want to see it in writing."

The judge sighed wearily. "We can drag out the books if you like, honey, but that won't change the truth. Do you think I do so much business that I don't know every depositor's balance to the penny? I'm sorry to say that I don't." He shook his head sadly. "I'm sorry, Maggie."

"But what happened? What about last year's cattle drive?" The annual cattle drive would have brought in thousands of dollars, more than enough for expenses, more than enough to pay for an exclusive girl's school and the expensive clothes Aunt Judith had insisted that she needed.

"Your father didn't make a drive last year. He wasn't himself, you see, and he wouldn't do certain things. . . ." The judge's voice trailed off.

Maggie was angry now. "If he wasn't himself, then who was he? I'm tired of hearing half-truths about my father. If he didn't make a drive, there must have been a good reason for it. I don't care what anyone says, my father was never a fool!" It was a little too much for Maggie to accept. If her father had acted strangely, it was because something forced him to. Or someone. She had a pretty good idea who that someone was. "It was Jack Sinclair, wasn't it?" she asked suspiciously.

"Jack?" the judge asked, genuinely confused.

"Yes, Jack," she said, spitting his name as if it caused a vile taste in her mouth. "He did or said something to keep my father from making a drive. Maybe he threatened my father, maybe he planned to rustle the herd to bankrupt him, and Daddy found out. I don't know exactly what it was, but I know he was responsible."

The judge was frowning heavily. "Maggie, girl, you don't know what you're talking about. Jack did try to talk to your father, more than once, but the man just wouldn't listen to reason. You see, he wasn't well, hadn't been for a long time, and he started to mistrust people. There was some trouble with squatters. I guess you heard about that." She nodded stiffly. "After that, Cal just wouldn't do anything. He sat up there in that stone house and cursed out anyone who tried to talk to him, me and Jack and . . ."

"You and Jack," Maggie mimicked. "How cozy. What exactly did you and Jack try to convince him to do, sign the ranch over to Jack?"

The judge seemed startled at her suggestion. "Of course not, Maggie, we just . . ."

"And why haven't you been out to the ranch?" she demanded, her tone accusing. She was gratified to note the judge had the grace to blush.

"Your father ordered me off the place and told me never to come back," he admitted uncomfortably. "He wasn't himself, Maggie. . . ."

"So you said," she snapped, rising imperiously from her chair. "I would demand that you put my money in another bank, except for the fact that yours is the only bank in town, so that leaves me embarrassingly obligated to you."

"Maggie," he begged, rising also and extending a pudgy hand to her beseechingly.

"I suppose if worse comes to worst, you'll give me a mortgage on the ranch," she asked bitterly.

"Of course. . . ."

"I doubt that will be necessary, however," she continued. "We will make a drive this year and, of course, with me home now, there will be no more expenses for schools and such."

"Maggie, honey, listen. . . ."

"Thank you for your time, Judge Harris," she said with a small nod of her head, and she swept out in a flurry of emerald skirts.

Judge Harris, feeling suddenly very old indeed, slumped back into his chair and then fumbled in his bottom desk drawer for a small bottle. Pulling the cork, he raised it to his lips and uttered the word, "Women!" just before taking a good, stiff drink.

Maggie was a block away before she realized that she was almost running in her haste to get away. Forcing her steps into a sedate walk, she took several calming breaths, and then the pain hit her, the pain of betrayal. How could he? A man she had known since birth, a man she would have trusted with her life, the man her father had called friend for over twenty years?

Biting her lip, she managed to maintain a semblance of control until she was able to regain true control. Once she thought about it, things were really not that bad. Swede was planning a cattle drive, she knew. They were already rounding up cattle and branding the spring calves in preparation. The money in the bank would hold out until the proceeds from the sale came in, and if not, her credit would be good until then. If worse came to worst, as she had told Judge Harris, she could always mortgage the ranch, as much as it galled her even to consider it. Her father would never have considered it, she knew, but then her father had never been a woman in her position, either. Desperate situations called for desperate solutions. She was, however, far from desperate at the moment, she reminded herself, and giving her head a shake at being so silly as to let an old man's lies upset her, she turned her steps purposefully to the Merchantile.

Unknown to her, a pair of black eyes watched her progress with intense interest, and when she scooted across the busy street, just barely missing being run down by a passing freight wagon, Jack was off the sidewalk before he was even aware that he had moved. Cursing himself, and glancing around to see if anyone had noticed, he walked on across the street as if that had been his intent all along.

Green. She looked even better in green than she did in gold, he admitted. She had even looked good in that rag she

60

had been wearing that first day. She would, he confessed to himself, probably look good in a flour sack. Or in nothing at all. The thought brought a secret smile to his lips. He had imagined her that way more than once, and more often since the day she had scorned him in the schoolyard. He had also imagined all sorts of other things, ways that he might pay her back for what she had done. All of them concluded with a very submissive Maggie Colson in his arms, and he found that very disturbing. He knew, of course, that sex could be used as a weapon. He was a man of the world, after all, but he had never stooped to doing that himself, and had always rather looked down on those who did. Still, in a situation like this, the prospect held a certain degree of appeal, even if he knew he would never actually act out his fantasies. Maggie Colson needed a little humbling, all right, but unfortunately, he knew that time would take care of that, even without his help. Meanwhile, he would be patiently tolerant, just as the good people of Bitterroot expected him to be, and when the time was right, he would step in to rescue a very humble young lady. That would be his revenge. It would have to be.

Maggie paused a moment in the doorway of the enormous Merchantile building to allow her eyes to become accustomed to the light. After a few seconds she could see clearly, and she saw that Mr. and Mrs. Alexander were standing behind the front counter observing her cautiously. She gave them a friendly smile, which they did not return. What was wrong with them? They, too, had greeted her at church and had been friendly enough then. She walked boldly up to the front counter.

"Good morning," she greeted them, and they nodded an acknowledgement. Something was wrong, very wrong, she decided, and wondered with a sickening dread if her father had neglected to pay their bill or something. Pinning on a falsely cheerful smile, she said, "I've come to take care of my bill today, Mr. Alexander."

Alexander looked puzzled. "Your father usually paid it after the spring cattle drive, Miss Maggie," he told her. "It's not even due yet."

Well, at least that wasn't it, Maggie thought with relief. "Oh, how silly of me. I guess I've forgotten. I've been away too long, I suppose," she said with a small laugh.

Alexander smiled politely. "That's all right. Something I can get for you today?" he asked.

"The usual supplies," she told him, producing a list from her pocket that she and Swede had made up earlier. "I have a wagon out front," she added unnecessarily, since she knew Alexander would have seen them drive up. He nodded automatically, casting a practiced eye down the list. "I'll have these things loaded for you in a few minutes," he told her, and disappeared into the storeroom.

Mrs. Alexander still stood where she had when Maggie had first entered the store, and she still had not spoken. "You've enlarged the store," Maggie observed conversationally.

"Yes, last year," Mrs. Alexander agreed. "Look around if you like," she offered.

Gratefully, Maggie proceeded to do just that. Why were they treating her as if she were a stranger, and a slightly dangerous stranger at that? She had been born here, after all, had known these people all her life. It made no sense.

Forcing her wandering thoughts into order, Maggie began to notice that the quality of merchandise had improved in the years in which she had been away, and she began to look around in earnest. She really did not need any clothes, if sheer numbers counted for anything, but when she considered what her wardrobe consisted of, she really did need some things, she decided, fingering a yellow workshirt. It was a small size, and with a little altering it would fit fine. Over at the fabric table, she chose a heavy denim to use to make a riding skirt. She would have preferred to wear pants, as she had as a child, but she was no longer a child, she

62

reminded herself sternly, hoisting the bolt and carrying it to the counter.

A few minutes later she had chosen a pattern and told Mrs. Alexander how much material she would need. While the woman measured and cut, Maggie wandered over to where hats were displayed and chose a very pretty black hat of Spanish style, with a flat crown and a wide brim. If she were ever free to ride again, it was just what she would need. Silently, Mrs. Alexander wrapped her purchases and stacked them neatly. Mr. Alexander had been going back and forth from the storeroom carrying sacks of flour and beans and coffee and such and loading them in her wagon. He was just going past with another load when Mrs. Alexander spoke to Maggie. "We're getting a church," she mentioned casually. Maggie missed the suspicious look Mr. Alexander flashed his wife.

"Oh, that's very nice," Maggie said, with genuine pleasure. The town had long needed a church, but somehow it had never gotten built.

"We think so," Mrs. Alexander sniffed. "It's all due to one person that we're getting it, too."

The thought that one person had donated enough money to build the church was a little surprising. Westerners were a proud lot and would look on such a gesture as charity, at best, or as an attempt at self-aggrandizement, at the worst. No one would attend a church built by one man for his personal glory. "Someone donated the money?" Maggie asked skeptically.

"Even better than that," Mrs. Alexander told her. "He said he'd match whatever money was donated, dollar for dollar. That way, everybody could have a part, even though they knew he was giving the most. It got to be a challenge, like, to see how much folks could make him give."

Maggie could understand the glow of pride in the older woman's eyes. It was the kind of thing people would enjoy, and they could take pride in both the giving and the finished

63

building. "And who is this pillar of generosity?" Maggie asked, amused.

Mrs. Alexander's eyes glowed even brighter, this time with triumph. "Jack Sinclair," she announced, savoring Maggie's startled reaction. "He's done other good things, too, things he doesn't want talked about. If we had more men like him . . ."

But Maggie was no longer listening. She just bet he'd done things he didn't want people to talk about. Public opinion must be cheap, indeed, if it could be bought with a church building, or half a church building, in this case. No wonder the Alexanders had treated her so coldly. She had insulted their idol. Well, she could tell them a thing or two about Jack Sinclair. Not that they'd listen, of course. Apparently, he had them completely fooled, probably had the whole town fooled, for that matter.

That was it, Maggie realized with a start. That was why no one had come to see her. They were all angry with her on Sinclair's account. As ridiculous as it seemed, it must be true. They were willing to side with a man like that over a woman who was one of their own. It was an infuriating thought, and Maggie was infuriated. Picking up the stack of neatly wrapped packages, Maggie turned away in a huff. "Put this on my account, please," she called testily over her shoulder, aware that Mrs. Alexander had still been talking, praising Jack Sinclair to the skies, and that she had cut her off in midsentence.

She almost collided with Mr. Alexander, who had just returned from loading the wagon. "I'll get those packages for you, Miss Maggie," he offered, but Maggie swept past him without even hearing. At the doorway she almost collided with yet another man who was trying to enter at just that particular moment. Backing off a step with an impatient sigh, she waited for him to move, and when he did not, she glanced up over the top of her stack of packages to give him a piece of her mind. The sight of two amused black eyes stopped the rebuke trembling on her lips.

It had just been too much of a temptation. Jack had resisted it as long as he could, but then he had just had to follow Maggie into the store. He knew she would have no kind words for him, but weighed against the prospect of seeing those flashing green eyes again, that counted for nothing. She was a little hell-cat, all right, standing there ready to spit and hiss at him. A small smile tilted his mustache. "Good morning, Maggie," he drawled.

Maggie stiffened her spine against the tremors that threatened at hearing her name roll so easily from those lips. He was the most unsettling man, but she must not let him know it. Lifting her chin as she had been taught that a lady does to express disdain, she said, "Excuse me, sir," in her most chilling voice.

Vastly amused, Jack dipped his head and bowed himself backward out the door, urging Maggie past him with an exaggerated sweep of his hand. She was magnificent, he thought, as she rustled past him, her emerald hem brushing the toes of his boots, the scent of lilacs trailing her. So engrossed was he in noticing the tempting way she moved beneath her clothes that he was almost a second too late to prevent disaster.

Basking in her triumph, Maggie brushed by Sinclair, her nose in the air, her packages clutched tightly to her bosom. He would never guess how her heart was dancing in her chest or how her body had tingled from just one whiff of Bay Rum and cigars. Too late she realized that her concentration on appearances had been entirely too narrow and that she had neglected to watch for the steps. She knew instantly that she had missed them when her foot struck nothing but thin air. Instinctively, her arms flailed out to break the fall, releasing packages, which flew in all directions, but just as a startled cry escaped her lips, strong hands clasped her from behind and hauled her roughly back.

She knew one blessed instant of relief as she sagged weakly

65

against the long, hard body that supported her, but when the panic of the moment subsided, she became aware of the scent of Bay Rum and cigars and, dear God, the two firm hands that gripped her protectively. One was clutching her waist, but the other, oh, Lord, the other cupped her breast! With a gasp of outrage, she wrenched herself free, somehow managing not to fall off the raised wooden sidewalk again in the process.

Every nerve in her body tingled as she whirled to face him, and she had to fight the urge to cover the breast he had held with her own hand in order to put out the fire that burned there. She could feel her nipples puckered in response to the shock of his violation, and crimson scalded her cheeks in shame at her reaction. Fury warred with embarrassment in her beleaguered body, until she saw the faint glint of amusement in the dark eyes that flickered over her bodice; and then fury won. Maggie threw back her arm and swung with all her might, but the crack of flesh against flesh startled even her. As if watching someone else, she saw her own hand strike the handsome cheek and that noble head jerk sideways from the impact, and then she quickly drew her stinging palm to her bosom. Ever so slowly, his face turned back to her, black eyes reflecting shock and a growing anger.

"You . . . don't you ever touch me again!" Maggie hissed in a voice that trembled alarmingly. Now that she noticed, her whole body seemed to be trembling, though whether it was from her fall or her rescue, she took no time to decide.

Though the dark eyes glittered dangerously, the answering voice was as cool as always. "As you wish, Maggie. Next time I'll let you fall on your pretty face."

Maggie's muscles tensed and her palm itched to slap him again, but reading her thoughts in her expressive eyes, Jack warned, "Don't even think of it, Maggie. I can excuse you once, but never twice."

A shiver prickled up Maggie's back as she saw the menace reflected back to her from two black pools, and for a

66

moment she knew real fear of what this man might be capable of if pushed too far, but fear was an emotion she could never reveal to Jack Sinclair. "And don't call me 'Maggie,'" she said with a bravado she was far from feeling.

Jack blinked once in surprise, the anger draining out of him instantly as he saw that proud little chin tip up in defiance. Yes, she was magnificent, no doubt about it, a woman a man could enjoy completely. Amusement again quirked his mouth, and he delighted to note how irritation turned Maggie's eyes dark. "As you wish, Miss Colson," he said with exaggerated civility and a small tip of his hat.

"Miss Maggie! You all right?" Swede's voice interrupted their exchange, and Maggie marvelled that she felt as if she had been rescued a second time by her foreman's arrival.

Turning away from Sinclair's black gaze with an effort, Maggie found Swede standing at the foot of the steps she had so recently missed, his long arms akimbo and his red face even redder from having run the length of town from the saloon, where he had heard an eyewitness account of the incident even as it was occurring. By now every living person in Bitterroot would know that she had slapped Jack Sinclair. Swede only hoped he was in time to prevent a further disaster.

"Swede, will you pick up my parcels, please, and put them in the wagon. We're going home," Maggie said regally, and managed to sweep down the stairs this time with both dignity and poise, even though her knees were still dangerously weak and her heart was still beating itself to death against her ribs.

"Home? We just got here," Swede protested even as he bent to pick up the parcels. A visit to town usually meant an entire day spent seeing the sights.

"I said, we're going home. My business here is complete," she informed him frostily, and he knew better than to argue with her in that mood. She waited until he had put her purchases in the back of the wagon with the other things, and

67

let him assist her into the wagon seat. She was only too aware that Jack Sinclair still stood watching every move she made, and she did not wish to attempt the climb herself and risk another fall. She did not dare glance in his direction, so instead, she stared stonily ahead until Swede had lumbered into his seat and started the wagon on its way out of town.

They had gone several miles before she felt able to relax a little and let down her guard. Even then she could not relax completely for fear that reaction would set in and she would weep, as she felt very close to doing whenever she remembered her reaction to Jack's hands on her.

"What happened, Miss Maggie?" Swede asked when he noticed that she no longer looked quite so stiff and formal.

Maggie hated the flush that rose from her throat, but ignoring it, she said as casually as she could, "I almost fell and Mr. Sinclair caught me."

Swede grunted. "That why you hit him?" he asked skeptically.

She was hoping he wouldn't know about that part, but she guessed that that was too much to ask. Everyone would know by now, anyway. How could she explain that Sinclair had had his hand on her? "I'm afraid I was a little upset and didn't know what I was doing," she lied, and her flush grew more vivid as Swede grunted once again. Plainly, he did not believe her, but she knew he would not challenge her on it. He was too much of a gentleman.

No one else challenged her on it, either, and for the next few days Maggie worked herself to a frazzle taking care of her father and concocting treats that she thought might tempt his failing appetite and inventing projects to take up any spare moments that might occur. At no time did she allow herself a minute to reflect on the powerful effect Jack Sinclair had on her person. It was enough that she knew that she hated him. She reminded herself of that fact several times a day.

Sunday came around again, and Maggie knew that it was a church day, but she chose not to go, knowing that no one would miss her, and not wanting to give everyone another reason to disapprove of her when she snubbed Jack Sinclair, as she knew she must if she ever saw him again. The safest thing to do was not to see him, and so she dressed as if it were any other day and went in to wake her father for breakfast.

At first she did not notice anything amiss. She greeted him cheerfully as usual, noticing in passing on her way to open the shutters that his eyes were open. He was usually awake when she came in, so that was normal. What was not normal was when she turned back after adjusting the shutters to let in the morning sunshine and noticed that her father was still staring fixedly at the ceiling. He always watched her perform this little task, and thanked her with a grimace that passed for a smile.

"Daddy?" she said tentatively, still uncertain that anything was really wrong, and not wanting her imagination to get the best of her. Her voice shattered what she now realized was the unnatural stillness of the room. She froze, her breath suspended in her chest, while her eyes frantically searched the figure on the huge bed for any sign of movement.

For one brief second she thought she saw the bedclothes rise and fall along his chest, but then her intellect told her it was a trick of the eye, the sunlight playing along the coverlet, and she knew that all was still, would always now be still. "Daddy," she repeated, but this time with despair, knowing that the man she addressed, the man she remembered, could not hear.

This time she did not fight the tears that rose and stung her eyes, but welcomed them, letting them fall heedlessly down her cheeks as she moved quietly to the bed and laid one hand against his sunken cheek. The chill of death repulsed her, and her hand pulled back of its own accord while a sob choked her. This time she touched him more purposefully, knowing what to expect, letting his coldness convince her as nothing else could that he was truly gone. Sinking to her knees beside the bed, she buried her face in the bedclothes and sobbed out her grief in one last and final cleansing.

How long she wept she had no idea, but when she rose, her knees were stiff. As she had once before, she found cold water in a pitcher and splashed her face, drying it on the clean towels she had stacked there just the day before in preparation for bathing her father today. She would indeed bathe him today, but in preparation for his burial.

She went to the doorway and called, "Wiley," in a voice that cracked slightly the first time. He did not hear her, and she was forced to go and find him. It was later than she had thought, and the men were gathered around the table when she entered the dining room. She dreaded making an announcement to the assembled group like that; it seemed so formal and cold-blooded, but she found that she did not have to say a word. One look at her tear-ravaged face told the whole story. After a moment, Swede rose from his place. "He's gone," he said in his matter-of-fact way, and Maggie simply nodded.

The next few hours passed in a haze of numbness, merciful numbness for Maggie, but only after her argument with Swede. He had wanted to send for the preacher, to set up a big funeral, the kind of funeral a man who had held an important place in the community deserved, but she would not allow it.

"They wouldn't come to see him while he was alive, and they won't get a chance to gloat now that he's dead," she had decreed.

"Funerals ain't for the dead, they're for the living," Swede had insisted. "You need folks to help you grieve."

"They didn't come to see me, either, and I don't need them for anything. I can grieve alone," Maggie had told him.

"Ain't right, not having a preacher," Swede had mumbled, and Maggie had begun to explain to him that no preacher who could be bought with a church building from Jack Sinclair was going to speak over her father's grave, but somehow her words kept coming faster and faster and louder and louder until she was screaming and crying at the same time. She was never certain whether or not Swede had actually slapped her, but her face was unnaturally red afterward, although that might have been from the brandy he had forced her to drink. After that, he had not argued, but had ordered the men to make a coffin and dig a grave next to the one occupied by Maggie's mother, and had allowed Maggie to prepare the body for burial.

Dressed in his best suit and laid out in the pine box, Cal Colson looked like his own ghost, a pale shadow of the man he had been during all the years it had taken him to find and settle and hold his valley. Maggie could not help but reflect that while men had feared his strength, they had despised his weakness, deserting him when he could no longer threaten them. When the men lowered the box into the freshly cut earth, she knew what it was to be alone, totally alone, the last of her kind on earth. She was the only remaining Colson, and it was an honor she would not forget. She would make them all sorry for what they had done to her father, and they would know that the Colson name was still a power to be reckoned with.

So engrossed was she in her plans for vengeance that she barely heard the words Swede said over the grave, and when she finally came out of her trance, she was alone at the graveside. Swede was standing several dozen feet off, smoking idly on a hand-rolled cigarette, waiting and watching, in case he was needed, Maggie knew. He would be needed, too, although not in the way he supposed. She would need him to help her fight, and she was certain he was the man to have beside her. Squaring her shoulders, she began the long walk back to the house.

When she came abreast of Swede, he threw down his smoke and crushed it with his boot. "You ready, Miss Maggie?"

Maggie allowed herself a small smile, thinking of all that she had before her to do. "I'm ready," she replied.

Chapter III

"It's the first of the month."

Maggie glanced up from where she sat at her father's huge old desk in the room that had served as his office and gave her foreman a small smile of greeting. He had come to remind her that it was payday, something of which she did not need to be reminded, but it was comforting to know that Swede had things under control.

"I've got the payroll all ready," she told him, going over to the ancient safe and turning the combination lock. Why they bothered to lock it was anybody's guess, since dozens of people knew the combination, and a good swift kick would probably smash the rusty old thing into a million pieces, but tradition demanded that it be kept locked, and so it was. When the door creaked open, Maggie hefted out a bag of gold Eagles, which she had carefully counted the night before, and passed it to Swede. It was only then that she noticed the strange expression on the tall man's face. "Is something wrong, Swede?" she asked, feeling a small twinge of alarm.

Swede's ordinarily red face turned even redder under her concerned gaze, and his blue eyes darted around, looking everywhere except back at her while he cleared his throat and shifted the money bag from one hand to the other. The gentle clinking of the coins as they were jostled sounded unnaturally loud in the suddenly quite room as Maggie tried to tell herself that Swede's strained expression was probably due to an advanced case of piles and his awkwardness to an understandable reluctance to admit it.

Just as she was about to convince herself, Swede cleared his throat again and said, "Miss Maggie, it's the men. . . ." He cleared his throat yet again, and Maggie waited in agony to discover what it was that he was having so much difficulty telling her. "They . . . they're quitting." Swede swallowed loudly, and Maggie watched in fascination as his large adam's apple bobbed. It was a far easier activity than trying to make sense out of what he had just said.

When it became apparent that Maggie was going to have no reaction to his statement, he repeated it, more forcefully this time. "Miss Maggie, the men are quitting. All of them."

At last she forced her mind to accept his statement. Quitting? All of them? *All* of them? That was impossible. In the few days since her father had died, life at the ranch had been business as usual. No one had spoken to her unless it was absolutely necessary, and then they had spoken in hushed tones, as if afraid she might shatter at the sound of a loud noise. Even Swede had seemed reluctant to approach her, and Maggie had wondered if her loss had put her into some mystical form of isolation or created around her an aura that others, more lucky, were loath to penetrate. Whatever it was, she had accepted it as her due, and had literally worked out her grief by scrubbing out her father's room and packing away all his things.

She had felt tempted to leave the room exactly as it was, as a monument to her father, but she could imagine his reaction to such a maudlin sentiment. That image had been enough to motivate her to strip the room bare of any traces that he had ever lived there. In the meantime, Swede had given her no indication that anything might not be exactly right with the men.

"What do you mean, they all want to quit? Is something wrong? Has there been some trouble that you haven't told me about?" Maggie was genuinely puzzled. Ranch hands were a notoriously independent lot, prone to pulling up stakes at the slightest provocation, imagined or otherwise, but usually they acted out such impulses as the rugged individuals they were, not as a cohesive group.

"No, no trouble, not exactly," Swede told her, the coins still clinking in his restless hands.

"Then what exactly? Are they afraid they won't get paid? I'll pay them just fine. Give them a raise and tell them they'll get a bonus when the cattle are sold," Maggie ordered, her temper flaring at the attempted rebellion of her men. Who did they think they were dealing with? She was a Colson, and she would hold the ranch together, just as her father had before her.

"It ain't money, either. It's . . ." Swede paused and cleared his throat again. Maggie thought if he did that one more time she would cheerfully strangle him. "It's . . ." He looked away again, out the door, almost as if he wished he could leave. Maggie wished he could, too.

"It's what?" she snapped, impatiently stamping her small foot on the smooth boards beneath her feet.

"They don't want to work for a woman," Swede blurted, and his already crimson face flushed one shade darker still as he took a step backward in anticipation of her reaction.

That reaction was several seconds in coming, because Maggie could not quite believe her ears. "Don't want to work for a woman?" she repeated incredulously. Not that it was completely inconceivable. Maggie knew that few ranches were operated by women alone, and that few men felt comfortable taking orders from a female boss, but she was no ordinary female. She was Maggie Colson!

Maggie's mild question seemed to reassure Swede, and he ventured forward a little, although he was still being cautious. He knew enough about women not to trust one for

74

a minute. "Yes'm, now that your daddy's gone," he paused a second, shrugging one knobby shoulder in apology, "they don't like the idea of a woman running the place." His adam's apple bobbed once more. "It's a big job, running a spread like the CMC. Even a man would have a time of it."

"EVEN A MAN!" Maggie echoed shrilly. "I'll have you know I know more about ranching than most men alive, and certainly more about the CMC. I was born here, and my father taught me everything he knew. . . ."

"I know, I know," Swede assured her, moving backward again. He shifted the money bag into one bony hand and held the other up in front of himself protectively. "Don't get all riled up, Miss Maggie. It's just, some men you can't reason with, that's all."

Most men, Maggie corrected mentally, and crossed her arms across her middle in angry resignation. "All right, then, pay them off, every last ungrateful one of them." She turned with an indignant swish of her skirts and began to pace the room. "Hire some more men, as many as you can find. Spread the word that we're paying fighting wages. Lord knows we'll need fighting men what with Jack Sinclair on the prowl," she told him over her shoulder as she walked away from him.

"Miss Maggie?"

Something in Swede's voice stopped her dead in her tracks, and she turned slowly to face him, a small seed of dread sprouting in her heart. His face was red again, redder than she had ever seen it, and twisted in a sort of grimace that looked almost like pain. No, oh, no! her heart cried out, but she knew it was useless.

"I won't be able to do that, Miss Maggie," he said in a strangely hoarse whisper.

That was what she had dreaded, what she had feared, and hearing it made her want to cry, to beg him to stay, but Colsons did not behave that way. Instead she lifted the chin she had inherited from her father and tried very hard to look haughty. "You, too, Swede?" He actually winced under the accusations in her eyes, but he nodded, albeit reluctantly. "Whatever happened to the Texas I grew up in, where men protected women and orphans?" she demanded.

He was fairly squirming beneath her scorn, and instinctively, she plunged the dagger deeper. "Can't you bring yourself to work for a woman, either?" Hearing her own words, knowing that Swede had never given her any reason to think that he might have a problem with that, forced her to realize that that probably wasn't the reason the other men were quitting, either. "It's Sinclair, isn't it?" she asked suddenly, putting her new discovery into words.

Swede's face actually paled. "Sinclair?" he asked a little tentatively.

"Yes, Sinclair," she asserted, certain now that she had seen Swede's reaction. "You're afraid of him, aren't you? You're all afraid of him. Well, *I'm* not afraid of him. Maggie Colson is not afraid of any shifty land-grabber, any two-bit, fancy-pants thief! I'll fight him, you'll see, all of you! This is Colson land and it will stay Colson land, do you hear me?"

Swede figured just about everyone on the ranch could hear her, but he simply nodded and began to edge toward the door. "I'll pay off the men," he was saying, "I can stay a few days, if you want," he offered, but Maggie cut him off.

"Do you think I'd want you here?" she asked with perfect outrage. "Get off my land, all of you, right now. I never want to see any of you again. If I do, I'll blow your heads off for trespassing."

"Yes, ma'am," Swede replied agreeably, just before making good his escape. Maggie didn't hear his sigh of relief, but she noted with satisfaction the speed with which he crossed the yard to the bunkhouse. The other men were clustered on the bunkhouse porch, as if awaiting his report, a report he obviously gave quickly as he passed out the men's pay to them. In another few moments the men disappeared inside and then reemerged with their belongings tied in neat

76

bundles. They had, Maggie realized, already packed up their gear. They had only been waiting for Swede to break the news to her.

As they each roped out a horse from the corral, Maggie wondered idly if they had a legal right to take those horses or if she could have them hung as horse thieves. It was certainly something worth looking into, she decided, stepping out onto the porch to watch them ride away.

Head held high, feet planted firmly, her arms crossed defiantly, she stared at them accusingly as they rode by her on their way to the front gate. With the Texas wind whipping her skirts and teasing the loose tendrils of her hair about her face, she made an imposing figure, even if they could not see her eyes, which blazed green fire at them as they passed. Not one of them could resist the temptation to look up at her, but none could hold her gaze for more than a moment. It was a sorry procession that Swede followed, being the last to leave the ranch. He dismounted a moment to close the gate behind him, and when that task was completed he cast one last look at the figure standing forlornly before the great stone house. Instinctively, he raised one hand in a gesture of farewell, but that gesture was not returned, and he slowly remounted his horse and rode away.

Maggie forced herself to stand there until the last man was out of sight, and she valiantly fought the tears that threatened to destroy her righteous pose. She didn't need those men; she *didn't,* she kept telling herself. Tomorrow she would go to town and hire a new crew, a crew who would owe its loyalty to her and her alone.

When Swede's horse had become an indistinguishable blur on the horizon, Maggie forced her sluggish legs to carry her inside the house. Entering the office, which had its own private entrance from the porch, she looked around the room she had left just minutes earlier as if she had never seen it before.

What was wrong? What had changed? Feeling a sudden

unease, she hurried into the main room. Something was different here, too, and in the dining room, the kitchen, even her own room, when she finally found her way there. It took her a long time to figure out just what had changed, and when she did, the knowledge sent a shiver up her spine.

She was alone. Completely alone. Never, ever, not once in her life had she ever been completely alone. Oh, she had been alone in her room, here at the ranch, at her aunt and uncle's home, at school, but there had always been other people, many other people, just outside, just within the sound of her voice. A ranch was always teeming with people, Aunt Judith's home swarmed with servants, and Miss Finley's school, with lively schoolgirls. Never, in all the years she had lived here, had she ever known the CMC to be completely deserted, as it was now.

Maggie listened to the silence for a long time before she thought to be afraid. It was a silly thought, she tried to tell herself even as she went to the gun rack and took down a shotgun. Silly, yes, but it never hurt to be prepared, she decided as she checked the loads. The gun was dusty, but loaded and serviceable. She carried it with her when she went to the kitchen to prepare herself a cold supper, and she leaned it against her chair all evening while she tried to read. Overcoming the temptation to keep the thing beside her in bed, she compromised by laying it on the bedside table within easy reach if one of the many creaks and groans the old house made proved to be an intruder.

She had even tried to lock the doors, but found it a futile effort. The doors had no locks, had never had any, and until now, had had no need for any. She would, she decided as she tossed and turned on her feather mattress, get someone to come out from town and remedy that situation, just as soon as she had hired a new crew. Until then, she would stay at the hotel. It wouldn't take long. The town was always swarming with men looking for work.

Maggie tossed like that a long time, pausing only when she

78

heard a suspicious noise and waited to ascertain its origin. When she had determined it was nothing but the wind or the house groaning, she resumed her tossing, cursing Jack Sinclair as the cause of all her difficulties, and vowing revenge against the black devil who tormented her.

In the morning Maggie woke up, which was how she knew that she had, at long last, fallen asleep, although she would have sworn that she hadn't closed her eyes all night. In any event, she rose and dressed, choosing a black broadcloth skirt and matching jacket in deference to her mourning. She didn't put the jacket on, of course. She just laid it out to take with her when she went to town, and went around the house packing a few changes of clothes as well as her night things, wearing the skirt and a thin cotton shirtwaist. Since the outfit did not require a corset, she packed the dreadful thing along with the rest of her clothes in a carpet bag.

That done, she fixed herself a hearty breakfast and forced herself to eat it, knowing she would need her strength if she was to accomplish all that she had set for herself to do. She had just finished taking some money out of the safe to use on her journey when she heard the sound of hoofbeats in the yard.

Maggie chose to believe the fire that heated her blood at the sight of Jack Sinclair was pure, unadulterated anger. It had to be at least partly anger, she reasoned, because she was absolutely furious that he would dare to show his face here. Not that that should have surprised her. Jack Sinclair had already proven he dared practically anything. She had a notion to send him on his way with a load of buckshot, and then realized suddenly that she had left the shotgun lying on the table in her bedroom. Swiftly, she retrieved it, just in time to see Sinclair dismounting his stallion out by the corral and tying the animal to the corral fence.

He stood by the fence for a long time, looking around at the empty buildings. Taking inventory, no doubt, Maggie thought bitterly. Well, he had another think coming if he thought he'd ever get his hands on anything belonging to the Colsons.

After another long look around, Sinclair began the long walk up to the house. Hating herself for it, Maggie watched him, taking in every detail of the black suit he wore, the polished boots, the immaculate Stetson, the smooth grace with which his body moved at every step. As she had the first time she had seen him, she began to feel very young and gauche and not quite equal to the task of meeting him head on. It was not a way she wanted to feel, so she drew herself up and began to recall all that she had been taught about putting a man in his place. It was a simple matter of logistics, she decided, and not wanting to be caught at a disadvantage, she stepped out onto the porch to meet him, cradling the shotgun in her arms like some deadly metallic infant.

Sinclair broke stride only slightly at the sight of her, and then came on with a steady pace, his face expressionless but his eyes glittering wickedly. He stopped at the foot of the steps and raised both hands in mock surrender. "I assure you I am unarmed," he said, after a meaningful glance at the gun she carried.

Maggie could have sworn that she'd laced her corset too tight, except for the fact that she wasn't wearing it. Why did she always have such a hard time breathing when that man was around? Her heart seemed to be having a hard time, too, as it pounded out a warning tattoo against her ribs. Too much more of this and it might quit altogether, it was saying. Maggie told herself she was just apprehensive because they were all alone, and gave a well-bred sniff. "A rattlesnake doesn't carry a gun, either, but he's pretty dangerous all the same."

That perfectly shaped black mustache lifted on one end. "Are you afraid I'm going to bite you, Maggie?" he asked mockingly. "I have no intention of it, although the idea does have a certain appeal. . . ." he added, letting his dark eyes play over her in a way that made her face, and various other parts of her, burn.

"What do you want?" she ground out between tightly clenched teeth, and only when she saw one black brow rise suggestively did she realize she had once again said the wrong thing.

Sinclair, however, chose not to pursue it, but replied, "Business, Maggie. I came to discuss business." He had lowered his hands, and now his long fingers curled into fists, and Maggie watched his face turn cold, all traces of mockery gone. "May I come in?" he asked, with an inquiring tip of his head.

She didn't want to invite him in. It was bad enough to be as close to him as she was without going inside between four walls, but she guessed she had no choice. "Suit yourself," she invited ungraciously, and stepped aside as he came up the stairs. She carefully moved so as to block the door to the living room, and indicated with a small hand movement that he was to enter the office. At his questioning look, she replied, "You said it was business."

Sinclair gave her one of his sardonic smiles, pulled open the screen door, and gestured for her to precede him. Maggie bristled at his sarcastic courtesy, knowing he was only trying to bait her, and not wanting him behind her in any case. "After you, Sinclair," she said, shifting the shotgun to a more comfortable position and noting with pleasure the way those black eyes narrowed in irritation.

With an audible sigh, he passed through the door and allowed it to slam shut behind him so that Maggie had to juggle the shotgun awkwardly in order to get it open again. She was beginning to feel a little foolish holding the gun, but it did give her something to do with her hands. Resolutely, she clutched it to her as she marched into the room to face Sinclair.

He was standing in the middle of the room, his back to her. He had hung his Stetson on a peg by the door, and he had his hands thrust into his pants pockets, his annoyance radiating from every pore. He was a lot more than annoyed, too, if she had only known it. He was just admitting to himself that he had been a fool to come here alone like this. In the weeks since their last encounter, he had been nursing his anger against her, not allowing himself to remember exactly why she could make him quite so angry.

After the incident in town when she had slapped his face in full view of everyone, he had been unable to overlook the suspicious, sidelong glances or the whispered conversations that ceased abruptly when he approached. Everyone was wondering why her reaction to him had been so violent, and since no one dared to ask him to his face, God only knew what stories were circulating.

He did know that people had been noticeably cooler toward him, more cautious, as if they were certain he could not really be as dastardly as Maggie had said, but thought there might be a grain of truth in there somewhere. To a man who had always enjoyed complete respect and had even, although he would never admit it to himself, felt that a certain amount of deference was his due, such caution was galling. And how could he defend himself against an accusation that had really never been made? How did a man prove he was not evil? How did a man, a gentleman, at any rate, explain that a young lady reacted violently to him because of the tremendous sexual attraction she felt for him?

Jack had given the matter a great deal of thought and that was the conclusion he had reached. It was only natural, when you thought about it. She was an attractive girl, and he had felt that attraction immediately. It was only logical to assume she had felt it, too. He knew his own powers over women, knew that women thought him handsome, knew he had a certain kind of charm that women found irresistible. It was not immodest of him to assume that Maggie Colson had succumbed to that charm. The fact that she thought of him as her enemy had turned her reaction into something quite unnatural, though. What should have been . . . oh well.

It was also damned inconvenient for her to cause the whole town to question the uprightness of his character, especially when he had gone to such great lengths previously to establish the impeccability of that character. A Sinclair of the Virginia Sinclairs did not suffer such an insult lightly, and Jack Sinclair was taking this one very heavily, indeed.

Standing alone in the room with her now, he felt the full weight of it. He didn't even have to turn around to feel the full effect of her presence, to know exactly how she looked, exactly how that auburn hair curled around her face, exactly how that cotton waistshirt clung to her breasts. One look at her outside had been enough to refresh his memory on all the very appealing details, but one look at the shotgun had convinced him that even if she had the appeal of a Cleopatra, too much animosity lay between them for him ever to entertain any romantic thoughts. Not to mention the fact that if she once more called him a thief to his face, he would throttle her. That decided, he turned to face her, surprising a look of uncertainty on her face. That pleased him and made him feel decidedly more pleasant. "Mind if I sit down?" he asked politely.

Maggie nodded toward one of the worn stuffed chairs that sat beside the fireplace, deciding she wouldn't mind sitting down herself. She perched on the chair opposite his, still clutching the shotgun and wondering how she could gracefully put it down without being too obvious about it. In the next moment she stiffened in alarm, grateful for the protection the gun offered her, when she saw one of his hands disappear inside his coat.

Noting her reaction, Jack stiffened, too. Did she think he was going to shoot her down, for God's sake? he asked himself as he drew a cigar from an inside pocket and held it up for her inspection. "It's not loaded," he informed her, gratified to notice the roses blooming in her cheeks.

"I didn't think it was," she said tersely, propping the

shotgun against the wall, grateful for an excuse to rid herself of the weapon.

"Will it bother you if I smoke?" he asked, hoping against hope that she would give him permission. As a general rule, he never smoked when a lady was present, but in this case he felt a genuine need to have something to do with his hands.

"No, not at all. My father always . . ." Her voice trailed off. She had been about to say that her father always smoked a cigar after supper, and she enjoyed the smell, but that hardly seemed like an appropriate topic to discuss with her father's murderer. Lifting her chin, she amended herself. "Go right ahead. I don't mind," she told him coolly.

With nothing better to do, she watched his fingers fish a small golden penknife from his vest pocket, cut the end from the long cigar, and toss the stub into the empty fireplace. Then he placed the uncut end to his mouth, rolling it to moisten the tobacco against his lips, and Maggie found herself remembering how those lips had felt against her palm and wondering how they would feel against her own lips. Unconsciously, her lips parted, her tongue coming out to touch the top one, just where his mustache would touch if he . . . Maggie caught herself just in time before her imagination went completely wild. She had to keep in mind that this man was her enemy, that she hated him. Sobered by that thought, she quickly closed her mouth, praying that he hadn't noticed her betraying action.

He hadn't. Jack was more concerned with getting his cigar lighted before his hands started to shake. Why in the hell did she have to watch him so closely, anyway? he grumbled mentally as he dug in another vest pocket for a match. Finding one, he struck it unthinkingly on his thumbnail.

Maggie jumped as the match flared. It was a trick she had seen a thousand times, but one she had never imagined Jack Sinclair performing. He seemed much more the type to strike it on his shoe sole or on the stone hearth, she reflected as he touched the flame to the end of his cigar and puffed encouragingly. The rich, acrid scent of the tobacco wafted over to her, carrying with it memories of happier times, but memories, too, of the few times she had stood close enough to Jack Sinclair to notice that he smoked cigars. A small shiver shook her even as she fought the recollection. Conscious of a need to end her close observation of Jack Sinclair, she called up her reserves of ingrained etiquette and remembered why they were sitting here. "You said you had some business to discuss," she prompted.

Jack took a fortifying puff and nodded. "Business," he repeated around the cigar, and then removed it from his mouth. For a moment he toyed with it, studying the burning end rather more closely than was absolutely necessary, and then he continued, still not looking at her. "I've come to make you an offer on the ranch." Ignoring her outraged gasp, he went on. "I'm prepared to offer you ten dollars a head for the cattle. I know that's far less than you could get if you drove them north, but then you won't have the expense of a drive, and I'll be buying all the cattle, not just prime steers, so it probably averages out to what you'd realize from a drive."

Only then did he chance to look at her, and her expression was just as he would have imagined. She was furious, her eyes flashing green sparks, her lips pressed tightly together, her hands clenched into tiny fists. Even her nipples were angry, he noticed, as he watched the taut peaks strain against her shirt with every indignant breath. Forcing his attention back to the subject at hand, he went on, "I want the house, too, and the land it's sitting on. Without the ranch, it wouldn't be of much use to you. I'm prepared to offer you . . ." He named a price, which he had determined was eminently fair.

"How dare you!" Maggie demanded, surging to her feet. "My father isn't even cold in his grave yet, and here you are, like some great, black vulture, to pick the bones!"

Jack rose, too, holding his temper in check. She was upset,

of course. He had known she would be, had known she might say insulting things, had expected her to put up a fight. She was absolutely lovely when she was angry, too, and he was prepared to enjoy the sight, but he was not prepared to lose the argument. "Be reasonable, Maggie. You can't run this place alone. . . ."

"You knew I was alone, didn't you?" she accused. "You never would have come if my men were still here. You never would have taken a chance on getting your precious hide perforated. Well, don't worry, I won't be alone for long. I was just on my way to town to hire a new crew, and this one will be even tougher than the last one. This crew won't run out because they're scared of what little bit of trouble you might stir up." Maggie lifted her chin in triumph, crossing her arms over breasts that heaved with indignation and raising her coffee-colored eyebrows in a silent challenge. It was a pose she had struck quite instinctively, but with which she was quite pleased. He could plainly see how little she feared him, how disdainful she was of his aspirations to steal her ranch, except that he did not seem to be paying attention. Instead, he was frowning at her.

"Did you say you were going to town to hire a crew?" he asked, scowling down into eyes that were rapidly turning brown.

"Of course," she replied with perfect hauteur. "As you so wisely pointed out, I can't run this place alone."

"Well, you can't hire a crew, either, not you, especially not a 'tough' crew. Don't you know what could happen?" he demanded, trying to put his hands on his hips in exasperation, but finding it difficult since he still held the cigar. Flinging the cigar impatiently into the cold hearth, he turned back to her, only to discover that she obviously did not have any idea what could happen. She was still standing there like the personification of outrage, and he fought the urge to shake her. "What happens when that 'tough crew' of yours gets lonely for some female companionship and decides to take its pleasure with you?" he inquired.

Gasping in shock that he would even suggest such a thing to a lady, she retorted, "They wouldn't dare!"

"They wouldn't dare!" he mimicked. "That's your favorite expression, isn't it? Well, I'll tell you something, there are a lot of things in this world that men would dare, and this is one of them."

He hadn't intended to kiss her, hadn't even intended to touch her, but before either of them knew what had happened, he was doing both. Maggie's breath and heart both stopped as Jack's hands clasped her arms and hauled her up against him, and when his lips closed over hers, she thought for a moment that she might faint dead away.

The feeling passed quickly, however, as his initial assault softened, and the mouth that had seemed so intent on punishing her began to move against hers with tormenting gentleness. The mustache that she had thought about before teased against her with the silkiness of a fairy's touch, and the hands that had grabbed her with such bruising strength eased around her back and gathered her in with a relentless tenderness that she was powerless to resist.

Maggie found that her own hands had crept up from their instinctive position of defense to grasp his lapels, and now were moving on to encircle his neck and bury themselves in that thick, dark hair. She could smell the smoke on his skin, taste it on his lips, and when his tongue teased at the corners of her mouth, and then forced its way into its warm recesses, she felt the bitter tang of the tobacco, absorbed it into her, as her own tongue tangled with his.

Maggie had long since ceased to think. She should have been appalled at herself for letting this man kiss her, but all rational thoughts had fled from her head. Instead she had become a woman, a woman with no name and no past and no future, only a present, a present that was fearfully dominated by the physical presence of one man. Maggie arched her body in a futile effort to get somehow closer, and he obliged her by tightening his hold, his large, fine hands molding her against his chest so that her strangely sensitive breasts had the contact they craved. Like a fawning kitten, Maggie moved against him, brushing aside the coat that kept him from her, and when his hand slid downward to cup one soft, round buttock, she sighed into his hungry mouth and then moaned softly as he drew her hips into intimate contact with his.

Jack groaned her name on his way to discover the sensitive spot just below her ear. Her skin was like nothing he had ever touched before, like velvet, only warm and alive, he decided, when his hand had worked its way under her shirtwaist to test the feel of it against his own. So very much alive, quivering beneath his touch, quickening as his fingers found the soft mound of her breast and played over the sweet swell until they found the tender tip.

Maggie heard a strange, strangled cry at the very moment when he touched the pebbled hardness of her nipple, but she never suspected it had come from her own throat. She was more concerned with the way her bones had suddenly turned to water, until she felt herself sagging in his embrace, barely aware that he was sagging, too. Only mildly concerned when he sank back into his chair, so long as he took her with him, she could only seem to concentrate on the lightning flashes that sped through her body. Radiating outward from the point of her left breast and stimulated by the ministrations of his magical fingers, they seemed to settle somewhere deep in her loins, starting a fire there that soon had her writhing from its searing heat.

He seemed somehow to sense her needs, for when his hand left her breast and she would have cried out in protest, his mouth swooped in, working a magic of its own. First tongue and teeth laved and tugged at the puckered peak, and then moved to treat its neglected twin to more of the exquisite torment. Then he brushed his downy mustache tinglingly across each one and began the whole maddening process again. Maggie was nearly delirious with pleasure, and in her distracted state she was only vaguely aware that he had found her hip. He was caressing it with a masterful hand that at once subdued and aroused, holding her still while stroking and stoking the fire that burned within.

She welcomed the invasion, when at last it came, when at last his tantalizing touch sought out and found the moist core that ached for him. He cupped her femininity through the thin barrier of her pantalettes, marveling at the turbulence of her passion, at the ferocity of her response to him. He had suspected, had told himself he knew, but he hadn't known at all, not at all. Maggie, sweet little Maggie, sweet little spitfire, who would ever have imagined it would be like this when it finally came? A few more minutes and she would be his, tamed and sated and so deliciously manageable . . . but not here. No, his impassioned brain insisted, he could not take her here, on the floor, like a savage.

"Where's your bedroom, Maggie?" he whispered against her heated skin.

"Hmmmmm?" she murmured back, unable to focus quite on his question while his fingers were tracing such intricate patterns on the insides of her thighs.

"Your bedroom, darling? Where is it?" he repeated, lifting his head to place a string of stinging kisses across her jaw and up to her startled mouth.

"My WHAT!" she demanded against his lips as the question sank into some still-sane portion of her brain, her eyes blinking open in shocked surprise.

"Bed-roooom," he enunciated quite clearly when he had lifted his mouth a fraction of an inch from hers. "I think we'd better find someplace more comfortable than this chair to finish this," he added with an indulgent smile and a very tantalizing twist of his fingers.

Even as the thrill shot upward from her loins, the shock of realization quenched it. She was sitting here, with Jack

Sinclair, in his very lap, half undressed, behaving like a . . . like a wanton! And feeling very much like one, too, if her quivering flesh were any indication. How could she have done such a thing? How could she have lost control? How could she have surrendered her body, the one thing she should have held inviolate, to the very man who would steal everything else she possessed?

With a cry of despair, she jerked herself free, pushing away the hands, the lips that had given her such pleasure only moments ago, with a violence that bordered on frenzy. Unfortunately, such violence was unnecessary. Jack had watched her face, had seen the emotions reflected there, had known the instant in which she had rejected him, and had already released her, so that her frantic reaction sent her tumbling to the floor at his feet in an ignominious heap.

Furious both at him and herself, shamed by her own actions, and humiliated beyond words to find herself dumped on the floor like a discarded plaything, Maggie struggled desperately to her feet. She had a time of it, what with having to wrestle with her skirts and her shirtwaist at the same time, both of which had been raised indecently to expose her charms. Her trembling hands seemed to be all thumbs, and when she was on her feet at last, her skirts back around her ankles where they belonged and her shirtwaist once again covering everything it was designed to, even though it was shockingly wrinkled and she had no hope of being able to tuck it back in, at least not with Jack Sinclair watching, she drew herself up to her full five feet, four inches, and managed a rather pathetic look of outrage. The words, "How dare you," trembled on her lips, but she had the good sense not to utter them, remembering just in time that that was what had prompted this whole disaster. Instead she clenched her unsteady hands into fists and hissed, "Get out of there!"

Jack raised his eyes heavenward for a second before closing them completely and running a weary hand across his face. He, too, was suffering a certain amount of reaction from their hastily interrupted passion, and was having a much more difficult time than Maggie making the transition from lust to anger. Damn it, he should have taken her right here on the floor. Maybe it would have humbled her a little, in addition to all the things it would have done for him. One of the curses of being a gentleman, he decided in that brief instant, was never being able to follow one's instincts with the proper degree of abandon.

"Maggie . . ." he began.

"And don't call me Maggie!" she shrieked, and immediately covered her lips with trembling fingers, appalled at her own vehemence and terrified that she might be becoming hysterical. She had already made a consummate fool of herself without adding a case of the vapors into the bargain.

Jack hauled himself to his feet, feeling suddenly very old and very tired. She was in a state, all right, and he winced when he saw the skittish way she backed away from him when he tried to approach her. "Miss Colson," he said, as calmly as was possible given the present circumstances, "what happened just now . . ." He knew it would be foolhardy to pursue that subject given the look of sheer panic that flashed across her face. "I deeply regret it, but don't let what happened between us influence you to do something you'll regret." He wasn't making any sense, even to himself, and certainly not to her, if her blank look was any indication. He tried again. "Listen, I've offered you a fair price. The next man won't offer you anything at all, believe me. Don't be a fool, Maggie."

So he took her for a fool, did he? Well, she was still her father's daughter, even if he had succeeded in breaking down her defenses for a moment. With practiced ease she lifted her chin defiantly. "If you think for one moment that I would sell out to a murderer, than it is you who are the fool, Mr. Sinclair."

"A murderer?" he asked in genuine surprise.

"Yes, a murderer," she replied, warming now to her new role. "You are as responsible for my father's death as if you had put a gun to his head. The law may not hold you responsible, but I certainly do. You, Mr. Sinclair, are a murderer!"

Shock gave way rapidly to a fury the likes of which Jack had never known, and now he had no trouble at all forgetting how just moments ago he had held this girl in his arms. Now he was fighting an overwhelming urge to put his hands around her throat! Curling those hands into fists, he had actually taken one menacing step toward her before he registered the stark terror in her eyes. He did not dare touch her, that much he knew. He would either murder her or rape her, possibly both, in his present state of mind, so he contented himself with shaking one fist in her face and uttering an enraged growl before forcing himself toward the door, and through it, and into the relative safety of the yard.

The stallion shied when he approached, but he grabbed his quirt and rapped the horse smartly across the nose before trying to mount again, thus insuring the beast's cooperation. He was halfway home before he realized that he had left his Stetson hanging in Maggie's house. With a smile of self-mockery he decided it would be far safer to simply buy himself a new one, rather than go back for it. Safer for whom, he wasn't sure, however, when he recalled Maggie's accusations.

She was the old man's daughter, all right. If he had had any previous doubts, they were laid to rest now. A more stubborn, unreasonable woman he never hoped to meet, and she was just like her old man in that respect. Well, he had made his offer. Now all he had to do was wait. Time would convince her that she had no choice but to accept it. Time and Sam Kincaid, he corrected himself grimly. Time and Sam Kincaid.

Maggie held back her tears until she could no longer hear his departing hoofbeats. The tears came slowly at first, trickling down her face like the first drops of a summer shower, but soon that shower became a deluge as the full force of the storm hit. Maggie found herself sobbing, great wracking sobs that shook her until she wrapped her arms around herself in a feeble attempt at self-comfort. At some point, without even being aware of it, she slipped to the floor, huddling there with her head pressed against the cushion of the very chair in which they had sat.

She had never felt shame before, never felt truly humiliated, and her grief was doubled by the fact that her traitorous body still quivered for his touch. Miss Finley had never taught her girls the facts of life, probably because she wasn't too clear on them herself, but she had been very clear on the point that a true lady did not permit a gentleman to take liberties. Maggie had never been exactly certain at what point a man's attention became "liberties," but she was absolutely certain Jack Sinclair had passed that point today.

And so had she. If he had forced himself on her, it would have been bad enough, but at least that would have been bearable. The fact that she had been willing, even eager for his caresses stunned and horrified her. What kind of a person was she? How perverted she must be to respond like a harlot to a man she professed to hate, to the man who had killed her father, to the man who would take from her everything that she held dear.

In the end, when her tears were gone and the sobs had become the tired hiccups that follow such a soul-shattering experience, Maggie gathered herself by sheer force of will and made her way to the kitchen. Bathing her face beneath the blast of water from the pump cleared her head somewhat, but brought no answers to the questions that haunted her still. Perhaps it was not important to understand why she had behaved as she had, but only to avoid behaving in such a way ever again. Now that she knew her weakness, she would be much more circumspect in the future, especially where Jack Sinclair was concerned, if indeed she ever encountered him again. It was something she would certainly never intentionally do, but it might possibly happen, and if so, she would be ready. In the meantime, she had a job to do. If she had a crew on the ranch, Sinclair would never dare show his face there again.

It was well after noon when Maggie had changed her shirtwaist for one more presentable and held cold rags on her swollen eyes until they were no longer red and puffy. Judging that she still had plenty of time to make it to town before dark, she went to the corral where Swede had left several horses penned and coaxed an old gray dobbin out. It had been a long time since she had even seen a buggy hitched, much less done it herself, but she managed well enough, and was soon on her way. The horse she had chosen carried her much more slowly than she would have liked, but she had to remember how patiently he had born her struggles with the harness, and she forgave him. Even so, she arrived in Bitterroot in time for supper.

Old Mr. Festus was still the desk clerk at the hotel. Maggie wondered idly how old he really was. It seemed that he had been an old man when she was a tiny girl, but now that she examined his withered face and his stooped shoulders and his faded eyes, she realized he was only now entering the stage of life in which one can be called truly old. "I'd like a room for the night, Mr. Festus," she told him.

Nodding, he handed her a pen and waited while she signed the register. "Kind of scary out at the ranch by yourself, ain't it?" he commented when she handed the pen back to him.

Maggie fought the feeling of annoyance that swept over her. She should not have been surprised that he knew. Swede and the men would have gone straight to town to squander their pay, and their story would have been all over town within an hour. Equally annoying as having everyone know her business, however, was the condescension in his voice. He obviously looked upon her as a little girl who would be so scared of boogey men at the empty ranch that she would flee to town for safety. Choosing to ignore the fact that that was precisely what had happened, she cast upon him her most withering look and informed him, "I have come to town to hire a new crew, if that's any of your business, and I will need the room for as many days as that takes me."

Festus's eyes blinked several times in surprise before he nodded his understanding. "You'd be better off selling out to Mr. Sinclair, if you was to ask me," he muttered.

"Well, I did not ask you," Maggie replied scathingly. "May I have my key now?"

Festus blinked again. "We got no keys, Miss Maggie. You know that." She did know that. For a moment she had forgotten herself and imagined herself in a fancy eastern hotel. The keys, if there had ever been any at all, were long ago lost or stolen or simply carried off and forgotten. In any case, she had no more need to lock her door in Bitterroot than she had at the CMC, at least, before the men had left.

With an impatient sigh, Maggie tried again. "What room, then, Mr. Festus, if you please."

"Two. First door, top of the stairs. I'll get your bag," he hastened to add when she stalked off toward the stairs.

"Don't bother; it's not heavy," she told him over her shoulder, wondering mentally if he could have made it up the stairs with it if she had accepted his offer.

The door to number two was open. The room was neat if not too very clean, and contained an iron bedstead made up with moth-eaten blankets (but no sheets), a rather rickety washstand with a remarkably serviceable bowl and pitcher, and a single straightbacked chair. The lone window looked out over the street.

Setting her carpetbag on the floor, Maggie took a moment to wash the travel dust off her face and hands with the water in the pitcher, and then she took her few clothes out of the carpetbag and hung them on the pegs that lined one wall.

She knew she should really go down to the dining room to eat some supper. She had not eaten anything at all since breakfast, but she suddenly felt so unutterably weary that the thought of even walking down all the stairs required for such a trip was overwhelming. She would lie down for a while, she decided, giving in to the temptation offered by the sagging bed. She would rest a little and then go down to eat. That was her last thought before she sank into the straw mattress. She was asleep almost before her eyes closed, and since she had slept little the night before and was emotionally exhausted from her confrontation with Sinclair, she did not awaken until morning.

At first Maggie had a hard time figuring out just where she was when the sounds from the street below woke her, and then it all came flooding back. She was a little dismayed to discover that she had slept all night in her clothes, but since she had barely moved, the clothes weren't too badly wrinkled, or at least no worse than the ones that had been packed in her carpetbag. She did feel remarkably refreshed, and so she forgave herself for doing something Miss Finley would no doubt have scolded her for, and hastily began to change into the dress she had brought for town wear.

It was her official mourning dress. Every well-dressed lady had such a dress in her wardrobe, and Aunt Judith had made certain that Maggie was a well-dressed lady. One never knew, after all, when one might be called upon to attend a funeral, and there was always the possibility, however distasteful to contemplate, that a member of one's own family might pass away, so it was best to be prepared.

For once in her life, Maggie was grateful for Aunt Judith's foresight. She wanted to appear in Bitterroot as the proper grieving daughter, a tragic figure who could inspire sympathy, however misplaced. She would need all the sympathy she could muster if she were going to beat Jack Sinclair.

Unfortunately, her mourning dress also happened to be one of the ones that required a corset, and a rather tight corset, at that. Maggie tightened the laces to what she estimated was the correct position, and then strapped herself into the torturous contraption, holding her breath until the last hook was fastened. It was lucky, she decided, eyeing her now tiny waist, that she hadn't eaten much the previous day. If she were one ounce bigger, she never could have gotten the cursed thing hooked.

In a few moments she had rustled into her three petticoats, tied on the wire birdcage device that supported her bustle, and slipped the elegant black taffeta dress over it all. At least a hundred tiny jet buttons fastened the dress down the front, and when she had buttoned them all, she proceeded to tame her unruly curls into a sedate chignon. She did not bother with the bonnet that she had brought, deciding that it was hardly appropriate attire for eating breakfast in Bitterroot, and she made her way downstairs.

The dining room was almost deserted when she arrived. Most of the townspeople had already gone to their places of business, but among the handful of people still lingering over their morning coffee, Maggie saw Judge Harris's familiar face. Choosing to ignore it, she found an empty table away from the doorway and sat down stiffly—the only way she *could* sit, considering her attire. Her bustle made it impossible to lean against the chair back, and her corset made it impossible for her to relax, in any case. But, she reminded herself, she was not in town to relax, and when a red-faced girl came to take her order, she decided on a very businesslike breakfast of steak and eggs.

While she was waiting for her food, sipping the bitter brew that passed for coffee in this establishment and pretending to be oblivious to the others in the room, the judge finished his breakfast and made his way over to her table.

"Good morning, Maggie," he said, his voice warm and friendly in spite of the fact that she returned his greeting with a bare nod and a sparse glance. "I'm real sorry to hear about your father. I would have come if you'd sent word."

"Which is precisely why I did not send word, judge,"

97

Maggie replied frostily. "I saw no reason why the friends who had deserted him in life should gloat over him in death."

The judge studied her rigid profile a moment and sighed wearily. "It wasn't like that, honey. If you'd just let me explain, tell you how it was . . ."

"I know just how it was," Maggie interrupted. "Just like a pack of wolves, when a leader gets weak, the rest turn on him and drive him out. They even kill him if they can." Bitterness darkened the eyes she turned toward him, and she did not understand the sadness she saw on his face.

"Just remember, if you ever need me, I'll be there for you, honey. Whenever, whatever, you just call. You hear?"

Maggie nodded stiffly, turning her face away lest he see the tears that threatened. His offer had touched her in some mysterious way, recalling, as it did, another time when she would have done just that. Knowing that she never would again was curiously depressing. After a moment he reached out a pudgy hand and patted her shoulder in a reassuring manner and then left, the worn floor creaking under his weight as he crossed the room.

Maggie followed him with her eyes, eyes that had been blinked free of tears, and fought the urge to go after him, to seek the help that he had offered. Only the knowledge of who that help would benefit stopped her and hardened her resolve to resist the very compelling urge to give it all up and surrender.

Maggie barely noticed when the girl put the plate of steak and eggs in front of her, and when the aroma of the meat finally penetrated her consciousness, she almost gagged. What had ever possessed her to order such a heavy meal? She forced herself to swallow a few forksful of the eggs, which she washed down with more of the murky coffee, but the appetite that had brought her to the dining room had somehow disappeared. Rising hurriedly from the table, she returned to her room, calling to Festus as she passed to put the meal on her bill.

For a few moments, once in the safety of her room, she thought that she might vomit the little bit she had succeeded in eating, but after a few deep breaths, or as deep as her corset allowed, the awful urged passed, and Maggie felt some semblance of calm returning. She would need to be calm if she was to gather a crew together today. No one would want to work for a woman who was spooked before the trouble even started.

That thought steadied her somewhat, and she found the bonnet she had not worn downstairs and put it on. It was a fetching little thing made of black satin ribbons, with a few graceful black feathers curving down to brush her chin. A delicate veil came down over her face and tied in the back. When it was in place she felt much more confident, knowing that no one could quite read her expression through the netting.

Completely satisfied with what she could see of her appearance in the small smoky mirror over the washstand, Maggie reassured herself with one glance out the window that the business day had officially begun. Wagons were rattling down the street, riders weaving in and out between them, and men loitered and women gossiped. The saloon was open, and although it was not doing much business at this early hour, she saw that a group of men had gathered in the shade of its porch. Those were the men she needed to see.

Once on the street, Maggie felt a little twinge of apprehension. After all, she had never been quite so close to a saloon. Ladies usually crossed the street rather than walk in front of it, and they certainly never spoke to the men gathered there.

This was different, however. Today she was not a lady, but a rancher, looking to hire a crew. All traditional etiquette could be waived in a situation like this, Maggie told herself, and marched determinedly across the dusty street. Unknown to her, a pair of black eyes marked her progress, black eyes that narrowed dangerously when they saw her destination.

The group in front of the saloon was comprised of exactly the type of men she needed. Neither too young nor too old, they were range-hardened men in their early to middle twenties, and they would not have been loitering on the town sidewalk at this hour of the morning if they had been employed.

Scanning the crowd, Maggie picked out one of the men as the most likely one to approach. She knew that she would command the attention of the whole group as soon as she addressed them, but she also knew that it would be better to single one man out, to honor him, as it were, with her attention. He would then influence the others to accept her offer. The only trick was choosing a natural leader, and that task had been simplified for her by the fact that one single man was already holding the group in thrall with some tall tale or another. Not only that, but he had seen her approaching from the corner of his eye and had been watching her with a discreet curiosity. He was nice looking, too, in a rough sort of way. If he fancied himself a ladies' man, the whole thing would be amusingly easy.

Maggie stopped a short distance from the circle of men, and caught the speaker's eye. "Excuse me, sir," she called with a small wave of her hand and a large smile.

The cowboy paused instantly in his narrative and looked around as if to ascertain that it was really he to whom she was speaking. "Yes, you, sir," she encouraged him, and he came forward, the crowd parting before him like the red sea before Moses. "Good morning," she ventured when he was close. Uncomfortably close, she decided, looking up into eyes that seemed suspiciously bright for so early in the morning.

The cowboy was looking her over and taking his time about it. Maggie thought him a little insolent, but then that was the sort of man who would be able to stand up to Jack Sinclair. "I'm Maggie Colson," she said, still smiling behind her veil, although her face was beginning to feel a little stiff the longer he looked at her.

"Pleased to meet you, Maggie," he said, his grin even more than insolent now.

"Miss Colson," she corrected sternly, letting her smile fade.

"Glad you ain't married, Maggie. I ain't married, either," he told her silkily. This remark brought a small chuckle from the group of men behind him and a slight flush to Maggie's cheeks, but she refused to be daunted.

"I'm hiring men. Are you interested?" she asked in her most businesslike tone, her hands clasping each other at her waist.

"Oh, I'm more than interested in anything you'd like to suggest," he assured her, drawing another laugh, although Maggie could not see anything funny in what was happening.

"I'm paying fifty a month and found," she said, still all business. That was almost twice what an ordinary cowboy made, fighting wages in anyone's book. That should tell him, and the others, without a doubt what was expected.

His reaction was a low whistle and a broad grin. "Mighty impressive, considering what might be 'found' with you around." This brought a loud guffaw, and Maggie could no longer deny that they were not discussing the same thing at all. Exactly what they were discussing, she was not quite sure. "You can keep your money, though. I wouldn't charge a honey like you one penny. I'd do it for fr . . ."

The force of a fist connecting with his jaw cut him off abruptly. Maggie had been only vaguely aware that someone was coming up behind her when that someone had jostled her roughly aside and very eloquently expressed his opinion of the cowboy's manners. That someone was fairly dragging her back across the street with one strong hand fastened to her elbow before she had a chance to realize that he was Jack Sinclair.

They were across the street and entering the hotel lobby

101

before she caught her breath enough to demand that he let her go.

"What room are you in?" he asked, totally ignoring her protests.

"None of your . . ."

"Room two," Festus supplied helpfully from behind the desk. He shrugged apologetically in response to the baleful look Maggie cast over her shoulder on her way to the stairs.

Always the perfect gentleman, Jack allowed her to precede him up the narrow stairs, but since he was virtually propelling her, she thought his courtesy lacked that certain something. Only when they were inside her room did he release her, slamming the door behind him.

Maggie knew a moment of panic. What was he going to do? He looked almost as furious as he had yesterday when she had thought he might murder her. "Open that door!" she commanded a trifle breathlessly. Her corsets and the rapid trip up the stairs had winded her abominably, and for a moment, with her hand pressed tightly to her diaphram, she thought she might faint. The black spots in front of her eyes were not encouraging.

Watching her closely, Jack crossed his arms and leaned back against the door. "Not yet. I've got something to say to you."

Now that she was still, breathing as deeply as the stays allowed, she recovered rapidly. The spots were fading. She would not faint. She lifted her chin regally. "Open that door at once," she insisted, much more confidently than she had any reason to sound.

"What's the matter, Maggie? Worried about your reputation?" he asked sarcastically. "Don't concern yourself. After that little scene on the street your reputation is already in shreds."

Maggie gasped in outrage. "*You* were the one who made a scene!"

"No," he corrected her with deceptive mildness. "I only

102

finished it. I'm sorry I had to interrupt your little business transaction, but I felt it my civic duty. It's bad for the town's reputation to have men selling themselves on the public streets." Maggie had no idea what he was talking about and scornfully told him as much. "Selling themselves," he explained patiently. "For stud service. Tell me, Maggie, how much did you offer him? I might be interested in the job myself."

Maggie hardly heard his outrageous offer. Her mind was frantically replaying her conversation with the cowboy. She had known he was twisting her words, changing them to mean something else, something that the other men thought was funny. He had said something about finding her, and not charging her, and how she was a honey and . . . "Oh!" she cried in despair, covering her flaming face with her hands.

"I warned you, Maggie. I told you you couldn't hire a crew," Jack reminded her coldly.

He had warned her, all right, but after he had practically attacked her, how could he have expected her to listen? He should have known she would do just the opposite of what he advised. If only he had explained . . .

"How much *did* you offer him?" Jack taunted.

Maggie uttered an inarticulate cry of rage as she swooped across the room at him, swinging her hand as she came, but he caught it, easily diverting the slap she would have given him. Twisting her hand behind her back, he hauled her up against him, and held her there, their bodies in intimate contact while Maggie squirmed in a futile effort to free herself.

"I warned you before about slapping me," he growled, jerking off her bonnet, veil and all, with his free hand. For one heartbeat he stared down into her face, taking in the emerald eyes in which the anger was rapidly turning to apprehension, and the trembling mouth that looked so inviting.

Maggie knew he was going to kiss her even before he knew it himself. She saw the desire flare up in those black eyes, saw those fine nostrils flare as he took in her scent, saw those firm, straight lips part beneath that black mustache, and heard the sharp intake of breath just before his mouth lowered to hers.

She met him eagerly, heedless of the arm still twisted behind her back, heedless of the pain his rough embrace inflicted, heedless of the fact that she was furious with him, that she hated the very ground he stood upon. None of that seemed very important at all in the instant when her breath mingled with his just before their lips met, and once their lips met, all else ceased to exist.

All that mattered was that he was close to her again, that his warmth was invading her, his strength supporting her as that strange, sweet weakness swept over her. Suddenly, her hands were both free, and she was clinging to him while his own hands explored her. She heard his moan of protest when the corset barred his access to her curves, heard her own moan of surrender when he found the softness of her breast through the stiff fabric of her dress. It was not enough, not for either of them. Too many barriers, too many constraints. Jack's lips groaned his frustration as they traced the sensitive cord along her neck, and Maggie's echoed it as she threw her head back to grant him access. She was only slightly surprised when he scooped her up into his arms. It seemed the most natural place in the world to be, but when the bed creaked under their combined weight, and she sprawled across him as he tumbled backward, she began to feel a faint tingle of alarm.

Something was wrong, very wrong. Even while her body arched toward him, molding itself to his, some nagging doubt scratched at her consciousness. He had wanted to take her to her bedroom that last time. When they had been kissing and touching, he had wanted her bedroom. Now they were *in* her bedroom, *in her bed,* and what was he doing?

104

Dear God, he was unbuttoning her dress! She was no longer on top, but half underneath him, his leg holding her hips, his mouth doing wonderful things to her throat and his fingers very busily working the myriad buttons. She had to stop him, she had to.

"Stop!" she cried, or rather tried to cry, but the word came out as no more than a breathless whisper. She should fight him, should at least struggle, but she found that her body refused to perform, refused to refuse him. It seemed that she had control over only a small portion of her brain and that the rest of her had switched allegiance to her enemy.

His lips found the opening of her bodice and breathed living fire onto the tender skin he had exposed. In another moment he had pushed aside the delicate silk of her chemise to find the warm, lush mounds that strained for his touch. Teasing them with the fur on his upper lip, he brought them to stiff, aching peaks, and then soothed them in the heated depths of his mouth. Maggie felt the heat spreading, seeping into her bones, smoldering into her belly, until she welcomed the hand that followed it there. He was having a time with her petticoats, and that gave her a perverse pleasure even as she thrashed impatiently for his touch, the touch that finally came, so gently and so knowingly. He knew just how to touch her, and where, and she moaned softly when his hand slid upward between the valley of her thighs to find the center of her desire. Instinctively, her hips lifted in response. This was what she wanted, what she needed, what she had been longing for for so very long. If only he would hurry. . . .

Maggie wasn't really certain about exactly what he should be hurrying to do, but she knew instantly that something was wrong when his head lifted suddenly from her breast and she heard his small, impatient grunt. He was doing something, something very difficult, and then she realized that he was undoing her drawers, or trying to, but the drawstring had knotted, and he couldn't get it untangled.

Maggie's eyes, heavy-lidded with passion until now, flew

open instantly at the knowledge. The sight of that dark head bent intently over her body, those fine hands working busily to unlock the secrets encased in the silk pantalettes, sent the alarm bells clanging in her head. If he goes any further, if he does what he's trying to do right now, she thought frantically, I will be lost. She had to stop him, somehow, she just had to, but if her body had refused to cooperate before, it lay completely paralyzed now. She would get no help from that traitorous source. She had only her mind, only her intelligence, to use against him, and that mind told her that she needed words, words that would stop him, since she had no other power. Where they came from she would never know, but no sooner did she need them then the perfect words came to her, the perfect, magic words.

"Fifty dollars," she whispered to the black head bent over her, and she felt the small tremor as he tried to shift his attention to what she was saying. "Fifty dollars," she repeated, more loudly, her voice still breathless but sounding more normal.

Jack raised his head, black eyes whose heat fairly scorched her searched her face questioningly.

"I offered that cowboy fifty dollars for his services. Will that be enough for yours?" she forced herself to say. Instantly she knew she had said the right thing, the perfect thing. The passion in those black eyes turned swiftly to the rage that was becoming equally familiar to her, and his whole body seemed to jerk with the force of his emotion. In another moment he was drawing away, not physically at first, but in some indefinable way that was equally apparent, and then he pulled away physically.

"Damn you," he breathed as he struggled off the bed and onto his feet. "Damn you to hell, Maggie Colson." He towered over her, his black eyes raking her with a contempt that made her cringe in a feeble attempt to hide the parts of her he had exposed. His huge body fairly trembled with the fury that he held in check, and Maggie knew that it must be

106

the slenderest thread of restraint that held him. Although she felt the urge, the almost overwhelming urge, to taunt him again, to tell him that his manhood wasn't worth fifty dollars, some instinct for self-preservation constrained her.

Instead she waited, cowering on the bed, just as he had left her, waiting and praying that he would simply leave, that she would not have to scream, would not have to call for help that might not come. Mesmerized, she watched his long fingers curl into and out of fists, and those black eyes glitter dangerously, while the tall body heaved in great, gasping breaths.

It was a titanic struggle, and for a moment Jack was not certain that he would win. In a way, he almost wished he would not, almost wished that he would lose control of himself and do what they had both wanted him to do just a moment ago. He felt a primitive need to subdue her, to crush her and conquer her in every way, to kill the spirit that he could see still shone from her eyes in spite of the fear she felt at the moment. Such an act would be the perfect balm to the pride that she had battered so many times now, and yet . . . What stopped him was the knowledge of what a tragedy it would be to kill that spirit. It was what he most admired about her, what had drawn him back to her time and again even when she had infuriated him as no other person had ever done, even when she insulted him as he would have allowed no other person to do and live.

It was indeed a titanic struggle, and he won it only by remembering that he still had the means to subdue her in another, less personal way. "You had your chance, Maggie," he told her when he felt he could control his voice. "I made you an offer, a very fair offer, and you refused it. Now you'll come to me on my terms and take whatever I damn well please to give you." He paused to take a ragged, calming breath, and to make a small decision. "When I've decided what that is, I'll be back," he told her, having decided that he had better take a little time away from her before setting his terms. His voice was still a little unsteady, but he still sounded threatening enough so that she believed him.

She believed him all right, enough so that she lay completely still while she watched him straighten his clothes and pick up the hat he had lost somewhere along the line and smooth his hair with a flick of his hand and put the hat back on and open the door. She wasn't afraid of him, she told herself. Not really afraid. It was only common sense to avoid tweaking the lion's tail, especially when the lion was in a rage.

He paused in the doorway, one hand on the knob, the other idly smoothing his vest. He was, once again, the cool aristocrat, the perfect gentleman in complete control of himself and the situation. "I'll be back, Maggie," he warned once more, and then he was gone.

For a moment Maggie did not move, but when the reality of his absence seeped into her consciousness, her courage returned. Bolting upright on the bed, she stared at the closed door a moment, recalling his last words. So he thought he'd gotten the best of her, did he? So he was coming back, was he? Well, she'd be ready for him. Defiantly, she lunged to her feet, and called out to the closed door, "And don't call me 'Maggie'!"

Whether he heard or not, she had no idea.

Chapter IV

This time Maggie didn't cry. She knew it was a waste of time, knew it accomplished nothing, and knew from bitter experience that it did not change the way she felt about Jack Sinclair. Resolutely, she knuckled the tears from her eyes and began to repair the physical damage he had done to her.

A few good tugs and her dress was straight again. With trembling fingers she rebuttoned her bodice, flushing hotly as she remembered how his mouth had traced the opening. Her bustle cage was a little bent, now that she noticed, probably from lying on it when he had her on the bed. She didn't even let herself remember that part of it as she struggled to bend it into its usual shape while it was still fastened securely behind her. It was a difficult maneuver, but she managed, and then she took a moment to look in the mirror. Her hair was an absolute disaster, just as she had feared, but by the time she had taken it down and brushed it and put it back up again, she was feeling almost composed.

She found her bonnet lying in a corner where Jack had tossed it. It was a little dusty, but not seriously damaged, and she tied it on determinedly. She did not have much time if she was going to do anything before Sinclair got back, and she did not intend to waste any of that time on any more vanities. When she was pleased with what she saw staring back at her in the mirror, she took one last, steadying breath and marched toward the door. She knew one second's hesitation after that door was open, but when a fast look revealed that the hallway was empty, she swiftly regained her determination and walked out of the room, down the stairs, through the lobby, and onto the street without so much as a backward glance.

As quickly as propriety allowed, Maggie made her way to the bank. She was no longer naive enough to think that she had any friends left in town, or anywhere else. She knew only too well that everyone in Bitterroot had sold out to Jack Sinclair, but she also knew that there was at least one person left whom she could trust. Not that she would trust him very far, but she knew he would tell her the truth, at least about the things she needed to know. It took a lot of courage to swallow the pride that had made her vow only a short time ago that she would never take Judge Harris up on his offer of help, but she was wise enough to realize that if there was any chance, any chance at all of beating Sinclair legally, that Judge Harris would know of it. He would tell her, too, if she asked him. Of that much she was certain, and it was that certainty that compelled her toward the bank.

The same pimply-faced teller whom she had seen before once again nodded her toward the judge's office, but this time she swept in without a hint of the warmth that had marked her last visit. The judge rose at the sight of her, his instinctive smile fading when he saw the same haughty look on her face that she had worn this morning. "Something wrong, Maggie?" he asked in very real concern. He knew her well enough to know that she would never have come to him after saying the things she had said to him in the hotel dining room unless something were very wrong indeed.

Maggie felt her skin prickle at his question, terrified that he might, somehow, have been able to tell by looking at her just how very wrong everything was. "I need some advice, judge, some legal advice."

The judge frowned thoughtfully. "Sit down, honey," he invited, indicating the chair with one short finger and then sitting down himself.

"Were you ever really a judge?" Maggie blurted when she had seated herself. That had been poorly put, rudely put, and she quickly corrected herself, recalling how she had so recently thought of asking him that very question out of idle curiosity. "What I mean is, do you have any formal legal training? Can you advise me on my legal rights?"

Judge Harris watched her for a moment, one finger tapping his upper lip thoughtfully, and then he replied, "I used to be a judge, a long time ago, before you were born. Unfortunately, being a judge doesn't necessarily mean a man has any formal legal training, and I didn't, but . . ." he hastened on, seeing her disappointment, "I can advise you on your rights. I've learned a lot about the law, even if you wouldn't call it 'formal training.' What do you want to know?"

Maggie felt certain he knew exactly what she wanted to know, but she refrained from saying so. Folding her hands tightly in her lap so that the judge would not see them tremble, she lifted her chin and said, "I want to keep my ranch. What legal recourse do I have?"

The judge studied her face for a long moment. She was her father's daughter, all right. There was no "quit" in her, and she just didn't have the sense to know when she was beaten. "Legally, you own the cattle, the ranch buildings, and the original homestead land." Maggie nodded. That much she knew. "There is no legal reason why you could not continue to run the ranch just as your father did before you, although I would strongly recommend that you take steps to lay claim to whatever government land you would like to continue to use as part of the CMC. However . . ." the judge paused and Maggie waited patiently, knowing that was not the whole story, by any means. He cleared his throat and continued. "However, as we both know, you cannot run the ranch,

111

legally or otherwise, without a crew, and as you learned this morning, hiring a crew will be a difficult proposition for you."

Maggie clenched her hands more tightly together and took a breath. This was the most difficult thing she had ever had to do, but she was willing to humble herself in almost any way, if by doing so, she could save her ranch. "Judge, you could hire them for me, if you would." It wasn't really a request, but they both knew that it was as close to begging as a Colson was ever likely to come.

But Judge Harris was shaking his round head, his old eyes sadder than she had ever seen them. "Maggie, darlin', don't you understand it yet? Of course I could hire them. I could have you a crew by this afternoon, but I won't do it. No honorable man would send you back to that ranch alone with a bunch of strange men. Maybe if you were fifty years old with a face like an old shoe, then maybe, just maybe, I might think about it, but a pretty young girl like you . . ." The judge shifted uncomfortably in his chair. "I hope I don't have to explain what could happen."

No, he did not. Jack Sinclair had already done that, quite satisfactorily, thank you very much. Maggie shook her head numbly. Surely, there was something else, some other way. . . .

"You're better off to take Jack's offer," the judge was saying. "I know how much he offered you for the place. You could be real comfortable. You could go back East, stay with your aunt and uncle. You'd meet a young man, get married. You could have a good life."

Maggie was staring at him in horror. Didn't he know? How could he think she would ever go back East? How could he think for one minute that she would ever be happy anyplace except her own valley? As for marrying one of the men she had met in Atlanta, the very thought made her shudder. "Isn't there any other way . . . ?" The judge shook his head at her unfinished question.

"For a woman, alone, no, there's no other way. Maybe if Deke and the old crew were still around, the men who were there when you were growing up, maybe then . . . but even still, you wouldn't be completely safe." The judge gave an apologetic shrug and waited.

For the first time in her life, Maggie felt the true weight of her heavy skirts. It seemed odd that only now would she begin to resent the limitations put upon her because of her sex. She had been a little resentful at first when her father had sent her away to school. She even remembered arguing that he would not have sent her away if she had been a boy, but he had replied that a boy had no need to grow up to be a lady. He had placed such importance on her becoming a real lady, like her mother, that she had come to believe it to be important, too. Instead of resenting it, she had seen it as another way she could please the father she idolized, and her studies had taken on new meaning. Now it all seemed so futile. Being a lady could only be a hindrance in fighting Jack Sinclair.

"Take Jack's offer," the judge was saying. "That's really the only choice you have."

Maggie had already arrived at that conclusion, but knowing it and being reminded of it were two different things. "Thank you very much for your time, judge," she said frostily, rising from her chair with the graceful, fluid movements she had learned so well at Miss Finley's. Turning in a rustle of taffeta, she was almost to the door when the judge called her name. The hint of alarm in his voice stopped her. She did not turn, but merely waited, her back ramrod stiff.

"Maggie, honey, don't do anything foolish," he cautioned, and without looking she could picture the worry lines that would have creased his face.

"Don't concern yourself, judge. Jack Sinclair hasn't even left me that option," she told him, still looking at the door, and then she opened it, making her escape first into the bank and then into the street.

If she passed anyone she knew along the way back to the hotel, she was unaware of it, conscious only of her own wild thoughts. With each step her fury grew, fury at Jack Sinclair, at her own mistakes, at her own impotence. By the time she reached the sanctuary of her room, she was in a state.

Slamming the flimsy door behind her, Maggie plunked herself down on the sagging bed and fought off the urge to cry. She would not let Jack Sinclair find her sobbing her heart out, would not let him think he had beaten her completely.

Looking out the dingy window, she could see a corner of the saloon, and the saddle shop. It wasn't much of a view, but then it wasn't much of a town, either. It had been *her* town, though, until Jack Sinclair had invaded it. How well she could remember coming to town as a child, how everyone had a smile and a greeting for her and her father, how everyone had always treated them both with the utmost respect. Rightly so, too, considering the town's very existence depended on the ranches that surrounded it, and the CMC was the largest of them all. In those days no one would have dared to treat her the way Jack Sinclair had treated her. He would have been horsewhipped or hung or . . . Maggie could think of no punishment quite foul enough for what Jack Sinclair had done, and so she stopped trying.

The fact remained that without her father to protect her, she was completely defenseless. The sting of her loss brought tears momentarily to her eyes, but she blinked them back. Now was not the time to mourn her father. Now she needed her wits about her for the coming confrontation with Sinclair.

The judge had told her to take Sinclair's offer. It had sounded so easy then, but now, in the privacy of her room, Maggie recalled the scene that had so lately been played out here, and how Sinclair had withdrawn that very generous offer. Now, he had said, she would take whatever he damn well chose to give her. She had a sinking feeling that that would be far less than what she had turned down. She had injured his pride, and from what little she knew about him, she was fairly certain that that was his most vulnerable spot. He would not easily forgive her, just as she could not forgive him either, but whether he would actually cheat her in retaliation she had no idea.

Whatever happened, she was certain of one thing, and that was that she must be careful not to anger him further. Obviously, she had no choice but to sell out to him now. She would need to get out of it as much money as she could, because if she had learned only one thing back East, it was that money is power. If she had some money, if she could use it to accumulate more, she could eventually get the power to beat Sinclair at his own game, and even if she had to sell her soul to do it, someday the CMC would be hers once more.

When she thought about it some more, she realized that she might very well have to do just that. Or at least sell her body. The judge had told her that a woman alone had no choices, but if she were not alone, if she had a man behind her . . . the idea was far from novel. Everyone knew that women often married for money and power. Many of her friends at Miss Finley's school had planned to do so without the slightest qualm. It had always seemed too cold-blooded to Maggie, but then, she had never known just how powerless a woman could be. In her present situation the thought of marrying a man who could help her fight Sinclair was quite appealing. Finding such a man would be the trick, of course, but Maggie knew that she was pretty, and if she had a comfortable dowry . . .

Maggie sat staring out the window for a long time, making plans that held little hope of fruition, but that comforted her, nevertheless. Someday she would pay Sinclair back in kind for the way he had humiliated her, and that knowledge would get her through what promised to be the very most humiliating interview of her life. At last she began to notice how the traffic in the street had thinned out, how the shadows of the pedestrians had lengthened, and how her stomach had begun to complain.

It must, she figured, be getting quite late in the afternoon. She had been sitting there for hours without realizing it, and somehow she had missed lunch altogether. Thinking back, she recalled that she had had only a few bites for breakfast and nothing at all the day before. No wonder she felt hungry! Well, if Jack Sinclair was coming, he could find her just as easily in the dining room as he could here, she reasoned. Besides, she would need fortification if she were going to pull off the conciliatory act she had planned.

That decided, she pulled off the bonnet she still wore, smoothed her hair, pinched some color into her cheeks, and made her way downstairs. The dining room was empty, but Festus had seen her, and he went to find the serving girl. The girl was less than pleased to be disturbed, but she grudgingly placed a cup of coffee in front of Maggie and went off to fry her a steak and some potatoes. The coffee was half gone when she saw Jack Sinclair in the doorway.

Fighting the urge to flee, Maggie forced herself to remain in her chair and to present a calm appearance. It was one of the most difficult parts she had ever played, but she thought she carried it off rather well, in spite of the fact that every one of her nerve ends sparked at the sight of him. She managed to glance up ever so casually as he approached, and she could tell by the lift of his eyebrows that he was impressed. He was wearing that same black suit that she thought suited his character so well, and a shirt that was just a shade whiter than any honest working man would wear.

"Mind if I join you, Miss Colson?" he asked, with just the faintest tinge of sarcasm.

So he had heard her parting demand, she realized as she gave him a frosty nod and he took a seat across the table from her. When he did not speak, she ventured a glance in his direction and found him studying her with grim intensity, his arms folded forbiddingly across his chest. She tried a small smile that fell sadly flat, and informed him as calmly as she could, under the circumstances, "I am prepared to accept your very generous offer for my ranch."

Once again his dark eyebrows lifted, but Maggie had a feeling he was not so impressed as amused. He let her wonder for a long moment. "It seems that you have forgotten that I withdrew that 'very generous offer' earlier today," he said at last.

To her horror, Maggie felt the blood rush to her cheeks at that memory and at the other memories that went along with it, but she pretended that she didn't, and took a calming breath before replying. "Then I am prepared to accept whatever you damn well choose to offer," she quoted him with another sad attempt at a smile.

Jack scowled in irritation. He did not like being reminded of the cavalier way that he had treated her. Under ordinary circumstances, he never swore in the presence of a lady. Under ordinary circumstances he never did most of the things he had done with Maggie Colson in the presence of a lady, but then Maggie Colson was no ordinary lady, either. No lady of his previous acquaintance would have called him a thief and a murderer to his face. Pondering her many sins helped soothe the irritation he felt at his own lapses in decorum, and helped stiffen his resolve to do what he had decided to do.

The decision had not been an easy one, but once made, he knew it was the perfect solution to all the problems Maggie Colson presented. He wanted her ranch, of course, and he was in a position to get it now, on any terms he cared to set, but he needed more from her. He did not dare let her go, either. He knew her well enough to know that she would not fade away into the wallpaper like a meek little flower, never to be heard from again. The judge had theorized that she would go back East, but he obviously did not know his little darling as well as he thought, even if he had known her since birth. No, she was the type to hang around, to cause trouble, to water the seeds of suspicion she had already planted, to make herself a tragic figure who had been wronged by the infamous Jack Sinclair. It was a role she would relish, he was certain, and it was a role she would play to the hilt. But, if Jack Sinclair had anything to say about it, it was a role for which she would never get a chance.

Jack smiled in anticipation of her reaction to his new offer, and noted with satisfaction her patent unease at the sight of that smile. "I'm not going to offer you anything at all for your ranch, Miss Colson. I'm going to take it from you, free of charge."

It took a moment for the meaning of his words to sink in. She had expected a greatly reduced amount, even a pittance, but she had not expected nothing. She had never guessed that even Jack Sinclair would stoop that low. The fluttering that had begun in her stomach was spreading until her whole body trembled. She clasped her hands together on the table top so that he would not see them shake. Fury and fear warred for preeminence in her heart, and fury won. "You'd steal my property, Mr. Sinclair?" she asked through gritted teeth. "That seems low, even for the likes of you." She had promised herself that she would not insult him, had sworn that she would be meek and sweet and cooperative, but he had pushed her too far.

Jack stiffened in reaction to her taunt, his lips whitening beneath the black mustache, but he forced himself to remain calm. After all, he held the upper hand. Her words could no longer hurt him. "No, not steal, my dear girl. It's considered perfectly legal when a husband assumes ownership of his wife's possessions."

Maggie blinked in surprise and then her mouth dropped open in very undignified shock as she realized the full implications of his statement. "You think that I would marry you? *You?* The man who killed my father?" she demanded, her voice becoming alarmingly shrill.

Jack looked around quickly. There was no one in sight, but someone was bound to be listening, ready to report the subject of their discussion to all interested parties the instant it was over. He would have preferred to conduct this meeting in the privacy of her room, but he doubted that he could get her there now with anything less than brute force, and a scene like that would just add more fodder to the gossip mill. "Keep your voice down," he hissed. "You know perfectly well that I did not kill your father, and stop behaving like a character in a melodrama."

Maggie felt very much like a character in a melodrama, except that she knew those people were only pretending. The terror she was beginning to feel was alarmingly real. The stomach that had fluttered before was churning now, and her trembling was becoming full-fledged shaking. Her heart had been beating madly just a moment earlier, but now it had slowed down to a dull, laborious thud, much like the pounding of a blacksmith's hammer. Each time it crashed against the steel stays of her corset, the echo throbbed in her ears and her throat and her wrists and a hundred other places. "I won't!" she whispered, unconsciously obeying his command. "I'd die before I'd marry you!"

Her obvious distaste, combined with the way her face had changed from scarlet to chalk white in a matter of seconds, galled him. There were any number of women in the world who would treat a proposal of marriage from him as a welcome honor, and none at all who would consider death a preferable alternative. None except Maggie Colson. "I'm afraid you will not have that choice, my dear," he told her, leaning menacingly across the table. "After you've thought it over for a while, I'm sure you'll come to your senses."

"Never! I'll nev . . ." she began, but he cut her off.

"I know just the place to send you to think, too. I have this friend in Amarillo. Her name is Mrs. Gibson, but they call her Madame Helen. She has this lovely little house, where you'll have your very own room and where you'll be allowed to entertain visitors. . . ."

He did not have to explain further. Maggie knew exactly what kind of a house he was talking about. She also knew what would happen if she went there. Not that she knew the physical things that would happen, at least not exactly, but she knew that once she had been inside, just across the threshold, she would be ruined. Even if no one laid a hand on her, even if they locked her up and no one ever came near her, she would be ruined just the same. "That's ridiculous," she told him, but her voice lacked a certain amount of conviction. "I'll get the law, the Texas Rangers. I'll tell them what you did, how you stole my land . . . my Uncle Edward, he'll come . . ."

"And just how much will they believe when they discover that they have to pay for the privilege of your company?" he taunted.

He was right, of course. Even Uncle Edward would be only too happy to wash his hands of her if he found her in a place like that. Her mind was racing, searching for an escape, and then she found one. "You'll never get me there!" she told him triumphantly. "Amarillo is a long way from here. Even you would have a hard time transporting a woman who fought you every step of the way." Lifting her chin, she managed a smug grin, in spite of the fact that she was still quivering from head to toe. She had him there, and she knew it. The people in Bitterroot might look the other way if he cheated her, but they would never allow him to carry her off bodily, not if she let it be known that it was against her will.

Jack smiled benignly into her upturned face. "You underestimate me, Maggie," he told her, his black eyes glittering like diamonds. "It only takes a few drops of what is commonly called a Mickey Finn to render a person your size unconscious for far longer than it would take to get you to Amarillo. Someone could slip it in your coffee, for example. . . ." He let those dark eyes rest meaningfully on her half-empty cup.

Maggie cried out in outrage, lunging to her feet, ready to do battle with this most despicable of enemies, but as soon as she was out of her chair, she knew that something was very wrong. For some reason she could not seem to get her breath, and the room was spinning and tilting in a most unnatural manner. The black spots that she had seen before her eyes earlier in the day were back with reinforcements, and suddenly his words rang in her memory. "A few drops . . . Mickey Finn . . . in your coffee . . ."

Maggie stared in horror at the half-empty cup. "You . . . you drugged me. . . ." she gasped as the darkness closed around her. He was rising from his chair, reaching out to her, but he seemed so very far away. She heard him say her name, or thought she did, and then the floor came rushing up, very fast, and she knew no more.

Maggie was having the most delicious dream. She was so very tired, and someone big and very strong was holding her, cuddling her so that she could feel warm and safe while she slept. Warm hands touched her, stroked her, made her feel so nice. They seemed to know just how to do it, just how to move and where. She wanted to help them, to show them where else she wanted to be touched, but her own hands just wouldn't seem to move. She wanted to open her eyes, too, to see to whom those wonderful hands belonged, but her eyelids wouldn't cooperate either, so she simply lay there, enjoying that good, safe feeling.

Then something was tickling her mouth, something very familiar, something that smelled like cigars, and tasted so good that she was kissing it. It felt so right that she wanted it to go on and on, but when she tried to move, tried to reach out and hold on, her body still would not respond. It was so frustrating that Maggie moaned aloud. Instantly, the good feelings stopped. Whoever had been there was no longer there, and she was alone. She felt so cold, so lonely, that she moaned again, and this time the sound of her own voice woke her up.

Her eyes fluttered open, and she saw that she was lying down, staring up at a cracked ceiling. She still felt cold, or a little cold, and instinctively she wrapped her arms around herself, only to encounter a surprising amount of bare skin. Looking down, she saw that she was clad only in her chemise and petticoats. Funny, she didn't remember getting undressed, or lying down either. All she remembered was . . . and then the memories came crashing down on her. She had been in the hotel dining room, and Jack Sinclair had just threatened to drug her and carry her off to a brothel and then she had . . .

A small noise drew her attention to a far corner of the small room where she saw a man standing. His back was to her, he was staring out the window, but she recognized him in any case. Her cry of outrage brought him around to face her. She couldn't quite read the expression on his face, but he seemed distant, oddly unfamiliar for just that one moment before his mustache tipped sardonically in that way that she knew so well and he said, "Are you finally awake?"

The next few moments passed in an agony of embarrassment as Maggie bolted up to a sitting position on the bed, only to remember that she was just partially dressed, and had to scramble for the corner of the blanket. She somehow got it over her, at least enough to cover her bosom, and then treated Jack Sinclair to the full force of her fury. "You . . . you *ruined* me!" she accused, green eyes blazing with the force of her anger. He had, too. She was sure of it. He had brought her to this awful place, and taken her clothes, and done unspeakable things to her when she was unable to defend herself.

Maggie had no way of knowing just how charming she looked with her hair coming loose in curls around her face, and her slender body only barely covered by the blanket she

122

clutched. Jack rolled his eyes heavenward for a moment, as if seeking divine strength, and sighed heavily. "Let me guess," he said when his black eyes rested on her again. "Your next line is 'How dare you?'"

Maggie longed to charge across the room and slap his insolent face, but she thought better of it when she remembered her skimpy attire. How dare he, indeed! To make fun of her after what he had done. Almost choking on her anger, she made a strangled noise in her throat, and then gritted, "You drugged me!"

"Don't be ridiculous!" he snapped in annoyance. "You fainted. Not surprising, considering how you were trussed up in that damn corset, and the girl downstairs said you hadn't eaten your breakfast or been back to eat since. By the way, Maggie," he asked, his eyes narrowing suspiciously, "when *did* you last eat?"

Maggie shook her head in confusion. "I don't remember," she mumbled. She probably could have remembered if she had tried, but she wasn't really concerned about that now. She was too busy trying to make sense of what he had said. He had said, "The girl downstairs . . ." Maggie looked around, and for the first time since she had come to she realized that she wasn't in a brothel at all, but back in her own hotel room. A glance outside showed her the sky was still light and that not very much time had passed since she had lost consciousness. Still, she recalled, glancing down at her petticoats . . . "What did you do to me?" she demanded, her anger coming back in a rush.

Jack's long fingers curled into fists for just a moment before he forced himself to remain calm. "Not what you so obviously think," he said tightly, unaccountably irritated that she thought him capable of such a dastardly act. "You overestimate your charms, Maggie, if you think I'd get any pleasure from making love to you while you were unconscious." He let that sink in a moment, and then smiled wickedly. "Especially when I know how much fun you are

123

when you're awake."

Maggie almost did get up then. The urge to scratch his insolent eyes out almost overwhelmed her, but the blanket she had covered herself with was caught on a spring or something, and when she lunged forward, it stayed where it was, exposing her thinly clad bosom for just a moment before she managed to recover it. That bosom was heaving in indignation by the time she had restored her modesty. "You took my clothes," she raged impotently. He might not have raped her, but he had taken liberties no gentleman had any right to, and her eyes crackled out the silent accusation.

Jack gave a disgusted snort. "Somebody had to get you out of those torture devices before they strangled you," he told her with a derisive gesture toward the heap he had made of her discarded dress, corset, and bustle. It was then that Maggie noticed that strange expression on his face again, the one he had worn when she had first awakened, the one that made him look so unfamiliar. It took her a moment to identify it, and when she did, she could hardly believe her own eyes. He was embarrassed! He was actually . . . well, not quite, but almost, blushing! His neck was red, at any rate, and he could not meet her eyes. But why . . .

Then Maggie recalled her dream, that delicious dream that she had not wanted to end. Her own face flamed when she realized that he might not have raped her, but he had certainly done a lot more than simply undress her. With a jolt, she realized he was coming toward her, and she cringed involuntarily.

Jack made an exasperated noise at her reaction and jammed his hands in his pockets. She was just too tempting sitting there on the bed. He had to get out of here. "I'm going downstairs to get you something to eat. When I come back, we'll finish our little discussion." At her blank look, he explained, "The one you interrupted with your theatrics down in the dining room." He started for the door, but paused with his hand on the knob. "And get some clothes

124

on, too . . . but not that corset," he added, jerking his head to where the item in question lay on the floor. "If you put that damn thing on again, I'll strangle you myself." With that threat he left, slamming the door behind him with unnecessary force.

Maggie's whole body jerked at the noise, and she sat for a moment completely numb with the relief that he was gone. That relief only lasted a moment, however, before she remembered that he would return, and soon. Scrambling off the bed in a tangle of petticoats, she snatched the traveling outfit she had worn the previous day off its hook and began to pull it on. It took only a few moments for her to button up the shirtwaist and slip on the black skirt. She found one of her shoes under the bed and the other half-buried underneath her mourning dress, which Jack had obviously dumped on the floor in disgust. The dress was hopelessly creased, and when she looked a little closer she saw that several buttons were torn off. He had been in a hurry, too.

For a moment she tried to picture the scene, Jack tearing her clothes off, frantic with concern, and then she shuddered. It hadn't been that way at all, she scolded herself. He had probably been furious, afraid she would die before he could get her land and whatever else he wanted from her.

That thought jogged her memory further and brought back the subject of the discussion they had been having in the dining room when she had fainted. The memory stunned her momentarily, so that the mourning dress slipped from her suddenly nerveless fingers and fell to the floor once more. They had been discussing marriage—*their* marriage. Or rather, Jack had been discussing it and she had been objecting to it. It seemed incredible that he had actually proposed marriage to her. Well, not proposed, exactly. It was more like an order or a command that he expected her to obey. Why on earth had he decided to do a thing like that? She knew that he wanted the ranch, and she suspected that money was no object, being fairly certain that he was capable of paying her the price he had originally quoted her. He had her where he wanted her, too, so that he didn't even have to pay her more than a token amount for her cattle so that the law would be satisfied. Why, then, had he suddenly decided he needed to marry her in order to get the land? Unless . . .

Maggie smiled slightly. It seemed incredible that he might actually *want* to marry her, to marry her for herself. Was he secretly in love with her? Had she stolen his heart? She almost laughed out loud at the thought. Jack Sinclair had no heart, of that she was certain. No, if he thought it was necessary to marry her, then he had a very good reason that had nothing to do with sentiment. Perhaps he knew something about the legal entanglements that she did not. Briefly, she considered the idea that the judge might have lied to her, but she soon dismissed that. The judge might have lied to many people, but she would have staked her life on the certainty that he had told *her* the truth, or at least the truth as he knew it. Marrying her did make things neat for Jack, though, regardless of what the law had to say. Maggie could never charge that he had cheated her or stolen from her. As his wife she would still possess the same benefits from the ranch that she had always possessed, with the additional advantage of having a man to protect her.

The thought startled her. Just a few hours earlier, in this very room, she had come to the conclusion that having a man to protect her was the very solution to her problem. Of course, she had envisioned a man who would fight Sinclair, and not Sinclair himself, but now that she thought about it, it all came out the same. If she were married to him, she would have no need for an elaborate scheme to get her ranch back. She would already have it. Oh, he would be in charge, at least at first, but if she could get rid of him . . .

Maggie smiled a slow, secret smile and sank down on the creaky old bed. She knew relatively little about marriage, having observed few such relationships firsthand. Her own mother had died when she was very young, so young that

Maggie scarcely even remembered the ethereal Margarite, much less recalled the way her parents had felt about each other. She had, however, had occasion to observe her aunt and uncle's marriage at close quarters, and had learned a great deal.

Maggie had always hated having to spend holidays and summer vacations at her Uncle Edward's plantation house, and she had known that her Aunt Judith resented her presence. Judith had taken out her resentment on poor Uncle Edward, who endured her shrewish attacks with the patience of Job. Judith had often, and in public, berated him for his follies and foibles, and for his lack of ambition.

In private, things had been even worse. When she had not felt constrained to maintain a ladylike demeanor, Judith became a harridan, turning life at the lovely plantation house into a veritable hell. Maggie knew firsthand, thanks to Aunt Judith, just how miserable a woman could make her husband. That she could do the same to Jack Sinclair, she was certain. It would take a while. She would have to get to know him, to know his weaknesses, but she already knew where to start. She had already pricked his pride a number of times and that would be a good place to start. If she could humble him, humiliate him, in the same way he had humiliated her in front of the whole town, she could drive him away.

Recalling the way Uncle Edward had sought solace in a bottle, Maggie tried to picture Jack Sinclair doing the same, but she could not. No, Sinclair would never sit back and endure, drowning his sorrows. When she had destroyed him, he would leave. Back-stabbing bullies like Sinclair always ran when the going got tough, and she would make the going as tough as possible for him.

Lost in her plans, she did not hear his approach until he called her name through the door. The sound of his voice startled her, and she jumped nervously up from the bed and instinctively backed away, until he called again with growing impatience. "Maggie, open the door! My hands are full."

Swiftly, Maggie obeyed his command and found him standing in the hall juggling a tray of food and looking far from happy about it. When she simply stood there staring, he lifted one eyebrow sardonically and asked, "May I come in?" with exaggerated politeness. Whatever embarrassment he had felt before had evaporated, Maggie noticed as she quickly stepped aside to allow him to enter the tiny room.

After a quick look around, Jack went over and placed the tray on the seat of the straight-backed chair that sat in the corner of the room, and then lifted the whole thing, chair and all, and carried it over to the bed. Satisfied, he straightened from the task and cast a baleful look at Maggie, who was still standing by the open door. "Close the door, Maggie," he ordered softly, and she did, without asking herself why. Jack nodded his approval and then pointed to the bed. "Now sit down and eat."

Maggie considered refusing, but the prospect of dealing with his wrath combined with the fact that she truly was hungry, convinced her that that was a foolish thing to do, and she scurried to take her place on the bed beside where he had placed the tray.

Looking down at the tray, she realized that he had brought up the same lunch that she had ordered downstairs, fried steak, fried potatoes, biscuits with gravy, apple pie and coffee. It looked appealing, but she wondered if she would be able to swallow one single bite with Sinclair glaring down at her. Resolutely, she picked up her knife and fork and cut off a piece of steak. She had it halfway to her mouth when she looked up and met his steely-black stare. "I can't eat with you glaring at me like that," she complained with exasperation, lowering the fork back to the plate.

Jack grunted with an exasperation of his own. "Excuse me, Miss Colson," he grated, and turning on his heel, he strolled over to the window. He stood there in front of it, apparently absorbed in what Maggie knew to be a perfectly awful view, but when she had satisfied herself that he was going to leave her alone to eat in peace, she picked up her fork and began to do so. After a few bites, Maggie admitted to herself that she was ravenous, and she finished off the food on the tray with much more dispatch than Miss Finley would have considered seemly.

Since there was no napkin, Maggie wiped her mouth discreetly with the back of her hand, and then looked up at Sinclair expectantly. He did not turn right away, and so she had a moment to study him. It was the first chance she had had to do so since deciding that she would marry him, and she made some surprising discoveries.

First of all, she decided that she would not mind having him around, physically at least. He made a very good appearance, knew how to dress well and conduct himself in company, even if his private manners could stand some improvement. She would not mind being seen with him, and she even was vain enough to think that they would make a striking-looking couple. As for the rest, she would be much more circumspect than Aunt Judith had ever been. Maggie knew that when a woman degraded her husband publicly, she degraded herself, too, so Maggie would confine herself to private humiliations that would corrode that proud exterior until she was able to turn the tables on him. With that decided, she cleared her throat to draw his attention.

His head swiveled around immediately, and seeing that she was finished, he came over. He came slowly, but with a deliberation that made Maggie a trifle uneasy, although she took great pains not to let it show. He stopped a mere foot away from where her feet rested on the floor beside the bed. "We were discussing our marriage," he began peremptorily.

Swallowing the lump that rose unbidden to her throat, Maggie forced herself to look up and meet that dark gaze. She even managed a small semblance of a smile. "Yes, we were," she agreed politely.

Her meek reply seemed to irritate him and he took a

ragged breath. "We're getting married, Maggie," he stated. His tone brooked no argument, and Maggie gave him none.

"All right," she said, her voice only slightly affected by the way her stomach was starting to churn. She shouldn't have eaten so fast.

He opened his mouth, ready to override her objections, but then his jaw simply dropped in surprise as the meaning of her reply sank in. After a second he closed his mouth with a snap, and his eyes narrowed suspiciously. "What did you say?" he asked warily.

Pleased that she had somehow gotten the upper hand, Maggie treated him to her best finishing school smile. The churning in her stomach was settling down to a slight flutter, and her hands were hardly even shaking. This was going to be far easier than she had imagined. "I said all right, I'll marry you. Don't look so surprised. It's not as if you gave me any other choice, you know," she sniffed, managing to look both put out and put upon at the same time.

Jack, on the other hand, was looking baffled, stunned and incredulous, all of which he felt. Something had happened, something very important, that he had somehow missed. That something had changed the Maggie Colson he knew into an entirely different creature. For just one instant he looked down at the tray, at the empty cup, and entertained the rather far-fetched notion that someone had indeed drugged her, but then he dismissed that notion just as quickly as he had thought of it. No, she hadn't been drugged, not any more than she had changed. She wasn't any different, he realized with certainty as soon as the idea occurred to him. She was simply acting different, with *acting* being the key word. She had chosen to play a new part in their little drama, the part of innocent victim. Well, let her, he decided. It suited his purposes admirably. If only she could sustain it until after they were married, then she could do whatever she damn well pleased, and it wouldn't matter. Once he had her as his wife, once he took her to his bed . . .

A knock on the door interrupted his thoughts, and he turned to answer it. Maggie was a little startled, and she rose nervously to her feet. She didn't want anyone to find her in a compromising position with Jack Sinclair, even if they *were* getting married. The door opened toward her so that she could not see who was there, but she immediately recognized the voice that asked, "You sent for me, boss?"

Swede! Maggie darted across the small space and pulled the door from Jack's grasp, flinging it wide. It was Swede, all right, and he looked more than little surprised to see her, surprised and a little embarrassed when he had a moment to think it over. "Miss Maggie," he murmured in greeting, cringing slightly under the condemnation in her eyes.

"Boss!" she mimicked furiously. *"He's* your *boss?"* she demanded with a contemptuous gesture at the tall, dark man beside her.

Swede's homely face had gone beet red, and he shifted uncomfortably from one large foot to the other. "Yes, ma'am," he said in a voice that cracked slightly.

Maggie stared at him in horror for a long moment as the extent of his treachery became clear to her. That explained everything, why he had left her, why the other men had left. "You've been working for him all along, havn't you?" she accused. "You took Colson pay and rode for the Colson brand, but all the time you were working for him, helping him steal my land, weren't you?"

She wasn't exactly screaming, but she was close, and Swede looked nervously up and down the hall to be certain no one was within earshot. "It wasn't like that, Miss Maggie, not exactly. . . ." he ventured, but Jack had decided that he had had enough of this little drama.

"We're getting married, Swede," he said, effectively ending any further discussion on the subject of Swede's loyalty. He took Maggie's arm in an authoritative grip and gave it a small warning shake.

She glanced up, and even though he wasn't looking at her,

131

she got his message: She had better shut up or else. Pressing her lips tightly together, she managed to bite back the words that she longed to say, words expressing her opinion of men who sold their loyalty to blackguards. Instead, she contented herself with the knowledge that soon she would have Jack Sinclair all to herself, to sink her verbal claws into at will, and if Swede was going to be around, too, so much the better.

"Married?" Swede's surprise was genuine. He had had no inkling that Jack had such plans for poor little Maggie. His pale eyes cast her a pitying look that was wasted because she was too busy glaring up at Jack to notice, but Jack saw it, and his eyes narrowed dangerously.

"Go find someone to marry us," Jack ordered between clenched teeth.

Swede's eyes grew large with amazement. "Now?" he asked in disbelief.

"Right now," Jack confirmed coldly.

Now it was Maggie's turn to be surprised. She had not imagined that the proposed union would take place quite so quickly. She had had no time to make her plans, no time to think things through completely. "But . . ." she tried to protest, but neither man was paying any attention to her.

"The preacher ain't in town till next week," Swede was saying.

"Then get someone else. There's a priest down in Spanish town, isn't there?" Jack asked, referring to the section of town where the Mexicans lived.

Swede wasn't sure about that. "I don't think he'll come. . . ."

"He'll come. Offer him a new bell for his church or something. He'll come," Jack said with a confidence Swede decided not to dispute.

"I'll try," he promised, turning from the door with a notable lack of enthusiasm. "Wouldn't hurt to wait a few days," he muttered just before Jack slammed the door behind him.

Looking down at his prospective bride, Jack realized he was still gripping her arm in a way that could hardly be described as gentle, and jerked his hand away as if her skin had suddenly burned him. What in God's name had gotten into him? He was behaving like a barbarian. Swede probably thought he had lost his mind, and he wouldn't be far from wrong, either, Jack decided. He hadn't been acting exactly rational for quite a while now, not since meeting Maggie Colson. Well, things were going to change now. He'd broken plenty of spirited mares in his time, and breaking this little filly would be a distinct pleasure. Then he would have some peace, and then he would be able to get back to the business of saving Colson's valley.

Maggie's voice startled him. "You planned this whole thing, didn't you?" she was saying, a look of profound amazement on her face. She had been going over the events of the past weeks in her head and dredging up every scrap of information she had learned about what had happened before she had come home. It was so clear to her now that she felt like a fool for not figuring it out before.

Sinclair had sent the nestors to cause the trouble that had broken up the old Colson crew. Deke and the others had either been killed or scared off, so that her father had been forced to hire strangers. Swede had stepped right in, hiring men who would be loyal to Sinclair, so that when the end came, there would be no one to fight him. She had been the only fly in the ointment, but her refusal to go along with his plan had been only a temporary setback. All Sinclair had to do was withdraw his men, leaving her totally alone and defenseless. Why he felt he had to marry her, too, was incomprehensible, but if he was willing to give her that weapon against him, then she would take it. Knowing the full extent of his perfidy only hardened her resolve to carry out her original plan.

She looked very small and vulnerable standing there

absently rubbing the arm he had so recently gripped. Her cheeks were smudged with color from the fury that she felt at his sins, both real and imagined, and her hair still curled wildly around her face. Her eyes weren't vulnerable, though, not at all. The green had faded almost completely to brown, a brown of bitter antagonism that he accepted as a challenge. It would be gratifying to change that antagonism into something else entirely. Yes, gratifying and extremely pleasurable, but not just yet, he decided reluctantly. Not with Swede coming back at any moment with a priest. There would be plenty of time for that later. He smiled at the thought. "No, Maggie," he told her in response to her previous question, "I didn't plan it all, but it's worked out rather nicely just the same, don't you think?"

She did not think so at all, but she did not say so. Not now, not with Swede coming back at any moment. Later there would be time for that, for that and all the things she had planned for him. He wouldn't be smiling then, either, she consoled herself.

"I think I'll wait for Swede downstairs," he said, his voice the cool polite one he used in public, not the one she was used to hearing at all, and she wondered at his abiity to cover his emotions so well. When he was gone, she sat down on the bed for a moment to try to make some sense of all the emotions she had gone through herself in the last hour. It was an exhausting list, but when she thought about it, she had to agree with Jack that perhaps things *had* worked out for the best. Being married to Jack Sinclair might not be the life she would have chosen for herself, but it would provide her with the weapons she needed to fight him, and that was all she asked.

A remarkably short time later, Maggie heard the sound of several people coming up the stairs, and men's voices raised in anger. She recognized two of them as belonging to Swede and Jack. The accent of the third voice marked it as belonging to the priest. She rose hastily as the door flew open and all three men entered.

No one paid her any attention at all. The priest was babbling in Spanish, and Swede was arguing with him, also in Spanish, and Jack, who obviously did not speak Spanish, was arguing in English and demanding to know what was being said by the other two. Maggie, who understood both languages equally well, could not suppress a giggle.

At the sound of her laughter, all three men ceased speaking and gaped at her.

"Por Dios!" the priest breathed fervently when he had taken in the rumpled bed, the clothes still on the floor, and Maggie's disheveled hair.

"What are you laughing at?" Jack demanded, totally ignoring the priest's reaction.

"He said he can't marry us because neither of us is Catholic," she explained, unable to suppress a triumphant smile. Some things even Jack Sinclair could not buy.

Jack took a moment to think this over, while Maggie studied the ridiculous scene before her. The two tall Anglos stood staring down impotently at the tiny priest, who was easily a foot shorter than either of them. His worn cassock testified to his vow of poverty and contrasted vividly with Sinclair's tailored suit. The man had begun to wring his small hands in distress and mumble incomprehensibly in his native tongue, seemingly oblivious to any threat whatsoever from his two formidable adversaries. He seemed, instead, to be overly concerned with Maggie's appearance and the disturbed bedclothes.

For a moment it appeared that the small clergyman had stymied the arrogant Sinclair, but then Jack thought of the perfect solution. "Tell him I'm Catholic," Jack ordered Swede.

Swede blinked in surprise and Maggie uttered a startled, "Oh," at his audacity. "You can't lie to a priest," Swede protested, but Jack's glare silenced him.

"I'll worry about my immortal soul. Just tell him," Jack

demanded once again, and reluctantly, Swede obeyed.

The priest barely glanced at Swede and nodded absently at the information. He was still staring at Maggie. Then he took a step toward her, still nodding, and said, "For you, señorita. I will do it for you," he told her in thickly accented English, and cast another dismayed glance at the bed.

It took Maggie only a moment to realize that he had finally agreed not because of Jack's lie, but because he thought she had been compromised. Jack seemed to realize it at exactly the same moment, because she heard his exasperated curse in the same instant that her face began to flame. As humiliating as it was to have him believe such a thing, still it suited her purposes for people to think that Sinclair was capable of it. Lifting her chin in a parody of wounded dignity, she murmured, *"Gracias, padre,"* and then added something else in swiftly spoken Spanish.

"What did you tell him?" Jack demanded, stalking over to her with such menace that even the little priest raised a hand to protect her, but Maggie forced herself not to cringe under his fury.

"I simply asked him to bear witness that I have been forced to marry you against my will," she informed him haughtily.

What Jack might have done was anybody's guess, but it probably wouldn't have been pleasant if the enraged growl he gave was any harbinger, but before he could so much as lay a finger on Maggie, Swede and the priest stopped him with their cries of "Jack!" and "Señor!" It took a moment for him to regain his self-control, but when he did, he straightened his vest with a jerk, and told Swede, "Tell him to get on with it, then."

Maggie was very glad that she was no longer wearing her corset. She was having a very difficult time breathing even without it, and her stomach was doing flip-flops or something. Not that she was really scared of Jack Sinclair, she insisted to herself, but even Swede had been a little alarmed at the murderous look on his face just a moment ago. It was gone, now, thank heaven. Maggie marveled once again at his ability to control his emotions, even such violent emotions, but she did not have much time to do so, because the priest, who introduced himself to her as Father Juan, had produced a small black book from the folds of his cassock and was reading the marriage ceremony.

Afterward, Maggie recalled little of that ceremony. She knew that she had responded at the appropriate times, and that Jack had, too, with a little prompting from Swede. When the time came to place the ring on her finger, Jack had rather awkwardly pulled a small gold ring set with an emerald from his little finger and placed it on her left hand. She couldn't help but stare at it, because it was quite obviously a man's ring, his ring, and yet she had never noticed him wearing it before, not even earlier today. That meant that he had gone somewhere and gotten it in anticipation of the wedding. She found the act strangely out of character for the man she knew as Jack Sinclair and thus, strangely disconcerting. Amazingly, the ring fit her quite well, but she found the weight of it uncomfortable, almost burdensome, and she had to cradle her left hand with her right to support it.

Before she had time to think, the ceremony was over. Jack was pressing something into Father Juan's hand, and he was protesting feebly and shaking his head, but he was no match for Jack Sinclair, and in the end, he accepted the very generous gift. Then he gave Maggie his blessing, and with a last, sad look at the bed, shook his head and left.

Swede started to leave too, obviously anxious to do so, but Jack stopped him with a word. "Have the buggy hitched up and bring it around to the hotel."

Swede started to protest, but then thought better of it, nodded, and left.

Maggie was painfully conscious of the fact that they were alone. What would happen now? She gave a nervous little laugh to break the silence that had fallen after Swede's departure. "Are we going someplace?" she asked, still cradling her newly ringed hand as if it bore a tremendous weight.

Jack turned his attention to her for the first time since the priest had pronounced them man and wife. "Yes, we're going to the ranch," he said matter-of-factly.

"Tonight?" Maggie glanced meaningfully out the window at the growing dusk. It would be dark long before they reached the ranch. It was foolish to make the trip now when they could just as easily wait until morning, unless . . . "You just can't wait to take possession, can you?" she accused. The knowledge that he now owned the CMC scalded her, and the fact that he could not wait even one more day to stake his claim infuriated her.

His dark eyes studied her intently, taking in the flushed cheeks and the stormy eyes. "No, I can't," he murmured, letting his gaze flicker over her suggestively for a long moment before beginning the lazy movement that drew her inexorably into his arms.

His mouth was on hers before she even had time to register his intention, and her response was immediate, much to her chagrin. Her body, it seemed, remembered his only too well, and her lips parted willingly at his insistence. Her hands slipped beneath his suit coat, seeking his warmth even as his tongue explored the moist secrets of her mouth. It was a long kiss, but it lacked the fevered passion that had marked their earlier ones. Instead, Maggie had the unsettling feeling that he was staking a claim on her, branding her with his lips in some mysterious way. Even so, she gave a small cry of protest when his mouth left hers long before she was ready.

His breathing was ragged, and he continued to hold her tightly as he gazed into her upturned face. Then his mustache tilted up in obvious pleasure at what he saw there. "No, I can't wait to take possession," he told her softly, "but I thought you would prefer to spend your wedding night at home."

138

It took a few seconds for the meaning of his words to register, and when it did, Maggie felt her whole body turn suddenly cold. Wedding night! Dear Lord, how could she have forgotten about that part of marriage? In an instant, Maggie recalled all the things that Sinclair had done to her, how he had kissed her and touched her, and she shuddered to think that now he had the right to do all that and more, much, much more. Exactly what, she wasn't certain, but she had a pretty good idea. Memories of stories she had heard, veiled hints of pain and blood and unspeakable acts, came back to her, and she paled under his scrutiny. If she had thought for one minute that he would not claim his conjugal rights, those thoughts were dashed when she saw the look of satisfaction settle across his features as he read her apprehension. No, he would take pleasure in humiliating her. Men did, or so she had been told, and she was certain that Jack Sinclair would.

"Pack your clothes, little bride," he told her with an annoying smirk. "I'm in a hurry to leave," he added, planting a swift, insulting kiss on her unresponsive mouth. When he pulled away, somewhat reluctantly, Maggie was appalled to realize that her arms were still clinging to him. How could she? she demanded of herself as she jerked her hands away.

Jack chuckled at her reaction. "I'll be back in five minutes," he warned gently as he let himself out the door, "to take possession."

Maggie's outraged gasp was delivered to the closed door.

Chapter V

The long ride back to the ranch was accomplished for the most part in silence. It was completely dark long before they arrived, as Maggie knew it would be, but even nature seemed to have given its allegiance to Jack Sinclair, and a bright moon lighted their way. The horse knew the road well, and that helped, too, so they arrived without mishap.

Maggie had spent the time trying to recall everything she had ever heard about wedding nights. The girls at Miss Finley's had discussed such subjects at length, but since no one involved in the discussions had had any firsthand knowledge, very little useful information had been exchanged. Having grown up around animals, Maggie had seen enough, in spite of heroic efforts to shield her from such things, to have a pretty good idea of what went where, but exactly how it was accomplished in humans, she had no idea. She knew it was done in bed. Of that much the girls at Miss Finley's had been sure, that and the fact that there was blood the first time. And pain.

Maggie had shivered at that thought, drawing a concerned question from Jack about whether she was cold. Disregarding her denial, he had removed his jacket and placed it around her shoulders. The jacket had smelled of cigars and Bay Rum and Jack Sinclair, and Maggie had wanted to fling it off of her and to snuggle down inside of it at the same time. It was a disconcerting feeling.

Between his jacket around her shoulders and his ring on her finger, she was beginning to wonder if she had not been just a little hasty in agreeing to this marriage. Twisting the gold that encircled her finger, she wondered once again just where it had come from, and what kind of a man would, when he was in the midst of forcing a woman to marry him against her will, take the time to hunt up a ring. Maybe, just maybe, Jack Sinclair had a soft streak, a romantic streak. The thought made her smile, but the proof was on her finger. If he did, and Maggie had to admit it was a very large if, then she had another weapon to use against him. That soft streak combined with his pride would make him vulnerable in ways of which only a woman could take advantage.

Of course, she was vulnerable, too, she acknowledged, recalling the way she had responded to his kisses. She wondered suddenly, with a surreptitious glance at Jack, whether the rest of it, the part of marriage she didn't know about, was as pleasant as those kisses had been. That was a very disturbing thought. How could she hope to nag him to distraction when all he had to do was take her in his arms . . . Maggie shivered again. She could feel her nipples puckering under her shirtwaist in anticipation of his touch. How could her own body betray her with such abandon? It simply wasn't fair.

Well, fair or not, it was still her body, and it would obey her commands, whether it liked it or not, she decided. She would simply discipline herself. Even if she felt pleasure, she would not show it. That should be simple enough. She would endure whatever he did to her, good or bad, with silent stoicism. If there was pain, she would not cry out, and if there was not pain . . . well, she would not cry out then, either. That was all there was to it. That decided, she felt immeasurably better. By the time they arrived at the ranch, she was self-possessed enough to notice that lights shone both from the house and the bunkhouse, and that men were milling about in the yard.

Jack did not stop the buggy until they reached the front porch, but as they drove through the yard, Maggie spotted some familiar faces among the ranch hands. They were the same men who had deserted her only days ago. An anger so bitter she could actually taste it welled up in her as she remembered Swede's perfidy. Although she had to hand it to Jack. It was a perfect plan. He might be the biggest scoundrel who had ever lived, but he was the best and the smartest, too. With grudging admiration, she once again examined the man who was now her husband. A worthy adversary, if ever there was one, she decided, as the buggy lurched to a stop at the foot of the porch stairs.

Jack paused a moment before climbing down from the buggy to give his bride a small smile. "Home at last," he told her with a trace of irony.

Maggie answered his smile with one of her own. "It's always been my home, Jack. The question is, will it ever be yours?" She watched with satisfaction as his grin turned into a scowl, and she knew that she had touched a question that he had himself considered. Simply owning something as massive, as vital, as the CMC did not make it yours. In a way, it owned you and made you a part of it, but only if it found you worthy. It might just as easily destroy you. Maggie was glad to know that Jack was aware of that fact.

Wasting no more time, Jack jumped lightly from the buggy and came around to assist Maggie. If his touch was a little less than gentle, she could only blame herself and her sarcasm. When she was safely on the ground, she slipped out of Jack's jacket and handed it to him with a polite nod. "Thank you very much," she said coolly, as if speaking to a stranger, and started up the porch stairs.

He watched her thoughtfully for a moment, enjoying the way she carried herself and savoring the idea that she now belonged to him, body and soul. Then he hastened after her, his long legs easily overtaking her, in order to reach the heavy front door first. Stepping around her to open it, he paused with his hand on the knob and cast her an inquiring look. "Shall I carry you over the threshold, Maggie?" he asked with feigned concern.

Maggie froze, knowing full well that every man on the ranch would be watching their every move. Fortunately, the darkness hid her scarlet cheeks. "Don't you dare!" she hissed threateningly.

Jack pretended to consider for a moment. "No," he decided at last, "I guess even I wouldn't dare, at least not in front of witnesses." Chuckling at her indignant huff, he opened the door and allowed her to precede him into the room.

A welcoming fire blazed in the huge hearth, cutting through the evening chill, and Maggie went straight to it, drawn by its warmth. A full minute passed before she thought to wonder who had lighted it, and when she glanced around the familiar room, she noticed some unfamiliar touches. Someone had cut some wildflowers and put them in a vase on one of the tables. The floor had been swept, too. Maggie knew because some of the furniture had not been replaced just exactly as it had always been. Someone new had been here, had been working in her home. She wanted to know who it was, who had the audacity to touch her things, but even as she opened her mouth to demand that information, an unutterable weariness settled over her. What difference did it make, after all? she asked herself, and was surprised to learn that she did not really know and was too tired to care.

Conscious of Jack, who still stood by the front door and was watching her every move, she suddenly wanted nothing so much as a little privacy. "I . . . I think I'll go to my room," she said to the fire and turned toward the hallway.

"Don't you want some supper?" he called after her, more than a hint of command in the question.

"I'm not hungry," she called back just as she reached the sanctuary of her room. The door didn't lock, of course, but just closing it gave her a small satisfaction. That satisfaction faded, however, when she realized that that invading presence had also been in her room. A lighted lamp bathed the room in a golden glow. A fire had been laid in the small stove, and even though it had now burned down to coals, it still sent out a pervasive warmth. A vase of wildflowers adorned her dressing table, and the water in the pitcher was warm. She poured some into the basin and splashed it on her face, and then used the scented bar of soap to wash her hands. No sooner had she dried them than she heard Jack's voice.

"Open the door, Maggie," he called, and without thinking she obeyed the command. Once again she found him at her door with a tray of food in his hands, and he brushed past her impatiently. Maggie could only stare as he carried the tray over to the large, overstuffed chair that sat beside the stove and set it on the small table nearby. When he straightened and turned, his mustache was set in a grim line. "You'll eat that," he said gruffly. "I won't have you fainting on me again." Maggie knew a small spark of rebellion at the order, but decided she wasn't up to an argument and merely nodded. She didn't need to fight about it. She would simply not eat it. She had not been lying when she had said she wasn't hungry.

Jack came back to where she still stood holding the door open. For a moment he studied her face, and then nodded as if giving silent approval of the meekness he saw reflected there. Then he cleared his throat. Maggie stared in surprise at the uncharacteristic sound. It was almost the way Swede cleared his throat when he was going to say something that embarrassed him.

"I'll give you some time alone now, to get ready," he said, and his hand went up to finger the gold watch chain that crossed his vest. "You do know what happens next, don't you?" he added, his eyes narrowing suspiciously.

For what seemed like the thousandth time that day, Maggie felt the blood rush to her face. It was bad enough that he was going to do it, but did he have to talk about it, too? Lifting her chin, she met his eyes, determined that he would not know how very frightened she was or how very ignorant. "Of course, I do," she informed him, and then stepped back with an exaggerated sweep of her hand that invited him to leave.

He looked almost . . . what was it? Almost relieved, Maggie thought, just before he turned to go, but he turned back just as she was closing the door and warned, "I won't be gone long, though."

No, she had already been certain of that. Closing the door this time gave her even more pleasure, and she wished once again that her father had installed locks when he had built the house. Not that she thought for one minute a locked door would have stopped Jack Sinclair, but it would have been amusing to see just how he would have dealt with it.

The thought lightened her mood for a moment, but only for a moment, and then the weariness settled over her again. The chair by the stove looked more than inviting, and when she sank into it, she could not help but notice the supper that he had brought her. She only needed a glance to tell her that Wiley's hands had never touched this food. The flat, perfectly round tortillas were artfully arranged around a tempting mixture of beef and beans. The crust of the apple pie actually looked as if it might flake if touched, and even the coffee smelled good. Unable to resist, she took a small sip, and then a larger one. It was strong, all right, strong enough to float a horseshoe, but for some reason it didn't taste as if a horseshoe had dissolved in it the way Wiley's coffee always did. The savory brew revived her somewhat, and she emptied the cup. She might even have tasted the food if she had thought that her stomach would have tolerated it, but instead she leaned back into the depths of

145

her chair and closed her eyes.

She should be doing something, she knew. She should be "getting ready," whatever that involved, but she just did not have the energy. She would get up in a moment, as soon as she had rested. With her eyes closed she could see, very clearly, the tiny padre in his frayed cassock and the emerald ring and the cowboy who had insulted her in front of the saloon and Judge Harris tapping his finger on his lip and Festus behind the desk at the hotel and Swede looking so embarrassed and Jack . . . and Jack. . . .

"Not ready for bed yet, Mrs. Sinclair?"

Maggie's eyes flew open to encounter two black ones, which were laughing back at her. She knew instantly that she had fallen asleep because even though her mind was alert, the rest of her was sluggishly unresponsive. Jack was squatting in front of her, his long, slender hands resting on the arms of the chair on either side of her, effectively blocking any escape she might have thought about making, if she had been able to move.

"I was hoping to find you waiting in bed for me," he was saying, "but I think I like this even better. Now I can help you undress." His voice washed over her in honeyed waves, his softly slurred accent lulling her while his hands began to work the buttons of her jacket.

He had the jacket open and had released the first two buttons of her shirtwaist before it really dawned on her what he was doing. "Stop!" she said a little too softly to be really effective, but at last she was able to make her sluggish hands move and she tried to push his hands away from her bodice. "You mustn't," she insisted, trying to blink away the cobwebs that still clouded her brain.

Amazingly, he did not seem angry, only more amused. "Oh, I forgot something, didn't I?" he said, allowing her to brush his hands away and rising to his feet. For one grateful second she thought he was going to leave, but instead he reached down and drew her up from the chair. Her legs were none too steady at first, but that didn't matter because he was holding her, and then his arms were around her and he was kissing her and she forgot about her legs entirely.

His kiss was amazingly gentle at first, as if his lips just wanted to play with hers, but Maggie's body remembered how it had been before and instinctively leaned into the kiss, demanding more. Her brain registered his satisfied hum, while her body settled into his embrace and her lips parted for his sweet invasion.

This wasn't right, this wasn't the way it was supposed to be, she knew. She had decided not to respond to him, hadn't she? She should probably just let herself go limp, except that she felt remarkably limp already. He had just pulled off her jacket and she hadn't even felt it. Now his lips were doing wonderful things to her throat while his fingers were undoing her buttons, and for some reason, she didn't mind a bit.

One button snagged, and Maggie was vaguely disturbed when he pulled it loose with a jerk that sent it flying, but he soothed that disturbance with his hands and lips. Gently sliding her shirtwaist from her, he warmed her bared arms and shoulders with a thousand tiny kisses. Her own hands were busy, too. For some reason she could not seem to stop touching him, running her hands over his back and shoulders, feeling the warmth of him through the fine linen of his shirt. When his mouth found the valley between her breasts, she buried her hands in his thick black hair and held him to her.

His grumbled protest against her bosom alerted her to the fact that he had begun to unbutton her skirt, and was having trouble. For some reason, she wanted to help him, but couldn't get her hands to cooperate. Instead she continued to cradle his head against her, smiling when she felt the tug and heard the tearing sound and then heard the buttons go skittering across the floor. Some distant part of her brain made a mental note to find them in the morning, while at the

147

same time she was registering his growing impatience.

The hands that had gently caressed just moments ago now where ripping at the ties of her petticoats. What was the hurry? she wondered as he stripped the petticoats and skirt down over her hips in one swift swipe. For one sobering moment she stood there in just her chemise and pantalettes, her skirts pooled around her ankles, before Jack scooped her up into his arms. Two long strides took them to her bed, and he laid her down on top of the quilt with a sort of quick carefulness.

Lying there, staring up at him, she felt all the fears she had harbored before come rushing back. He would take her now, now that they were on the bed. The nice part would be over and the bad part would start. Maggie swallowed the lump that tried to rise in her throat, and concentrated on meeting his dark gaze unflinchingly. He was watching her, looming over her on the bed, and then, instead of closing in as she had expected, he rose to his feet and began, ever so slowly, to release the buttons of his vest.

Maggie watched, almost hypnotized, as he removed first his vest and then his shirt, taking the time to remove the studs from his cuffs and put them in his pants pocket before tossing the shirt to the floor. Surely she had seen a man's chest before, but she could not remember ever seeing one quite so broad or quite so masculine or quite so dark before. The same raven hair that covered his head matted that chest in tiny curls, narrowing to a V just above his belt buckle. When his hand went to that belt buckle, Maggie felt her body tense, but she could not seem to turn away. Fascinated, she watched as he slipped off his trousers, shoes and socks almost in one continuous motion.

Clad now only in the snug cotton drawers that hung low across his hips, he looked like some magnificent sculpture, the whiteness of his body where it was shielded from the sun contrasting with the ebony of his hair. Maggie thought that she had never seen any sight so compelling, but when his hand moved to the buttons at his waist, she caught her breath in alarm. As pleasant as it was to look at him, she did not want to see any more.

Immediately sensing her distress, he changed his mind, moving instead to remove her shoes and stockings. The simple pumps came off with a flick of his wrist, but he peeled her stockings down carefully, pausing once to place a single kiss on the inside of one well-turned ankle.

Maggie gasped at this, and found the blood that she had thought had turned cold heating up again. Magic fingers danced a teasing tattoo up her body, starting at her feet, and then up her calves, pausing to discover a sensitive spot behind her knee, and then moving on, heating the silk that covered her thighs, darting around the part of her that was beginning to throb uncomfortably and pattering on to find the breasts that longed for his touch.

He paused there, too, fingering the puckered peaks through the fragile silk for just a moment before seeking out the silken flesh bared by the décolleté chemise. Those fingers found the pulse that now beat wildly at her throat, and rested there a moment, savoring this evidence of her arousal, before reaching up to catch the head that now tossed to and fro in silent denial of emotions that raged out of control.

Then his mouth captured hers, and in that first sweet contact, Maggie noticed something that had escaped her before, the sickly-sweet taste of alcohol on his breath. Oh, he was far from drunk, that much she knew, but had he needed a drink or two before coming to her? Dutch courage? She found courage of her own in that thought, and when he lifted his mouth from hers and reached to brush a stray auburn curl from across her eyes, she saw that the hand that performed this simple task was trembling.

For the first time she realized that he was trembling all over, his breathing ragged and shallow, those dark eyes she knew so well glazed with the same desire that throbbed in her own veins. He wanted her! The truth dazed her for a moment. She had thought . . . what *had* she thought? That he kissed her only to punish her or to distract her? Whatever she had thought, she now knew the truth, that as much as he made her want him, he wanted her that much and more. Instinctively she knew he had added another weapon to her arsenal, but before she had time to consider it, she felt the cool air touch her breasts. While she had been thinking, he had been working, loosening the ribbons of her chemise, exposing the pale mounds of her breasts, first to his heated gaze and then to his scorching touch, and then to his consuming kiss.

In spite of all her best intentions, Maggie found herself writhing with pleasure as his tongue curled around one pink tip while the pad of his thumb nudged the other to pebbled hardness. She was too busy following the track of his mustache across her heated skin to notice when he slipped her chemise down her arms and out from under her. Once her hands were free again, she used them to do some exploring of her own. If her skin was hot, then his was on fire, she thought, running her fingers across the broad expanse of his shoulders. He felt like satin wrapped around molten steel, his softness surprising her as much as the burning power she felt beneath it, and she could not seem to get enough of the feel of him.

She felt more than heard him groan at her touch. Reveling in this newfound source of power, she tested it to its limits with fingers that sought and traced and caressed and tormented, until, in desperation, he captured her hands and pinned them above her head.

"Little witch," he breathed against her parted lips just before claiming her mouth with a kiss that fairly drowned her in a sea of sensation. The tickle of hair against her nose matched the prickle of hair that teased against her swollen breasts, and this time it was she who groaned while she strained and arched against him. One large hand released her small wrist to still her writhing, and one long leg caught both of hers. He had found the drawstring to her pantalettes, and wasting no time on formalities this time, he snapped it between his fingers and slid the silk from her silkier hips.

Within seconds she lay naked beside him, and he took a moment to savor the sight of her pale, trembling body. "You're beautiful, Maggie," he whispered. Just as beautiful as he had imagined, and more so, because now she belonged to him. Or she would, in just another moment.

The cool air caressing her most private parts cut through the haze of passion that had surrounded her as Jack drew his warmth away in order to admire her. She was naked! How had that happened? She could not remember, nor did she care to. His compliment came to her from very far away, and then she went rigid when his movements told her that he was removing the last of his own clothes.

Curiosity tugged at her eyelids, but humiliation squeezed them shut. As much as she longed to see what made a man a man, she could not bring herself to look. Instead she frantically tried to cover herself, but once more he caught the hands that fluttered in a feeble attempt at modesty and placed them gently but firmly by her sides. Helplessly, she clutched up two handfuls of quilt, eyes still squinched shut, and swallowed her last vestige of pride to beg for some semblance of privacy. "The light, put out the light," she pleaded, her voice wavering with the panic building within her.

He denied her gently. "No," he murmured, touching a tiny kiss to one crinkled eyelid. "I want to see you," he added before kissing the other. She stiffened defensively when a warm hand reached out to caress her hip, but he did not draw away. Stroking, coaxing, in an attempt to soothe her fears, he moved his lips to the hollow behind her ear, and whispered, "I'll try not to hurt you."

A strange promise from a man who several times this very day had fought off the urge to murder her. He was the first to admit it. He had not intended to be so very tender with her,

151

had, in fact, looked forward to using a certain amount of force in subduing her. It would have been meager compensation indeed for the torment she had caused him, but he had forgotten all desire for revenge the moment he had come in and found her sleeping in the chair. She had looked so small and fragile and defenseless, and he had been faced with the fact that she truly was. Some primitive protective instinct that he had never suspected he possessed had taken hold of him at that moment, and all thoughts of vengeance had fled. He had been fairly certain that he could make her respond to his lovemaking, but from that instant it became imperative that she feel the same urgency, the same need that now consumed him. She would never know the force of will, the sheer grit that had held him from the ultimate possession until he could achieve that goal, and now that that goal was so close, he restrained himself with a renewed compulsion.

Gentle fingers traced her hip and then explored her thigh down to that special spot behind her knee, and her fear seemed to evaporate on the sigh that escaped her lips. She had vowed not to enjoy it, but where was the harm? she wondered as her legs parted obediently at his encouragement, granting him the access he demanded. Moaning softly at his first touch, at his first intimate invasion, she missed his small gasp of surprise.

She was so hot, so ready for him, that for one desperate split second he almost lost what little control he had left. Only the sound of her moaning constrained him. It would only take another minute, just one more minute, and then she would be as lost as he, he reminded himself.

Maggie was already lost, lost in a world where she was quite alone, a world that centered on one deliciously sensitive spot. Like a talented musician, Jack struck all the right chords, playing her body until every nerve, every fiber sang in a joyous chorus of desire. Her moans came with every breath, while her very toes curled with wanting, wanting.

"Please . . . please . . ." she begged, not knowing for what she entreated, but trusting that, somehow, he would.

He did. In a moment he was on her, testing, probing, prodding, spreading her to receive him. Gently, so gently that he quaked from the effort, he broke through the slight barrier of her innocence, capturing her small cry with his mouth, before claiming her completely.

The pain was as sharp as a bee sting, and as fleeting, quickly forgotten as she felt him fill her. It was so right, so good, that she could not remember what she had feared. He held her still, their bodies joined, for a long moment, while his mouth explored hers, his tongue duplicating the union they had made below. Maggie clutched him to her, her nails digging into the smooth skin of his back in an effort to meld his entire body into hers, and she moaned a protest when he resisted her embrace. For a moment she did not understand when he began to pull away, but when he plunged back again, sending waves of pleasure coursing over her, she understood instantly. At his urging, she tentatively met his next thrust, and found the waves rose higher still. Soon they were moving together in the pulsing rhythm, hands and lips caressing wildly, bodies locked into an ancient quest.

Maggie had never imagined that her body could feel so much pleasure, or that the pleasure could grow with each tormenting thrust. The pressure kept building, building, until she thought she might explode, and her breath came in ragged, pleading gasps and her blood raced in streams of liquid fire. Just when she thought, just when she knew that she could bear it no longer, not for another second, the explosion came, her body and her soul shattering into a million crystal shards that flashed the brilliance of the sun in the instant before its heat consumed her.

From far away, from beneath the tinkling remnants of

herself, she heard Jack call her name, felt his shudders of release, registered his sated stillness, but she was still too lost, too broken to quite care. As long as he was there, close and warm and holding her, she was content.

In the weariness that follows complete satisfaction, Jack slid the burden of his weight from her, but still cradled her against him with arms and legs that held and cherished. He knew that in another moment reality would intrude, that their passion-dampened bodies would begin to cool and that they would have to untangle themselves to struggle with quilts and bedclothes, but for the moment he simply held her. She was so very beautiful, lying there, still quivering in the aftershocks of the cataclysm that had shaken them both. Her face flushed and glistening in the golden glow of the lamplight, her long, coffee-colored lashes spreading fanlike across her cheeks, her honeyed breath sighing through lips still swollen from his kisses, she was the personification of all his dreams, of all that life had once promised and then failed to provide, and in that tiny sliver of time, he knew.

You are the one I have been looking for, little one, he thought. How could I not have realized it before? How could I not have understood why I could not let you go? I love you, little witch.

"I love you, little witch." He did not even realize that he had spoken the words aloud until he saw her eyelids flicker open, and saw the surprise, the horror mirrored in those green depths.

Maggie could not believe it. It was too incredible. How could she be lying here, naked and trembling, wrapped in the arms of the man who had destroyed her life and listening to him utter the most monstrous lie of all?

"Is that what you men do?" she asked, her voice a thin thread of sound that threatened to snap at the slightest provocation.

Still trying to make sense of her reaction to his declaration, Jack could only stare stupidly. "What?"

154

"What you do, what you say, to make it all right after you've raped a woman," she explained. No longer trembling, she was shaking now with the fury that rushed in to fill the void in her body left by his passion.

"Rape!" Jack was incredulous. The hands that only moments ago had cherished, now gripped her shoulders with bruising force.

"Yes, rape," she replied, ignoring the way she shook, ignoring the way his fingers were biting into her flesh, ignoring the way her voice was beginning to sound shrill and hysterical. "That's what it's called when a man takes a woman against her will."

"I didn't notice its being against your will," he gritted, responding with a fury of his own.

"Everything you've done to me has been against my will," she insisted, not letting logic interfere with her thought processes. "You've taken everything from me." She paused a moment and then repeated, "Everything," in a broken whisper that reminded them both of the last thing he had taken.

The protective instinct that had saved her from his anger before welled up once more. His punishing grip relaxed into a soothing caress. "You're my wife, Maggie," he murmured.

"And that gives you the right to take whatever you want from me," she hissed, her face contorting into a mask of rage, "but you can't make me believe your lies, your dirty stinking lies. How dare you speak of love to me, you thief, you *murderer!*" She was close to hysteria now, but there was nothing she could do to stop herself. Jack was shaking her, but he could not halt the flow of words that rushed from her lips like the pent-up waters pouring through a broken dam. She saw the hand rise and curl into a fist, knew he was going to strike her, but there was nothing she could do.

Instinctively, she cried out, a pathetic little squeal, before throwing her hands up protectively, but it was a wasted effort. The blow had not been aimed at her at all, and it struck the bed beside her head, jarring her, frightening her into silence. Then she was jarred again as Jack thrust her away from him with a vicious curse and pushed himself off the bed.

Through the fingers that covered her face, she caught a glimpse of lean flanks as he pulled on his trousers, and then he wheeled to face her, raking her body with contemptuous black eyes. "If that was rape, Maggie, then one of us is crazy," he told her in a voice that shook with rage, "but don't worry, I'll never take anything from you again." He drew a ragged breath in an attempt at calmness and raised one clenched fist heavenward. "In fact, I'll never even touch you again. So help me, God," he swore through gritted teeth, "not even if you beg me."

Maggie lay paralyzed, half by fear and half by shock, unable even to cover herself from him, but then he was no longer even looking at her. He was gathering up his clothes in swift, angry movements, and then he was gone, slamming the door behind him with a finality that made her cringe.

What had she done? In the past half-hour she had gone from the heights of ecstasy to the depths of terror. She had welcomed Jack Sinclair into the haven of her body with an eagerness that appalled her, and then she had driven him away in a fury that should have pleased her, but somehow did not. Wasn't that her plan? Hadn't she decided to marry him just for the opportunity to do that very thing? Then why did the victory seem so hollow? Why did she suddenly feel so alone, so abandoned?

The trembling that had ceased so abruptly at his blow began again, little quivers at first that quickly grew into convulsive shudders. She was cold, so cold, she decided, missing the warmth of that other body, and she reached with one palsied hand to draw the edge of the quilt over her. Wrapped in her patchwork cocoon, shielded from prying eyes, muffled from prying ears, she gave in to the sobs that had been tearing at her chest, granting them release. She knew that crying would not stop the pain, would not even ease it, but that made no difference. She had to weep, and weep she did, as if the salt tears could wash away the memory of his touch . . . or the desire for it. How long she sobbed she never knew, but at some time during the night, long after the lamp had sputtered into darkness, she slipped into the netherworld of sleep, a victim of exhaustion and her own tormenting emotions.

Jack was not quite so lucky. Denied the catharsis of a good cry, he pulled on the remainder of his clothes and went in search of Cal Colson's liquor cabinet. To his everlasting regret, he found it.

The sun was high when Maggie awoke. Stiff and a little sore, she stretched tentatively, and was surprised to discover that she was naked. Instantly she recalled the reason for that nakedness, as well as the events surrounding it, and she felt her face flame. She was developing an alarming habit of waking up in distressing situations, she decided. Snuggling back down into the warmth of the quilt, she compared her prior information to the facts of life as she now knew them.

There had been pain, a little anyway, but nothing too very dreadful. Nothing, at least, compared to the emotional pain that Jack Sinclair had inflicted. Then she recalled that she had inflicted a little pain herself. She could not recall exactly what she had said, she had been too upset at the time to really pay that much attention, but she vividly remembered his vow never to touch her again. That suited her fine, she decided. She had no desire to repeat the soul-shattering experience of the night before. Not even the glorious pleasure she remembered was enough to tempt her to put herself in Jack Sinclair's power again.

Then she remembered that there was supposed to have been blood. Had there been? Exploring herself with cautious fingers, she encountered a little soreness, and the dried residue of what might have been blood. That was enough to spur her to action, and in another moment she was out of bed and into the wrapper that hung on a peg by the bed.

The water in the pitcher was stone cold, but it served the purpose. After she had splashed some on her face, she dipped the corner of a towel in the icy water, and gingerly scrubbed the tender area between her legs. Only the faintest tinge of red stained the towel, thus alleviating her worst fears, and when she was free of this last trace of Jack Sinclair's invasion, she felt immeasurably better.

The next step was to pick up her scattered garments from the night before. Every one of them, she noticed with irritation, would have to be mended, and try as she would, she could not find one of the buttons he had torn from her skirt. Hiding the clothes in the bottom of her trunk where no one might chance across them and guess the shameful events of the night before, she proceeded to choose the clothes she would wear for the day.

The decision gave her a moment's hesitation. While she would have liked nothing better than to climb back in her bed and pull the covers over her head, never having to face another living soul, never having to acknowledge that she was Jack Sinclair's wife, in deed as well as fact, she knew that that would be a foolish thing to do. That would give Sinclair the upper hand, would make him think that he had beaten her, and that would never do. As unpleasant as the prospect was, she knew that she would have to dress and go about her business as if nothing had happened, as if Jack Sinclair had never held her in the night and made her cry out in abandon. She could just imagine with what delight the ranch hands would greet the news that the bride had cowered in her room the morning after her wedding, ashamed to face the world. That thought alone was enough to galvanize her into action.

She chose a simple calico dress, one she had previously rejected for ranch wear. It was white, with a sprinkling of green and gold flowers, and was, she determined, the most virginal of all her dresses. She would present quite a picture in it, too. She spent an unusual amount of time on her hair, partly because she had not taken it down and brushed it the night before and it was dreadfully tangled, but partly because she wanted it to look perfect, too. Instead of putting it up as she usually did, she left it loose to curl around her shoulders and tied a green satin ribbon around her head to keep it out of her face.

She had to pinch her cheeks and bite her lips to get some color into them, and even so she looked a little strained, but at least her eyes weren't red and swollen as she had feared. The little sleep she had managed had taken care of that situation, and she had to admit, when she stood back from her mirror to admire her efforts, that she looked every inch the abused innocent. Smiling at the thought, she suddenly realized that she was starving, and set out to hunt up some breakfast.

The house was quiet, as it should have been in the middle of the morning. The men would have long since eaten and gone off to work, and Wiley might even have cleaned up the mess by now.

When she came to the front room, Maggie paused for a moment, listening for sounds of life. She had thought that maybe Jack would be in her father's office, but a peek through the partially opened door to that room showed it to be empty. A slight tingle of apprehension crawled up the backs of Maggie's legs at the prospect of facing Jack in the light of day. He would still be angry, of that she was certain, but he would also have the satisfaction of knowing how she had responded to him. The prospect of seeing that satisfaction reflected on his face was daunting, and for a moment she considered fleeing back to her room, but then sternly reminded herself that that was the very reason she had decided to come out in the first place. She could not let him know that he intimidated her. Squaring her shoulders, she started for the dining room. Jack probably wouldn't be there, either, she told herself. He would have eaten with the men, and might even have ridden out with them. It was a comforting thought.

Maggie's comfort lasted only a few seconds, until she reached the doorway into the dining room, and then it was replaced by complete shock.

Jack was there, all right, sitting at the head of the huge table with a cup of coffee in front of him, but it was a Jack that she had never seen before. The raven hair that was usually so carefully combed was a mess, hanging down in his eyes in front and sticking up in tufts in other places. His fine linen shirt looked like it had been slept in, and slept in fitfully at that, and now that she noticed, it was buttoned crooked, with one extra buttonhole sticking up at his throat. His face bore a vicious-looking set of unshaven whiskers, and his eyes, when he finally lifted them to her, were absolutely awful. Maggie had never seen eyes so red-rimmed and bloodshot. It hurt her even to look at them, and unconsciously, her hand lifted to cover her heart in her distress.

When he saw her poised in the doorway, Jack, the consummate gentleman, rose. She would never know what it had cost him to perform that little courtesy. His head felt like someone had dropped an anvil on it, an anvil that someone was still pounding on, and he would have been roundly cursing Cal Colson and his poor taste in liquors if it hadn't been so exceedingly difficult for him to get his mouth to form words. Simply standing had been a major achievement.

"Good heavens, Jack, you look like you've been pulled through a knothole . . . backwards!" Maggie exclaimed, unable to resist. It had taken her a moment, but she had at last determined that he was suffering from a hangover, that he had spent the night disposing of a good portion of her father's liquor supply, and was quite a bit worse off for the experience.

He winced slightly at the volume of her voice, but managed a slightly crooked smile of self-mockery. "And you

160

are looking as lovely as ever, Mrs. Sinclair."

Maggie winced at that. How little she had considered when she had consented to this marriage. From now on, for the rest of her life, she would no longer be Maggie Colson, but Mrs. Jack Sinclair. The thought horrified her, but she tried not to let it show. Instead she schooled her face into a pleasant smile. "No need to be so formal, Jack," she chided lightly. "Now that we're married, you may call me 'Maggie.'"

A small sound alerted her to the presence of a third person in the room. Maggie's eyes darted to the door that led to the kitchen, and she realized for the first time that their little scene had been played out before an audience, and a very appreciative audience at that.

The Mexican woman standing in the doorway was grinning with approval at Maggie, sending her a silent message with her dark eyes that said she was proud of the way Maggie had handled her new husband. The woman, Maggie judged, was probably in her mid to late twenties, and was quite attractive in a full-blown sort of way. Her figure was buxom, large-breasted and large-hipped, but pleasingly so, without being in the least fat, and her face was smooth and brown, not at all pretty, but appealing, nevertheless. Maggie felt herself responding to the silent message.

Jack's gaze had followed Maggie's and he swallowed once, with difficulty, in preparation to making the necessary introductions. "Maggie, this is Consuela, my housekeeper . . . our housekeeper," he corrected himself. "Consuela, this is my wife, Maggie."

Maggie thought he put undue emphasis on the word "wife," but she tried to ignore it, and nodded politely to the woman. A thousand thoughts ran through Maggie's brain during that nod. She bristled at the fact that Jack would naturally have a woman to look after his needs, whatever those needs might be, and that explained his whiter-than-white shirts that only a woman could have produced, and the flowers in the house, the fire in her room, the hot water.

161

Consuela had been busy, had had the run of Maggie's home for quite a while, perhaps since the moment she had left it two days ago. How certain Sinclair had been that he would have it all in the end. But, Maggie reminded herself, the end had not yet come, and when it did . . .

"Is there any breakfast left, Consuela?" Maggie asked with more pleasantness than she felt.

"*Si,* señora, I will get you some," the woman replied, approaching the table. She was looking at Jack with some concern. "Señor Jack?" she asked, cocking her head inquiringly as he cautiously lowered himself back into his chair. "Some eggs, *por favor?*"

Maggie almost giggled at the look that passed over his face. Those awful eyes closed for a moment in horror at the mere suggestion, and she thought he actually paled, although he was so pale already it was difficult to be sure. "Just some more coffee," he said in a slightly strangled voice.

For a moment Consuela did not move, and when she did, it was not toward the kitchen at all but in the opposite direction. She returned almost instantly, carrying a familiar-looking bottle, which she placed beside Jack's cup before finally disappearing into the kitchen.

Maggie watched in amused silence as Jack picked up the bottle and splashed a generous portion of the amber liquid into what remained of his coffee. "A little hair of the dog, Jack?" she asked cheerfully, taking the seat to his immediate left.

Jack picked up the cup with a hand that was ever so slightly unsteady, drained it, and set it carefully back in its saucer before replying. "Don't feel that you have to make polite conversation, Mrs. Sinclair," he said quietly, but the look he turned on her held a warning that she had no difficulty understanding. Whatever else he had to suffer, he would not suffer her teasing.

Shrugging in mock apology, she said, "Yes, Jack," quite meekly, and folded her hands very primly in her lap, while

162

mentally congratulating herself on her decision to come out of her room. If she had not, she might have missed seeing Jack in this condition, missed knowing that however clever he was most of the time, he still made mistakes, just like normal people. That was important information.

Consuela soon came bustling back, bringing with her some coffee for Maggie and a refill for Jack, which she spiked for him herself. Before Maggie could think of anything to say or do that would sufficiently irritate Jack, the housekeeper returned, and Maggie soon realized that she could irritate him beyond measure simply by eating the very well-prepared breakfast that Consuela set before her.

Jack made a point of not watching her eat, but he could not ignore the sounds she made, sounds that Miss Finley would have been horrified to hear, but which Maggie took great pains to make. She also found it necessary to remark to no one in particular what a good cook Consuela was, and how she could not remember ever having eggs that had been prepared with quite so much care. From the corner of her eye, she had watched Jack go chalk white. When his skin had taken on a slightly greenish tinge, he could stand it no more. Lurching to his feet, he called, "Consuela," forgetting for a moment that he should not shout, and grasping his head with both hands as the reverberations echoed through it. When she did not come, he turned slightly toward Maggie without actually looking at her and asked in a carefully modulated voice, "Will you ask Consuela to bring some hot water to my room, please."

"I'd be glad to," Maggie replied around a mouthful of eggs, but Jack was already hurrying from the room. She watched him with a satisfied smile that faded slowly as a new thought occurred to her. As amusing as it had been to see Jack in this condition, she had to wonder why he had gotten himself in this condition in the first place. All amusement died when she remembered what had happened the previous night, how she had hurled her bitter accusations at him, how

163

he had left her in a rage. She had not been laughing then. She had been sobbing in pain and grief. Had he felt some of that pain, too? Men did not cry into their pillows, of course, that much she knew, but did they drown their sorrows in a bottle? She had often seen her Uncle Edward do just that when Aunt Judith's tongue became too much for him. The knowledge that she had driven Jack Sinclair to the bottle on the very first day of their married life should have given her great satisfaction. Somehow, it did not.

"The señor, he is gone?" Maggie glanced up, startled. She had not heard Consuela return.

"Yes, he . . . he went to his room," Maggie told her. Now that was strange, she realized. *His* room. Just where was that, she wondered, and was it different from *her* room? "He wanted you to bring him some hot water," she recalled absently as she pondered this new question.

Consuela made some reply that Maggie did not hear and left again, presumably to get Jack his hot water. Maggie finished her breakfast in the ensuing silence, and forced herself to consider her next move. Coming out of her room had been the right thing, that much she knew, and facing Jack had not been nearly as difficult as she had anticipated. Now she had to face the men. The thought made her cringe, knowing how cowboys loved to tease, knowing that as a new bride she would be subject to the most embarrassing kind of double entendres, but also knowing that it would be worse if she hid. She would have to face them sooner or later, and a Colson would make it sooner. If she were still a Colson, she would have to prove it, she decided, but how? It took her only a few moments to decide on the most natural way to encounter them.

Patting her mouth with the snowy-white napkin that Consuela had placed beside her, Maggie rose and marched resolutely back to her room. She came up short when she entered the hallway to the bedrooms and saw Consuela entering from the other end carrying a steaming kettle. The Mexican woman apparently did not notice her, but

164

proceeded to carry the hot water into what had been Cal Colson's bedroom. So *that* was his room, Maggie thought bitterly. He hadn't wasted any time taking over where her father had left off. Well, she didn't care where he slept, she told herself, as long as he didn't try to sleep with her.

Once in her own room, she quickly found the riding outfit she had purchased on her last trip to Bitterroot. One of the many projects she had undertaken to kill time had been altering the yellow workshirt she had found at Alexander's Mercantile and making up a riding skirt from the denim she had purchased. Her old riding boots were still in the bottom of her wardrobe, and when she had dusted them off, she found they still fit, even if they were a little stiff. When she had adjusted the flat-crowned hat at just the right angle, tucked in the tail of the yellow shirt for the third time and stood back to admire the picture she made, she felt ready to face anything, even a yardful of smart-mouthed cowboys.

The yard was indeed full of cowboys, she discovered, much to her surprise. She had not really expected to see more than two or three who had been assigned to work around the ranch buildings for the day. Pausing on the porch steps for a moment, she studied the crowd of men, and then saw the tallest one break away from the group and come loping over to her.

"Something wrong, Miss Maggie?" Swede asked when he arrived, panting, at her side.

"Why are all the men still hanging around?" she asked, forgetting for a moment that she had very good reason to be furious with the foreman.

"They're waiting for the lumber," he said obscurely.

Now Maggie remembered that she was angry with him. "What lumber?" she asked, resigning herself to the fact that if she wanted information from him, she was going to have to extract it piece by piece.

"For the new cookhouse," he replied, as if that explained everything.

Maggie sighed wearily. "Why do we need a new cookhouse?" she asked with exaggerated patience.

Swede frowned. "Jack didn't tell you?" he asked suspiciously.

Maggie glared at him until he flushed. "If Jack had told me, I wouldn't be asking you, now would I?" she informed him, and then gave him a very expectant look.

"He said . . ." Swede stammered, and then cleared his throat and tried again. "He said that he don't want the boys eating at the house anymore. Said you and him would dine alone." That, Maggie knew, must be a direct quote, since Swede would never use the word "dine." "He sent for some lumber so's the boys could build themselves a cookhouse."

Maggie felt her own face turning a little red. How they must have laughed at that, at the picture of her and Jack "dining" in romantic seclusion up in that huge dining room all alone. Now more than ever she wanted to get away. "I'm going riding, Swede. Saddle me a horse," she ordered and began to walk toward the corral.

It took a moment for Swede to register her command, and then he came charging after her. "I don't think you ought to do that, Miss . . . I mean Mrs. Sinclair," he was saying.

Maggie bristled at the sound of her new name on the foreman's lips. That, combined with his refusal to obey her, irritated her beyond words. "And why not?" she demanded, coming to such a sudden halt that Swede almost careened into her.

"I . . . you . . . I mean, you'd better ask Mr. Sinclair about that. Did he say it was all right?" he asked suspiciously.

Maggie fought the rage that rose up in her at the suggestion that she should ask permission of Jack Sinclair to do anything. Instead she let her eyes go wide and her face go slack in complete astonishment. "Am I a prisoner here?" she asked in perfect disbelief.

"NO! Of course not!" Swede insisted a little too loudly, and then looked around nervously at the other men, who had all paused to watch and listen with fascination. "It just . . . it might not be safe, that's all," he finished lamely.

Maggie lifted her chin haughtily and treated him to the full force of her contempt. "The only man I know of around here who 'might not be safe' is Jack Sinclair, and I don't think I have to be afraid of him anymore, now do I?"

Swede swallowed loudly. "N . . . no, ma'am," he allowed cautiously.

"Then saddle me a horse," she commanded, "and not some old nag, either. I want something with a little spirit."

Swede hesitated only another second before hurrying off toward the corrals, calling for Slim, the boy who handled the horses.

Maggie watched him for a few minutes, her foot tapping impatiently, and when she was satisfied that he was indeed going to get her a horse, she took a minute to glance around the yard. All the men were still standing there, watching her. If they felt like saying anything smart, it was not apparent from their expressions. They all looked a little surprised, and when Maggie started staring back at them, a little sheepish.

She let her gaze run over the group and then feigned a faint surprise herself. "You're all back, I see," she observed with just the tiniest bit of sarcasm. "I guess it's all right now, though, because you won't be working for a woman." A few of the men shifted uncomfortably under her scrutiny, and more than a few dropped their eyes.

One man, whom Maggie remembered was named Harvey, spoke up. "That wasn't our idea, miss . . . ma'am."

"No need to explain, Havey. I know exactly whose idea it was," she replied. "Just like I know who it was you've been working for all along." Turning on her heel, she strode to where Swede was holding the horse he had had saddled for her, so she did not see the uncomfortable glances that were exchanged at her parting remark.

Swede had chosen a bay gelding for her. He was not exactly the spirited mount she had ordered, but neither did he qualify as a nag, Maggie decided as she approached.

Swede bent and made a stirrup with his hands since he judged the saddle stirrup was too high for her to reach. To his great surprise, when he hoisted her up, she swung her right leg completely over and settled her feet securely in the stirrups.

They didn't have a real side-saddle at the ranch, but he had expected her to hook her leg around the horn and make do the way a properly brought-up young lady would. Instead she was sitting astride, the skirt that he had thought was a skirt falling away on either side to prove that it was not a skirt at all but some kind of loose pants. Then he noticed the way she settled herself into the saddle, and his eyes narrowed as he thought of something else.

"You shouldn't ride like that, Miss . . . Mrs. Sinclair," he blurted before he had a chance to think.

Maggie squelched a pang of irritation. "And why not?" she demanded, looking up to catch his eyes on her crotch. When he hastily lifted them to meet her own, his face turned that awful beet red she was coming to dread.

"You might hurt . . . I mean, you just . . . I mean . . . have a nice ride," he sputtered, backing away in an agony of embarrassment.

It took a moment for Maggie to comprehend his concern, and it was only when she felt a small twinge between her legs that she completely understood. A woman who had just been initiated into the marriage bed had no business riding astride. Her own face flamed as she wondered if *all* the men were thinking the same thing. Well, let them think, and let them wonder, too, she decided with a toss of her head. With a jerk of the reins she turned the gelding, and with a nudge from her heels she urged him from the yard.

In a hurry to escape from their prying eyes, Maggie kicked the horse again, and the gelding broke into a run, carrying her quickly, if not quite comfortably, away. Soon the ranch buildings had faded from sight, and Maggie slowed the pace to a trot until she reached a small rise where she stopped altogether.

From here she could see the sweep of the valley, and she paused to savor the panorama that stretched before her. It wasn't really a valley, of course. She had learned that in school. In order to have a valley, you had to have mountains, and there were no mountains in this part of the world. The valley was more correctly a basin, a cavernous indentation left by some prehistoric lake that had in turn deposited all the rich ingredients that made up the fertile soil that, in turn, fed the even richer grass.

As she walked the horse down the small rise and across the lush green carpet, she recalled Swede's words about the nestors. "Folks see that grass, they think anything'll grow here." It was an easy lie to believe, she admitted. If a person didn't know, if a person hadn't grown up around here and seen the years when not a drop of rain fell for six months at a time, and when it did fall, came in torrents, real gully-washers, that pounded and destroyed and then dried up to nothing in the heat of the next day, then a person might believe that he could grow a crop here. But Maggie knew better. She knew that only the grass could survive here, only the grass with its ancient roots that reached down deep into that rich soil and took what little was offered it and survived. The thought of ripping out those roots, of cutting into that soil, caused Maggie physical pain, as if someone had cut into her own soul.

And so they would, if they cut into the CMC, because it was as much a part of her as her soul, maybe even more a part of her. Or maybe she was part of it. She could not decide, but she knew that the distinction was not important. The important thing was to make sure that those awful things never happened to the CMC, that it remained intact for . . .

Once more Maggie pulled her horse to a stop as a new and very horrible thought struck her. She had once wanted to keep the CMC intact for those who would come after her, but she suddenly realized that if she had children, then her husband would have to father them, a husband she hated and had planned to drive away, a husband who had already sworn never to touch her again. The thought of having Jack Sinclair's children appalled her, but the thought of never having children at all was equally dreadful. Maggie rode on, heedless of the direction she was taking, as she considered once again how ill-advised had been her decision to marry Jack Sinclair.

The sight of a lone plume of smoke rising in the distance finally changed the direction of Maggie's thoughts. Looking around to get her bearings, she discovered that she had ridden much farther than she had realized or intended, and if she remembered correctly, the only dwelling off in that direction belonged to Mr. Snider, or rather, had belonged to Snider before Sinclair had driven him away. If her information was correct, no one lived there now, and if no one did, then where was that plume of smoke coming from?

The gelding was only too happy to oblige her by breaking into a run. Maggie pulled him up just within sight of the tiny shack, and what she saw stopped her heart.

Squatters. A whole family of them, if the amount of laundry hanging on the line was any indication. Yes, it was a whole family, she determined when she identified two of the figures in the yard as children. The third figure was definitely not a child, however, and he had a plow, a plow he was using on her precious grass. He had not made much progress, of course. He had obviously just started his destruction within the past day or two, but it wouldn't take him long, not at the rate he was going.

Maggie sat and watched the miniature man and horse carving dark streaks into the emerald-green landscape for a long time. Was this part of Sinclair's plan for the valley? Was he going to move in the nestors and carve up the valley? She could not help but remember Swede's assertion. "He's a cattleman. He hates nestors, same as you." She had been so

170

certain that he was behind the nestor trouble, and yet now, seeing the threat with her own eyes and knowing Sinclair a little better than she had before, she found it difficult to believe that even he could be involved in such a despicable plot. As much as she hated the man with the plow, she could not help but pity him, because even as he destroyed the land, the land would destroy him and his dreams, and he would be left with nohting. Would, *could* Jack Sinclair have planned such wholesale destruction? Her head insisted that he could and had, but her heart . . . ah, her heart denied it.

She could have ridden down, confronted the man with the plow, and demanded to know what he was doing on her property. That would have simplified her problem, because he could have told her who had sent him, but she resisted the urge. She knew that she would have to drive this man and his family away, and as long as they were total strangers to her, that would not be too difficult. But if they weren't strangers, if she knew his name, his children's names . . . no, she would not go down there, would not see the hope in their eyes that she would have to kill if she wanted to keep the CMC intact. Besides, if Sinclair *was* behind it all, she wanted to find it out from him.

Fingering the gold ring that symbolized her bond to the man, she tried to convince herself that the same person who would take time to hunt up a wedding ring would be callous enough to send a family like the one she was watching to its doom. Unable to, she turned the horse at last back in the direction of the ranch and rode away. It was an easy enough mystery to solve. All she had to do was tell Jack about the family living in the Snider cabin and watch his reaction. She could hardly wait.

Chapter VI

When she reached the ranch, she saw that the awaited lumber had arrived and that the men had wasted no time in constructing a floor for the new cookhouse. It would be located behind the bunkhouse and would spoil the perfect symmetry of the ranch buildings, but she had to agree that it was something that had long been needed. If a rancher wanted to present an aura of success, he simply did not eat his meals with the hired help, and he especially did not ask his wife to. The fact that Cal Colson had never cared a straw for what people thought was the only reason that the ranch hands had continued to eat at the main house. That, and the fact that it was simply easier.

Maggie climbed down from her mount with a groan of weariness and turned it over to Slim, the boy who took care of the horses. Her muscles, long unused to riding, were letting her know their displeasure, and she was also being painfully reminded of Swede's concerns for the more delicate portions of her anatomy. She probably should not have gone riding at all today after what had happened last night, and she most certainly should not have ridden so long and so far on her first time out in years, but now that the damage had been done, she would have to make the best of it. She would have Consuela fix her a hot bath and try to soak away some of the discomfort. The difficult part would be walking up to the house without letting anyone know the agony she was enduring.

After completing what Maggie had decided was the longest walk of her life, she paused at the top of the porch steps to rest a moment before finishing the trek to her room. From where she stood, she could hear voices coming from her father's office, and curiosity led her toward the office door. Through the screen she could see Jack and Swede seated in the same chairs she and Jack had occupied during their ill-fated conversation a few days earlier. They were discussing ranch business. Ranch business, not squatter business, she realized with a start. Did they even know about the intruders she had discovered today? Determined to learn the truth about Jack Sinclair's motives, she pulled open the door and marched into the room, her aching muscles forgotten.

Both men stood instantly as she approached them. Swede, she noted absently, was blushing furiously, as usual, and Jack looked thunderous. He had recovered somewhat from his indisposition. Although his eyes were still abnormally bloodshot, he had changed into fresh clothes that suited his usual dapper image, and he had shaved and combed his hair. Except for those eyes, he looked just like the old Jack, and just like the old Jack, he was angry. For some reason, Maggie found that very exciting.

"Did you enjoy your ride, Mrs. Sinclair?" he asked venomously. Obviously, Swede had been right to be concerned that Jack might not approve of her riding off alone, but she had no intention of getting into that now.

"Who is that family living at the old Snider place?" she asked, pulling off her hat and shaking her hair free.

It took a moment for her question to register with Jack, and when it did, his mustache dipped into a frown. "The Snider place?" he asked thoughtfully, and when Maggie nodded, he turned an inquiring look at Swede.

"They weren't there three days ago," the foreman said.

"Kincaid must have moved them in as soon as you and the boys pulled out the other day," Jack remarked almost to himself, and Swede grunted his agreement.

Kincaid. The name was vaguely familiar to Maggie but she could not remember where she had heard it. "Who's Kincaid?" she asked, but no one paid her any attention.

"You'll have to get rid of them," Jack was telling Swede. Swede's head was bobbing, but his homely face clearly registered his distaste at the prospect, and Maggie's heart suddenly turned cold in her chest, all thoughts of Kincaid forgotten.

"You aren't going to kill them, are you?" she demanded, remembering all too clearly the two children she had seen.

Jack glanced down at her as if surprised to discover that she was still there. He studied her upturned face for a moment and then said, quite matter-of-factly, "They're nestors, Maggie. You know what they'll do to the land. We can't let them stay. We can't let even one family stay."

His use of the word "we," as if he were a part of the valley as much as she, rankled, but she put that aside. "But they're a family, with little children. You can't just murder them," she argued. His face was totally expressionless, his eyes blank and hard, and at that moment Maggie thought that perhaps he very well could murder them. Gone was the man who had given her the ring, the man who had held her in the night, gone even was the man who had seconds ago been furious at her for riding alone.

"Why not?" he asked in that same flat voice. "I murdered your father, didn't I?"

Maggie's mouth dropped open in shock. Hearing him say it, just like that, made her realize how ridiculous her charges had been. Of course he had not murdered her father, not like *that*, at any rate, not in cold blood, but before she could respond, Swede's voice cut into her thoughts.

"Boss!" he said. It was an exasperated plea, which

snapped Jack out of his strange mood.

Sinclair's mustache quirked. "Anyway, I doubt that Swede would kill them even if I ordered him to," he told her. "I hardly think that will be necessary, in any case. A family man isn't likely to put up much of a fight. I think a simple show of force will be enough to send them back where they came from, so don't worry your pretty little head about them, Mrs. Sinclair."

Maggie was so relieved that she forgot to be irritated by the "Mrs. Sinclair." She listened with only half an ear as the two men discussed the alternatives and decided that it would be best to wait until morning to take care of the matter. Then she realized that Swede was leaving, and decided that she had best leave, too. She had no desire to be alone with Sinclair.

"Maggie!"

The edge of his voice caught her just as she reached the door into the front room, and she turned back to him with a tinge of apprehension. "Did you enjoy your ride?" he asked again, and this time he was not going to be distracted.

Maggie lifted her chin with a defiance she did not really feel. "Yes, thank you. It's been years since I had a chance to ride over the CMC."

"You are not to go riding alone again. Is that understood?" His voice was cold and hard, all traces of anger gone, but that frightened her even more, although she would never let him know that.

"Are you planning to keep me a prisoner here, then?" she asked, and was pleased to see his irritation register.

"With all this nestor trouble, it isn't safe for you to be out alone." He was making an attempt to keep his tone reasonable, but his clenched fist gave him away to Maggie, and once again she felt the excitement surge through her. For some reason, she could not resist the urge to taunt him, to test the limits of his self-control.

"Surely you don't expect me to go riding with *you*," she

175

said, curling her lip with distaste.

This time it was his jaw that clenched. "Take one of the boys with you, then," he snapped, and started to turn away, obviously intent on ending the discussion.

"I don't want to go riding with 'one of the boys,' either," she told him, perversely unwilling to let it drop. "I ride because I like the solitude. I want to ride alone!" Without realizing it, she had been walking toward him, stalking him, challenging him, and when he turned back, they stood toe-to-toe, the air between them vibrating with tension.

Instantly, Maggie knew that she had made a mistake. She was too close to him. She should never have come this close to him, not where she could smell the Bay Rum and the cigars, not where she could see every curling hair in his mustache, not where she could see that blue-black flame burning in his eyes.

He was the one who made the first move, she was sure of that, but whether he was responding to something he saw in her face, she was never certain. In any case, it came as no surprise when his hands reached out and grabbed her, hauling her against him with no pretense at tenderness, or when his mouth ground down on hers with a ferocity that took her breath. A weakness that she could not blame on horseback riding buckled her knees, forcing her to cling to him for support, but she would not have fallen anyway, so tightly was he holding her.

No! Her mind was screaming the denial even as her body pressed itself against him. As much as her physical self seemed to want him, her other self, her real self, recoiled in terror. Not again! She could not submit, could not lose control again, not if she were to beat him, not if she were to win.

At last he lifted his mouth from hers, and when her eyelids fluttered open, she saw him staring down at her with a look that scorched her face and melted her very bones. He wanted her! As much as he had wanted her last night, when he had

176

literally torn her clothes off in his haste to get at her, he wanted her now, that much and more. In spite of his vow, in spite of his anger, in spite of everything, he still wanted her, and the knowledge stunned her. She gazed up at him and breathlessly whispered her wonder. "You said you'd never touch me."

Her words cut him like a knife, and instinctively he recoiled, thrusting her from him in horror. She staggered and almost fell, catching herself at the last moment on the back of the chair, and he forced himself to watch without helping. He could not help, dared not help, because if he touched her again . . . God, if she hadn't reminded him, what might have happened?

That was a stupid question, he chided himself. He knew exactly what would have happened, and he wouldn't have cared if it *was* rape. He wouldn't have thought it possible to want a woman more *after* he'd had her, but he'd discovered upon seeing her again this morning that his head wasn't the only thing aching because of her. It would certainly never do to let her know her effect on him, though.

Resolutely, he straightened his vest, wishing he were wearing a jacket as well so that he could button it over the bulge in his pants. "I beg your pardon, Mrs. Sinclair. I'm afraid I forgot myself for a moment." Pleased that his voice sounded as calm and unaffected as he would have desired, he gave her a mocking smile.

Maggie hardly knew what to make of it. Mere seconds ago he had been kissing her passionately, and now he was standing there like nothing had ever happened, apologizing as if he had just spilled his tea or something. She knew she should be happy that she had gotten away so easily, relieved that he hadn't forced her to . . . to do *that* again, pleased that he was so easy to control, but for some perverse reason she was annoyed instead. She did not bother to decide why. Instead, she lifted her chin and took a deep breath to steady a body that seemed dead set on trembling.

177

"Certainly, Mr. Sinclair, as long as you never let it happen again," she informed him, and turned away with a haste that set her aching muscles to screaming in protest. Gritting her teeth against the pain, she stalked from the room, out the door, and into the relative haven of the front room.

Jack watched her go through narrowed eyes, absently noting how stiffly she carried herself and wondering if it were due to something he had done to her. The thought drove him to the amber bottle on the desk, and he had actually poured a drink and raised it to his lips before he realized what he was doing. With a cry of disgust, he slammed the glass back down on the desktop.

That won't solve anything, he told himself sternly. He could drink Texas dry, but he'd still want Maggie Colson. What had ever possessed him to make such an idiotic vow? Another stupid question, he decided. It was insanity, pure and simple. The same insanity that always overcame him whenever he was with her, the same insanity that had convinced him he could tame her once he had her as his wife, once he had her in his bed. Now he was beginning to think that *he* was the one being tamed. It was not a pleasant thought, and once again his hand reached for the glass resting on the desk. Well, he wouldn't go near her again; *couldn't* now, because it was a matter of honor. Even if he had to buy a woman, even if he had to send for Renita . . . no, he couldn't do that, no matter how desperate he got. That was a matter he had to take care of, should have taken care of long ago. He'd mention it to Swede. Swede could handle it for him. Before he realized it, he had drained the glass and poured another.

Maggie's step slowed from necessity once she reached the hall. She was simply too tired and sore to keep up the pace once she was certain Jack could no longer see or hear her. Wanting nothing more than to lie down for a few moments before finding Consuela and ordering up that hot bath, she rounded into the doorway of her room only to come face-to-face with that same Consuela. For a moment she stared, speechless, and the Mexican woman stared back before breaking into a hesitant smile.

"Did you have a nice ride, señora?" she asked.

Maggie was getting a little tired of that question, but she was even more annoyed at something else. "What are you doing in my room?" she demanded, her weariness sharpening her voice even more than she had intended.

Consuela seemed a little surprised, but covered it with a properly deferential smile. "I came in to straighten up and change the sheets," she explained pleasantly, gathering up a bundle of white bedding that Maggie had not noticed before.

Still not satisfied, still a little more than reasonably irritated to find a stranger snooping around in her room, Maggie challenged, "And what made you think the sheets needed to be changed?"

This time Consuela did not bother to cover her surprise. "I thought . . . I mean . . . there should have been blood. . . ." She let her voice trail off, watching closely to see if Maggie caught her meaning.

It took a minute, but eventually she did, recalling the vague rumors she had heard at Miss Finley's. There had been blood on her, that she remembered, but there would have been no blood on the sheets. They had not even turned down the covers. With a self-conscious glance at her bed, Maggie forced herself to look back at the housekeeper, to meet her eyes even though she felt as if her face were on fire with humiliation.

Consuela was smiling again, but this time it was conspiratorial. "Do not blush, señora," she told her in an urgent whisper, coming close as if to share a secret. "We are both women, and there is no shame. You should be proud! No other woman could have refused Jack Sinclair."

Maggie almost gasped in surprise. "Wh . . . what makes you think I refused him?" she stammered, the agony of embarrassment threatening to choke her. She almost

179

cringed at the knowing look Consuela cast her.

The housekeeper shrugged one rounded shoulder. "No blood on the sheets, and Señor Jack gets drunk. I have worked for him for many years, and I have never seen him do this. A man does not leave his bride's bed and drink himself to sleep if everything has gone well for him, no?"

The logic was impeccable, and Maggie was not about to argue with it. Let the woman think what she wanted. Maggie rather enjoyed the gleam of respect she saw in Consuela's eyes. She found herself smiling back at the woman. Still, she did not like the idea of someone's coming into her room. There were still the torn clothes hidden in the trunk that she didn't want anyone to see, least of all Consuela. "You don't have to clean this room anymore. I'll do it myself from now on. You have plenty of other work to keep you busy," she added, to soften the command.

Consuela nodded pleasantly and started to leave, but then she stopped and turned back. "I find this button on the floor," she said, reaching into her pocket and producing the item.

Maggie almost jumped at the sight of it. It was a button that Jack had torn from her skirt, the one she had been unable to find this morning. Unwelcome images, scenes from the previous night, flashed before her, and she had trouble concentrating on what Consuela was saying.

"I will sew it on for you if you will show me the right dress. I could not find the right one in your wardrobe."

"I'll do it myself," she said, snatching the button from Consuela's outstretched hand. "I mean, I don't have anything else to do, now do I, with Jack running the ranch and all?" she added, seeing Consuela's startled look.

"*Si,* señora, whatever you want," she murmured and started for the door again.

Before she left, Maggie fortunately remembered something else. "Oh, Consuela, could you fix me a bath? A hot one?" she asked. When the woman turned back, she explained. "I went riding today and I'm afraid I'm feeling the effects."

Consuela shook her head sympathetically. "*Si, señora,*" and then she gave a ribald laugh. "That should keep the señor from going riding again tonight, no?" Laughing even harder at Maggie's crimson blush, she turned once more and left, carrying the discarded sheets with her.

Gingerly, Maggie lowered herself to her bed to wait for her hot water, and after a minute she found herself smiling. Consuela certainly had a lively imagination, but Maggie couldn't fault her conclusions. If the woman wanted to believe that Maggie had successfully repulsed Jack Sinclair, then let her. She was even free to spread the word if she were so inclined. That could only help Maggie's cause. And if Jack kept his word, if he really had no intention of touching her again, of sharing her bed, then Consuela could spread that around, too. A man who couldn't bed his own wife would not command much respect, she was certain, and stripping Jack Sinclair of his self-respect was part of her plan. If clean sheets could accomplish that . . . An unpleasant thought occurred to Maggie. There had been no blood on the sheets, but might there be some somewhere else?

Reluctantly, she began to examine the multicolored quilt that covered her bed, trying not to picture how the two naked bodies must have looked upon it last night, entwined in mutual passion. It took her a few minutes, but at last she found it, a small spot to be sure, but unmistakably blood. Her blood. Her innocence, sacrificed to Jack Sinclair's lust. That thought helped her block out the more disturbing visions that threatened her, and with as much haste as her stiffening muscles allowed, she got up and wet a towel and scrubbed away all traces of her defilement.

Defilement. Yes, that was the proper word, she decided when her task was done. Jack Sinclair had defiled her, but that was nothing compared to what she intended to do to him.

The bath was just what Maggie needed, and she soaked for as long as the heat held out. Afterward she put on her nightdress and asked Consuela to serve her supper in her room. Somehow she had missed the noon meal altogether on her ride, and even though it wasn't quite time for the evening meal yet, she was starving. Besides, she was still having a little difficulty sitting, and since the men would be eating at the house for a few more days until the new cookhouse was finished, she didn't relish the thought of sitting on a pillow where they could see her. Heaven only knew what construction they would put on that.

After she ate, she read for awhile, or tried to. In reality she kept finding herself pausing to listen to the sounds in the house. During the meal, she could hear the men's voices. Were they quieter than usual, or were they just muffled because she was so far away? It was a silly question, but she used it as an excuse for listening, not wanting to admit that she was trying to pick out Jack's voice from among them. Was he there or had he, too, taken dinner in his room? It would be simple enough to find out, of course. All she had to do was go across the hall and look, but then, she really didn't want to know if he were that close. It was disturbing enough to know he was somewhere in the same house.

When everything got quiet, when she knew that Consuela would have finished cleaning up and gone to wherever it was that she stayed, and all the men would be down at the bunkhouse, Maggie found herself listening all the more closely. She told herself that she only wanted to know where he was, only wanted to be ready if he tried to force his way into her room again, but she finally had to admit to a certain disappointment when she heard nothing. All was quiet, and if Jack Sinclair were anywhere nearby, he was keeping it quite a secret. In any event, he was not making a beeline for Maggie's room, a fact that should have pleased her immensely, but didn't. At last the listening bored her to fatigue, and that, combined with her physical weariness, forced her to bed.

Funny, she had never noticed before just how large her bed was, and how small she felt curled up all alone on the big feather mattress. Blaming her aching muscles for her inability to find a comfortable position, she tossed and turned for a long time before finally drifting off. She did not hear the footsteps that paused outside her door for just a moment before proceeding into the room across the hall.

Swede and the men had already gone on their unpleasant errand when Maggie awoke the next mornig. Somehow she had completely forgotten about the squatters and all her other problems the moment Jack had kissed her yesterday. They had never even settled the argument about whether or not she could go riding alone, she realized with some consternation. Well, she would just go, and let Sinclair try and stop her.

The dining room was empty when Maggie arrived, the huge table cleared, except for one place setting that she assumed must be for her. Consuela came at her call, and asked with friendly concern how she was feeling. Maggie was happy to report that, although she was still a little stiff, she thought she might live.

When Consuela came back later with her breakfast, Maggie asked with what she hoped was disinterest, "Where's Jack this morning?" Part of her was hoping that he was lying in a drunken stupor somewhere, but the other part of her . . . was just curious, she told herself.

Consuela frowned. "He go with the men. He say he want to talk to the people himself before they leave," she said with obvious disapproval.

Maggie felt a tingle of alarm go up her spine. "Do you think there might be trouble?" Jack had been so certain that there wouldn't be, but still . . .

The housekeeper sniffed. "A man does not give up his home so easy, no? Even a farmer will fight for his family."

"But not against so many," Maggie argued, picturing the men who worked for the CMC armed to the teeth. They would be very intimidating to a simple sod-buster.

Consuela shrugged her shoulder. "Maybe not," she allowed. "We will see."

Her calm acceptance was of little comfort to Maggie, who spent the morning pacing the large front room and fighting off the urge to ride off after them and see for herself what had happened. She kept trying to tell herself that if there had been shooting, if somebody had been killed, she would hear about it soon enough, and she really didn't need to see it firsthand. What she didn't think about was exactly whose safety she was concerned about. It was enough to know that she didn't want *anyone* to be killed on the CMC.

After what seemed an interminable wait, during which time Maggie managed to pace off what soreness remained from her horseback ride the day before, she was relieved to hear the sounds of horses returning to the ranch. Running to the front window, she eagerly scanned the group of horsemen. The tension that had held her all morning rose into her throat in an aching lump when she did not see the black stallion for which her eyes had unconsciously been searching. Where could he be? What could have happened to him? A thousand questions flashed through her mind in that second between when she did not see the stallion and when she did see the man.

He was riding another horse today, a mean-looking roan gelding who nevertheless seemed under his complete control. Of course. It was stupid of her to think he would ride the high-strung stallion into such a potentially volatile situation. He still rode like no other man she had ever seen, like a . . . like a prince. From the way he was sitting his saddle he wasn't the least bit hurt, either. That thought surprised her back to her senses. What did she care if he were hurt or not? Forcing herself to look over the rest of the men as they rode into the ranch yard, she made note of the fact that none of them seemed to be hurt, either. That meant that there had been no fight, or not much of one, anyway. That was what she cared about. That was all she cared about, she insisted.

It seemed to take an inordinate amount of time for the men to dismount and unsaddle and turn their horses loose in the corral. It would have made sense for Jack to let someone else care for his horse, but he did not, choosing instead to do it himself. By the time he had finished that task and exchanged a few words with Swede and made his way up to the main house, Maggie was having an extremely difficult time restraining herself from charging out the door and demanding to know what had happened. She blamed her fluttering heart on her impatience.

As he came up the stairs, he glanced up and caught sight of her standing in the window watching him. His pause was almost imperceptible, and then he came on, just as if the sight of her hadn't shaken him to his boots. She was still standing by the window when he went inside, only she had turned to face him now. She was wearing one of those dresses that made her look very young. She had her hair tied back with a ribbon and the sun behind her was turning it into a red-gold halo. Her hands were clenched together and he knew she was trying not to fidget, trying to look as calm and expressionless as he did, but she was failing miserably. She simply did not have the years of practice that he had had, and those eyes of hers gave away her every thought even when she was able to control the rest of her. He fought down an almost overwhelming urge to take her in his arms, aided by the vision of how she would laugh if he exhibited his weakness to her one more time, and instead contented himself with simply saying her name.

"Maggie." He pulled off his hat and hung it on a peg by the door, the same peg where she had hung it that very first day.

Then he shrugged out of his suit coat and hung it up, too. By the time he trusted himself to look back at her, she was fit to be tied.

"Well?" she demanded, taking an impatient step toward him. Maggie had had just about all the waiting she could stand, and if he didn't tell her something soon, she might very well beat it out of him.

"Well what?" he replied with infuriating denseness. He loved the way her breasts rose and fell underneath the thin calico of her dress, loved the way her chin lifted, the way her eyes flashed green when she was angry.

"What happened!" she said with forced calmness. She really wanted to stamp her foot in fury.

She couldn't be sure, but she thought the corners of his mouth twitched just a bit before he said, "They were squatters, all right." Then he strolled over to one of the horned chairs and sank down in it. He was teasing her, but he knew just how far to go, and when he saw her take a breath in preparation for the explosion he knew would follow, he added, "A man and wife and three children. The youngest is just a baby."

The memory of the woman holding that baby to her breast and staring up at him with those frightened eyes would haunt him for a long time. "We got there right about dawn, so we caught them by surprise. They didn't put up any fight at all, although the man did argue a bit. It was just like we thought; Kincaid put them up to it."

Maggie had been about to give him a piece of her mind, a rather sharp piece, too, when he had saved himself by launching into his story. His words had drawn her closer, and now she stood not more than an arm's length from his chair. "Who's Kincaid?" she asked. She had asked the same thing yesterday and gotten no response.

Jack looked up in some surprise. "Sam Kincaid. He's . . . I don't know who to tell you he is. He's just Kincaid, a man who came to Bitterroot to cause trouble. Nobody really

186

knew what he was doing before. He just showed up one day and opened an office in town. He never did any business that anyone could see, and then the squatters started showing up. That was before I got here, so I don't know exactly why he was never connected with the trouble then, but there were rumors, and eventually everyone just came to accept the fact that he had been behind it all. When the trouble died down, people just forgot about it, I suppose."

Maggie sat down in the chair opposite him. "Do you think he'll bring in more people, more nestors?" she asked, completely unaware that she had forgotten her anger and all her other feelings for him for the moment.

Jack gave a mirthless laugh. "I'm sure they're already on the way, if they aren't here already. He was only waiting for your father to die before he moved in."

Maggie stiffened in surprise. It was odd that the pain of losing her father had eased to the point that she could hear it mentioned without feeling anything more than a deep regret. Her anger over Sinclair's treacheries had overpowered it, but now it seemed that she had been right about those treacheries, except for one small but very important detail: Jack Sinclair had not been the man behind it all. But, she reminded herself, he had had a plan of his own. "Just as you did, Mr. Sinclair," she pointed out acidly. He, too, had moved in as soon as her father had died, and he had taken much more than her land.

Jack smiled, conceding her point. "You make a very tempting target, Mrs. Sinclair," he told her, letting his dark eyes play over her in a way that said he found her tempting in more ways than one.

His look made her go hot all over, and then the heat seemed to settle in the most disconcerting places. To cover her discomfort, she asked, "What happened to the people, the family?"

Jack leaned back and crossed one dusty boot over his knee. "We moved them out. The men helped load all their belongings onto their wagon, and when they were finished, we tore down the shack and burned it. There was no point in leaving it standing. It would be much too easy for them or someone else to move back in."

Maggie nodded. She could imagine that it hadn't taken much more than a good swift kick to knock down Snider's cabin. It hadn't been much more than the shack Jack had called it. Maggie tried to think of another question while she noticed how well his boot molded along his calf. He really did have wonderful legs, so long and straight and strong, just like the rest of him. . . . Her face flamed at the direction her thoughts were taking, and she almost jumped out of the chair in her haste to get away from the source of her adulation. "I . . . I'd better go help Consuela with dinner," she said, turning with a swish of her skirts.

"Maggie!" As always, his voice caught her just as she was about to escape. Taking a deep breath and twisting her face into a mask of placid inquiry, she turned back to him. "We'll be going to town tomorrow morning."

"We?" she asked, hoping that "we" meant himself and Swede. She had no desire to go to town just yet. Word of her hasty marriage would be all over by now, and she would rather die than face the knowing looks she was sure to receive.

"Yes, you and I and Swede and a few of the men," he clarified.

She took a step toward him and lifted her hand in an unconsciously imploring gesture. "I don't want to go to town," she said. "I . . . I need to stay here. There's so much to do and I have to help Consuela. . . ."

Jack sighed impatiently. "I have some business that may take me several days. I have no intention of leaving you here alone all that time. God only knows what mischief you might get yourself into."

Maggie's body stiffened indignantly. How dare he . . . several days? The new thought distracted her. "What's going to take you several days?"

Jack fought to keep the smile from his voice. Really, she was delightful to watch. "I have to do some snooping around, talk to some people and find out just how far Kincaid has gone. Then I need to have a little discussion with Kincaid himself and see if we can't settle this whole thing peacefully. Don't forget to pack a few things, enough for two or three days. We'll stay at the hotel," he added.

At the hotel! The thought of going back there, to the place where her marriage had begun, horrified her, but even worse was the thought of sharing a hotel room with Jack Sinclair. It was difficult enough in this barn of a house where she at least had her own room to go to for some privacy, but there she'd be confined with him in one small room, in one small bed. . . .

Jack was frowning in concern. "What is it, Maggie? What's wrong?" He had never seen that expression on her face. She looked almost . . . what was it? Frightened, that was it. What on earth would frighten her about a trip to town?

How could she tell him? How could she explain? Even now, the mere thought of being alone with him in the night was turning her whole body to jelly. If he ever really did get her alone in the night, she knew she stood no chance, no chance at all, of resisting him. She would respond with the same mindless abandon as she had on their wedding night, and how he would laugh at her lack of control. She could never accuse him of rape again, not a second time, not if she reacted the way she knew she would, the way she wanted to even now.

"Maggie?" He was getting up, coming toward her, a worried frown on his face. How tall he was! Funny how she always forgot how very tall he was. A vision of him the way he had looked that night, standing there like a beautiful statue, flashed in front of her eyes, but she blinked it away and backed up a step. He was getting entirely too close, and she felt the panic welling up inside of her. If he put his hands on her again . . .

"You promised you wouldn't touch me," she blurted, seeing the hand he had raised reaching out to her.

Her words stopped him instantly, the hand that he had lifted instinctively curling into a fist. Was the thought of his touching her *that* distasteful? Enough to make her actually pale, because she was pale, pale and trembling. Good God, what had he done to her to make her react like this? She was terrified of him. Jamming his hands into his trouser pockets, he backed up a step himself, showing her she was completely safe, but he could not keep his jaw from clenching in frustration. "Is there some reason why you don't want to go to town?" he asked through stiff lips.

Maggie was fervently wishing that the floor would open up and swallow her, but she knew that she would never be that lucky. She would have to give him an answer sooner or later because he certainly did not look inclined to let the matter drop or to let her stay at the ranch simply because she preferred it. She would have to tell him. Swallowing the lump of apprehension that had lodged in her throat, she spoke, choosing her words carefully. "I don't wish to share a hotel room with you."

The small twitch in his cheek was the only clue he gave her to the violence of his reaction to her statement. He was stunned, and angry at himself for being so. Odd, he had never even considered this aspect of their visit to town, not thinking beyond the necessity of keeping her nearby where she could not get into trouble or cause him any, yet it had been the very first thing that had occurred to her. It had terrified her, too. The supreme irony of it was that the strange compulsion he had felt to protect her now compelled him to protect her from himself. "Then we won't share a hotel room," he told her in a voice washed clean of expression. "Will that suit you?"

Maggie was learning to distrust that blank look that

closed down over his face like a mask, clearing it of all emotion, and that flat, bland tone of voice sent warning chills along her spine. She knew him well enough to know that her request had struck a stunning blow to his pride, and that such a blow would infuriate him, but he was letting none of that show. His calmness was somehow more frightening than his fury. "Y . . . yes," she replied, hating the way her voice quivered, but unable to stop it.

They stood there for another moment, facing each other, each trying to see beyond what the other was showing, each searching for an opening, an openness, but each was disappointed. "May I go now?" Maggie asked. She tried to sound sarcastic instead of desperate, and thought she even succeeded a little.

"Certainly," he agreed, the irony coming to his voice with practiced ease, but he frowned as he watched her go, and the breath he drew was not quite steady.

By the time she got to the kitchen, Maggie had recovered somewhat. Simply being away from Jack Sinclair was a calming influence, she was discovering. The door to the kitchen stood open to catch the breeze from the open dog-trot, and Maggie was inside before she noticed that Consuela was not alone.

Not alone was an understatement. She was standing on the other side of the room, near the door that led to the back of the house, and she was being embraced by a very amorous cowboy. The man stood almost a head taller than Consuela, but he was stooped over some to accommodate himself to her, and both of his hands were resting in an extremely familiar manner on the curve of her behind, holding the lower portions of their bodies in intimate contact. Consuela's ample breasts were pressed against his shirtfront, while her hands played restlessly across his shoulders.

Maggie had never seen anyone embracing quite so passionately, or anywhere near so passionately, for that matter, and she could not help but stare, feeling her mouth go dry as she did so. She could not help but listen, either, because for some inexplicable reason they weren't kissing but were talking. How anyone could converse while being fondled in such a scandalous manner, Maggie could not imagine, and it took a minute for her to realize that they were discussing her.

"The boys couldn't believe it when she went riding, but I guess it must be true. You mean they don't even *sleep* together?" the cowboy was saying.

"Not even in the same room," Consuela affirmed, "and the señora does not even lock her door."

Maggie stifled a gasp. How dare they discuss her in such a manner? But even as she felt the scarlet blush of humiliation staining her cheeks, she heard the note of pride ringing in Consuela's voice. "She will not let him steal *everything* from her," the housekeeper was saying, and then they both laughed, a pleasant, intimate sound that made Maggie feel like the intruder that she was.

Backing silently from the room, she felt the flush of her own humiliation fading as she considered the amount of humiliation this would cause Jack. She had already realized that a man who could not bed his own wife would get no respect from the men of the CMC, and now Consuela was unwittingly helping her achieve her goal.

But would *she* get respect from all of this? An interesting question, one she decided to answer immediately. Taking a determined breath and making as much noise as possible, she went back into the kitchen. "Consuela?" she called, and pretended to be surprised at the couple hastily separating in the corner.

"Señora," Consuela said, smoothing her clothing with a nervous hand. "What did you want?"

Maggie allowed herself a knowing smile at the flustered cowboy. "I thought you might need some help in the kitchen, but I see you already have some."

The cowboy raised a protesting hand. "Oh, no, ma'am. I

192

just came by to say hello. I'm on my way." He was a nice-looking man, not quite handsome but very pleasing, with dark hair and eyes. His coloring and features bespoke some sort of mixed blood, but exactly what sort, she couldn't determine. Maggie realized with some surprise that she had never seen him before.

"Who are you?" she asked with a degree of severity. As the lady of the house, she had every right to be shocked to find a stranger in her kitchen kissing her cook.

The cowboy flushed to the roots of his hair, but Consuela seemed to know that Maggie wasn't really mad and smiled. "This is Lee Parker," she said. "He works here."

"Then why have I never seen him around here before?" Maggie demanded, thoroughly enjoying her new role.

The cowboy might have been capable of speaking for himself, but Consuela didn't give him a chance. "He was working for Señor Jack over at the old house until we all came here," she explained.

Maggie gave a haughty sniff. "Did he work in the kitchen over there?" she asked sarcastically.

"Oh, no, ma'am, I . . . I was just visiting Connie here," he explained nervously.

"He is my betrothed," Consuela added with a sly grin, and Maggie noted with some amusement that this came as somewhat of a surprise to Lee Parker.

"He had better be," Maggie said with some asperity, letting them both know that she had made note of their earlier activities. "And now he'd better leave if we're going to have any dinner today." Maggie had to bite her lip to keep from laughing at the haste with which Lee Parker exited the kitchen. His "See you later, Connie," was almost an afterthought as he made a dash for the bunkhouse.

"Your betrothed?" Maggie asked dubiously.

Consuela shrugged in a characteristic gesture. "It does not hurt to put the idea in his head, no? He is a good man. A woman could do much worse."

Yes, Maggie had to agree, a woman could do *much* worse, but now was not the time to lament that fact. "Do you need any help with dinner?"

Consuela seemed shocked that Maggie would make such an offer, but after a few minutes of discussion, Maggie made it very clear that she had every intention of helping out in her own house whenever it suited her, and it suited her now. Consuela gave in with good grace and let her peel some potatoes. Both women agreed that they would be glad when the new cookhouse was finished and the men could take their meals down there with Wiley doing the cooking. The poor man had been sulking like a spoiled child ever since Consuela had evicted him from the big house.

Maggie would have been just as happy to help serve, but Consuela insited that she should sit at the head of the table as befitted her position. She must show the men that Jack Sinclair had not broken her spirit. They had already begun to suspect as much by the way she had hidden in her room the night before. Consuela managed to convey this information in some mysterious fashion without ever actually coming right out and saying any of it, and Maggie was grateful. Maggie also concluded that she was still somewhat of an awesome figure, from the way Lee Parker had reacted to her, and if he spread the story about the separate bedrooms, as she felt reasonably certain he would, then she would become even more awesome. With that in mind, she took her place at the table with an aplomb that even Jack Sinclair's raised eyebrows could not shake.

Jack took his seat at the opposite end of the long table, at what Maggie liked to think of as the foot, although Jack might have given her an argument on that. Although he gave little evidence of it, he was conscious of her every move, her every expression, even of exactly how much she ate. She was up to something, he decided as he noted how she took great pains to speak pleasantly to the men seated near her. If she were trying to win their sympathy, she looked far too poised and confident to succeed, and if she were trying to win their admiration . . . a sharp stab of something very akin to jealousy caused him to shift in his chair. Well, it wouldn't do her any good. He knew these men. He had hand-picked every one of them, and every one of them owed his loyalty to Jack Sinclair. It would take more than a pretty face and a pair of . . . it would take more than that to turn them against him. Did she have to lean so close to the men when she talked? Harvey was going to be drooling on her bodice if she wasn't careful.

Although she appeared to be completely engrossed in her conversations with the hands, Maggie was watching Jack, too, and noting with some satisfaction that he had barely touched his dinner. More than likely he would give her a lecture on not getting too friendly with the hired help, but that would be just fine. Then she could tell the ranch hands that she was forbidden by her tyrannical husband from speaking to them anymore. That would certainly work to Jack's disadvantage, making him look as if he were afraid some cowboy were going to steal his bride right from under his nose. Maggie had a hard time biting back the smile that threatened at such a thought. It was with great difficulty that she followed what Harvey was telling her.

"We've been having a time of it, Miz Sinclair, finding all the cattle. Some way back in the brush ain't seen a man in a hundred years, it seems," he said.

Why had they been beating the bushes for all these lost cows? Oh, yes, he had said something about changing the brand. "Did you say you were rebranding all the cattle?" she asked with feigned interest, and then grew cold as the meaning of her words sank in. Changing the brand, *her* brand, the brand her father had created? Without the CMC brand, it just wouldn't be the CMC anymore.

"Yes'm, it sure is a job," Harvey asserted.

"Just what does the new brand look like?" Maggie asked with credible calmness.

"Oh, it's just like the old brand only . . . here, I'll show you," he offered, pushing his empty plate away and picking up his knife. Using the blade, he scratched some lines in the tablecloth forming the standard CMC brand. "We're just adding the J is all," he explained, showing her how and where. The tablecloth seemed to shimmer in front of her eyes for a moment as she examined Harvey's artwork. Why had she never noticed it before?

Somehow the significance of the formation of the letters of the CMC brand had escaped her, and in all the years that she had seen the configuration, she had not realized, had never dreamed . . . and knowing her father, would never have suspected. He had been a romantic! The letters had stood for their names, of course, Cal and Margarite Colson. That much she had taken for granted, but she had never considered why the second C had been turned backwards. Seeing it now, drawn on the pristine tablecloth, she realized that the two C's formed a heart, a heart enclosing the M that represented her mother's name.

And Jack Sinclair had defiled that, too! The alteration had been to form a J out of one of the straight lines of the M, thus enclosing the M and the J within the heart. It was an abomination, and Maggie had to clench her fists to contain her rage and blink several times to clear her eyes of the tears that threatened.

"You all right, Miz Sinclair?" Harvey was asking with some concern.

"What? Oh, yes, I'm fine," she assured him, snapping out of the black mood that had held her for a moment. "It's just . . . the change is such a surprise. It's been the CMC for so long."

Harvey was frowning. "A surprise?" he said apprehensively. "Maybe I shouldn't have told you." He was smoothing the marks from the cloth. "Maybe Mr. Sinclair wanted to tell you himself."

Maggie was certain that he did. It was the kind of thing he

would love to gloat over. "That's all right. I won't let on that I know. I wouldn't want to spoil his fun," she lied. At least she was forewarned. Now when he did spring it on her, she could pretend that she didn't care.

After the men finished and left to resume their work for the afternoon, Jack excused himself to his office, leaving Maggie to her own devices. She helped Consuela clean up the kitchen and then headed for her room. She still had a trunkful of clothes that needed mending and the sooner that job was done, the safer she would feel. Somehow she could not stand the thought of Consuela's finding them in their present condition.

Passing through the front room, she stopped dead in her tracks as the scent of cigar smoke caught her. How could the mere smell affect her so? she wondered as she took a minute to savor the aroma wafting out through the office door, marveling at how it sent a wave of warmth spreading over her. He was in there, probably going over the books or hatching some new plot. The thought should have angered her, but for some reason it did not.

"Where are you going, Maggie?"

The sound of his voice startled her out of her reverie, and the sight of him standing in the doorway was positively unnerving, considering that she had just been having almost pleasant thoughts about him. Then she remembered to be irritated by his question. "None of your business," she snapped, and started to walk away.

"Excuse me, Mrs. Sinclair," he called after her, and his syrupy sarcasm stopped her. "I only wished to know if you intended to go riding this afternoon."

Slowly, cautiously, Maggie turned back to face him. This was one argument they had never settled, and now was as good a time as any to do it. "And if I am?" she challenged, lifting her chin.

His mustache quirked in the way that irritated her no end. "If you are," he mimicked, "then have a good ride."

197

Maggie blinked in surprise. That was all? That was it? Her eyes narrowed in suspicion. "Aren't you going to tell me that I'm not allowed to go alone?"

He gave her a full-fledged smile at that. "And what good would that do? You'd simply sneak away by yourself anyway," he pointed out reasonably. He was right. That was exactly what she had planned to do if he had insisted on having his way. "No, you may ride alone, just as long as you tell someone where you're going."

That was eminently fair and only common sense. Even Maggie could think of nothing to which she might object. She gave him a grudging nod of agreement as she watched one fine hand lift the cheroot to his lips. And then she thought of the perfect comeback. "But I wasn't planning on going riding today, anyway," she informed him saucily, leaving the room in a swish of skirts. She never knew how close he came to going after her.

Chapter VII

They got a late start the next morning. It wasn't that Maggie was purposely slow, at least not exactly, but she had a hard time forcing herself to get ready. The thought that Jack might be irritated by her tardiness was also a contributing factor, and so the day had gotten off to a pretty fair start before their buggy pulled through the ranch gate.

Jack's stern silence told her that she had successfully irritated him, and gave her a chance to go over the events of the previous evening in her mind. She had managed to keep to her room for the afternoon, mending the garments that he had torn on their wedding night, and sorting through her clothes with an eye to the fact that she was now a matron and no longer a schoolgirl. Later she had gone to the kitchen to help Consuela with supper. Supper itself had passed uneventfully, with Jack sitting opposite her as he had at dinner. He seemed to pay even less attention to her than he had at the noon meal, and she, in turn, was even more charming to the cowboys who sat near her.

After supper Jack had disappeared into his office again—odd how she had begun to think of it as *his* office—and he and Swede had been in there most of the evening. Once or twice Maggie had found an excuse to wander over to the closed door, but their voices were no more than a murmur.

She really should have gone on in, and demanded to know what they were planning. It was, after all, her ranch, and she had every right to be included in their discussions, but she didn't. It wasn't that she was afraid to go in, she told herself. It was more that she dreaded the possibility that Sinclair would tell her to run along, as if she were an annoying child. That was what she feared most, and it was that fear that kept her in the front room, seated in front of the fire with a book in her hands.

It had been late when Jack had finally come out of the office. Maggie could hear Swede going out the other door, onto the porch and off into the night, and then Jack had appeared. He looked tired, she noted, and she wondered absently if he had had as much trouble falling asleep the previous night as she had. He hadn't noticed her at first and had paused a moment to rub the back of his neck wearily. Then he had seen her sitting across the room. His hand had dropped and he had straightened, as if embarrassed by his betraying gesture. He would not, she realized, want to exhibit any weakness before her.

He had slanted her a wry smile and asked, "Still up, Mrs. Sinclair?"

Maggie had instantly regretted her decision to wait until he came out. It had seemed far preferable to sitting in her room waiting to see if he was going to try to join her there tonight. She had no reason to think he would, after all. He had given her his word, and Maggie had a suspicion that his word meant a great deal to him. He might be dishonest in a lot of other ways, but he still considered himself a gentleman, and a gentleman's word was his bond.

Not waiting for her answer, he had gone over to the cabinet where Cal Colson had stored his liquor. Maggie recognized the squat bottle that he found there, but not because she had ever seen such a bottle in her father's house. It was a brandy bottle. Her Uncle Edward often drank brandy in the evening, a practice her father probably would have scorned as "dandified." A real man drank whiskey, or so she had often heard him say. Now, watching Jack pour the amber liquid into the snifter—another new addition to the cabinet—she had to wonder if her father had been right.

He had poured just a small amount, and then replaced the stopper with the care of a man who likes the little things done just so. Maggie watched the way his hands moved, those long slender hands that had never done an honest day's work, but that were so lovely to watch all the same. Then he had scooped the snifter up, cupping it to warm the brandy, and turned back toward her.

He had caught her staring, and she had quickly lowered her eyes to the book in her lap. It seemed as if a lot of time went by before he asked, "What are you reading?"

Maggie had been pretty sure that he didn't really care, which was just as well because she wasn't really sure what the book was called. It was just one she had pulled out of her trunk, a leftover from Miss Finley's. "Nothing important," she had replied, closing the book and lifting her eyes to him again. He had been watching her, watching and swirling the brandy in his glass. "You and Swede must have had a lot to discuss," she remarked to his impassive face. It was as close as she would come to admitting she had been curious about exactly what they had been discussing.

She had seen his eyebrows lift, had known instantly that he had no intention of telling her his latest schemes, and although the knowledge irritated her, she was more interested at this moment in the way his mustache tilted up at one corner when he was teasing her. "We were just swapping lies," he told her dismissively. "Nothing important."

Maggie had rankled at hearing her own words repeated back to her so sarcastically. Why had she ever considered waiting here for him in the first place? She must have known he would never tell her anything. Then she remembered. She had had another reason for waiting for him, the reason she had decided not to go to bed, to lie there waiting for the sounds of his footsteps in the hallway. Tonight she was going to walk out on him, say good night and repair to her room with a poise and dignity that told him she was no longer the silly schoolgirl who had panicked this afternoon at the thought of sharing a hotel room with him. She would show him that she could handle their relationship with the same cool detachment that he did. She had decided all this during the time it took for Jack to down his brandy in two swallows.

Straightening her shoulders, she collected her book, and prepared to rise, but his words stopped her. "I hope you won't be offended if I leave you, but it's been a long day, and I'm tired. Good night, Mrs. Sinclair." He had set the snifter on the liquor cabinet carefully, and sketched her a small bow before strolling nonchalantly from the room, leaving her staring after him in disgruntled surprise.

How dare he! she had fumed when he was gone, but it had done no good because he *was* gone, taking her audience with him. Fighting an urge to fling her book after him, she had forced herself to wait a respectable interval before going to her own room. She could never let him know that she had only been waiting up for him.

Once she had gone to her room and prepared for bed, sleep had eluded her. Her bed had still seemed extra large and empty, and she had still been unable to find a comfortable position, just like the night before. That was probably why she had overslept the next morning.

Consuela had awakened her when she had brought in a breakfast tray, and then the Mexican woman had scolded her playfully for not having packed a bag to take to town with her. Maggie should have resented her presumption, but instead it made her feel a little homesick for Miss Finley's, of all places, and she had smiled and exchanged friendly banter with her housekeeper. In the past two days she had come to know Consuela, and while she should have been suspicious of the woman who had worked so long for Jack Sinclair, she found that she liked her very much. And trusted her.

It hadn't taken long for Maggie to figure out that for some strange reason she had won Consuela's respect, and that for some equally strange reason, the housekeeper was seeing to it that she won the respect of the ranch hands as well. Consuela was even more conscious of appearances than Maggie, and she was not above dropping Maggie a hint now and then as to how she should conduct herself. The conversation that Maggie had overheard between Consuela and Lee Parker proved that she was working behind the scenes, too. As embarrassing as Maggie found it to have her personal business discussed by the hired help, she was realistic enough to realize that they would be discussing it anyway and that they might as well be seeing her in a good light.

This morning Consuela had helped by dropping the hint that Señor Jack hated to be kept waiting and would be furious when he found out that she had overslept. Maggie had taken the hint by insisting that she be allowed to pack her own bag, thus delaying their departure even more. Jack had indeed been livid, but he did not betray himself with so much as a word. Maggie had to content herself with noticing his clenched jaw and the jerky movements with which he stuck her bag behind the buggy seat next to his own.

Now they were halfway to town, and Jack hadn't said more than three words. It was satisfying but a little boring. Not to mention the fact that Maggie was beginning to feel uncomfortably aware of how close they were sitting in the privacy of the buggy. The last time they had ridden like this had been just after their wedding and Maggie had been engrossed in speculation over what her wedding night would be like. Now that she knew, she had even more reason to be concerned.

Risking a glance at his profile, she decided for the thousandth time that he really was a very handsome man. He could be charming, too, when the mood took him, and when he touched her . . . if she weren't careful, she might find herself falling under his spell, just the way the rest of Bitterroot had. Maggie shifted uneasily in her seat as a funny little anticipatory tingle danced up her thighs. It certainly wasn't a bit helpful that her own body was so traitorously weak, either. All this silence was unhealthy, giving her imagination too much time to work, she decided when her gaze settled on his hands, and her stomach fluttered at the way those long fingers worked the reins.

Would it compromise her carefully laid plans to have a little civilized conversation with him? After a bit of consideration, she decided that it would not. She needed the distraction to curb her wayward thoughts. It also wouldn't hurt to find out a little more about the man. After all, the more she knew about him, the more easily she could get to him. Trying to recall all that she did know made her realize that she knew precious little. She could start at the beginning. "Where are you from?" she asked.

Jack seemed a bit surprised that she should speak after so long a time of silence, but his innate caution prompted him to give an evasive answer. "From all over."

Maggie was not to be easily dissuaded. "I mean originally. That's not a Texas accent, although I can tell it's southern."

He could not help the grin that tugged at his mouth. She was determined to get some information out of him, so he might as well humor her. "Virginia," he said. "Jack Sinclair of the Virginia Sinclairs, at your service," he told her with a patronizing nod.

She had never heard of the Virginia Sinclairs, of course, but she could tell by the way he said it that it was not something he had made up on the spur of the moment, but something he had been used to saying once upon a time. It gave her an uneasy feeling to think that he might belong to a very respectable family. "And just what do the Sinclairs do in Virginia?" she asked, trying to sound only mildly interested. With any luck they would prove to be rumrunners or pirates or something equally unsavory.

Her luck did not hold. "They raise horses," he told her, and then added with a note of pride, "The Sinclairs have raised horses in Virginia for almost a hundred years."

Well, now, that would account for the masterful way that he rode, as well as the way he controlled that beastly stallion of his. He had spent his life with horses, much as she had, but without the distraction of the cows. It must have been an exciting life, watching the gangly spring foals grow up, breaking them, training them, breeding them. . . .

Maggie jerked her thoughts back to the present, slightly shocked at the direction they had taken. Simply being around Jack Sinclair was an evil influence, she decided. Casting about for something else to say, she thought of the genteel poverty in which her aunt and uncle lived on their plantation. The war had been over for a long time, yet the effects were still being felt in the South. "Didn't the Yankees put you out of business during the war?" she asked. She wouldn't have put it past some relative of Jack Sinclair's to have made some sort of deal with them to preserve the Virginia Sinclairs.

Jack chuckled. "Actually, it was the Confederacy who almost put us out of business. Somehow the Yankees never quite made it to our neck of the woods, but the Rebels always knew just where to find good horseflesh. They 'requisitioned' every bit of saddle stock we had on the place. Fortunately, my father was able to convince them to leave him some good breeding stock, since it was in their own best interest to provide for the future. After the war it took a long time to get the place back on its feet again, especially since my father had taken payment from the army in Confederate money, but good horses are always in demand, and my father always raised the best."

Maggie mulled over this information for a while, and then she remembered that he had spoken of his father in the past tense. "Is your father still alive?"

She thought his hands tightened a little on the reins. "No," he said after a brief pause. "He passed away several years ago."

His voice was expressionless, that flat, toneless voice that made Maggie suspect that he still had strong emotions about his father, but whether they were good ones or bad ones, she had no way of knowing. "Your mother?" she asked tentatively.

"She's been gone more than ten years now," he said, and this time Maggie could tell by the faint note of sadness that he grieved for his mother, but had come to terms with her loss long ago. They had that in common, then, the loss of both parents. It made her feel a kinship with him that she did not want to feel.

Maggie was beginning to feel as if she were cross-examining him, but he did not seem inclined to volunteer any information, and she was certain that when he grew tired of answering her, he would stop. "Any brothers or sisters?"

Jack shot her a look, his dark eyes narrowed suspiciously for an instant, his whole body suddenly tensed. Maggie stared back in surprise at his reaction to her innocent question, and then grew even more amazed when, just as quickly, he relaxed and assumed that blank expression again. "No . . . brother. Or sisters."

A thousand new questions popped into her mind, but Maggie judged it would not be prudent to ask them, especially the ones that had to do with the brother he did not have. Instead she would use the Westerner's roundabout way of discovering the truth. "Who runs the family business, then?" she asked skeptically. Somehow she could not picture Jack Sinclair leaving anything in the hands of a stranger.

"I have a cousin who runs it. He does very well, too," he added.

So, she had been right. He did have an independent source of income, but she still needed to know just what kind of a financial position he was in. "And how well is that?" she asked casually.

Jack turned to her then, a look of frank amusement tilting his mustache and lighting those black eyes. "Really, Mrs. Sinclair!" he chided. "I'll get the idea that you only married me for my money!"

Maggie gasped in outrage. "How could I have married you for your money when I didn't even know if you had any?" she blurted and then tried to correct herself, "I mean, you know I couldn't have . . . I mean, you didn't . . . I didn't . . . oh!" Maggie gave up in disgust. He was laughing at her now, and not even trying to hide it, and she could feel her face flaming. He had been teasing her, just like he always did. He knew just how to get her goat, too, accusing her of a thing like that, as if she'd had any choice about marrying him at all. Furious, she turned her face away from him so that at least he wouldn't have the satisfaction of seeing her blush.

A lot of scenery went by before she heard him say, "Maggie?" His voice was soft, wheedling, daring her to look at him. She could not ignore the challenge.

Very carefully, she blanked her expression. She would not give him the satisfaction of seeing how angry he had made her. She could not know that the blazing green of her eyes gave her away. "You should be more careful about asking so many questions, you know. You might offend someone," he cautioned her, but she knew he was still teasing, could tell by the way his mustache still tipped. "However," he allowed, "I suppose that as my wife, you have a right to know these things." He put undue emphasis on the word "wife," but Maggie pretended not to notice. "I inherited Sinclair Farms when my father died. My cousin manages it and keeps half of the profits for his trouble. Fortunately, he is a very good manager, and has made me a rich man even on a half share.

"How nice for you," Maggie observed acidly. "I guess that leaves you free to go about despoiling the West."

She had meant her barb to sting, but she had not expected

207

the frown that instantly creased that fine forehead. "Is that how you see me, Maggie? As a despoiler?" he asked thoughtfully.

Maggie cringed inwardly at her choice of words, but she had to stand by them. He *was* a despoiler, of young women as well as of land. Not deigning to answer, she merely lifted her chin and turned her head away again. Let him worry about how she saw him, if he cared at all, which she doubted.

But he did worry, and the frown deepened as he watched her proud profile turn away from him. How ironic, he thought as he tried to return his attention to his driving. He now had everything that he had been working toward for over a year, and while he knew only too well that his problems with running the CMC were just beginning, he should have felt a measure of satisfaction that he was at least in a position to run it.

The fact that he felt none he could attribute to Maggie. She had called him a thief and a murderer, and although he was neither of those, she had made him feel guilty, nonetheless. Now she had called him a despoiler, a man who ruined things. Had he ruined things? From her point of view, he knew the answer was yes. He had taken over her ranch and her life and even her body, for however short a time. Those were violations he knew she would have a difficult time forgiving, if indeed she ever could. It had all seemed so simple that day in town—had it only been three days ago? All he had to do was marry her, and the ranch would be his and she would be under his complete control. What had ever made him think that Maggie Colson would ever be under anyone's control? It was difficult to remember now, but it had to have been insanity, pure and simple. It was not the first time he had come to that conclusion.

Neither of them spoke for the remainder of the trip, neither being willing to pursue the subject of despoiling, and both were relieved when the buggy rolled into Bitterroot. Jack pulled up in front of the hotel and instructed Swede, who had come along right behind them on horseback, to take the buggy over to the livery. Then he got down and came around to help Maggie out. It was an awkward business, with each of them avoiding the other's eyes and both of them trying to pretend that nothing was wrong. No matter what passed between them in private, they were loath to let the general public suspect the truth.

Jack had brought along two other men besides Swede, and one of them came forward and unloaded their bags from the buggy. Jack offered her his arm, and when she had taken it, albeit reluctantly, they strolled into the hotel lobby.

Festus was dozing behind the desk, even though it was not quite noon, but he woke right up when Jack cleared his throat rather loudly. Jumping to his feet, he treated Jack and Maggie to what Maggie could only assume was his best professional smile. "Mornin', Mr. Sinclair, Mrs. Sinclair," he said with a nod to each of them. Maggie knew that word of her marriage would have spread by now, and that Festus would probably have been the first to spread it, since he had witnessed the priest going upstairs that day, and then later, her leaving with Jack. Still, it made the whole thing seem so final, so real. "You want a room?" he asked perfunctorily, automatically turning the register book for Jack to sign.

Maggie had released Jack's arm as soon as they had reached the desk, and now she stepped back, unconsciously reacting to the renewed prospect of sharing a room with Jack. He had promised her she would not have to, but she had not realized then how embarrassing it would be for him, a bridegroom of only three days, to ask for separate rooms. She knew enough of the Sinclair pride to doubt that he would do it, and the familiar panic was teasing at the edges of her mind.

Jack signed his name with a flourish. "Yes, Festus, the best room in the house," he was saying. That was a joke, of course, since all the rooms were exactly the same and none would qualify as "good," much less "best." Then he

209

pretended to consider for a moment and said, "Now that I think of it, why don't you give us two rooms. I'll be needing a place to conduct some business meetings, and I wouldn't want to disturb Mrs. Sinclair."

Festus's graying eyebrows rose. *"Two* rooms?" he asked with more than a casual interest as his shrewd eyes glanced from Jack to Maggie and back again. He seemed delighted.

"Yes, two rooms, right next to each other," Jack said. His voice was even, but Maggie knew that it was too even, and she could tell by his suddenly clenched fist that he was more than annoyed by Festus's interest in the subject.

Festus rubbed his chin thoughtfully. "Well, now, them walls is kinda thin, Mr. Sinclair. Iffen you don't want to disturb the lady, you'd best take a room across the hall," he advised.

Jack smiled with barely suppressed fury. The old man hadn't actually said anything out of line, had made no accusations, had not even hinted that he suspected, and yet Jack knew with certainty that the old goat knew that he and Maggie would not be sharing the same bed. Good God, did everyone in town know that he and Maggie did not sleep together? At that moment he thought it appallingly likely. Of course, one would have been hard pressed to read his thoughts on his face, which was blanked of expression.

He pretended to think over Festus's sugestion and then turned to Maggie. "What do you think, my dear?" he asked blandly.

Maggie was already biting her lip to keep the laughter from gurgling out, and when she read the fury in Jack's blank eyes, she almost lost control completely. She should have suspected that Consuela's gossip would have made its way to town by now. It had already been twenty-four hours since she had heard her telling it to Lee Parker, and such news would spread with the speed of a grass fire. Swallowing with difficulty, she managed to reply quite meekly, "Whatever you say, Jack."

Nothing she could have said would have angered him more, and she knew it, but she decided that it was worth whatever retribution he exacted later to see the slow flush that worked its way up his neck.

"Well, then," he said with a false bravado, turning back to Festus, "I guess we'll take your suggestion. I certainly wouldn't want to disturb Mrs. Sinclair in any way." Maggie heard the irony in his voice and the laughter died inside of her. She knew what he was telling her, that he had no intention of disturbing her in the night, as well as in the day with his meetings. That information should have pleased her, should have at least relieved her, but for some reason it only disturbed her all the more.

Festus gave them rooms one and two, the two rooms at the top of the stairs, and Maggie found herself back in the same room in which she had been married. Jack did not even try to follow her inside. He merely set her bag inside the door and told her he would come back for her in about half an hour to take her downstairs for the noon meal.

Later Maggie was both relieved and disturbed to discover that they were to share a table with Swede and the other two men. She tried to tell herself that she only wanted to be alone with Jack so that she could needle him a little about their separate rooms, but she didn't really believe it. She didn't really feel like discussing it at all, if the truth were known. That was why she felt relieved. They wouldn't be able to discuss anything personal with the other men there, but she couldn't help wishing that they weren't there all the same. She couldn't help wondering what they might have talked about had they been alone.

When they were finished eating, Jack told her that he had some business and that she was free to shop or visit or do whatever she wanted, and that he would meet her back at the hotel for supper. Watching the four men leave the dining room, Maggie felt suddenly very alone, and she almost called after Jack, demanding to know why he hadn't left

211

someone to guard her. It was childish, she knew, to feel so cowardly. She didn't want to have to face the townspeople alone, but on the other hand, she would have been furious had Jack left someone to escort her, or worse yet, chosen to escort her himself.

She lingered over her coffee as long as she could, and made an unnecessary trip to the outhouse out back, and went up to her room to check her hair, which she had just checked a half-hour earlier, and when she could delay no longer, she made her way out of the hotel, into the bright afternoon sun of Bitterroot.

Maggie was halfway to the Merchantile, and was beginning to think that her luck was exceptionally good today, and that she wouldn't run into anyone she knew on the street, when she heard someone calling her name.

"Maggie! Yoo-hoo, Maggie!"

Maggie cringed, but managed to pin a polite smile on her face for Miss Milligan, no, Mrs. James, she mentally corrected. Her old schoolteacher was scurrying across the street, waving a handkerchief at her.

"Oh, Maggie!" Mrs. James exclaimed a little breathlessly when she finally caught up with her. "We were all so happy to hear the news! My best wishes to you!"

Maggie kept smiling and hoped her face would not crack. "Thank you," she said through gritted teeth.

Mrs. James did not seem to notice her constraint. "Some people were surprised at the news, I don't mind telling you, but I wasn't a bit surprised. I told Mr. James, more than once, too, that there was something going on between you two. Anyone could see the way he looked at you that he was madly in love. . . ."

Maggie almost choked at that, but managed to restrain herself by marveling instead at the elaborate fictions that people could construct out of whole cloth.

". . . and you'll just have to come over for dinner on Sunday," Mrs. James was saying.

Maggie had no intention of subjecting herself to such an ordeal. They would expect her and Jack to act like besotted lovers, and Maggie simply did not feel up to the task. Besides, she had not forgotten that Mrs. James was one of the people who had snubbed her for snubbing Jack way back in the beginning. She wasn't quite ready to forgive and forget, either. "I'm sure we'd love to, but I'll have to check with Jack first," she hedged, hating even the lie that hinted she might need his permission for anything.

Mrs. James nodded knowingly. "If you're busy this week, there's always next week," she said encouragingly. She would have gone on all day, gushing about Maggie's romantic elopement, but Maggie managed to extricate herself with an abruptness that bordered on rudeness, and left Mrs. James standing on the wooden sidewalk with her mouth hanging open in midsentence.

Feeling lucky to have escaped, Maggie made her way into the Merchantile, only to remember that there she must face Mr. and Mrs. Alexander. The last time she had seen them had been the day that she had almost fallen off the sidewalk and Jack had caught her. She had just finished letting Mrs. Alexander know her opinion of Jack Sinclair, and now she wondered just how she was going to justify that opinion in view of the fact that she had married the man.

She need not have worried. Mrs. Alexander had apparently been cutting things from the same whole cloth as Mrs. James. "Mrs. Sinclair!" she called the moment Maggie stepped across the threshold, rushing to greet her. "Congratulations! Oh, no, I mean best wishes. You aren't supposed to congratulate the bride, now are you? That makes it sound like she did the pursuing, doesn't it?" Mrs. Alexander gave Maggie a smile that was entirely too smug for Maggie's liking. Did the woman think that Maggie had actually chased Jack Sinclair? After the things she had said about him? After the way she had slapped his face in front of this very store?

"Thank you," Maggie murmured halfheartedly, studying the woman for signs of insanity.

"I guess you had a good laugh at me, the way I defended Mr. Sinclair to you, when all the time you and he . . ." she stopped, letting her voice trail off suggestively, and then shook her head with a knowing smile. "You're a sly one, all right. Every girl in the county was bending over backward to be nice, and then you come along and spit in his face. Who would have guessed that that was the way to catch him, eh?"

Mrs. Alexander had a good laugh, while Maggie just looked on in amazement. The woman *was* crazy! Maggie almost felt sorry for her. Almost, but not quite. She remembered only too well how Mrs. Alexander had taken such great pains to let Maggie know that she was the only one who didn't think highly of Jack Sinclair. This was something else she would not forget or forgive, and she had a hard time stomaching the extravagant good wishes of people who only days ago had barely had a civil word for her. Jack Sinclair certainly had this town in the palm of his hand, she concluded rather glumly. Her marriage to him had transformed her from pariah to patron saint in the twinkling of an eye.

"Excuse me, Mrs. Alexander," Maggie interrupted her, reaching into her reticule for a slip of paper. "I have this list of things that we need out at the ranch. I don't know when we'll be leaving, though. We plan to be in town a few days, so could you just have them ready for us?"

Mrs. Alexander blinked in surprise at the coolness of Maggie's voice. "Yes, of course," she murmured, taking the paper from Maggie's hand.

"Thank you. Now I think I'll look around the store, if you don't mind," she added brusquely and walked away without waiting for a reply. There, she thought, that should let her know that she can't get back in my good graces quite so easily.

Strolling to the far back corner of the store, Maggie

proceeded to examine just about every piece of merchandise in stock. It wasn't so much that she was interested as that she didn't have anything better to do. She was engrossed in deciding whether to buy a piece of green ribbon or a piece of blue ribbon when someone spoke to her.

"Mrs. Sinclair?" the voice asked hesitantly, and Maggie looked up into a face she had never seen before. The woman was a few inches taller than she and a few years older, but there was something about her eyes that made her seem much older still. It was the mark of suffering. Maggie had seen too much of it to be mistaken, but while she usually saw that it had hardened the person it had marked, in this woman she saw something completely different. The deep blue eyes that looked back at her hazel ones were full of kindness and compassion, a compassion that reached out to Maggie and touched her heart.

"I'm real sorry to hear about your father," the woman said. She meant it, too. Maggie was certain of that, and she felt the sting of tears in the back of her eyes. She would not cry, though, not here.

Forcing a brave little smile, she whispered a heartfelt, "Thank you," and realized suddenly that this woman was the only person besides Judge Harris who had mentioned her loss. The rest of them were too amazed at her marriage to even recall that one of the greatest men who had ever lived had just died. But this woman had, and from the sadness on her face, Maggie knew that she felt the loss, too. Then a very disturbing thought occurred to Maggie. Just exactly how well had this woman known her father? She tried to imagine the two of them together, but could not.

Never once, in all the fifteen years she had lived with her father, had she seen him with a woman. After her mother's death he had closed off that part of his life, and had never, at least to her knowledge, shown any interest in other women. But Maggie had been gone for three years, and a lot could happen in three years. The woman was attractive, too. Not a

215

beauty, by any means, but nice looking. She had a full figure, with large, round breasts and soft curves, the kind of figure that would tend to fat if she wasn't careful, but she was obviously careful. She certainly didn't look the part of a mistress, however. Her clothes were clean, but serviceable instead of fashionable, her blond hair tucked neatly into a style that was more practical than becoming. She looked more . . . well, more motherly. That bosom was more the type to offer solace than seduction, a place for laying one's head and sobbing out grief rather than . . . but then, Maggie didn't have any idea how a man would see her. Maybe a man would see her differently, and maybe her father had needed a woman like this.

"How . . . how well did you know my father?" she asked, a little reluctantly, but anxious to know.

The woman smiled, a kind and understanding smile. "Not real well, but he was a good friend to me when I needed one. Oh, where's my manners. I'm Abigail Wheeler." She extended a work-roughened hand, and Maggie shook it. Abigail Wheeler's grip was as firm as a man's.

"Pleased to meet you, Miss Wheeler," Maggie told her with a friendly smile. Whoever this woman was, she hadn't been her father's mistress. On that Maggie would have staked her life.

"It's Mrs. Wheeler, but I'm Abby to my friends," the woman said, her eyes telling Maggie that she very much wanted them to be friends.

Maggie wanted the same thing. "And I'm Maggie to my friends. How long have you lived in Bitterroot?" she asked.

"Going on two years now," Abby said, and then looked around to see if there was anyone near who might overhear, and lowering her voice, she went on, "I guess I'd better tell you this now, so you don't hear it from someone else later. You might not be too glad to be my friend when I tell you." Maggie knew a moment's apprehension that she might yet learn something she did not want to know about her father,

216

but she nodded encouragingly. "Me and my man, when we first come here, we squatted on your ranch."

Maggie almost sighed with relief. If that was all, she could easily forgive it. "You don't live there now, though," Maggie commented. The Wheelers must have been part of the earlier nestor trouble she had heard about.

Abby grinned. "No, your men ran us off, of course. We sneaked back, though, and set up again." Abby paused, and a frown marred her pleasant features. "Things might've been all right, though, if Wheeler hadn't have gone into town and got drunk and started bragging how he was gonna beat the whole CMC. He picked a fight with one of your men and got himself killed."

Maggie gasped, both in surprise at the news and in shock at the matter-of-fact tone of voice in which it was delivered. "Oh, I'm so sorry," she offered, angry that her words seemed so inadequate for expressing the compassion she felt.

Abby, however, did not seem upset, but merely shrugged. "Wheeler had needed killing for a long time," she said quite honestly. "He wasn't worth the powder it would've taken to blow his brains out, but his killing was an accident, and all his own fault, when you come right down to it."

When Maggie realized that she wasn't going to offer any details, she asked, "How did it happen?"

It was obviously not a subject that Abby liked to discuss, but she explained, "Like I said, he was at the saloon, and drunk. Some of your men came in, and he was spoiling for a fight. One of the men finally gave it to him. It was just a fistfight, nothing very important, but Wheeler fell real hard and cracked his head on the corner of the bar. Knocked him out cold, but he didn't wake up. He was like that for a couple days, and then one morning he was dead, just like that." Seeing the pained expression on Maggie's face, she hastened on. "Really, Mrs. . . . Maggie, the world's a better place without him in it."

Maggie could only marvel at Abby's attitude. What a

217

despicable creature Mr. Wheeler must have been to have earned his wife's contempt. She thought of Aunt Judith and the way she was constantly criticizing Uncle Edward. Maggie had always thought that theirs was an unhappy marriage, but she also knew that should anything happen to Uncle Edward, Aunt Judith would mourn him for the rest of her life. Even as much as she hated Jack, if he should die . . . quickly Maggie forced her thoughts back to Abby Wheeler's problems. "Is that when my father was a friend to you?" Maggie could easily imagine her father feeling responsible for a woman widowed by the actions of one of his men. It was a soft side of him few who knew him would even have suspected he possessed.

"That's right, although some said he just wanted to get me off his land. I knew different, though, and I guess you do, too." Maggie nodded. "He wanted to send me back where I came from, but I didn't want to go back, so he helped me set up in business. I run a boardinghouse at the end of town. That big gray house. Maybe you've seen it?" Maggie had noticed it. It was one of the buildings that had been built since she had gone away to school. "He loaned me money, and I paid him back a little at a time, out of the profits. Matter of fact, I still owe some. I have it all written down, if you want to look over my books. I guess I owe you the money now."

Maggie could have wept with joy at this information. Not that she cared about the money, but here was proof positive that her father had been the man she remembered, the man that everyone had been telling her had changed so much, had "not been himself." And here was someone who had respected him the way he had deserved to be respected. "You don't owe me any money, Abby," Maggie stated. Abigail Wheeler's kind words had repaid any debt she might have owed the Colsons.

"Oh, yes I do. . . ." she started to protest, but Maggie interrupted her.

"I mean your debt is canceled. You owed the money to my father, and he's gone. That's all there is to it." Maggie lifted her chin belligerently. She would brook no arguments, and Abby knew it, but she felt obliged to try it, just the same.

"It ain't right. A person needs to pay her debts." Abby frowned in disapproval.

"If that's the way you feel, then consider the ledger books still open, Abby," Maggie said, a sly smile on her lips. "Who knows, maybe someday you'll be able to return the favor my father did you, and then we can call it even. Until then, I don't want to see any of your money."

"Well, all right," the older woman agreed reluctantly.

"Maybe you could start by being my friend. I've discovered that I don't have any friends left since I've come home, and I could use one," Maggie suggested, and Abby brightened at the prospect.

"I'm afraid I don't have many friends, either," she confided. "Seems like I'm too old to be friends with the single women in town, and the married ones think I'm after their men."

Maggie couldn't help the laughter that bubbled out at Abby's distasteful expression. Obviously, Abby did not consider the men of Bitterroot worth chasing, and Maggie had to agree. The only one worth having was Jack Sinclair, and she . . .

"Maybe you could come for a visit sometime," Abby was saying, and Maggie gratefully turned her attention back to the conversation. "Are you going to be in town long?"

"Yes, at least another day, I'm sure. How about tomorrow afternoon?" she suggested.

Abby readily agreed, and they decided to meet at Abby's home the following afternoon. Abby had to get back to the boardinghouse to finish her chores and prepare the evening meal, and Maggie hated to see her go, knowing that she had the long afternoon ahead of her to kill, but at least she had the promise that the next afternoon would not be so long.

Of course, she could have done some visiting on this day, as well, but the prospect of sitting with some of the town women and listening to them rave on and on about Jack Sinclair was more than she thought she could bear. Instead, she chose to spend some of Jack's money on things she really didn't need. When she got back to the hotel in plenty of time to get cleaned up for supper, she was laden with packages.

When Jack came to fetch her for supper, she was inordinately glad to see him, blaming her enthusiasm on the boring afternoon she had spent. She would have been glad to see Attila the Hun if he could have made intelligent conversation. He inquired politely about her day, but answered noncommittally when she asked him about his. Then he told her that Judge Harris would be joining them for their meal, and by that time they were in the dining room. The judge was already at the table, and he hauled his round little body up out of the chair to greet her.

"Maggie, darlin', you're looking well," he said, taking both her hands in his.

Maggie couldn't remember if she should be angry at the judge or not, so she decided not to be. It was an arbitrary decision, but she saw no need to ruin the evening by pouting. Besides, she was really glad to see the judge. She had missed him. "And so are you," she replied, offering her cheek for his kiss. He hesitated only a moment before brushing his lips across her soft skin in the ancient ritual that had seemed so inappropriate at their last few meetings.

When he pulled away, he continued to hold her hands for another moment while he searched her face for some clue to her change in attitude. She gave him a sad smile that said there was no reason to hold a grudge against him. What Jack Sinclair had done was not his fault, and she did not hold him responsible. He read the look, and then squeezed her hands, his eyes growing suspiciously moist for a moment, before he let her go and seated her at the table.

Jack was on his best behavior, Maggie noted, and the

meal passed in a haze of quiet, meaningless conversation. He seemed to be going out of his way to avoid controversial subjects, and he even refrained from teasing her. She should have been grateful, she knew, but for some reason, she felt oddly disappointed, even more so when he explained that he and the judge still had some things to discuss at his office and asked her to excuse them.

Her disappointment couldn't have been caused by a desire to spend the evening with him, of that she was certain. She was just bored, bored stiff, and now that she thought of it, she was also furious at Jack Sinclair for bringing her to town and then leaving her to her own devices. If he'd let her stay home, she could at least have found things to do to keep busy. And she'd had just about enough of his courteous reserve. How he could act so cool and calm in public when in private he was so passionate . . . and that was another thing; how could he turn his emotions off and on so easily? There had been a time when he couldn't seem to keep his hands off of her, and now . . . now it seemed as if he had to force himself to touch her. Not that she wanted him to touch her, of course. She was actually very glad that he wasn't pawing at her anymore, but the change had been so sudden, and so great. Well, it just went to prove that he was the liar she had always thought him, pretending a grand passion for her one minute and being coldly civil to her the next. To think that he had actually said that he loved her! It was unbelievable. And preposterous. And very, very disturbing.

It disturbed Maggie all evening as she sat in her lonely hotel room and tried to embroider a sampler that she had bought that day, and it disturbed her even more when she arose the next morning to discover a note that he had slipped under her door telling her that he would be gone most of the day. He wanted to talk to some of the other ranchers, the note said.

Maggie was furious. If he was so concerned about her getting into trouble when he wasn't around, then why hadn't

221

he taken her with him? How dare he leave her here all by herself with nothing to do? She had half a mind to order up the buggy and ride back out to the ranch by herself. She would have done that very thing, too, if she hadn't already promised to visit Abby that afternoon. As it was, she still had the whole empty morning ahead of her, and the prospect was quite bleak. Just wait until she saw Jack Sinclair again. She'd give him a lesson or two on how to treat a wife. She was so angry that she didn't even realize that she had begun to think of herself as Jack's wife.

Abby's boardinghouse was on the edge of town, built as an afterthought in the town's construction. It was a tall, three-storied house, with a modest amount of gingerbread decorating the eves. That would have been her father's idea, she decided. Abby was much too practical to waste money on something so frivolous, but her father would have insisted that the house look fashionable. The large front porch would have been Abby's idea, though, a place to congregate in the cool of the evening, a place to rest after the work of the day was done.

Smiling to herself as she climbed the steps to that front porch, Maggie wondered what made her think she knew so much about Abigail Wheeler's character. Either she was getting very astute in her old age or else Abby was a very easy person to read.

Abby was waiting for her at the front door, and inside she had a tray of tea and hot scones waiting. Maggie was surprised to discover that she liked Abby even more today than she had yesterday. She found the woman remarkably easy to talk to. Too easy, perhaps, because she soon found herself discussing things she would never have mentioned to another living soul.

"You haven't been married very long, have you?" Abby asked when they had exhausted all the pleasantries.

"No, just a few days," Maggie replied, amazed to note that it was true. For some reason, her marriage seemed of much

222

longer duration. Her marriage. The word still sounded so strange to her. And then there was the matter of its unseemly haste. What were people saying about *that,* behind her back? Would Abby know? "I . . . I guess you've heard the gossip," she said cautiously.

Abby looked genuinely puzzled. "What gossip?"

"You know, about the way we got married, so soon after my father's death, and all," Maggie prompted.

Abby was still puzzled. "I heard that you'd gotten married, and that it was all kind of fast. Didn't you have a priest come to the hotel or something like that?" Maggie nodded stiffly. "That's all I heard, but I hadn't considered it gossip. Was there more to it than that?"

Once again Maggie nodded, this time in an agony of indecision. Could she trust this person, this virtual stranger? Should she even consider it? She struggled with her doubts for a moment, but her need to confide in someone won out. "I only married him because I had to," she blurted.

Abby looked a little surprised, and then a little shocked, and then very understanding. She reached over and patted Maggie's hand. "It's nothing to be ashamed of, honey. It happens to a lot of girls, and besides, having a baby's about the nicest thing that can happen, no matter how it got started."

It took Maggie a moment to figure out how they had suddenly gotten on the subject of babies, and when she did, she flushed crimson. "Oh, no!" she protested. "I didn't mean I had to marry him because of *that!* I had to marry him because he made me, so that he could get my ranch."

Now Abby was really puzzled. "What do you mean, he had to marry you to get your ranch? Couldn't he just buy it from you?"

Maggie sniffed in disgust. "That's what he was planning to do at first. He even made me an offer, but I turned him down. I never would have sold the CMC, and he knew it." That wasn't quite true, of course. In the end he would have forced

her to practically give it away. "And then I made him angry."
Maggie recalled all too clearly the time she had called him a
thief and a murderer and the events immediately preceding
those accusations. And then there was the time in the hotel
room, the time he had finally withdrawn his offer. Looking
back, she wondered why he had not murdered her on the
spot, and she recalled her fear at the time that he might do
just that. "Then he got the idea to marry me. That way he got
my ranch, for free, and he got me, so that he could get his
revenge." She had expected some sympathy from Abby, but
instead the other woman was frowning again.

"Revenge? I don't understand. Why would he marry you
to get revenge?" Abby asked.

Maggie opened her mouth to reply and found that she
had no ready answer. It was true, she was sure it was true, but
if it was, she should have an answer. "So he could have me
around to . . . to torment and to keep as a prisoner and . . ."
She couldn't think of anything else, try as she would. She
was sure that he had tormented her, but then she had
tormented him just as much, if not more. He hadn't exactly
kept her a prisoner, either. He had even told her she was free
to go out whenever she wanted. She hadn't liked being in
town, of course, but she was hardly a prisoner here, either.
Even if he had used her body for his lustful purposes, she
would have had something to accuse him of, but he didn't,
not anymore, and the one time that he had used her body had
not been entirely unpleasant. She was at a loss, and how
could she hope to make Abby understand if she could not
understand herself?

"It don't make any sense, Maggie," Abby decreed. "I don't
know Mr. Sinclair very well, but I do know that a man don't
shackle himself to a woman for life just to get revenge.
That'd be pure suicide. Even a fool knows a woman can
make a man's life pure hell if she sets her mind to it, and I
imagine you'd be the type who could set her mind to it good
and proper."

Maggie's mouth dropped open at this insightful evaluation of her character. Had she not married Jack Sinclair with that very thought in mind? But *he* had to have had a reason for marrying *her*. She knew he wasn't madly in love with her, no matter what Mrs. James might think. "My ranch," she announced triumphantly. "He married me to get my ranch."

Abby was unimpressed. "You said yourself he offered to buy it, and I heard what happened, about your hands leaving you and all. All he had to do was wait and you'd be begging him to take it off your hands." Now she leaned forward, searching Maggie's face. "He's not an evil man; I know that. I don't think he'd do anything to hurt another person, not without a good reason. . . ."

"Not an evil man!" Maggie fairly shouted. "How do you account for the fact that he killed my father then?"

This time Abby looked downright stunned. "What do you mean, killed your father? Nobody killed him. He got sick and died." She was looking at Maggie as if she suspected the girl might be one brick short of a full load.

"But he was the one who made him sick. He caused him to have the stroke," Maggie insisted.

"Who gave you a wild idea like that?" Abby demanded.

"Swede. He told me the whole story."

"He couldn't have told you the *whole* story, if that's what you think happened," Abby declared, pursing her lips in disapproval.

"Well, what did happen, then?" Maggie wanted to know.

"It's sort of a long story," Abby hedged.

"I'm listening," Maggie said, crossing her arms in silent challenge. Let her try and exonerate Jack Sinclair. Just let her try.

"You remember I told you how my man and I came and settled on your ranch?" Abby began. At Maggie's nod, she continued. "It was Kincaid who brought us." She said the name Kincaid as if it left a vile taste in her mouth, and

Maggie almost stopped her to ask about him, but then decided that that could wait. "He took every penny we had, and never told us that the valley he'd talked us into moving to was already somebody else's property. We weren't the only ones who came, either. Most of them are gone now. Your father's men drove them off, Mr. Perkins and the others who used to work for him. There was trouble, a lot of fighting, and folks were getting killed, but Maggie, the reason it all started was because your father had been sick, and Kincaid figured that all the fight had gone out of him."

This information struck a familiar chord in Maggie's memory. "What are you talking about? What do you mean, he was sick?" she asked.

"I don't know exactly. It wasn't anything you could see, more like he just started getting feeble, and started acting funny in his head," Abby explained.

Maggie did not like hearing that her father's mind had gone bad, but Abby was not the first person to mention this to her. "How did he act?"

Abby thought this over for a minute. "He wasn't crazy or anything like that, that's for sure. The few times I talked to him, he was fine, and then he helped me out with the house and all. It was more like he started suspecting things about people that weren't true. Oh, it was true that Kincaid was out to steal his valley, all right, but he stopped trusting everybody, even his oldest friends. He had a big fight with the judge, said the judge was plotting against him, and threw him out of his house, told him never to come back." Maggie could only nod her understanding, not trusting herself to speak. The judge had told her pretty much the same story. "And then Mr. Sinclair came."

Unconsciously, Maggie leaned forward. This was the part she really wanted to know about. "Mr. Sinclair saw what was happening, and he didn't want Kincaid to get his hands on the valley any more than your father did, but he knew that it was only a matter of time. Your father was getting old, dying right before our eyes, you might say. Mr. Sinclair had

226

this idea; he tried to convince your father to split the valley with him. It's too much land for one man to hold, anyway. Always has been." Another time, Maggie would have argued that point, but now she let it pass. "He figured the two of them together could stop Kincaid, but your father didn't want none of it. They fought about it more than once. The last time they fought, your father had the stroke. The doc said that he might have had one or two smaller ones before. That might have been what changed him, made him so feeble. Anyway, we all knew it was only a matter of time before he . . . Swede and the men made it pretty clear that they wouldn't let anybody squat while they were around, so Kincaid just bided his time. As soon as Mr. Colson was gone, he moved in."

The story Abby told was pretty much the one Maggie had already known. It was amazing how the addition of a few facts could make a difference. It was difficult for her to imagine her father behaving so irrationally, but she had no reason to doubt Abby's word. The woman had nothing to gain by lying to her. Still . . . "Who told you all this?" she asked. That could explain a lot.

Abby shifted a little uncomfortably, and Maggie noticed a slight bloom of color come to her cheeks. "Swede."

If it hadn't been for Abby's unusual reaction, Maggie might not have thought to be surprised by that information. Even so, with all this new information running through her mind, it took her a moment to be amazed. Swede? The man who never spoke unless compelled? The man who never volunteered a thing had told Abigail Wheeler all of this? And when would he have had an opportunity? Under what circumstances had he met with the widow? Only one possibility occurred to Maggie, and she almost dismissed it as preposterous, yet she could think of no other explanation. "Swede?" she asked with a sly smile and a suspicious lift of her eyebrows.

"Don't look like that," Abby insisted, fussing nervously with the tea things. "It isn't like that at all. He comes over

227

sometimes to help around the place, do the things it takes a man to do. He's just lending a hand, that's all. It's not like we're . . ."

"Courting?" Maggie supplied, delighted. It was almost novel enough to get her to forget her own problems, and it was certainly a more pleasant topic of conversation than what they had been discussing. Maggie tried to picture the buxom, talkative Mrs. Wheeler and the skinny, silent Swede together. It was an amusing picture. How on earth did she get him to talk? Did he blush all the time the way he did whenever he spoke to Maggie? Did he ever try to kiss her? Maggie doubted it. How dull it would be to be courted by a man like that. Not at all the way it had been when she and Jack . . . well, you couldn't call what they had done "courting" exactly, but at least it had been exciting.

Anticipating all the questions that Maggie would have for her, Abby quickly changed the subject. "Like I said, Mr. Sinclair would never have married you for revenge. You're gonna have to think up a better reason than that. And don't tell me any windies about how he wanted your ranch. He could've gotten that without tying up with you, and we both know it." Abby considered for a moment. "You want a good reason, maybe you'd better look in the mirror."

Did Abby think he'd married her because he *liked* her? "Oh, no, it couldn't be that," she assured her friend. "He doesn't even . . ." Maggie caught herself just in time. She hadn't meant to say that.

It didn't matter, though. Abby already knew to what she was referring. "I'd heard that," she mused, "but couldn't hardly believe it. Could it be he lets you sleep alone because that's the way you want it?"

Maggie was shocked. Of course that was the way she wanted it. How could she want anything else? Just because that one time he'd made her respond . . . Maggie forced herself not to think about that. Besides, she knew enough about Jack Sinclair to know that if he wanted her, he'd take her, without a thought to what her own feelings in the matter might be. Hadn't he already proven that? But then there'd been that time in the office when he'd kissed her and she'd thought that maybe he did still want her. Oh, it was all so confusing. And what did it matter, anyway? Nothing could negate the fact that he had stolen her ranch and forced her to marry him. It didn't matter whether he liked her or not. She could never forgive him for those things. Or could she?

Looking up, she realized that Abby was watching her with an amused expression on her face. "Is it what you want, Maggie?"

Was it? Did she want to be married to a man who slept in a different room, who was barely civil to her? "I . . . I don't know," she answered quite honestly.

After that the pleasure seemed to go out of her visit, and Maggie took her leave. On the long walk back to the hotel, Maggie went over her conversation with Abby in her mind, reviewing all the things she had learned about her husband. He hadn't really set out to steal the whole valley, the way she had thought, but then he'd certainly grasped the opportunity when it arose. And he really had had no right at all to suggest that her father split the valley with him in the first place. But then, her father hadn't really been in a position to hold on to it alone, either. And then there was the way he had treated her, alternately bullying her and seducing her to get his own way. Was he really the blackguard that she had painted him in her mind, or was he merely a strong-willed man, used to having his own way regardless of the consequences? And what had been his *real* reason for marrying her? Was Abby right?

Maggie could find no answers to those questions in her own experience, but she determined then and there to find them. She would start tonight, as soon as Jack came back from wherever it was that he had gone. She would study him and question him, and she would find out. Even if it meant being nice to him. Even if it meant . . . well, she'd cross that bridge when she came to it.

Chapter VIII

Maggie had been in her hotel room for some time when she finally heard Jack's step on the stairs. Not bothering to analyze why or how she happened to know that it was *his* step, she took one last look in the mirror to check her appearance before stepping out into the hall. She had used the time after her visit to Abby to change into her emerald-green dress. She could not have said why she had thought to bring it with her to town, but now she was glad that she had. She wanted to look her very best for her next encounter with Jack Sinclair.

Jack was tired. He had ridden a good thirty miles that day while making the rounds of all the ranchers south of town. In addition to being tired, he was irritated, because his visits had profited him nothing. All the other ranchers had heard about the nestors, but they did not feel they were a serious threat. Jack felt certain they would change their tunes when the nestors started setting up housekeeping on their land, but until then, he didn't think he could count on them for much help. Now he would have to meet with Kincaid knowing that when he spoke, he spoke for himself alone. Kincaid needn't know that, of course, but it weakened his bargaining position somewhat, nevertheless. Now all he wanted was a change of clothes and a hot bath and a good supper.

He was halfway up the stairs when he heard a door open and looked up. The hand that had been massaging the weariness from the back of his neck stilled immediately, and he forced it back down to his side as his eyes took in the sight of her. She was wearing that green dress, the one that turned her eyes to jade, the one that outlined the beautiful breasts that he remembered so well. Her hair was up, but not really up, caught back from her face, but all those auburn curls were cascading down her shoulders. She looked good enough to eat, with her face scrubbed all shiny and bright, he thought, as he almost—but not quite—missed the next step. And dear God, she was smiling at him! What was she up to now? After the day he had just had, he didn't need that, too.

Maggie couldn't help smiling. Something about seeing him, after not seeing him all day, made her feel so strange. It was like a heavy lump had settled in her stomach and then cracked open and the most wonderful feelings had curled up out of it. She simply felt glad, glad to see him, and her face showed it.

"You look tired," she remarked when he reached the top of the stairs and stopped in front of her. He did look weary, but wary, too. She wondered why. When he did not reply, she asked, "You went to see the ranchers today?"

Jack would have thought that after the riding he had done that day he would have been impervious to Maggie's charms, but he discovered that that was not so. Inhaling the scent of lilacs that always surrounded her, as he drew in a fortifying breath, he nodded. "They aren't as concerned as we are about the nestors, it seems," he remarked, fighting off the urge to finger the glossy curl that rested on her breast.

His face, as usual, was expressionless, but his eyes looked so funny, sort of glittery, almost the way they looked when he was angry, but not quite. "Oh," she said. It was all she could think of. She had forgotten what they were discussing, and her heart had suddenly started beating so hard in her throat that she was afraid it might pop out of her mouth if she said any more. He smelled of sweat and leather and horses, but faintly of Bay Rum and cigars, too. And something else, something she could not name, but something she found very compelling. She couldn't seem to stop looking at him.

Jack watched in fascination as the green cameo brooch pinned at the throat of her dress trembled with each heartbeat. He couldn't remember ever having seen a green cameo before. It shouldn't be trembling like that, though. *She* shouldn't be trembling like that.

"Mr. Sinclair?"

Festus's voice calling from the bottom of the stairs broke the spell that had held them both. Jack stepped guiltily back, instantly dropping the hand he had raised to touch her, and jamming it into his trousers pocket to disguise something else that had risen. When he turned to look down at Festus, all emotion had been wiped clean from his face. "Yes?"

"You folks gonna want your rooms again tonight?" Festus asked.

"Yes, but I'm not certain about tomorrow. I'll let you know," Jack replied, no hint of his irritation in his voice. Why couldn't the idiot have waited five more minutes to ask his question? he wondered before turning back to Maggie.

The smile was gone from her face, and in its place was . . . what? Disappointment? Don't be a fool, he told himself. It was probably relief. Suddenly, he was conscious of how dirty and uncomfortable he felt. She would probably have cringed if he had touched her, and who could blame her? "I was just coming up for a change of clothes, so I could go to the barber shop for a bath. When I get back, I'll take you down to supper," he told her in a carefully controlled voice.

"All right," she replied, surprised that her voice sounded so normal when she felt so breathless. She'd probably laced her corset too tightly, she decided, fighting off a wave of disappointment. She'd been almost certain that he was going to touch her, and then Festus had interrupted them. As far as Maggie was concerned, that desk clerk's days were numbered.

Not that she'd wanted Jack to touch her, of course. It had just been an experiment. She had just been testing Abby's theory, trying to discover whether or not Jack really did care for her. For a moment there, she'd been so sure, but when he'd turned back, he had been the same old cool, calm Jack, the look she had thought she'd seen in his eyes gone.

At her agreement, he disappeared into his room, and she could hear him moving around, gathering up his clothes. More than anything, she wanted to stand there and wait for him to come out again, to see how he would look at her this time. She wondered if maybe his strange expression had been because he didn't like her dress. Or her hair. Maybe he didn't like her hair down like this. It wasn't really a proper style for a married woman, and she had seen him staring at it. Maybe if she put it up? But no, she decided. Let him stare. And he certainly wouldn't find her still standing in the hall like a lovesick schoolgirl, waiting to catch a last glimpse of her heart's desire. Whirling in a rustle of taffeta, she went back into her room and closed the door, not even bothering to feel irritated that after having waited for him all day, she had to wait for him some more.

When he came back for her, Jack felt immensely better. He had soaked out his stiffness and scrubbed off the grime, and in his clean shirt he felt like a new man. Or at least, almost new. There had been one certain ache that no amount of hot water could soak away, an ache that had started immediately after his wedding night, and which he saw no present hope of easing. Not for the first time, he cursed his hasty tongue just before rapping on her door.

This time Maggie calculated her smile, but it was no less genuine. Soap and water couldn't enhance his appeal, but they certainly helped to make it more visible, and he was appealing, she had to admit. Adding that to the "handsome" that she had already acknowledged, he was a pretty potent package. Fortunately, she knew too much about him to be fooled by it.

He didn't offer her his arm, since the stairs were too narrow for them to walk side by side, but he did offer her a little bow as she passed, and then followed her down. He couldn't help but notice how all those curls bounced when she walked, and wonder what else might be bouncing under all that green taffeta.

The crowd in the dining room had thinned out by the time they arrived, and Jack chose a table against the far wall where they wouldn't be disturbed by people walking by. He spoke to several people as they moved through the room, but briefly, so that they would not be encouraged to join them. He still wasn't sure what Maggie was up to with all this smiling, but he didn't think he wanted any witnesses.

Maggie had decided to be on her best behavior, and when they had placed their orders, she inquired politely about how he had spent his day, deciding not to berate him for leaving her alone all day. That could wait until another time.

Just as politely, Jack told her about his visits to the ranchers and how they had not seen fit to put up much of a fight. "They don't want to see a range war started, and I can't really blame them. On the other hand, it's not their land these folks are settling on, either."

Maggie did not think it would be wise to point out that it was not *his* land, either. "No one likes to see a range war start. Too many innocent people get hurt," she said.

Jack wondered if she considered herself one of the innocent people who had already gotten hurt, but decided not to ask. Instead he inquired about how she had spent her day.

"I had a very nice visit with Abigail Wheeler," she said, watching closely for any reaction. Did he know about Swede and Abby?

234

He seemed mildly surprised. "How do you know Abby?" he asked.

"We met yesterday in the store. She said some nice things about my father, and I liked her immediately," Maggie explained. "She seems very nice . . . for a squatter," she added tentatively, hoping that Jack would react to that.

His only visible reaction was to lift his dark eyebrows in surprise, until he realized that she was only testing him. "That wasn't her fault. Her husband brought her," he said, "and he was a dirty, no account . . . well, I won't speak ill of the dead, but he got what he deserved."

"What was he like?" Maggie asked, dying of curiosity now that she recalled the things Abby had said about him.

Jack shook his head. "Ask your friend Mrs. Wheeler to tell you," he advised just as their dinner arrived.

They did not talk much while they ate, but Maggie found herself lingering over her apple pie, not wanting the meal to end. What would happen afterwards? Would he go off and leave her again? She found the thought curiously depressing.

Jack studied her over the rim of his coffee cup. What now? He knew what he wanted to do, and that was take her right upstairs, get rid of all that green taffeta and make love to her until dawn. Not even the certainty that she would probably scratch his eyes out and scream bloody murder if he even tried it had the power to dampen that desire. At the ranch he might even have taken the chance, but here at the hotel, with its paper-thin walls, he didn't dare. No, the most he could hope for was to take her upstairs, try for a good-night kiss, and hope it led to more. He could remember several times when it had, and if she were in the mood . . .

Unfortunately, it was much too early to take her upstairs. "Would you like to take a stroll around town?" he asked. It was the only alternative activity he could think of.

"Yes, I'd love to," Maggie agreed, with much more enthusiasm than the prospect warranted. She knew that she shouldn't have seemed so eager, but she'd just been so relieved that he wasn't going to send her off to her room alone again tonight that she hadn't been able to help it.

The street outside was quiet, most of the buildings dark. All the townspeople had gone home to supper, except for the few who had stopped at the saloon.

"Do you mind if I smoke?" he asked, still being excruciatingly polite.

"No, go right ahead," she replied, thankful for this little exchange that lent a hint of normalcy to the situation. She suddenly felt very alone with him on the dark, empty sidewalk. Jack took a moment to trim and light the cigar, and when he had it going well, they started down the street.

They had gone a few steps before Jack thought to offer her his arm. Maggie hesitated only a second before accepting. It was dark, she excused herself. There was no reason why she should be proud and maybe stumble and fall on her face. His arm felt reassuringly strong and steady.

Jack looked down at the small hand tucked into the crook of his elbow and a flash of gold caught his eye. Her wedding ring. *His* ring. He'd won the thing years ago in a poker game, and although he'd never worn it himself, he'd always kept it. Something about the color of the stone had caught his fancy, and now he realized that it was the same color as Maggie's eyes when she . . . but it was hardly an appropriate ring for a lady. "We'll have to get you a proper wedding ring, Mrs. Sinclair," he commented, expecting her to agree.

"No!" she said without thinking, and then flushed at her vehemence, thankful that the darkness hid her color from him. Would he guess how much she had come to like the ring? The thought of trading it for another, more traditional one held no appeal. She did not stop to ask herself if the thought that the ring had been Jack's, had been the one he had remembered to provide for their wedding despite the unusual circumstances, influenced her opinion of it. She only knew that she did not want to give it up.

Jack frowned. No woman of his previous acquaintance

236

would have turned down the offer of jewelry of any kind. What was her objection? Of course, he mused. Why had he not thought of that? She certainly didn't want *another* wedding ring from him, not when she hadn't even wanted the first one, not when she didn't even want him. "Of course, if you're happy with the one you have, then I won't force you," he drawled, not quite able to keep the bitterness completely from his voice.

Now Maggie frowned. She was happy with the one she had, but he didn't sound as if he really thought she could be. How could she explain without betraying feelings that were best kept secret? She settled for a murmured "Thank you," and then fell silent, as did he.

Neither could think of anything to say for a while, so they simply walked, down one side of the street, across, and up the other. They were almost abreast of the hotel again when the stage rattled past them and pulled up farther down the street in front of the Merchantile.

Jack took a puff of his cigar, and commented, "The five o'clock stage is early tonight."

Maggie looked up in mild surprise. "Early? It must be after seven!" she contended.

"It is, but the five o'clock stage usually doesn't arrive until after eight, so that means that it is early," he explained very patiently.

Maggie didn't need to see the tilted mustache to know that he was teasing her. Now that was more like it, she decided. She knew how to handle that. "Shall we go see who's arriving?" she asked, letting her smile show in her voice.

Jack scowled down at her. "Do you think we have time?" he replied with mock alarm. "We want to be sure to get back to the hotel in time to see Festus empty the cuspidors. That's always the highlight of the evening in Bitterroot."

Maggie barely stifled a griggle. "You're forgetting about the sidewalks," she chastised him.

"The sidewalks?" he asked suspiciously.

237

"Yes," she said quite primly. "Rolling up the sidewalks is always much more exciting than emptying the cuspidors, don't you think? I always make a point of watching it when I'm in town."

She was expecting a bantering remark from Jack in retaliation, but when she glanced up at him with her eyes stretched wide and her mouth puckered prudishly, she was surprised to see that he was not looking at her at all, but was staring off in the direction of the stage with a look of pure shock on his face. He had stopped dead in his tracks, forcing Maggie to do the same. With more than a little trepidation she forced her own gaze to follow the direction of his.

She could see nothing shocking. The stage had stopped up ahead and the passengers were getting off. They were about fifty feet away, and Maggie could see them clearly. One was a middle-aged man who she thought looked vaguely familiar, and the other was a young woman whom she had never seen before. Neither looked particularly shocking, although she had to admit the young woman was quite beautiful, in a dark, sultry sort of way, but before she had a chance to question Jack's reaction, she heard him mutter something that might very well have been a curse, and then he was hustling her off the sidewalk and across the street.

"What's going on?" she demanded as he fairly dragged her into the hotel.

"Swede!" he called down the street just before they entered the lobby, and when they were inside, he bent down to her and said, "I just remembered some very important business I have to attend to, my dear." His voice was as calm as always, but Maggie could hear an undertone of urgency that she had never heard before, and it alarmed her.

"What kind of business?" she insisted. Did it have to do with that man on the stage? Was that Kincaid? Was he going to confront the man now? Before she could ask her questions, however, Swede came tromping into the room.

"Swede, take Mrs. Sinclair up to her room, please. She's

238

had a busy day, and she'd going to retire early. See that no one disturbs her," he told his foreman.

Swede nodded, but Maggie was too upset to notice the silent messages being passed between the two men. She was more worried about being hustled off out of the way. "I did not have a busy day, Jack Sinclair. I had a very restful, boring day, thank you very much, and I am not going to be sent off to bed."

Jack ignored her. "You know that the stage just arrived?" he asked Swede. Swede nodded again, the grim set of his mouth alarming Maggie even more.

"What's going on? Who was on the stage?" she demanded, but the two men weren't even looking at her.

"I saw," was all Swede said, but Maggie had a feeling he meant a whole lot more than that, and she was becoming even more frightened.

"Maggie, Swede will take you up to your room," Jack said, turning back to her at last.

"He most certainly will not! I'm not going upstairs until you answer some questions!" she stated, crossing her arms over her chest in defiance. If he thought he could send her to her room like a naughty child, he had another think coming.

Jack stared down at her, his irritation building by the minute. He had to get her out of the way and fast, but from the set of that little chin, he had a feeling it would take a stick of dynamite to do the job. Then from the corner of his eye, he caught sight of Festus standing behind the front desk. The clerk was listening raptly to every word they said. Jack's lips curled in amusement as he slipped an arm around Maggie's waist and began walking her toward the stairs. Bending his dark head down to hers, he whispered, "Don't look now, Mrs. Sinclair, but you're making a scene."

Maggie's mouth dropped open in outrage, but before she could launch into the tirade he felt certain she had planned, he went on. "We won't air our dirty linen in public, darling. You will go to your room now, and I will explain everything

239

to you later." Turning her toward him, he placed his hands on her shoulders and squeezed with a little more strength than was warranted. "Good night, sweetheart," he said, loudly enough for Festus to hear, and placed a chaste kiss on her forehead.

Maggie was mad enough to spit. How dare he call her "darling" and "sweetheart" and treat her as if she were in the way? She was just about to ask him that very thing when she noticed that even though he was smiling, his eyes were glittering the way they did when he was angry. In fact, they were glittering *exactly* the way they did when he was angry, and now that she noticed, he was probably going to leave bruises the way he was gripping her shoulders. A warning prickle went up the back of her neck, but still she could not resist lodging a protest. "I don't like being treated this way, Jack," she gritted.

His false smile broadened, but his voice did not sound happy. "I'm sure you don't, and knowing the way you love scenes, I know you are showing remarkable restraint, and I'm very proud of you. Now try to remember that you are one of the Virginia Sinclairs and that Festus is over there taking notes on everything we say and do, and run along upstairs like a good little girl. I don't like this any more than you do, believe me." It was true, too. He'd planned an entirely different ending to the evening, one that definitely did not involve sending Maggie off to her room alone.

He watched with great interest the small battle being fought across her face. Meek acceptance simply was not in her nature, but she also recognized when she had met a will stronger than her own. Her eyes were almost completely brown when she finally said a gruding, "Good night." She was agreeing on the outside, but he knew good and well that she was still rebelling on the inside. That was not a matter for consideration, however. The important thing was to get her out of the way—now.

Maggie hesitated one more moment, casting a glance to

make certain that Festus was still watching. When she saw that he was, she flashed him a totally false smile, which caused him very suddenly to find something of great interest to do down behind the desk. Satisfied that he had been taken care of, she flashed Jack a warning look, and then turned on her heel and flounced up the stairs. She paused once to look back, but Jack was still standing where she had left him, obviously waiting until she was safely ensconced in her room before doing whatever he had to do that was so urgent. He didn't look to very happy about her delay, so with an exasperated sigh, she climbed the rest of the steps, and went into her room. It was a great temptation to slam the door, but she recalled Jack's warning about making a scene, and her pride rebelled at giving Festus any more gossip fodder, so she closed it with infinite care. Still fuming, she plunked herself down on the bed, but once there she suddenly remembered the reason that Jack had sent her up here, and she completely forgot her anger at being dismissed. He had been going to do something that he didn't want her around to see! How could she have forgotten that!

As quickly as her skirts allowed, Maggie darted to the window. Fortunately, it faced the street, and Maggie was in time to see Jack crossing that street, his long legs making quick work of the job. The man she had seen getting off the stage was standing on the sidewalk in a puddle of light from a lantern hanging nearby, waiting for his baggage to be unloaded. He was smoking a cigarette and looking rather sinister to Maggie's way of thinking. The tiny knot of fear that had formed in her stomach tightened as she watched Jack coming closer and closer to him, and her heart seemed to be beating somewhere behind her eyes in a relentless tattoo, and she wondered frantically if Jack had a gun. And if he would need one.

Jack had waited only until he heard her door close before wheeling toward the hotel door. Swede had been standing in the opening, watching the activity across the street. "They just about got the stage unloaded," he commented as Jack brushed by him.

Jack broke his stride long enough to turn back to Swede and whisper, "Don't let her come back out." He made an upward motion in the direction of Maggie's room, and Swede nodded his understanding.

"Good luck," the foreman said as he dug into his vest pocket for his Bull Duram sack. Jack's reply was a vicious curse as he strode across the shadowy street.

The stage had just been unloaded, and the two passengers still stood by while the driver separated their bags from the rest of the load. Jack could see the man smoking in the lantern light, watching his approach with great interest, and he cursed again, wishing the fellow to Kingdom Come. Still he did not hesitate, but kept on toward the stage and toward certain disaster. It would have been easier without so many witnesses, but it was too late to worry about that now. The sooner he got this confrontation over with, the better.

He was at the stage now, and as he stepped around the rear of the vehicle and up onto the sidewalk, the fellow who was smoking tossed down his cigarette, ground it out with his heel, and stepped forward. "Evening, Mr. Sinclair," he said as Jack stalked by.

Jack acknowledged him with a barely perceptible nod, his mouth stretched into a grim line. At the sound of his name, there was a startled cry from the other side of the pile of luggage, and then the second passenger came forward in a rustle of silk petticoats.

Both arms outstretched, her beautiful face radiant with a smile that could haunt a man's dreams, she would have embraced him, but he caught her hands and brought them together in front of her, restraining her.

"Jack," she said, and the one word held a wealth of meaning. She said it the way a man longs to hear his name spoken in the dark by the woman he loves. It held the promise of endless delights and undying devotion and much,

242

much more.

Jack was unmoved. "What are you doing here, Renita?" he asked through gritted teeth.

The woman drew her lovely mouth into a pretty pout and managed to look quite repentant. He was still holding her hands, and she would have used the contact to draw him close, but when she tried, he would not budge. Instead she drew herself close, letting his hands brush the bodice of her dress before he hastily pulled them away. "You are angry," she said in dismay. "You should be flattered, *querido*. I could not stand to be away from you a moment longer."

"I told you to wait until I sent for you," he said, keeping his voice low in deference to the listening ears so close by. The driver had paused in his labors to watch them.

"And what was I supposed to do while I waited? Knit?" she asked, laying both hands against his chest in a gesture of erotic supplication. "You have not been to see me in months," she whispered up into his face.

It was true. He had not been to see her in months, and being reminded of it only made him madder. In the year and a half that he had been in Bitterroot, he had kept Renita in a distant town, recognizing immediately the folly of parading his mistress in front of the good people of Bitterroot if he wanted to win their respect. That hadn't kept him from enjoying her, however. Until recently, he had managed to visit her at least several times a month. But that had been before Maggie Colson had come home. Since that first day, that first time he had met her, he had not gone to see Renita once. Looking at Renita now, he wondered why he had been such a fool, but that did not negate the fact that her arrival severely complicated his life just now.

"I think we had better discuss this at the hotel," he said tightly, removing her hands from his chest.

"Oh, yes, *querido*," she purred, her dark eyes sparkling up at him. "I knew you would not be able to wait. It has been a long time."

Jack sighed in exasperation. "Do you have a bag or something?" It was an idiotic question. Renita would not have gone across the street without a change of clothing.

With a coquettish smile, she pointed out a fairly large trunk and two carpet bags. Jack hefted the smallest of the bags, and told the driver he would send someone over for the others. "Come on," he told her, without even bothering to sound polite.

Her laughter tinkled out into the evening darkness as she took his free arm to cross the street. She was delighted. It was always better when he was a little angry. At other times he tended to be much too gentle for her taste. Tonight should be wonderful, making that ghastly stage trip almost worthwhile.

From her post Maggie could see everything that had happened. She felt like such a fool! There she had stood, terrified for Jack's life at the hands of some vicious killer, and all the time he had wanted her out of the way so he could meet that woman. When she had seen the woman rush to meet him, throw her arms out for a welcoming embrace, Maggie had thought she might not be able to bear the pain. It had come so quickly that she was totally unprepared for the gut-wrenching agony that had torn her insides. The cry of outrage that had escaped her lips when that woman had put her hands on him had startled her back to reality, however, and helped her replace her pain with fury.

Once or twice she tried to tell herself that the woman was probably a relative, a sister, but then she had remembered that he had no sisters, and no close relatives, either. Now, watching them cross the street, that . . . that *person* clinging to Jack as if afraid he might escape, Maggie could no longer delude herself. The woman was something more than a relative or a friend or an acquaintance.

For a moment Maggie had wondered if the woman might possibly be his wife, if his marriage to her had been a sham, a bigamous union in order to facilitate his theft of her property, but she quickly rejected such an idea. Jack's sense of honor would have rebelled at bigamy, that much she knew of him. She also knew him to be the type of man who would not think twice about accepting a woman's favors outside of marriage. Had he not tried to seduce her, more than once, prior to their wedding? No, this woman was not his legal wife. She was his . . . his . . . Maggie could not think of the appropriate term, but the word "paramour" sprang to mind. With it came the pain again, like a hot knife twisting into her vitals, until she could feel the sting of tears behind her eyes.

Why she should feel so badly, she had no idea. After all, she despised the man, and she certainly had no desire for his attentions. She should be glad that he now had someone handy with whom to slake his lust. She need have no worries now that he would bother her again. For some reason, that thought brought with it a wave of despair.

Swede was still standing in the hotel doorway when Jack and Renita arrived. He stepped out of their way, still smoking his hand-rolled cigarette and studying the newcomer through narrowed eyes.

She flashed him a smile. "Hello, Swede," she sang out. She had never liked the tall, blond man, but tonight she was willing to forget that.

Swede gave her a curt nod. "Miss McFadden," he said, as she swept past on Jack's arm. He had never liked her much, either, and it was something he would never forget. He followed them inside.

Jack almost faltered when he approached the desk and saw the avid curiosity on Festus's face. This would have to be handled very delicately. "Festus, the lady would like a room, please," Jack said, not letting his hesitation show in his voice.

Festus took a moment to look the "lady" over. "Well, now," he said, licking his lips, "would she be wanting a room next to yours or across the hall?"

Since they both knew perfectly well that Jack's wife

245

occupied the room across the hall, Jack found the question more than a little offensive. His expression did not change, but he could not stop the red flush he felt crawling up his neck. "Just any room that you have available will be fine," he said through stiff lips.

"Oh, yes, sir, Mr. Sinclair," Festus said in a flurry of reconciliation, trying to act as if he hadn't really meant to offend Jack. He turned the register book for Renita to sign. "Pleased to have you, Miss McFadden," he said, reading her name from the book. "Excuse me if I offended you or anything. It's just I ain't used to seeing Mr. Sinclair with two such pretty ladies all in the same day."

Renita cocked her head, her smile fading. "*Two* ladies?" she asked, but before Festus had a chance to answer, Jack was steering her toward the stairs.

"Swede, go fetch Miss McFadden's bags, will you?" he called over his shoulder. "What room, Festus?"

"Seven," Festus replied with a smirk. Room seven was at the far end of the hall, as far away from Jack and Maggie as possible. Jack could not have been more pleased, but he still felt reasonably certain that he would throttle the old man at the first opportunity.

"*Two* ladies?" Renita asked again when they were halfway up the stairs, her suspicion growing. Perhaps there had been a good reason why she had not seen Jack for so long. Perhaps he was getting his fun somewhere else now. Renita was not worried, however. She knew that now that she was here, in the flesh, she could overcome any possible competition. She would start the process as soon as they were alone.

Jack did not answer her, acutely aware that they were passing right by Maggie's door. He had been too angry before to realize that sending Maggie to her room was hardly a solution when that room looked out onto the street and she might very well have witnessed the entire meeting, anyway. He wouldn't compound the damage by letting her hear him talking to Renita in the hallway. If she heard them walking by, well, there was no way she could know that it was he. Besides, there was no light coming from under her door. Maybe she had gone to bed. Maybe she had missed the whole thing.

What Jack could not know was that Maggie would have known it was he in the hall even if she had not watched what had happened at the stage. Once again she recognized his footsteps, and once again she fought off the tears that threatened. She could not help but hear the woman's voice and her question, and it did not take much imagination to guess who the two ladies were. Although she hated sitting there in the dark, hiding her pain, she also could not bring herself to light the lamp and let Jack know that she was witnessing this humiliation.

When the sound of their footsteps died away, and she heard the door at the end of the hall close, she waited a moment to be certain that Jack was not coming back, but had indeed gone into the woman's room with her. Certain now that her worst suspicions were true, she began tearing at the buttons of her emerald dress. It was ironic, she realized, how she had dressed to please him tonight, how she had thought to discover if he really did care for her, when all the time he had just been waiting for *her* to arrive. No wonder he had not come back to Maggie's bed again. How boring he must have found her after having been with that woman.

Maggie recalled the brief glimpse she had had of her rival, recalled the dark beauty that had so impressed her. How much more it must appeal to a man—especially a man with the passionate nature of Jack Sinclair.

Mechanically, she hung up her dress and stepped out of her underthings. She wasn't the least bit tired or sleepy, but she put on her nightdress from habit, and crawled into the lumpy bed as if it were a refuge. The silence from the hall mocked her, goading her with the message that Jack had not come out, that he was there with *her*, right now. Maggie closed her eyes against the pain that assailed her, but she could not shut out the vision of two bodies entwined as hers and Jack's had been that night. A silent sob shook her, and she snatched up her pillow and buried her head in it, muffling the next one, which was not silent at all. This time she could not stop the tears that scaled her eyes, and with every wrenching breath she cursed Jack Sinclair and tried to convince herself that it was only her pride that he had wounded by bringing his mistress to Bitterroot.

Renita looked around the room with a jaundiced eye. It was certainly a poor excuse for a hotel room, but not the worst she had ever seen, not by a long shot. She would make the best of it until Jack moved her to a better place, as she had no doubt that he would. Jack had always been more than generous with her. It was only his stupid sense of propriety that had kept him from living with her openly, and now that she was here, in the same town with him, she felt certain that she could overcome even that.

Turning back to him, she could see that he was still quite angry. One thing he had never been able to tolerate was open defiance of his orders. He had rarely refused her anything, and so she had personally never had any occasion to test him. Now she did, but she was not worried. No man had ever been able to resist her charms when she had decided that he would not.

Carefully, she removed her hat pin and lifted the confection of ribbons and feathers that she wore from her head and hung it on a peg. Then she unbuttoned her jacket and slipped it from her shoulders. Jack usually rushed to help her with such things, but this time he simply watched from where he still stood leaning against the closed door, arms crossed forbiddingly across his chest.

"Aren't you at least glad to see me?" she asked with a coaxing smile. "Not even a little bit?"

Was he? Jack asked himself the question, even though he already knew the answer. He wasn't, not a bit, not even a little bit, even though he should have been. Renita was the kind of woman men dreamed about: beautiful, charming, intelligent, and sensuous, willing to try anything once. That her passion was, for the most part, faked did not lessen her appeal, or at least, not much. She was a good actress, and she could make a man think he was the most exciting bed partner she had ever had, even if reason told him differently. She had never given Jack cause for complaint, until now. Of course, he couldn't blame her. A woman with Renita's highly developed sense of self-preservation would have perceived immediately that she was losing her hold on her man and would have followed the only logical course of action. If he had been thinking about it, he could have predicted her appearance here, but the problem was, he hadn't been thinking about it, or about her, at all.

"I know that you told me not to come," she was explaining in that soft, husky voice that she reserved for intimate moments. "You have to admit that I was a very good girl and waited very patiently, even when you did not come to see me for so long. And then I heard that the old man was dead, and I knew that there was no longer any reason to wait."

Jack stiffened at the mention of Colson's death. He still felt bad about it, even if he wasn't quite as guilty as Maggie made him out to be. "There was a complication," he said, wincing inwardly at the thought of Maggie's being called a "complication." She was that, and more, however, especially at this moment. "Colson had a daughter."

Renita dismissed the daughter with a flick of her hand. "I do not think that Jack Sinclair would let a silly girl stand in his way. I am right, no?" she asked with a smile, as she came to him and slipped her hands inside his coat.

Her characterization of Maggie as a "silly girl" made him smile. "Not exactly, Renita," he told her, grasping her wrists and pushing her away. He walked to the center of the room and turned back to face her, wondering if there was an easy way to break the news of your marriage to your mistress. It wouldn't matter how he said it, though. She'd still be furious, and he couldn't blame her, but he was certainly dreading the scene she was bound to make. "In order to get the ranch without any legal problems, I had to marry Colson's daughter," he lied.

It took a moment for the meaning of his words to sink in, and when they did, Renita had one unguarded instant when she let her true feelings show. Her chocolate-colored eyes snapped with fury in that second before she regained control, but not before Jack saw her reaction. He wondered then if he had ever before seen an honest emotion reflected on that lovely face, and he knew that he had not. The vision of another face clouded his memory momentarily, a face that could never hide its emotions, a face that revealed passion and pain and anger and pleasure with equal clarity, and when he had managed to shake free of that vision, Renita had regained her control.

"Married, *querido?*" She laughed with just the proper degree of disbelief. "That is a drastic step to take, even for a ranch like the one you told me of." She never doubted for a moment that he had done it, however. He would never tell her a lie like that simply to get rid of her. If he were finished with her, he would say so, and he had not said so, yet. There was still hope. A marriage of convenience would never satisfy a man with Jack's needs, and he might still want her. No, he *would* still want her. She would make sure of that. The fact that she had hoped for a more permanent arrangement with him herself would not matter. She would simply lower her goals, and hope that he would continue to keep her.

She studied him for a moment, looking for certain signs that would tell her what she needed to know. He had pushed her away several times, but she had felt his instinctive response, nevertheless. He was wound as tight as a spring.

250

Married or not, he wasn't getting any satisfaction from his bride. On that she would have bet the pearl necklace he had given her last Christmas, and on that she would base her plan of attack. "You have hurt me, *querido*," she began, adopting the role of the wounded party. "Oh, I know that you have done this thing for business, but to a woman, a woman who has thought that she had your love . . ."

Jack had never mentioned love to her, not even in the heat of passion, and it irritated him that she should mention it now. They both understood the bond that had held them together, and it was a bond that had little to do with the more tender sentiments. Each had had something that the other wanted, and they had made an even exchange. More than even, from Jack's point of view, considering how infrequently he had visited her and how much she had cost him.

"But this need not interfere with what we have together," she was saying. "We can go on, just as before, except that I will live here, close to you. A married man cannot keep making trips, and there is no reason for it. It will be even better than before, you will see. . . ." She had gone to him again, her hands moving under his coat once more. She could feel the tension in him, and her hands told him that she knew just how to ease it.

With practiced skill, she began to arouse him, pressing her body against his, lifting her lips for his kiss, but it was a kiss that never came. Frustrated, her movements became more urgent, and she whispered promises of the delights they would share against the warm skin of his neck. Still his body remained stiff and unresponsive, and when she sought out the proof positive, she found that the one part of him she had always been able to control was no longer susceptible to her charms. "Jack?" The word was a cry, a plea, and his reply was to set her away from him.

He found the act surprisingly easy. For some reason he had doubted his ability to break off with her, to resist the temptation she had always presented. Now he discovered

251

that she no longer tempted him at all. Compared to Maggie's innocent response, Renita's carefully rehearsed performance left him cold. "I won't leave you penniless, of course," he said, knowing that she had realized the truth. "You may keep all the jewelry I have given you, and I'll make you a settlement." He named a figure that might have astounded her with its generosity if she had not already been so furious. "I'll also continue to pay the rent on the house for another six months. By then you should have found . . ."

"Do you think I would go back to that hovel?" she shrieked, fury radiating from her sleek body. "Or that town, where the people spit at me because I am a kept woman? Keep your little house. It will be a good place to put your next mistress when you get tired of the cold comfort your wife can give you. Then you will curse the day you sent me away. Think of that the next time you want a woman and can't find one in your bed!"

Any pity he had felt for Renita died in that instant. It was bad enough that he did not share Maggie's bed. He did not need to be reminded of it by the likes of Renita. The fact that if she had not arrived this evening, he might very well have been sharing that bed right now did not help her case, either. Jack felt his own temper snap, but a knock on the door sealed forever the words he might have spoken.

It was Swede with Renita's trunk and other carpet bag. Jack opened the door and rushed to help his foreman with the awkward load. When he had set down his burden, Swede hazarded a glance at Renita and then one at Jack. "You told her, huh?" he observed mildly.

"Get out of here, you stupid *pelado,*" she hissed. "Get out of here with your snake's eyes and your bloodless face. GET OUT!" Swede had started for the door, but he wasn't moving quite fast enough for Renita's taste, so she hurried him on his way by picking up the empty water pitcher and hurling it at his head. Fortunately, her aim was poor, and the pitcher fell far short, smashing to the floor with a resounding crash.

252

"Get out, both of you!"

The two men were only too glad to oblige her, but Jack took his time, refusing to be cowed by her display of temper. "I'll have them send you up another pitcher, my dear," he told her just before closing the door behind himself. He could hear her cursing through the door.

"All horns and rattles, ain't she?" Swede remarked as they walked down the hall, and Jack grunted his agreement, even as Swede's assessment made him smile.

The foreman paused outside Jack's door, waiting to see if he had any more orders. Jack stopped, too, and could not keep his eyes from Maggie's door. There was still no light and no sound. Was she in there, listening to everything that had happened, or was she sleeping peacefully, oblivious to Renita's little drama? Jack discovered that he really did not want to know, at least not yet. After the day that he had had, he could not face one more scene. "Come on, Swede. I'll buy you a drink," he offered, slapping the foreman on the shoulder. Swede grinned his agreement, and the two men went down the stairs.

Maggie stood wide-eyed in the darkness. The sound of the smashing water pitcher had brought her off her bed in a flash, and she had heard the woman yelling, although she could not quite make out the words. She had already heard the thumping on the stairs and recognized Swede's tread as he had hauled the woman's luggage by. Only when she had heard Jack's voice and her breath had escaped in a sigh of relief did she realize that she had been holding it. Jack had come out of the woman's room! And from the sound of it, they had had a terrible fight. Maggie did not need to tax her imagination to determine what that fight had been about, either, and she could sympathize with the mysterious woman on that subject.

The only thing that Maggie did not know was whether they would make up again. Would Jack have broken off with her? It seemed unlikely. Why should he deny himself the

253

comforts she could offer when he so obviously felt no desire for his wife? On the other hand, *she* might have broken off with *him*. Perhaps she had no wish to be allied with a married man. It seemed a little far-fetched that a woman like that could have scruples, but maybe she did. Or maybe she was simply jealous. Maggie recalled the glimpse she had had of the woman. She had recognized traces of Latin blood in the woman's dark beauty, and everyone knew how volatile those people were.

Then Maggie grew impatient with herself. What on earth was she doing, standing there in the dark, tears still wet on her face, hoping that Jack's woman had broken off with him? What did she care? What did she care if he had a hundred women or no woman? As long as he stayed away from her, she didn't care. After she had told herself that a few times, she almost began to believe it, and then she made her way back to her bed.

She didn't care, but just let him try to set his mistress up in Bitterroot. Just let him try.

Chapter IX

Although she lay awake a long time, Maggie still did not
hear Jack come back. He and Swede had made an evening of
it, and although they were far from drunk when they got
back to the hotel, Jack felt reasonably certain that he had
had enough fortification to walk past Maggie's door
without a qualm.

When Maggie awoke, the sun was already good and up,
and the street noises told her that the day had fairly begun.
Bathing in the cold water still in her pitcher brought her fully
awake, and only then did she stop to consider her best course
of action. Should she confront Jack, demand to know who
this woman was and what she wanted? Should she insist that
he send her away? Maggie decided that such a demand
would be foolish. It might make him think she was jealous,
and then there was always the possibility that he would
refuse. Then what would she do?

After careful consideration, Maggie decided to wait, to see
what would happen. If the woman disappeared, then she
would know that Jack had sent her away. If the woman
stayed, then it would only be a short time until public
outrage would bring the situation to Maggie's attention, and
she could then insist that he get rid of her, strictly for
appearances. With that settled, Maggie tried not to notice

the hollow feeling in her stomach, blaming it on hunger.

She dressed once again in her green dress, perversely wanting to look her best once more. If she had to come face to face with that woman, as she very well might, considering the size of the town, then she would need every bit of confidence she could muster. This time she put her hair up, pinning it into a very proper chignon in hopes that that would make her look older and more sophisticated. Still, she frowned back at her reflection in the poor mirror. Compared to the person she had seen at the stage last night, she still looked like a schoolgirl playing at being grown up. She could not know how appealing that combination was.

Now, where would Jack be? she asked herself. He would either be still in his room or already in the dining room or . . . Maggie did not let herself think where else he might be, but there was always the possibility that when he had come back the previous night he had wanted some female companionship, and God knew, he hadn't come to her room. Screwing up her courage, she opened her door and marched across the hall, hesitating only a second before knocking authoritatively.

She heard a slight scuffling sound, and she knew a moment of relief that he was, indeed, inside, but only a moment. What if he were not alone?

"Who is it?" he growled irritably through the door.

Maggie stifled a sudden urge to reply, "Your wife," and said instead, "It's Maggie."

Instantly the door flew open and Jack was there, filling the doorway, his dark eyes narrowed in concern. "Maggie!" he said, taking her in from head to foot in one swift glance and then darting a quick look up and down the hallway. "Is anything wrong?"

Something was very wrong, and Maggie found that she suddenly did not have the breath to reply. It was silly, she knew. She had seen him without a shirt before. She had seen him without a lot more than a shirt, too, but somehow, coming face-to-face with him like that, so unexpectedly, simply took her breath. She had forgotten just how broad his chest was, and how the dark hairs curled all over it, tapering to a V down to his waist. Forcing herself to look at the part of him that was clothed, she lowered her eyes to his trousers, but was appalled to note that below those trousers he was barefooted. Odd, she had never noticed his feet before. They were long and slender, like his hands, and they had dark hair on them, too, just like his chest, just like his hands, just like his . . .

Feeling suddenly indecent for staring at the man's feet, she jerked her chin up until she was looking him squarely in the face. That did not help much, however. Those black eyes were still full of a concern that weakened her knees, and the bottom half of his face was covered with shaving lather. The combination was unnerving, and Maggie felt totally unnerved.

"N . . . No, nothing's wrong," she stammered. "I . . . I just came to see if you were ready to go down to breakfast, but I see you're not." She gave a nervous little laugh. "I . . . I'll just go down to the dining room and wait for you."

Jack's relief was obvious. He had been afraid for a moment . . . but that was silly. He was just getting ready to agree to her plan, when another though struck him. Renita was still running loose somewhere in the hotel, and although he had never known her to be an early riser, you couldn't be too careful where Renita was concerned. The thought of Maggie's coming face-to-face with her without his protection horrified him. For the moment he had totally forgotten that his little wife could more than hold her own, even with him.

"No," he said, a little too quickly, and then seeing her surprise, softened his voice. "Why don't you come in and wait for me. I won't be long," he coaxed, but his hand had grasped her wrist, and he was already pulling her inside with a force that she would have been hard pressed to resist.

Maggie was certain that she had laced her corset too tightly. Why else would she be having such a difficult time getting her breath? She was a silly widget for being nervous, too. There was absolutely nothing wrong with her being in his hotel room. They were married, after all. Why, then, did she feel so delightfully wicked?

"Sit down," Jack commanded, but then noticed that his clothes were draped across the only chair. "I'll move those," he offered, rushing to do so, but Maggie demurred.

"I'll just sit here," she said primly, lowering herself to the rumpled bed. Instantly, she knew that she had made a mistake. The bedclothes reeked of Bay Rum and Jack Sinclair, and she found the combination a trifle heady. At this rate, she would never catch her breath. She folded her hands in her lap, fighting the urge to trace her fingers over the indentation of the pillow where his head had lain, and pasted a small smile on her face. She only hoped that she did not look as rattled as she felt.

Jack was feeling pretty rattled himself. She was just lucky he'd thought to pull his pants on before asking who it was or she might really have gotten a shock. As it was, he felt pretty disreputable. "You'll have to excuse my appearance. I don't usually shave in my shirt," he said. Or my pants, either, he thought.

"That's all right," she lied, trying not to stare and slipping her fingers between her knees to keep from fidgeting. If only he'd hurry!

Jack stepped back to the washstand where the hot water he had ordered was rapidly cooling. Wetting his shaving brush, he once again worked up a lather in his soap mug and remoistened the soap that had dried on his face. Then, ever so carefully, because he was conscious of the two hazel eyes that were watching his every move, he lifted the straight razor and began to scrape away the foam.

Maggie couldn't seem to make her eyes behave. They kept drifting back to Jack. Funny, she'd never seen his bare back before. She'd felt it, though, and she could remember only too well how those muscles had bunched beneath her fingers and how warm and smooth his skin was when slicked with his passion.

Maggie's throat was dry. With difficulty, she worked up a swallow, but it sounded suspiciously like a gulp. Nervously, she glanced up to see if Jack had heard it, and her eyes clashed with his in the mirror.

He had been watching her cameo, the same green cameo he had noticed yesterday. It was trembling again. And so was she. And if he didn't get this lather off his face soon, he would be, too. "Interesting ritual, isn't it?" he commented when he caught her eye.

"W . . . What?" she asked, licking her lips. Now she was certain that she'd laced her corset too tightly. Her breasts were beginning to feel like they would burst free of her bodice, and her heart was starting to beat in the strangest places.

"Shaving. It's an interesting custom," he clarified. Why did her eyes look so green? Was it just the dress or was it something else?

"Yes, yes, it is," she agreed. "I used to watch my father shave when I was little girl," she remembered.

"It's a wonder he didn't cut his throat," Jack muttered, scraping the last of the soap from his own.

"What did you say?" she asked, leaning forward slightly. It seemed important to catch his every word.

"Nothing," he replied, and then, "Oh, damn!"

"What is it? Did you cut yourself?" Why she felt so concerned, she could not imagine. Shaving cuts were rarely fatal, after all. She should have been glad to see him bleed a little. He had made her bleed, after all. . . . Blushing furiously at the thought, she made herself sit back down, amazed to discover that she had halfway risen from her seat on the bed.

"No," he replied in disgust, "I just cut off part of my

259

mustache." Now how in the hell had that happened? He'd had the damn thing for almost ten years and had never done a thing like that before.

Maggie had to bite her lip to keep from smiling, and then another thought sobered her. "Is it ruined? I mean, will you have to cut it off?" For some reason, the thought of Jack without his mustache was upsetting. Without it, Jack just wouldn't be Jack. Why it should matter she had no idea, but it did.

"No," he grumbled, squinting into the mirror and measuring with the edge of the razor. "I'll just take a little off the other side so it won't be lopsided."

Fascinated, she watched him make the adjustment, and then swiftly finish off the rest of his face. If his hand trembled just a trifle, she did not notice, so intent was she on watching the way his shoulder muscles moved beneath his skin. He really was a magnificent specimen of a man, she decided, comparing him to some sculptures she had seen once in a museum, but then, she had always thought so.

Jack almost sighed in relief when the last of the lather disappeared onto the razor. Swiftly toweling his face, he reached for his bottle of Bay Rum and splashed some on, hissing in his breath as the alcohol burned his freshly shaven skin. When the stinging stopped, he turned, managing a smile at the little witch perched so innocently on the edge of his bed. If she only knew how tempting she was, and how tempted he was. He indulged himself in a momentary fantasy of what it would be like to sample the delights underneath those flowing green skirts before forcing himself to walk over and reach for his shirt.

Maggie had thought for a moment that something very strange was about to happen. The way those dark eyes had stared at her had turned her blood into a molten lava that semed to scorch wherever it passed, and at the rate her heart was beating, it was passing everything a mile a minute. All she wanted to do was get out of this room, and the sooner the better. She saw instantly that he was coming for his shirt, the shirt that was draped over the back of the chair that stood right next to the bed. In an intense desire to help, to speed things along, she reached for it in the same instant that he did.

She touched it first, and his hand closed down over hers, the shock of that touch going through her like a bolt of lightning. She was never certain afterward if she had actually cried out or not. Perhaps it had really been no more than a whispered sigh, but it didn't matter, because he caught it with his lips and gave it back to her in a kiss that blotted out the sun and the morning and the room and even their own identities. Nothing mattered except the feel of his mouth on hers or the way his skin came alive under her fingertips.

She barely heard the creak when the old bed took his weight, and hardly noticed when he laid her back against his pillow. Could a person get drunk from just the smell of Bay Rum? It did not matter. Maggie was thoroughly intoxicated with it anyway, possible or not. All her thought processes seemed scrambled, registering only partial images, the way his mustache tickled her upper lip, the way his hot breath seared her skin, the way his tongue traced moistly against her lips, seeking the entry that she oh, so willingly, granted him.

With sweet thoroughness he explored her depths in imitation of the possession that he craved and that she, even now, was pleading for with hands that stroked and clung and clawed.

Feverishly he plucked at the buttons at her throat, but found them sealed tight by the cameo brooch, and had to content himself with palming her thrusting breast through the stiff fabric of her dress. Her moan of frustration echoed his as she arched herself to his hand, and he could feel the pebbled evidence of her need.

She could not seem to get enough of him. The more she touched, the more she wanted to touch. The more she kissed, the more she wanted to kiss, and she found herself tasting the skin of his shoulders even as her hands were trying to force their way beneath his waistband. He was busy, too, seeking out the warmth of her beneath all the petticoats. She started to tell him not to tear anything, but then she forgot and then his hand was on her belly, petting, smoothing, and then she remembered. She remembered what it was that she wanted from him, remembered how it was to have him, to have all of him, to have him fill that aching, empty void.

He heard the tiny pleading sounds, but mistook them for something else. "I can't stop now, Maggie," he rasped, wrenching her pantalettes from her.

That was fine. She did not want him to stop, not at all, and when his searching fingers found the center of her, she rewarded him with an impassioned moan.

"Oh, Maggie, darling Maggie," he murmured as he loosened his own clothes. Almost wild from wanting her, from the triumph of finding her so ready for him, he took her in one swift stroke, catching her gasp of surprise in a drowning kiss.

Had it been like this before? Maggie could not remember. Surely if it had, she would never have turned him away, never have let him leave, she thought. Her hands and legs clung to him, demanding that he feed the fire that he had started, meeting him thrust for thrust, making the blissful discovery that her pleasure mounted with each plunge.

The fire raged out of control now, searing them, melding them into one entity. In that feverish union, they strove together to that white-hot central flame, the vortex that swept them up and blazed over them, purging all else save that one sacred moment of fulfillment.

Maggie cried out her joy as the spasms wrenched her. Her soul scattered into a thousand flaring embers that burst across the heavens in a dazzling conflagration and then fell back to earth, into her heart, slowly, one by one, until she was herself again. Herself, but new, refined in the furnace of passion, purified by the fire of her love.

Her love. Somehow the thought was not as frightening as she would have expected. Holding him now, cradling him through his own conflagration, accepting the seed of promise from his beloved body into her own, she was no longer afraid to love him. Indeed, she could do nothing else, nor did she even want to try.

He had slid his weight from her, but he still held her against his chest where she could hear his heart beating out the slackening rhythm of slaked passion. She lay there for awhile, her heavy-lidded eyes creating for her a private twilight world where she could savor that weak, boneless feeling that came after, and where she could listen while her nerve endings sang out his name, over and over, in an ardent litany.

"Maggie?" Her name came to her from far across the peaceful aura that surrounded her, so that when her eyes flickered open she was a little surprised to discover that he was so close. Surprised and pleased, too. She never wanted him to be very far away again.

She could not help the small smile of contentment that curved her lips. Only then did she notice his expression. She had to exert her lazy brain to identify it, and when she did, she felt a mild surprise. He was worried! What did he have to be worried about? Was he afraid she would accuse him of rape again?

That was exactly what he was afraid of, and if she did, he would not be responsible for his response. After what had just happened between them, he knew that he would never be able to stay away from her again. How he had lasted this long he had no idea, but he knew that he had been an utter fool to vow never to touch her again. Now he had to know what she was feeling. That he had pleasured her he was certain, but whether that pleasure was enough to offset the hostilities that lay between them, he wasn't sure. The sight of her smile was reassuring.

Quite unexpectedly, Maggie recalled that only yesterday

she had been wondering if Jack might really care for her. The fact of their separate bedrooms seemed incontrovertible proof that he did not, but now . . . She remembered his whispered words: "I can't stop now." He had wanted her with the same uncontrollable need that she had experienced, in spite of his promise never to touch her again. Her smile deepened.

"You said you'd never touch me again," she marveled, noticing the way his expression lightened at her teasing accusation.

"I know," he said, the worry smoothing from his brow.

"Not even if I begged," she taunted, touching the tip of her nose to his.

"That's right," he agreed, shifting slightly to place a kiss on that impudent little nose.

"It's funny, but I don't remember begging," she said, frowning in mock concentration.

Jack's mustache tilted. "You begged me with your eyes, little witch," he informed her.

Those eyes, so very green in the aftermath of their lovemaking, widened in amazement. "I did?" she asked. "I guess I'll have to be more careful, won't I?"

He saw the laughter in her eyes, the flirtatious teasing that she did so naturally, but oh, too seldom, and he wanted her all over again with an urgency that hit him like a physical blow. "Yes, you will," he rasped, lowering his mouth to hers, but before their lips touched, the sound of someone knocking at the door startled them apart.

Neither of them moved for a moment as they lay there, bodies still intimately entwined, and then Maggie felt compelled to say, "Someone's at the door." It sounded inane, even to her ears.

"Ignore them. They'll go away," Jack advised, moving in for the kiss once more, but once more another knock, more forceful this time, stopped him.

Maggie only barely stifled a giggle at his muffled curse. "It doesn't sound like they're going to go away," she observed. "I guess we'd better answer it."

A third knock, the loudest one yet, decided him. "All right," he grunted, and then called, "Just a minute," to the knocker. "I think," he added softly, looking down at their tangled bodies, "that you'd better go. You're a lot closer to being decent than I am." He was referring as much to the swollen evidence of his renewed desire as he was to his state of undress, and when Maggie's gaze automatically followed his, she blushed in a confusion of feelings, at least one of which was pleasure at her husband's reaction to her.

Reluctantly, Maggie extricated herself and tumbled to her feet, managing to get her skirts down around her ankles at the same time. Amazingly, her dress did not look too bad after a few adjustments. She supposed that the elaborate drape in the front served to disguise the fact that it had been seriously crumpled during the last few minutes. Smiling at that thought, she started for the door.

The sensation of her stiff petticoats rubbing against her bare legs reminded her that she had been relieved of her pantalettes at some point. She really should find them and put them back on, but she would do that later. For now she would enjoy the deliciously wanton feeling of going without.

Jack could not help watching her until she was completely covered again, delighting in the glimpse of slender leg that he caught before she had put herself to rights again. As soon as they got rid of whoever was at the door, he'd get more than a glimpse. And whoever was at the door had better be armed. If it was Swede . . . well, the foreman had better have a damn good reason for hammering on the door, and if it was Festus . . . Jack grinned at the prospect of tossing the meddling old fool down the stairs. Then he heaved himself up, pulling up his trousers and then reaching for his shirt as Maggie opened the door.

Maggie couldn't help her gasp of surprise. Her only

265

comfort was that the woman on the other side of the door was just as surprised as she. It was the woman she had seen at the stage last night, and close up, Maggie noticed that the woman was even more beautiful than she had at first thought. Her coal-black hair was pulled into a classic chignon, emphasizing her fine features. Dark brown eyes set into an olive-tinted face gave evidence of her Mexican heritage, but the rest of her face was as aristocratic as Jack's, right down to the haughty expression she had assumed. Well, Maggie could be just as haughty. How dare this person come to her husband's room? How dare she think that Maggie would give up her husband without a fight? Of course, Maggie had no reason to think that the woman even thought that, but Maggie had no intention of giving her that idea. It was a matter of pride, she told herself. She would never have turned Jack over to another woman even if she hadn't wanted him for herself. Now, of course, she did want him for herself. She would examine the reasons why later. For now, it was enough that she knew her destiny and acted accordingly.

Pulling herself up to her full height and lifting her eyebrows disdainfully, she gave the woman a withering look and asked, "May I help you?"

Renita was furious. She had never intended to come face-to-face with the little bitch. Damn that nosy desk clerk! He had told her all about the Sinclair marriage, how Jack had forced poor little Maggie into it, and how he didn't even share a room, much less a bed with her. Renita's plan had been perfect. She would come up here, find Jack alone, tell him she had decided to forgive him and take him back. From there it would have been only a few steps to his bed, and once she had refreshed his memory with her skills, she had been certain that things between them would have been just as before. A good night's sleep had convinced her that she would be a fool to give Jack up. He had been the most generous and least demanding of her "protectors," and what did she care if he were married or not?

Now she knew that her plan would never work. Desk clerk or no desk clerk, it was obvious that even though the Sinclairs had rented two rooms, they were only using one. It only took one look at the girl to know that they were making very good use of it, too. Her tousled hair, her swollen lips, her creased dress. Good God, she could even *smell* it. Couldn't he even wait to undress her? Renita had never known him to be that eager, and she would have thought that she had seen him in all circumstances.

Making the best of a bad situation, Renita feigned a new kind of surprise. "Oh, I'm so sorry," she said. "I seem to have come to the wrong room." Whether the girl was fooled or not, Renita neither knew nor cared. The fact that she had suddenly noticed that the girl was quite pretty was taking up most of her attention. So much for Jack's claim that he had only married to avoid legal entanglements with the ranch. She should have known that that was a lie. Jack never would have tied himself to a woman for such a mundane reason. He would have considered it a challenge to get around the law instead. No, Jack's reasons for marrying the little *puta* were more basic.

Hearing Renita's voice, Jack strode to the door and jerked it out of Maggie's grasp, throwing it completely open. He glared down at his former mistress with a warning look that she could not mistake. "Yes," he said through gritted teeth, "you do have the wrong room."

Renita got his message. Obviously, the girl did not know who she was, and Jack intended to keep it that way. Well Renita would play along, for now. "Please excuse me," she simpered sarcastically, eying his half-buttoned shirt and bare feet. "I hope I didn't interrupt anything." From the way the girl blushed, she knew that she had scored a hit. Having done so, she turned on her heel and flounced down the corridor to her room.

Seething with anger, Jack watched her go and then closed

the door. One glance at Maggie told him their intimate mood had been destroyed. What he was not sure of, however, was why. Had she seen him with Renita last night? Did she suspect their relationship? Or was she just feeling upset at being "caught in the act"? He gave her a tentative smile, testing her mood.

Maggie's mind was racing. Why had that woman come to Jack's room? Had they arranged a tryst that Maggie had interrupted? It seemed unlikely, considering that Maggie was sure to expect to see Jack at breakfast. Unless he no longer cared for Maggie's opinion. But how could he have made love to her the way he had just now if he no longer cared? Only minutes ago she had been so sure. Why was she so confused? And what should she do now? Should she let Jack know that she had seen the two of them together last night? Should she demand an explanation? Should she demand to know what that woman was doing coming to his room? But what if he told her it was none of her business? What if he told her that he intended to keep his mistress and his wife, too? What if . . . Maggie couldn't think anymore. She had to get away, alone, for a few minutes. But she couldn't let Jack see how upset she was. She met his smile with one of her own.

"I wonder who she was looking for," Maggie commented, hoping her voice sounded normal. Not waiting for his reply, fearing what it might be, she dodged his outstretched hand and went back over to the bed, looking for her pantalettes. She found them on the floor, half under the bed, and snatched them up, wadding them into a discreet bundle. Turning back to Jack, feeling suddenly quite awkward and self-conscious, she tried to look casual and said, "I'd better go back to my room and freshen up before breakfast."

She didn't have to go back to her room, and he knew it. She could do any "freshening up" right there, but he knew as well as she that that was not her real reason for wanting to leave. He, too, felt the sudden awkwardness. Wanting nothing more than to take her in his arms and kiss away her uncertainty, he restrained himself, sensing that such a move would panic her, and he did not feel that he could cope with her rejection just now. Instead he accepted her statement at face value, hoping against hope that she did not suspect the truth about Renita, hoping that when she had had a few minutes alone, she would have regained her composure.

"I have a little freshening up to do, myself," he told her. "Why don't I call for you when I'm ready?"

Maggie nodded gratefully, and slipped past him, out the door that he had opened for her. She paused once, when she was in her room, to look back, and he was still standing there in the doorway, watching her. He gave her a smile that warmed her to her toes, a smile of remembrance and a smile of promise. She could not help but return it.

It was the more familiar Jack who came for her, the immaculate Jack in his tailored suit and faultless shirt, but the lazy way those dark eyes played over her told her that he was remembering their earlier intimacies. She remembered them, too, and could not help the blush that stained her cheeks. Was the hand that took her elbow warmer than usual, or was she imagining it? She only knew that *she* was warmer than usual, the heat that radiated outward from his touch disturbingly reminiscent of the heat that had consumed her before.

Maggie was grateful when he released her to go down the narrow stairs. She only hoped that her vagrant thoughts did not show on her face, and smiled to think what Festus would make of it if they did.

As usual, they were late for the meal, and the dining room was empty when they came in. Maggie would have expected the girl to be surly at having to serve extra customers, but she had not counted on Jack's charm. As it turned out, the girl was only too glad to wait on them, bringing them coffee as soon as they were seated. Jack ordered them both a hearty breakfast, commenting to no one in particular that he had worked up an appetite. Maggie concentrated on placing her napkin in her lap, hoping that her face was not as red as it felt and lamenting the fact that since meeting Jack Sinclair her face had done little else but change color.

When they were alone, an uncomfortable silence fell, and Maggie cast about for something to say. "Are we going home today? I mean, are you finished with your business?"

Jack frowned. He had almost forgotten that he had the most unpleasant part of his business yet to do. "No, not quite, although I think I can finish up this morning. We should be able to head back out to the ranch this afternoon."

This was pleasant news to Maggie, but she did not like the scowl on Jack's face. "What else do you have to do?" she asked, amazed to realize how she had lost track of the running of the ranch. Except for ordering supplies at the store, she had played no active part in its management since her marriage, and for some strange reason, she did not feel the least bit resentful.

Jack's scowl deepened. "I have to meet with Kincaid," he said, already dreading the encounter. He had only seen Kincaid a few times, but that was enough to know that he would not like the man, not at all. Fortunately, he did not have to like him to deal with him, and considering exactly how he would have to deal with him, that might even be an advantage. Still, he knew the type, and Kincaid would drive a hard bargain. Ordinarily, Jack would have looked forward to such an encounter, relishing the challenge, but today he could think of little else except getting Maggie home to that huge four poster bed back at the ranch. He would never have suspected how marriage could take a man's mind off business.

Maggie didn't notice the way Jack's attention had strayed. All she could think of was that he was going to meet with Kincaid. Last night she had been terrified thinking that he was going to shoot it out with the mysterious land grabber, but that had been because Jack had been acting so strangely.

Studying him now, she realized that he was not the least upset at the prospect of meeting with the man, and she tried to tell herself that she should not be, either. "Is he . . . dangerous?" she heard herself ask.

Jack seemed mildly surprised. "Of course, he's dangerous, but not in the way I think you mean. He'll take the CMC, if he can, and that makes him dangerous, but I doubt that my life will be in danger when I go to see him."

Maggie could not help the sigh of relief that escaped her, berating herself when she saw his mustache tilt. The black eyes softened in a way that made her stomach, and various other parts of her, flutter in response, and he whispered, "Were you worried about me, Mrs. Sinclair?"

She had been, of course, desperately so. Odd that only yesterday she would have been only too happy at the prospect of becoming a widow. Or would she have? It was difficult to remember when Jack was looking at her like that, as if he'd like to carry her off somewhere and . . . a flurry of movement somewhere over Jack's left shoulder caught her eye, and when she focused on it, all other thoughts were wiped clean from her mind.

Renita had entered the dining room. She had known that they would be there, of course, but she had no intention of causing a scene. She would just be there, a silent reminder to Jack, an irritant to his bride. If the girl suspected anything, Renita's mere presence would be enough to start trouble. Carefully, she took a seat at a table across the room from them, sitting so that her back was to them.

Jack sensed the change in Maggie immediately. Had he said something, done something? "What is it? What's wrong?" he asked. He had not noticed Renita, had not been able to concentrated on anything but his wife.

Loath to let him know how upset she was, she tried to smile. "It's . . . our friend," she said, settling on the most innocuous term she could think of. "The woman who . . . knocked on the door. She just came in." Maggie felt almost faint from all the emotions roiling in her. Embarrassment and shame and fear and dread were all fighting for preeminence, and she hated herself for feeling any of them.

Jack's head jerked around, but when he saw that Renita had taken a seat and did not seem bent on causing trouble, he turned his attention back to Maggie. "So it is," he commented blandly, his face void of expression, his dark eyes trying to read hers.

Now Maggie was really frightened. Before, in the room, he had seemed angry at seeing the woman, but now he was hiding his feelings from her. What feelings could he be having that he did not want her to see? She longed to ask him, just ask him outright who this woman was to him, and know once and for all. The only thing stopping her was her abject terror that he would tell her something she did not want to hear. Love, she concluded, did strange things to people. Why, oh why, had she gone to Jack's room this morning? Before she had known that she loved him, she could have handled this situation calmly, treated it as a breach of etiquette instead of as a disaster. Still, in spite of her fear, she had a perverse urge to test him, to goad him into an admission. "She . . . she's very beautiful," Maggie observed.

Jack's eyes never left Maggie's face. What did she really want to know? he wondered. Was she looking for reassurance? What did a man have to do? After this morning, he would have thought . . . but with a mental shrug, he played along. "Is she?" he asked coolly. "I find it difficult to notice other women when I'm with you, Mrs. Sinclair."

Did he mean it or was he simply using his practiced charm to allay her suspicions? In spite of her doubts, his words soothed her, the sensation spreading over her like warm honey. The smile she gave him told him of her pleasure, but before she could respond, their breakfast arrived.

Neither of them spoke while they ate, each absorbed in

private thoughts, and each conscious of the third occupant of the dining room. Jack was able to do justice to his meal, but Maggie could only pick at hers, her appetite suddenly gone. She needed to be alone with her thoughts for a while. The few minutes that Jack had allowed her upstairs had not been nearly enough to sort through them all, and she longed for solitude.

Jack pretended not to notice that she was not eating. They had enough problems without his acting like a nagging parent. He hated leaving her alone, too, but he had no choice, not if he wanted to get them out of town today, and he certainly did. The farther Maggie was from Renita, the better. He would also have to see about getting some money to Renita. The sooner she got it, the sooner she would be on her way. He could get Swede to take care of that so he wouldn't have to meet with her again.

There was an awkward moment when they rose to leave the room, but Renita pretended not to notice them, and they returned the favor, so they made it to the lobby without incident.

"I think I'll go on up to my room for a while. I can pack our things and then we'll be ready to leave right after we eat dinner," she said, trying to sound as if she were not afraid for his life. As much as she wanted to be alone, she could not forget that he was going to meet Kincaid.

Once again that mustache tilted in amusement. "You'll pack *our* things, Mrs. Sinclair?" he asked, his dark eyes twinkling. "I think you may be getting the hang of your wifely duties."

Wifely duties! Maggie felt the flash of irritation that he had intended for her to feel. Why, he was making her sound like a meek little serving girl! But before she could make the stinging retort that trembled on her lips, she recalled some "wifely duties" that did not require any type of serving, the kind that she had been engaged in up in his room not too long ago. She hadn't minded those duties at all, and the

273

memory twisted her lips into a teasing smile.

"Yes, I am," she replied sweetly, lowering her eyelashes provocatively and stepping very close to him. "I'm new at this, but I'm sure with practice, I'll get better and better." As she spoke, she let the fingers of one hand play over his belt buckle, and insinuate themselves up under his vest and into the opening of his shirt, between two buttons, until she touched warm, lightly furred skin.

His sharp intake of breath was her reward for her boldness, but it only hinted at the raging emotions that washed over him. The naked lust left him so weak that for a moment he could not even move, could not even think of moving, and then her hand was withdrawn, and she was heading for the stairs. He had taken one step in pursuit, instinctively following the tantalizing scent of lilacs, when she looked back over her shoulder.

"I'll be all ready to leave when you get back," she taunted, reminding him of his own "duties."

Her words stopped him, but still he lingered until she disappeared from view, and then he smiled grimly, remembering her words. "With practice, I'll get better and better." He wasn't certain if she *could* get any better, but he intended to see that she got plenty of practice. That decided, he forced his attention to the meeting with Kincaid, and headed out the door and down the street to the man's office.

Kincaid had set up shop in the storefront of a two-story building. He had his business office in the downstairs, and he lived upstairs. It was a convenient arrangement, if not too elegant, but then Kincaid made no pretense at elegance. He was a pragmatist, pure and simple.

Jack walked in without knocking, and paused a moment to let his eyes adjust to the interior dimness. The room was fairly small, the building having been divided into two offices and this one being by far the smaller of the two. Within a few seconds, Jack could make out a desk with a young man seated behind it. He had seen the boy around but

274

did not know his name. The boy rose now, assuming an air of authority that weighed heavily on his slender frame. "May I help you?" he asked, seeming to insinuate that Jack needed all the help he could get.

Jack chose to be amused rather than offended. "Is Kincaid in?" he inquired, taking in the boy's dirty blond hair, pale, beardless cheeks and nervous blue eyes in one disapproving glance.

The boy stiffened under the scrutiny. "Yes, but he's busy right now—" he started to say. Jack cut him off.

"He'll see me," Jack said, brushing past the desk without a backward glance, ignoring the boy's protest.

The door to the rear office was half open, and Jack stepped inside, closing it behind him. "Kincaid," he said coldly, by way of a greeting to the man seated behind the desk.

Kincaid lifted his large head from where it had been bent over some papers on the desktop and looked at Jack through two beady eyes that seemed lost in his broad face. Kincaid was a big man. Not tall or even fat, just big, his large frame covered over with slabs of flesh that looked as if they might be soft, but Jack doubted this. He moved slowly, almost lazily, but that, too, was deceptive.

"Sinclair. I've been expecting you," he said. His voice was strangely soft to come from such a huge source, and also strangely devoid of emotion. Kincaid prided himself on never expressing emotion of any kind. His thick lips stretched into what might have been a smile on someone else. On him it was more of a grimace.

Jack looked into eyes that were the color of slate and just as flat. Most men gave away their thoughts in their eyes, and as a man who had once made his living playing cards, Jack was an expert at reading eyes. Kincaid, Jack grudgingly allowed, would make an excellent poker player. "All right, Kincaid, tell me what you want so we can come to terms," Jack snapped.

Kincaid never even blinked. "I want Colson's valley," he replied in that same soft voice.

"Don't we all," Jack murmured, half to himself. "And how much would it take to convince you to move along and set up shop in another place?" He never doubted for a minute that Kincaid could be bought. Every man had his price, and if Kincaid's wasn't too high, Jack would gladly meet it. It would cost him a pretty penny to fight the man, and he much preferred simply paying him off. There was no sense in starting a war if one could avoid it.

"You haven't got that much money, Sinclair. I want the valley, and that's all I'll settle for." Kincaid still had not even blinked, and Jack was becoming irritated at the man's lack of response. Still, he did not let it show.

"Look, you know that we'll fight you," Jack explained patiently. "We've got men and guns, and we'll run off whoever you send out to homestead. We can keep it up forever if we have to, and sooner or later you'll run out of people who want to take a chance. I'll do it if I have to, but personally, I'd rather not see a lot of innocent pople get killed in the process."

"And that's why I'll win," Kincaid said, his dull face showing the first sign of life. As if a small candle had been lit inside his head, his eyes began to glow, and he rose slowly to his feet. "See, I, personally, don't care how many innocent people get killed, and that's the difference between us. You'll fight, I know. You'll fight for a while, but a man like you can't keep it up for long. You with your fancy clothes and Sunday School manners, you won't be able to sleep nights, seeing the faces of all those 'innocent people.' You won't be able to stand having your hands dirty with their blood, and that's why, in the end, I'll win." His lips twisted into that parody of a smile again. "You could have saved yourself the trouble of marrying the girl, Sinclair," he added.

Jack fought down the surge of anger that followed Kincaid's remark, and then felt foolish for the violence of his reaction. He wasn't even certain if Kincaid had meant it as a taunt or as a simple statement of fact, and he had no way of judging. He would have liked nothing better than to beat an apology out of the man, but he doubted whether the satisfaction he would gain would justify the effort involved. No, better to beat Kincaid where it would really hurt him. That would take more time, but it would be far more satisfying. "Oh, it wasn't any trouble at all, Kincaid," he said, noting the slight lifting of the man's pale eyebrows in surprise. "I doubt that you'll be much trouble, either, when all is said and done."

"We'll see, won't we?" Kincaid challenged mildly.

"Yes," Jack agreed just as mildly. "We'll see."

Jack found Swede holding down a chair in front of the hotel. The blond man put down the paper he had been reading when he heard Jack approaching. "How'd it go?" he asked when Jack stopped by his chair.

Jack reached into his coat, pulled out a cigar, and took his time about lighting it. When he had it going well, he took one deep puff, and blew it out into the street toward Kincaid's office. "He said he didn't think I'd want to get my hands dirty in a fight," he told the foreman.

Swede's pale eyes grew wide with amazement, and then his red face cracked into a grin. "That's all he said?"

Jack nodded, taking another puff. "He thinks he'll win because I won't fight. That's what it boils down to."

Swede shook his head in disbelief, still grinning. "I'll be damned."

"Let's hope it's Kincaid who gets damned, shall we?" Jack suggested, the ends of his mustache tipping upward, and Swede nodded. "Come on, I'll buy you a drink," Jack offered.

Swede's grin twisted into a suspicious scowl. Jack had been buying him far too many drinks lately. He had to be up to something, and Swede had the unpleasant feeling that he knew just what it was. "Kinda early, ain't it?" he asked cynically.

Jack managed to hide his irritation and looked aggrieved. "When is it ever too early for a man to buy his friend a drink?" he asked, thinking that while it was comforting to have people around whom one could trust, it was also annoying when they got to know you too well. Swede was suspicious, and he had every right to be. Just wait until he found out what Jack wanted him to do. Then he'd be downright mad.

"You know I get dyspepsia if I drink hard liquor before sundown," Swede reminded him.

"A beer, then," Jack suggested helpfully.

"Why not just tell me what you want me to do. I know I'll probably wish I wasn't cold sober when I hear it, but go ahead and shoot." Swede set his thin mouth into the stubborn line that Jack knew only too well.

Sighing with defeat, he glanced around to see if anyone was near who might overhear, and then squatted down beside Swede's chair. "I have to pay Renita off," he whispered.

Swede swore, uttering one brief, succinct phrase that summed up his feelings and his understanding completely and brought a reluctant smile to Jack's lips.

"You know it would never do for me to be seen giving her money, or even going to her room again," Jack pointed out reasonably, but he needn't have bothered. Swede knew that as well as he, and his expression told Jack so. "Look at it this way," he added, knowing only too well how his foreman felt about his former mistress. "It's the last time you'll ever have to see her." That was an argument that even Swede had to agree was good.

Still he was far from pleased, and he replied with a string of profanity that had Jack chuckling in admiration. Swede didn't say much, but he could swear like a master. Jack sat back on his heels and enjoyed the display of this dubious talent, until the blond man ran down. Then he slapped him on the back. "Let's go over to the bank and see if Judge Harris has enough cash on hand. Cheer up. You don't have to actually give it to her until after dinner," Jack informed him jovially. He ignored the withering look Swede flashed him as they crossed the street to the bank.

When Jack came back to the hotel, he found that Maggie had kept her word about packing his things. Usually a stickler about having everything just so, he could find no fault in Maggie's work. She had been as neat and thorough as he himself would have been, and he smiled to think that she had done this small thing to please him. Perhaps there was some small thing he could do to please her in return, he thought wickedly. He would be only too happy to do just that, but when he went to her room he found it empty.

A hurried inquiry at the desk brought him the information that Maggie had gone to the Merchantile to arrange to have their order filled in time for them to leave today. Festus had grinned knowingly as he had supplied the news, but Jack had been so relieved that he didn't even mind. He really was going to have to do something about his overactive imagination. He couldn't keep on panicking every time she got out of his sight.

What he could not know was that Maggie had experienced her own version of that panic. When Jack had left for Kincaid's office, Maggie had stood by her window, watching him every step of the way until he had disappeared inside, and then waited, motionless, counting the seconds, until he reappeared, safe and sound. She didn't need to be told that all had not gone well with Kincaid. How she knew, she could not have said, but she knew, nevertheless. It was something about the way he walked or the way he carried his head or something. She didn't really care about the meeting, though, as long as Jack was all right.

She had waited expectantly then for his footsteps on the

279

stairs, because she had seen him disappear from her view near the front of the hotel, but then, to her disappointment, she had seen him crossing the street with Swede on his way to the bank. Irrationally irritated that he had not been as eager to see her again as she had to see him, she had stormed into his room, determined to stuff his clothes into the bag like so many rags. She had not bargained for the memories that would assail her when she reentered his room.

Once inside, she had closed the door behind her as if to keep out prying eyes. The room smelled of cigars and Bay Rum and Jack Sinclair, and her own scent, although she could not smell it. When she had touched his things, it had been like touching him, or part of him, and she found herself placing each item in the carpet bag with tender care.

Was this what love was? Did love make a person irrational? Make her put value on inanimate objects just because they had once touched the one beloved? Once she would have laughed at such nonsense, but no more. Yes, love did make a person irrational. Only days ago she had hated Jack Sinclair, had held him responsible for every bad thing that had ever happened in her life. She still did, when it came right down to it. Nothing else had changed, and he hadn't changed, not one bit. But she had. Oh, how she had changed. To think that once she had scoffed at women who had succumbed to his fatal charm, and now she had fallen harder than any of them. Was that justice, or divine retribution? She wasn't certain, and decided that it didn't matter. What did matter, however, was keeping it a secret. It would never do for Jack to find out his hold over her. He was insufferable enough as things stood. If he ever found out that she worshipped the ground he walked on, the very tie that hung around his neck . . . Unless he felt the same, she knew it would be foolhardy to admit her weakness. More than foolhardy, if that woman was still around. She would have to wait and see what happened, and meanwhile, try to keep her secret safely hidden.

It had taken her only a moment to pack her own things, finding no need to linger over each item as she had with Jack's. When she was finished, he and Swede still had not emerged from the bank, and Maggie had decided that if Jack had to fill the judge in on everything that had been happening the past two days, he would be in there a while. He would not find her cooling her heels, waiting for him, either. Remembering a legitimate errand when she tried to think up an imaginary one, she had gone to the Merchantile to tell Mr. Alexander to load up their supplies, since they would be returning to the ranch that afternoon.

Jack looked up the instant that Maggie came out of the Merchantile. He was sitting in the chair that Swede had vacated earlier, and had been enjoying a cigar while contemplating the sights of Bitterroot, but the moment Maggie had come into view, he had sensed it. She certainly was a lovely little thing, he decided, watching as she strolled down the long sidewalk toward him. Not lovely enough to justify the way he felt about her, however. For sheer beauty, Renita certainly had her beaten, as did many other women he had known. No, it wasn't just her physical attractions that made him want to protect her, to hold her next to his heart where no evil could ever touch her. Not for the first time, he considered the irony of the situation. It had only been days ago that he had been one of the evils from which she needed protection, and now he was ready to move heaven and earth for her. Was it sex? He doubted it. It seemed unlikely that an inexperienced virgin could so captivate him, and besides, he admitted grudgingly, it had started even before he had made love to her.

Thinking back to that night, their wedding night, he remembered his words of love, the words that had made her so angry. He had never uttered them to another woman, because, until now, they had never been true. He had often laughed at men who were obsessed with a certain woman, never having experienced the emotions inherent in such an obsession. Now, however, he understood only too well. He loved Maggie Colson, adored her, worshipped her. There was no other explanation for the way he felt toward her. Unfortunately, it was something he could not tell her, at least not yet. He recalled only too vividly how she had reacted the first time. He was not worried, though. Knowing his power over women, knowing that she had enjoyed their little encounter this morning as much as he, he was confident that he could win her innocent little heart. It would just take time. Until then, he would simply have to keep his secret.

Chapter X

Maggie had been watching Jack watching her all the way down the sidewalk, and she was enjoying it thoroughly. She didn't even have to wonder what he was thinking about because she had a pretty good idea that he was thinking about the same thing she was thinking about. At least she hoped he was. She hoped he wanted to get back to the ranch so that they could be alone. The prospect sent little shivers up the backs of her legs and caused her breasts to pucker in the most shocking fashion. Feeling totally depraved and loving every minute of it, Maggie purposely slowed her steps to prolong the anticipation of seeing Jack again.

He rose as she approached, dropping his unfinished cigar into the cuspidor that stood beside his chair. It took all his will power to keep from grabbing her and kissing that impudent grin off her lovely little mouth. So she thought she had a hold over him, did she? Thought that just because he hadn't been able to resist making love to her this morning, she now had the upper hand. He was especially irritated because he knew only too well that those things were true. Well, there was no use letting her know it. He wanted her to think it took a lot more than a quick tumble to conquer Jack Sinclair.

He schooled his features into stern disapproval. "Where

have you been, Mrs. Sinclair?"

At first she thought he was teasing, but the cold glitter in his eyes disabused her of that notion in a hurry. He seemed almost angry. Her smile sank into a frown, and then she remembered how he had gone to the bank after meeting with Kincaid instead of coming to see her, and her frown became a scowl. Did he expect her to sit around all day waiting for his return like some meek little . . . some meek little wife! If so, then he had a surprise coming.

Lifting her chin defiantly, she met his disapproving stare with one of her own. "I had some errands to run before we leave town. Do I have to ask permission to go to the Mercantile now?" she asked sarcastically.

Jack gave her a smile that never reached his eyes. "If you aren't more polite, Mrs. Sinclair, you'll even have to start asking permission to go to the outhouse."

Maggie could not help her cry of outrage, but managed to stop herself before actually slapping his face, twisting her small hands into tight fists instead. She had to remember that they were standing on a public street in full view of the whole town, and if she slapped him, she would cause a scandal. Slapping him before they were married was one thing, but now . . . Maggie actually trembled at the strain of holding her fury in check, biting her tongue to hold back the insults she longed to throw at him. Even worse was the pain that settled in when the first hot rush of anger had subsided. How could she love a man like this, a man who could make passionate love to her one minute and insult her the next? She had been right to keep her love a secret. "Going to the outhouse is far preferable to being in your company," she told him haughtily. "If you'll excuse me," she added, brushing past him to enter the hotel lobby. If she stayed with him one more minute, she could not be responsible for her actions.

Jack watched her go with mixed emotions. He had accomplished his purpose all right, but that was hardly the

284

way to make the woman fall in love with him. On the other hand, she was so cute when she was angry. Automatically, he followed her into the hotel and up the stairs, catching her door just when she would have slammed it in his face.

Resolutely, he pushed the door open, forcing her to step back and allow him to enter.

"Did you want something?" she inquired coldly as he closed the door behind him. She did not want to be alone with him, not when he was acting like this. It hurt too much.

Then he completely disconcerted her by smiling apologetically. "You didn't ask me how my meeting with Kincaid went," he pointed out mildly.

Resisting the urge to stamp her foot in frustration over his quicksilver changes, Maggie managed to remain reasonably calm. "Well, he didn't murder you. That's fairly obvious. Judging from your pleasant mood, he didn't offer to give up, either. Is there anything else I need to know?"

"Aren't you at least glad that he didn't murder me?" he teased, but his playfulness only made her more angry.

"Not in the least!" she lied, turning to the mirror so she could remove her bonnet. "If he had, I'd be a rich widow, wouldn't I?" Placing her bonnet on the washstand, she turned back to him, startled to see that his face had gone blank.

"Would you like that, Maggie?" he asked in that flat voice that she hated. The Jack she knew had disappeared behind that frozen mask of a face. What emotions was he hiding from her? Had her careless lie hurt him in some way?

Feeling her anger drain from her, she tried to smooth it over. "Everyone wants to be rich," she said with a nervous laugh.

"You're already rich, Maggie. Would you like to be a widow, too?" he asked ruthlessly.

Maggie almost cringed, blinking back the tears that sprang to her eyes at the thought of losing Jack. She should lie, she should say that yes, she'd love to be a widow, but she knew the words would choke her. Feeling as she did about him, the mere thought of it was agony. "Jack, please . . ." she pleaded, not knowing how to phrase her request, only knowing that she could not talk about it anymore. Drawing a ragged breath, she tried again. "Can we go home now? I'm so sick of this town. . . ."

He nodded absently, his mind replaying her words. At least she had not said that she wanted him dead, and the thought had seemed to upset her. Maybe she was just softhearted, though. Maybe she was thinking about her father. Maybe . . . maybe any one of a hundred things, none of which had anything to do with him. She was right about one thing, though. They needed to get out of this town, back to the ranch. Maybe there, without the threat of Renita hanging over them, they could work things out. "Let's eat first," he suggested. "It's almost noon, and we'll be awfully hungry if we wait until we get back to the ranch."

Maggie doubted if she would ever be able to eat again, but she agreed readily. Anything to get them on their way. They were a little early for the dinner hour, so they did not have to wait long for their food, and they ate quickly and in silence. Neither quite knew what to say to the other, especially since the room was rapidly filling up with people and they could so easily be overheard. Several people stopped by their table to say hello and wish them happiness, and Maggie forced herself to smile, hoping no one would notice what a sad bride she made.

When they were finished, Jack brought their bags down, recalling as he did how pleased he had been that Maggie had packed for him. He would have done better to mention that to her when he had first seen her in front of the hotel instead of pretending to be angry with her. Maybe it wasn't too late.

Downstairs, Maggie waited impatiently in the lobby. Only a few more minutes, and they would be safely away. She was beginning to hate this whole town. But she discovered that she was not to get away quite so easily. While she stood

286

there, tapping her foot testily, that woman walked in the door. For the first time Maggie noticed her clothes, and a brand new wave of irritation washed over her. The dress she was wearing was pure watered silk and had taken the hands of an expert dressmaker to construct. Maggie tallied up the possible cost of such a garment mentally, and knew a sense of outrage that her husband's money had probably paid for it.

Renita had paused to take down her parasol, and then she caught sight of the little bride standing over in the corner all alone. A quick glance around the lobby showed no signs of Jack, and Renita decided that she could not resist the temptation. Strolling over to where Maggie stood, she smiled her most calculating smile. "Well, hello again," she said sweetly, as if she and Maggie had met previously under the best of circumstances.

Maggie stiffened, unable quite to believe the other woman's boldness. "Hello," she replied cautiously, without the slightest hint of civility.

"What! All alone!" Renita observed, glancing about. "Your friend hasn't deserted you, has he?" she inquired solicitously.

Maggie felt her face heating up, hating herself for this small betrayal. "My husband went to get our luggage," she informed Renita, feeling fairly certain that the woman would not be surprised at their relationship.

Renita pretended surprise, nevertheless. "Husband, is he? How charming!" she gushed. "You'd best be careful, though, *chiquita*. He looks like a hard one to hold." Laughing outright at Maggie's obvious rage, Renita swept into the dining room before Jack could come down and catch her tormenting his bride. It would not do to antagonize him until after he had given her the money he had promised. Once she had it, however, things would be different, and if he thought he could get rid of her that easily, he was in for a surprise.

Maggie was trying to remember all the things Miss Finley

287

had taught her that a lady never does so that she could fantasize about doing them right this very moment. She wanted to throw things, and scream and cry, and most of all, do severe bodily harm to that female person in the other room. Maggie had learned a lot of swear words growing up on a ranch, and she ran through them all mentally, cursing both the woman and Jack Sinclair. How dare he bring his mistress to this town and flaunt her in front of his wife? What would people say? How they would laugh at her behind her back for not being able to hold on to her husband for even a week. That the woman's words had been a warning she had no doubt. The question was, were they a warning that she intended to heed? Would she fight for Jack? Would she try to win his love? *Could* she win his love from such a formidable adversary? Added to her fury was the pure misery of not knowing the answers to those questions.

When Jack finally did come down with their bags, Maggie was fit to be tied, and it didn't help a bit that he had such a pleasant look on his face. "Where have you been?" she snapped. "You took your own sweet time." Turning on her heel, she stormed out to the street where the buggy awaited them.

For a moment Jack simply stood there staring after her, his mouth gaping open in surprise. Now what had gotten into her? She'd been fine when he'd gone upstairs. Shaking his head in puzzlement, he followed her outside. No use trying to figure it out now. The best thing to do was get her away from this godforsaken town before anything else happened.

The long ride home was accomplished in silence, brooding silence on Maggie's part and baffled silence on Jack's. Claiming a headache that wasn't entirely imaginary, Maggie went to her room until suppertime. Solicitously, Consuela brought her a wet rag for her forehead and some herbal tea that made her drowsy. Later, the housekeeper brought her supper on a tray and fussed over her until she felt a little ridiculous for hiding in her room any longer. Still, the thought of facing Jack again today was unbearable, so she kept up the charade and allowed Consuela to plump her pillows and massage her neck. When she finally left, Maggie lay in the growing darkness worrying over her problems like a dog worrying a particularly interesting bone.

Finally, when she heard the parlor clock strike eight, she decided that she was foolish to continue thinking about it any longer, especially after the kind of day she had had. Her emotions had run the gamut since early morning when she had first gone to Jack's room. What she needed was a good night's sleep to give her a fresh perspective.

With that decided, she rose and began to undress, smiling sadly at the green taffeta gown that she had worn this morning with such high hopes and that now was so limp and creased. Laying it over the back of the chair to be pressed, she slipped out of her petticoats, shoes and stockings, and then unlocked her corset. She had just removed her camisole when she heard Jack's footsteps in the hall.

Her reaction was instinctive, even though she hated herself for it. Her heart was pounding madly, her breath coming in anxious gasps. Frantically, she tore off her pantalettes, her only thought being to get into her nightdress as quickly as possible and then get into bed, so that she could feign sleep. But she was not fast enough.

The rap on the door was light, in deference to her headache. "Maggie?" he called softly through the door.

"Go away!" Maggie called back, realizing too late that she hadn't sounded sick at all, only shrewish. Frantically, she reached for her nightdress, but her hand froze in midair when the door flew open.

"Maggie, we have to tal. . . ." Jack's words died on his lips when he saw her standing there, her ivory body glowing in the twilight shadows.

Neither moved for a long moment. Jack simply stared, taking in every detail of the vision before him, and Maggie

289

stared back, fascinated by the stunning effect she had had on him. At last he murmured hoarsely, "I'd forgotten how lovely you are."

The sound of his voice helped break the spell that held her motionless, and her frozen hand finished its mission, grasping the nightdress that hung on a nearby peg. In one swift motion, she snatched it up and clutched it to her bosom, effectively concealing most of her nakedness from his intense gaze. "What did you want?" she tried to demand, but it came out more like a breathless plea. She cursed herself for the weakness invading her traitorous body even as she blushed at the inanity of her question. It was painfully obvious what he wanted, and it was the same thing she wanted, too, as much as she would have liked to deny it.

Ever so slowly, Jack reached behind himself and closed the bedroom door. The click of the latch sounded like thunder to Maggie's supersensitive ears.

Jack's mustache quirked, but Maggie knew he was not amused. "I was going to say that we have to talk, but I've changed my mind," he said, his husky voice sending ripples of sensation across the room to stroke along her quivering nerve endings. "How's your headache, Mrs. Sinclair?" he asked then.

Maggie could only shake her head, unable to recall whether she had ever had a headache or not. She would have swallowed, but the pulse in her throat tried to choke her and she gave up the attempt. Invisible fingers tingled along her bare back and down her legs and up into the most secret parts of her, until her very core became a molten mass of need. Marveling at how the mere sight of him could trigger such violent reactions, she watched as Jack very carefully loosened the watch chain that stretched across his middle and began to release the buttons of his vest.

"I know a very enjoyable way to cure a headache, my darling," he told her, shrugging out of the vest and moving toward her.

"Will it be enjoyable for me, too?" Maggie heard herself ask, amazed at the bantering tone of her voice. Why didn't he hurry?

"Most assuredly," he replied, peeling off his fine linen shirt and dropping it to the floor beside his vest. Her eyes were sea green now, deep and stormy, mirroring his own passion. Her breath came in tiny gasps through gently parted lips, and he could see the edges of her nostrils flare to take in his scent.

When he came close, she felt a blast of heat, as if someone had opened a forbidden door into the earth's molten core and allowed some of the primal energy to escape to charge between them. She could see every curling hair across that expanse of chest, and the two flat, dark nipples that were now as puckered as her own. Her fingers, longing to reach out and touch them, curled more tightly into the clutched nightdress as she drew a shaky breath.

Jack's own breath rasped as he reached out, fighting the urge to take her in his arms. From where he drew the strength to resist, he would never know. If he hadn't already had her once today—had it been today? It seemed so very long ago—he knew he could never bear it. As it was, his self-control hung by a fragile thread, and only the knowledge that he was prolonging their pleasure by prolonging the anticipation kept him sane. His long fingers closed around the delicate material of her nightdress and drew it inexorably from her grasp.

Maggie resisted at first, but the smoldering determination radiating from those obsidian eyes defeated her, and she surrendered the garment to him. It slithered soundlessly to the floor.

"Maggie." Her name was a tortured growl dredged up from the depths of his soul, and his eyes took her in as one dying takes in the sight of paradise. "You're so very beautiful," his strangled voice declared even as he lamented the inadequacy of the praise. Had it only been today when he had thought others more so? He had been insane. Never had

291

he seen, never had he known another to compare. His worshipful gaze took in her full, proud breasts now straining for his touch, the smooth plane of her belly, the cluster of auburn curls, the long, slender legs. She was perfect, so perfect.

Maggie knew that she should feel ashamed standing before him like this with nothing hidden, but something in those dark eyes forbade shame. Instead she felt adored, and proud, and desirable, and all the things she wanted to be for him. It gave her power, but it was a power that made her helpless, too, so helpless that she almost cried out in despair when he turned away.

Drawing on the last of his will power, Jack walked away from her on legs wooden with reluctance, knowing instinctively that this part was important, so vitally important, that he dared not even touch her for fear of ruining it. He wanted her, and he would have her, but this time it would be because she chose it, too, and not because he seduced her. Stopping beside her bed, he paused a moment, taking in the rumpled coverlet where she had lain before, and then, in one swift movement, he swept the bedclothes back. Staring for a long heartbeat at the pristine sheet, he took a breath and turned back to her.

He reached out one hand and said, "Come to me, Maggie." His words were half-plea, half-command, but yet neither, and Maggie responded, recognizing in them the summons of her soul's mate. She went to him. She could do nothing else.

Silently, her bare feet hardly seeming to touch the floor, Maggie went to him, lifting her own hand to meet his. His fingers closed over hers in a grip that might have caused pain had she then been capable of feeling anything but pleasure at his touch. He drew her into his arms, at last, at last, but still his embrace was gentle, restrained, as if he were afraid to surrender the iron control he held. For an instant his kiss was as gentle as his touch, tasting, testing, seeking, but only for an instant. When he felt her softness under his mouth, under his hands, against his naked chest, that last frail shred of control snapped and he clutched her to him, drinking in her essence, devouring her, knowing he could never get enough.

Maggie surrendered eagerly, clutching back, her nails unconsciously raking furrows where they gripped and causing a pleasure-pain that Jack only vaguely felt. She barely noticed when he lowered her to the bed, registering only the very welcome weight of his body on hers and the chance to hold him closer still.

Their mouths were busy reexploring familiar territory, and when Jack's tongue invaded, Maggie no longer felt the intrusion strange. Instead, she used her own tongue to tangle with his in a sensuous duel that left them both gasping when at last Jack drew back in amazed surrender.

"My God," he whispered, raising up on both elbows and resting his forehead against hers in an effort to curb the emotions threatening to run rampant.

But Maggie wanted none of such restraint. She knew exactly what she wanted, exactly what should happen, and it could not happen soon enough. She wanted him, wanted that delicious oblivion that came when he was inside of her, and she wanted it now. She lifted herself to him, telling him her needs with hands and lips that searched out sensitive spots and then moved on to eliminate buttons and barriers.

Only when he caught those hands and held them fast, eluding those lips until he had successfully pinned her motionless to the bed, did she notice that he was laughing. No, not laughing, exactly. Chuckling.

"Slow down, little witch," he was saying. "We've got all night."

All night! Maggie could not wait all night, and the hips that churned against his told him so. The green eyes that blazed up at him pleaded for the release that he alone could give. In the light of her need, his amusement faded into sober determination. There was no reason they could both not have what they wanted.

Still holding her arms prisoner, he lowered his head to her breast, pressing a kiss on first one pink peak and then the other. Maggie shifted restlessly, arching temptingly, but he moved on, leaving a string of stinging kisses across her ribs and down to her navel. There he paused to trace a moist circle around the tiny cavern with his tongue and then to dip in for one tormenting taste, before moving on.

Only when he planted a kiss into the auburn nest did she realize his destination, and she went stiff with humiliation. He shouldn't be kissing her *there*, but before she could think to protest, his tongue snaked out and touched. The effect was magical, sending vibrations singing out to the far corners of her being and back again to center in her center where he was working still more magic, making her forget her inhibitions, her embarrassment. She even forgot what else she wanted from him as her awareness turned inward, focusing on that one spot where all sensations converged into pure delight.

Her hands were free now, and she used them to hold him closer, fingers weaving into his soft, dark locks. She did not recognize the impassioned moans as coming from her own throat, knowing only that she could not bear this pleasure much longer. It shouldn't happen this way, she knew it shouldn't, but she couldn't stop it, didn't even want to. Crying out his name, she arched her neck, burying the back of her head in the pillow as release throbbed through her. Wave after wave crested and broke, the initial fury gradually subsiding until the last one finally ebbed away, leaving her limp and sated and content.

Content, except for one niggling little doubt. As reason slowly returned, she realized that while she had had her sweet moment of oblivion, he hadn't even . . . reluctantly, she forced her eyes open, and instantly wished she hadn't. There he was, still lying between her outstretched legs, propped up on his elbows and watching her. One hand idly stroked the inside of her thigh.

His mustache tilted. "Feeling better, Mrs. Sinclair?"

Maggie wanted to die. How could she have opened herself up like that to a man? How could she have lain there, writhing, while he . . .

Jack levered himself off the bed, his eyes never leaving hers. He could easily read her confusion, her embarrassment in those expressive eyes, and he could not help the small surge of triumph that he felt. She might hate him at other times, but at least he had this power over her. If he were ever to win her love, her trust, this was the way to do it.

As soon as he moved away, Maggie drew her legs together, growing more mortified by the second. She simply could not believe what had just happened, and now he was leaving as if . . . no, he was not leaving. Maggie's eyes grew wide as she watched his long fingers working the buttons of his trousers.

With impatient swiftness, Jack stripped off what remained of his clothes, enjoying Maggie's reluctant curiosity. She had even forgotten that initial stab of modesty that had forced her legs together. He had expected that she would try to cover herself, but now she seemed to have forgotten her own nakedness in the face of his. He had not forgotten though, and he let his gaze linger lovingly on every rolling swell, thoroughly enjoying the telltale signs that she had enjoyed his lovemaking.

Maggie's eyes had grown wide at the sight of his manhood. She had never had more than a glimpse of him before, but now, for the first time, she could see him, all of him, and the sight both terrified and intrigued her. It was so huge; how did it ever fit? But it did fit, as she remembered oh, so well, and to her amazement, in spite of what had just happened, she began to feel the same aching emptiness that she had felt before. What was he going to do? Was he going to stand there all night, just looking at her? Was he going to leave?

Somehow Maggie was certain that he wasn't going to

leave. Not the way he was looking at her, not the way those black eyes were glowing. No, he wasn't going to leave. What, then, was he waiting for? Licking suddenly dry lips in an unconsciously provocative gesture, Maggie put all her questions, all her doubts into one word. "Jack?"

He could not have said why he had waited, perhaps he had wanted a sign, a signal from her telling him that she still wanted him. Whatever he had needed, the sound of his name on her lips met that need, freeing him to go to her.

Her body was soft and still warm from her passion, and for a moment he simply held her, absorbing that warmth, savoring it. Then silken arms slipped around him and honeyed lips came seeking his, and the raging desire that he had held in check so long broke free.

The blaze of his kiss cremated all of Maggie's doubts. His mouth on hers was savage, almost hurting in his attempt to devour her. He forced her lips apart and plundered her sweetness, never even giving her the chance to respond, and then he moved on, pressing kisses on every part of her face until he found the sensitive spot below her ear.

Maggie was busy, too, her hands running over him almost frantically, reveling in the soft-hard feel of him, the heat that radiated from him, scorching away all inhibitions. Still she could not bring herself to touch him below the waist, and each time her fingers grazed into forbidden territory, she pulled them guiltily back to begin her limited explorations all over again.

Meanwhile Jack was sampling her throat, nipping and tasting the tender skin, and marveling at how delicious she was. Then he sampled the valley between her breasts before moving on to feast on the tender peaks.

Maggie gasped when she sensed the edge of his teeth against her delicate flesh, but that gasp became a sigh when he stopped tantalizingly short of pain and then moved on until he had pricked every inch of her breasts with his precious love-bites. Maggie was moaning out her pleasure with every breath, clutching him to her as her blood once again turned to liquid fire and the need that she thought he had satisfied raged once again.

"Touch me, Maggie." His ragged whisper stilled her thrashing.

She was already touching him, had been touching him all along. What did he mean? Puzzled, she lifted languorous lids to meet his dark, commanding gaze.

He had already captured one small hand and guided it to his chest. For a moment he held it there, letting her feel the pounding of his heart, and then he moved downward, across his ribs and the flat plane of his belly, but when he tried to take it lower, she resisted.

"I can't," she protested feebly, but she knew that she could, knew that she wanted to, oh, how she wanted to, but she was afraid.

"It's all right," he assured her, and because he was stronger and because she wasn't nearly as reluctant as she wanted to be, he moved her hand.

Tentatively at first, her fingers encircled him, but his sharp intake of breath emboldened her, and she began to explore. He was so soft, like warm satin, but so strong, too. His strength, his power awed her, and for a moment she forgot all else save the wonder of her discovery.

"Oh, God, Maggie." Jack pulled her hand away, capturing it as he had before and drawing it back to his chest as he sagged down into the mattress. "I can't take too much more of that."

Confused, Maggie could only stare, trying to reconcile the strain in his voice with the hammering of his heart. "Did I hurt you?" she whispered. She hadn't meant to, of course, but she had been so curious that she had forgotten herself.

The strain that twisted his features relaxed, and she could make out the familiar twist of his mustache. Then those dark eyes opened slowly, and she saw that teasing light that she had come to love. Before she could guess his intent, he lunged toward her, half-covering her body with his own, his face mere inches from hers. "Did you think you were hurting me?" he asked, black eyes dancing.

"I . . ."

But he wasn't interested in her reply. "Tell me, does this hurt?" One long finger had insinuated itself between her thighs to caress her most sensitive spot, and no, it did not hurt at all.

"No," she squeaked. Was that what he had felt? Why on earth had he stopped her? It was starting all over again for her as his skilled fingers moved over her, but as much as she wanted it, she wanted it to be different this time. "Not like this," she said, trying to pull his hand away. "Not this time."

He wasn't cooperating, not a bit, and even though the room was now almost completely dark, she could still see the slash of white teeth as he grinned down at her. "How *do* you want to do it?" he taunted.

Still wrestling with his hand, Maggie felt her face burn at the topic of conversation. "I want to do it right!" she snapped, irritation adding an urgency to the need building inside her.

In one smooth movement, he was over her, on her, smothering her struggles. "There isn't a wrong way to do it, honey," he informed her.

She might have continued the argument except that he was doing what she wanted now, making her forget everything else.

Jack bit back a groan as he sank into her velvet depths. It had happened so quickly this morning that he had not been able to remember if it had truly been the best he had ever had. Now he knew. Never had it been like this, never had he felt so much pleasure, never had he felt so much a man. It was like coming home. Dear God, he adored her.

And she adored him, although she was gritting her teeth to keep from saying so. She could not tell him, not yet. She couldn't quite remember why, but she knew that she could

298

not, and so she didn't, and when he began to move inside her, she was no longer able to.

Slowly, ever so slowly, he stroked her, savoring his possession, exulting in her response. He could make her love him, he knew he could, and he would. He would succeed. He had to.

Maggie clung to him, meeting him thrust for thrust, her body locked into the ancient rhythm and her soul pulsing to the throbbing beat. This was so right, so right that she could forget all the things he had done. She could even forget how she had once hated him. Her emotions now were just as intense, but the ferocity of her hatred had somehow been converted into seething passion. She did not care, either. The only thing that mattered was that they were together, struggling, striving for that perfect union.

Maggie lost herself in the effort, oblivious to all save the fusion of their bodies into absolute harmony. The symphony of sensation washed over her, drowning her consciousness until she knew nothing except that blissful oneness that boiled up and up and finally over. Liquid joy coursed through her veins, while delight blazed before her eyes and the soaring symphony deafened her to her own cry of ecstasy.

Jack heard it, though, and caught it with his own hungry mouth. He held back another second until her body stilled, and then he plunged into her with his own release, filling her with the living seed that sealed them into one entity.

For a long while Maggie simply lay there, absorbing his weight the way she had absorbed the fruit of his passion, but then his weight grew burdensome, and she longed to draw a deep breath. Feebly, she pushed against him, and with a groan of protest, he reluctantly slid the top half of his body to one side, leaving them still joined below. He was not ready yet to sever that sweet connection, and Maggie did not object.

They lay like that for a time, enjoying first the euphoria

and then the delicious contentment. Jack could not remember ever feeling so fine, and he knew a tug of irritation that they had wasted the whole day snarling and snapping at each other. Whatever had he been thinking of to allow it? And what had come over Maggie to keep her in her room all afternoon and evening? Lazily, he lifted first one eyelid and then the other. He could only see her profile, that cute little nose, that stubborn little chin. She looked as if she might be asleep.

"Maggie?" His voice was soft but coaxing, and Maggie's eyes flickered open in response.

She had not really been asleep, only dozing. Groggily, she turned her head and her attention to him. "Hmmmm?"

He could barely make out her features, but he could guess at how green her eyes would be. "Why were you hiding in your room all day?" he asked.

His voice stroked over her like a warm hand. "I wasn't hiding," she protested sleepily. It wasn't his voice at all, it was really his hand that was stroking over her, but that was all right, too.

"Then why were you pouting in your room all day?" he insisted.

Maggie came fully awake. "I was not pouting," she said, trying to ignore the way his hand was cupping her breast. "I had a headache."

As punishment for her lie, he tweaked one puckered nipple, and then grinned in the darkness. "Is it gone now?"

Maggie could not believe this was really happening. Here they were, lying naked in her bed, still . . . intimately entwined, and having a conversation. Did normal people really do things like this? She thanked heaven for the darkness that hid her chagrin and practically everything else, and tried to remember what they had been talking about. Oh, yes, her headache. "Yes, it's gone," she said as normally as possible under the circumstances.

"Good," he said, and she didn't have to see him to know

that he was smiling. After a slight pause, he asked, "And did I 'do it right'?"

Now Maggie really did want to die. It was mortifying enough that she had actually said such a brazen thing, had actually behaved in such a brazen manner, but to discuss it, as if they were discussing the weather . . .

Well aware of her feelings, Jack had no patience with them. If she was ashamed of her feelings for him, how could he hope to channel them in the right direction? "Now that we've done it 'right,' why don't we try doing it 'left'?"

Before she could even think to ask what on earth he was talking about, his hands had slipped down to grip her hips, and in one swift movement, he flipped both of them over so that she was lying on top. Somehow he accomplished this feat without breaking the intimate contact of their bodies.

Maggie came up on her elbows, sputtering. "What are you doing?" she demanded.

"I'm discovering what a very nice bottom you have, Mrs. Sinclair," and he was, too. "I don't believe I ever had a chance to do so, before. What a shame to disguise it with a bustle."

Maggie knew that she should be outraged in addition to being thoroughly humiliated, but the oddest sensations were curling up inside of her, and they distracted her. "Jack . . ." she tried to protest, but his mouth had found her nipple and she forgot what she was going to say. She did not even have time to marvel that her body was responding to him yet again before she was caught up in the swirling vortex. Gentle hands and whispered commands guided her in this new variation on a now-familiar theme, and soon they were moving once more in unison. It took much longer this time, their passion building slowly to the crescendo, but Maggie thought her very soul had shattered in the cataclysm.

This time it was she who lay sprawled and unmoving until he pushed her away. Even though her love-slickened body had cooled and the night chill had settled over them, she still could not move. At last it was Jack who found the strength to reach down and pull the covers over them, and when they were warm and snug, he drew her back into his arms.

"I told you there wasn't a wrong way to do it," he murmured into her damp hair.

"Jack . . . ?" She had so many questions, she hardly knew where to begin. What had happened? Was it like this all the time? Was she supposed to feel like this? And most important, how did he feel? Was it like that for him, too? And could he make love to her like that and not really love her? And should she tell him that she loved him?

He never gave her a chance to ask anything, though. His fingers rested gently against her swollen lips. "Shhhh, not now, Maggie. Don't say anything. You might accidently start a fight, and since I have every intention of sleeping right here with you tonight, I'm not going to give you a chance to throw me out."

How silly. Maggie didn't want to fight, not at all, but now that she thought about it, she didn't really want to do anything else, either, except go to sleep. And so she did, curling herself into the crook of his arm. Her questions could wait until morning.

Maggie's nose twitched. Her arm was cramped, and she needed to roll over, but when she tried to turn her head, it wouldn't turn. She tried harder, but that only caused her pain, and when she opened her eyes to discover what was holding her, she was startled to see a human face mere inches away from her own.

It was Jack, of course. He was lying on her hair, which was why she hadn't been able to move her head. Cautiously, so as not to disturb him, she eased her cramped arm into a more comfortable position, and then waited, every muscle tensed. He did not wake up, and gradually her tension eased. She could not move away, so she used the opportunity to study him. He was lying on his side, facing her, both arms wrapped loosely around her, and one leg thrown over hers.

Trying not to remember that they were both still naked under the covers, she examined his face. With those dark eyes hidden and his features softened in sleep, he looked almost harmless. And very appealing. Except for those whiskers. They were certainly vicious looking, and she fought off the urge to run a finger over them to test them. She wondered if they would grow into a beard as silky as his mustache, and imagined how such a beard would feel whisking over her sensitized skin. Gooseflesh prickled that skin at the thought, and she was conscious once again of his nearness, of the warm comfort of his presence. It would be quite pleasant to wake up with him every morning like this, to spend every night . . . memories of the previous night came drifting back, snatches of sensation, glimpses of images burned into her brain by the heat of passion. The memories were pleasant, far too pleasant, and terrifying in the light of day.

All her questions of the night before rang in her ears. What had happened to her to make her lose control like that? And why had he been so tender, so loving with her? And so very ardent? Considering that he had a mistress in town, he no longer had a reason to come to Maggie at all. Unless he wanted to.

Could it be that he wanted to? Could it be that he cared for her, that he wanted her? Of course, she knew he didn't love her, not the way that she loved him, but if he wanted her, then that was a beginning. Still, she was frightened. What if he didn't care for her? She knew little of men and had no way of knowing whether a man could make love without being in love. Until she was certain, until she better understood his feelings, she would have to be careful not to reveal her own. She knew Jack Sinclair well enough to know that if he didn't really care for her, he would use her love as a weapon, as a means for keeping her in line and controlling her. No, until she was sure, she would keep her secret.

So involved was she in her thoughts, that she did not really hear the knocking. It wasn't on her door anyway, and so she did not pay any attention. If she had, she might have spared herself some embarrassment.

"Señora! Señor Jack is not in his room. I have looked everywhere. . . ." Consuela had burst into the room without bothering to knock, so certain was she that there was no need. Now she realized that she had been wrong, and she stood gaping, her unfinished sentence completely forgotten.

Jack had come instantly awake, his whole body jerking with surprise, just as Maggie's had done. It took a moment for him to figure out where he was and how he'd gotten there.

"Madre de Dios!" Consuela's muttered exclamation reminded him of what had awakened him. Instantly he released Maggie, but it took another moment of awkward fumbling to free her hair from under his head and then to snatch the blanket up to cover them both decently. Maggie, he noticed, was blushing furiously, and his own face felt unusually warm. A wave of annoyance washed over him. There was absolutely nothing to be embarrassed about. They were married, for God's sake.

Consuela, however, seemed to think he had a lot to be embarrassed about. Her dark eyes were taking in the entire room, beginning with his clothing scattered about the floor, and then moving on to Maggie's nightdress, which was lying in a heap in the middle of the room, and at last settling on the couple in the bed. She did not speak, did not utter a sound, but her disapproval was as evident as if she had been shrieking condemnation. Planting her fists on her ample hips, she cocked her head as if awaiting a suitable explanation for such scandalous behavior.

Maggie fought a desire to pull the covers over her head. As frightened as she had been of revealing her love to Jack, she was just as frightened of losing Consuela's respect. Would the housekeeper think less of her now, knowing that she had surrendered to him? If she ever found out how much Maggie had enjoyed it . . .

But Consuela's disapproval was reserved for Jack alone, and when her brown eyes clashed with his, it was he who flinched. "Did you want something, Consuela?" he asked through gritted teeth.

Consuela gave a final, censorious sniff, and said, "You have a visitor."

Jack's eyes narrowed as he wondered for one awful moment if Renita would have had the gall to come out to the ranch. "Who is it?"

Consuela gave an eloquent shrug, clearly conveying her displeasure at having to converse with such a depraved person. "He would not say his name. He said you are old friends, but *I* do not know him," thus implying that he was not worth knowing at all.

Jack scowled, forgetting his compromising position for a moment. "What does he look like?"

Consuela shuddered slightly, her condescending look twisting into a mask of revulsion. "He is *mucho* ugly. *Dios*," she said shuddering again and crossing herself piously. "He has a scar." She pointed to her own cheek, and Jack sat bolt upright, heedless of his nudity.

"A scar?" he demanded, and Consuela nodded, puzzled.

Maggie had watched the whole exchange with curiosity, and now she felt the alarm that had gone through Jack. Who was this man with the scar and what did he want? And what would it mean to her and Jack? She watched Jack's face grow thoughtful for a moment and then saw that blankness settle over it. He was hiding something, something very unpleasant.

"Well, tell him he'll have to wait," Jack said, giving no indication of the tension that Maggie could sense he felt. "And bring me some hot water," he added, plainly dismissing the housekeeper.

Consuela, however, took one last opportunity to cast a

reproachful look around the room before tossing her head haughtily and stomping out.

Jack muttered a curse. If that woman wasn't such a good cook . . . Then he remembered Maggie, who was still cowering under the blanket. He let his gaze drift down to her. Her color was still high, but she no longer looked embarrassed. Instead, she was studying him intently. He tried a grin. "Good morning, Mrs. Sinclair."

Maggie ignored his attempt at charming her. She was dying to ask him who the man with the scar was. "It's kind of early for visitors," she ventured.

Jack squinted in the direction of the window. "I don't think so. Seems like we slept rather later than usual. Perhaps because we were so . . . active last night." His eyes twinkled, reminding her of the delights they had shared.

She could feel her skin prickle in response, but she fought it. "Wonder who he could be," she said, prodding him to tell her, mentally begging him to.

"Probably just some drifter looking for a job," he said. His lie was smooth, but it did not fool Maggie. Instead, it had the opposite effect. The fact that he was trying to hide the man's identity from her convinced her that the man was a danger. As usual Jack was treating her as if she were a child who needed protection. Odd that she should only realize that now, but it was true. He had never seen fit to confide anything about his problems with the ranch or with Kincaid unless she had absolutely insisted. Did he think she couldn't handle such problems? Did he think she was so fragile that she would grow hysterical if he told her who this visitor was and why the man's presence had upset him?

Of course, he did. Maggie knew it instinctively. Oh, she was perfectly suited as a bed partner, for enjoying the physical pleasures to which he had introduced her, but other than that he considered her just an empty-headed ornament. The knowledge inflamed her with a swift fury.

Jack didn't notice. He was still smiling, half of his brain

still worrying over his visitor, but the other half regretting having to leave Maggie's bed. "I apologize for this interruption," he was saying. "I had very different plans for this morning." He leaned over to place a kiss on her very tempting mouth, but she stiffened and pulled away, avoiding his lips.

"No need to apologize," Maggie said acidly, the bitterness of her anger spilling over into her voice. "The sooner you get out of here the better!"

Jack could only stare, completely baffled by her fury. What in the hell had come over her? After last night, he had expected her to wake up purring like a kitten. All his problems with her would have been solved, and he would have been free to concentrate on Kincaid and the nestors. Now he not only had to worry about Kincaid; but Paul Crescent, the scarred man he was certain he would find waiting for him, had crawled out of the woodwork to see what havoc he could wreak. On top of that Maggie had changed overnight from a cuddly kitten to a scratching, spitting hell-cat, and he hadn't a clue as to the reason. "What's the matter with you?" he asked in exasperation.

"Nothing's the matter with me," Maggie replied, adjusting the covers more modestly about her. "I've never been overly fond of your company. That shouldn't come as a surprise." She gave him what she hoped was a condesending glare. She really did want him to leave. She was having a hard time sustaining her anger in the face of his naked chest, and for some ridiculous reason she felt the urge to cry. Why, oh why couldn't he see her as a woman, a complete person and not just a warm body to fill his bed? Last night he had been so sweet that she had almost believed that he could care for her, and this morning he was telling her charitable lies as if she were a child he had to protect from the harsh realities of life.

"You didn't seem to mind my company last night," he pointed out ruthlessly, gratified to see the flush crawl up her throat.

"What choice did you give me?" she said after an agonizing moment. Never, she would never admit the truth, not as long as he treated her like a . . . like a kept woman!

Jack swore, briefly and succinctly, and then he threw back the covers and swung his long legs to the floor. His trousers were still lying beside the bed where he had discarded them the night before, and he snatched them up and jerked them on furiously. Damn her. If Crescent wasn't waiting . . . he smiled grimly. If Crescent wasn't waiting, he would take great delight in making little Maggie beg his forgiveness. But Crescent *was* waiting, and knowing Crescent, it wouldn't be too wise to keep him waiting very long. Maggie could wait, though. Let her stew in her own juice for a while. If she didn't want his company, she could damn well go without it. Knowing her passionate nature as he now did, he knew she couldn't go without it for long, any more than he could go without hers.

His irritation evident in every movement, he scooped up his scattered clothing and headed for the door. He paused just a moment to cast her one last, long look before pulling the door open, and then he was gone.

Maggie lay there a moment, hardly daring to believe that she had gotten rid of him so easily. When he had stopped at the door, she had been terrified that he would say something cruel, some last, hateful remark that would be the last straw in crushing the frail, protective shell she had built around herself. As soon as the door latch clicked behind him, she felt the sting of tears, and the next breath she drew turned into an ignominious sob.

She felt like an absolute fool, but somehow she could not seem to stop the tears that coursed down her cheeks. Pride drove her to bury her head in the pillow so that no one would hear her weeping. Pride, and the knowledge that if she had had to explain her crying, she could not have given a reason for it. Disappointment played a major role, of course, but there was far more than that involved in this fit of despair.

She could not seem to reconcile the facts that she wanted both to be in Jack Sinclair's arms and to be as far away from him as was humanly possible. Added to that was the shame of having responded to him so eagerly when he quite clearly had no deep feelings for her at all, and the knowledge that she would do the very same thing again if he so much as smiled her way. Love, she concluded, was a horrible emotion, degrading and humiliating.

Perhaps if she had heard Jack yelling at Consuela, she might have realized that he felt exactly the same way, but with her head buried in the bedclothes, she could not.

"In here," he barked when he heard Consuela coming down the hallway with his hot water, and the housekeeper brought the kettle into his bedroom. Her expression was one of stoic tolerance, but Jack barely spared her a glance. "Bring me some coffee, too."

Instead of rushing to serve him, she stood there a moment, arms crossed over her bosom, waiting until he grudgingly met her relentless gaze. "What did you do to that poor girl?" she demanded.

It took a concerted effort, but Jack held his temper. "That 'poor girl' is my wife, Consuela, and you are nothing but the housekeeper. This is none of your business." His voice was cold, his black eyes glittering dangerously, but Consuela did not even flinch. She was far more than the housekeeper, and she knew it.

"You will never make her love you if you take her by force," she said. This time she did flinch at the raw fury that actually shook him. His face went white with the effect of containing it, and when Consuela saw it, saw him losing control, a thing she had never seen, she backed away, heading for the door.

"I . . . I will bring your coffee," she promised before ducking out.

Jack stood there a long moment trembling with the rage that had exploded within him so unexpectedly. Poor

Consuela, she could not have known that she had said the one thing calculated to turn him into a madman. If one more person accused him of raping his own wife, he was very much afraid the consequences could be fatal. Shaking his head to clear it from the red haze that had temporarily blinded him, he mechanically went about the process of shaving. He tried not to notice the slight tremor in his hands.

Maggie didn't even hear Consuela come in until she was standing by the bed. "Señora?" she inquired tentatively.

Maggie jumped at the sound of her voice so close, and when she lifted her head, she found the Mexican woman leaning over her. Consuela was actually wringing her hands and her smooth face was the picture of concern. "He hurt you, señora?" There was pain in the softly accented voice, and Maggie's aching heart responded to it. She nodded. "Do not worry, I have some herbs. Is there much blood?"

Maggie blinked in surprise at the strange question, and then she realized that she and Consuela were talking about two very different kinds of hurt. "No . . . Oh, no, he did not hurt me," she assured the housekeeper, wiping the tears from her eyes with the back of one hand, while still clutching the blanket to her bare bosom with the other. She made a halfhearted effort to sit up, and Consuela assisted her, adjusting the pillows for her.

Consuela clucked sympathetically. "There is no need for shame, señora. We are both women. The first time is always hard, and when a man uses force . . ."

Maggie was shaking her head vigorously. Later she would think that perhaps she should have allowed Consuela to believe the lie, but that was later. Now she only felt a perverse desire to defend the man she loved. "No, it wasn't like that. He was . . . gentle." Gentle was perhaps the wrong word, but it was as close as she could come to describing what had happened in that bed the night before. "And it . . . it wasn't the first time, either," she admitted reluctantly. Now

Consuela would lose all respect for her. Maggie had to force herself to meet the brown eyes staring down at her.

To her surprise, they held not condemnation but relief. Consuela was nodding, and her pleasant mouth was stretching into a smile. "I should have known. It is as you say. Señor Jack is a gentle lover. He would never hurt a woman."

She said it with such certainty, with such conviction, that her words stabbed Maggie like a knife. The pain was agonizing, but even so she could remember thinking how typical it was that Jack had a woman taking care of him. Consuela was not the beauty that the woman at the hotel was, but she was very attractive and certainly available. "You? You and . . . Jack were . . ." She could not even say the words, and at first she thought Consuela was only pretending not to understand.

The housekeeper tipped her head in puzzlement, studying the tragic eyes, the small, pale face, and tried to make sense of her question. When she did, she stared back in equal horror. "No! Oh, no, señora!" she assured her, shaking her head in vehement denial. "I clean his house and cook his food, that is all! I never . . . oh, no, señora. I have only heard Renita say . . ." She caught herself, but it was too late.

"Renita?" Maggie's pain had eased, but only for a moment. She believed Consuela, knowing instinctively that they had never been lovers. She should have known, having seen them together, that they never could have been, not the way they treated each other now. But . . . "Who is Renita?"

Consuela was shaking her head again, but not so vehemently this time. "She is no one, no one," she said, but Maggie knew differently.

"She's very beautiful, isn't she? She's taller than I am and she has long black hair, doesn't she?" Maggie said, surprised that her voice sounded so calm when her insides were screaming in agony.

311

Consuela hesitated a moment, plainly wanting to deny it, but also very curious. "You have seen her?" she asked in amazement.

"She was in town. She arrived on the stage night before last. I saw Jack meet her." The bare facts sounded so harmless that she found she could recite them without faltering.

Consuela scowled. This was a development she never would have considered. How could the señor have done such a thing?

"And she came to his room yesterday when we were . . . there," Maggie was saying.

"He told you who she was?" Consuela asked in patent disbelief.

"Oh, no, he pretended not to know her," Maggie said. A strange numbness seemed to have gripped her heart, sealing in the pain. Otherwise she could not have borne it.

Consuela considered this a moment. "He has not gone to see her for a long time," she said almost to herself.

Maggie grasped at this straw. "How long?" she demanded.

Consuela shook her head. "A long time, long before you were married." Her brow furrowed in concentration, and then suddenly cleared as the truth dawned on her. "He has not gone to her since you are come home," she announced triumphantly.

It was too much to hope for, but Maggie couldn't help hoping anyway. Could it possibly be true? "Are you sure?" she asked, hating herself for the weakness that forced her to voice the question.

Consuela nodded with certainty. "That is why she comes, don't you see? She is afraid to lose him, so she comes to see why he stays away. Why did I not think of it before?" Consuela's smile seemed to brighten the room. It certainly lightened Maggie's heavy heart.

"Do you really think so?" she asked hopefully.

The housekeeper shrugged. "Was he happy to see her?"

312

Maggie thought this over. "Not particularly," she decided.

A sly grin twisted Consuela's mouth. "Especially when she comes to his room when you are both . . . there?" She put a special meaning on the word "there" and Maggie could not help the blush that stained her cheeks. She nodded painfully.

"And you and Señor Jack please each other, no?" Her grin had not faded, and she fingered the edge of the sheet suggestively.

"Consuela!" Maggie cried in reprimand, but the grin only widened.

"Why would he send for his fancy woman when he has such a pretty, willing wife?" Consuela asked reasonably, and in spite of her embarrassment, Maggie had to agree. Of course, she hadn't been quite so willing at first. Maybe he had sent for Renita because of his promise not to touch Maggie ever again. If that were true, then she had sent him right back to that woman's arms this morning.

"Do not be sad, señora. You can hold him. As long as he comes to your bed. . . ."

"I thought you were the one who told me not to . . . to sleep with him!" Maggie reminded her.

Once again Consuela gave her eloquent shrug and smiled aplogetically. "Sometimes a woman cannot help herself, eh señora?"

No, sometimes she could not help herself, Maggie admitted silently.

"I think he will send her away," Consuela theorized.

"And if he doesn't?" Maggie asked, not really wanting to hear the answer.

"Then you will have to fight for him, no? Will you fight for him, señora?" Consuela's eyes narrowed in speculation as she waited for Maggie's response.

It was a long time coming, but in the end, she knew that there was no other answer. "Yes. Yes, I will."

Chapter XI

In profile, Jack's visitor looked ordinary enough. He was dressed in range clothes, although they were just a cut above what the average cowboy would wear, and riding boots, although they were also a bit too fancy. If the tied-down gun he wore was smooth from too much use, it wasn't something the casual observer would notice. The left side of his face, the side visible to Jack as he entered his office, was actually quite handsome, and it was only when he turned his head to reveal his full face, as he did when Jack entered the room, that he looked truly menacing.

The scar ran from the corner of his mouth up almost to the outside end of his eyebrow, and it had puckered the skin of his face, twisting it into the grotesque parody of a perpetual smile. It ruined what had once been actual beauty, and the contrast between the disfigurement and the shadow of what had been made the deformity all the more horrifying.

Two clear, blue eyes, one of which drooped slightly, met Jack's black ones, and Jack felt the hate radiating from them like a physical blow. Still, he smiled his cool, impersonal smile, and said, "Well, now, look what blew in with the tumbleweeds."

The good side of Paul Crescent's face smiled back, but it was not a friendly smile. "Looks like you really fell into it here, Sinclair. This is quite a setup." He lifted one well-shaped hand to gesture toward the ranch buildings, noting with satisfaction the way Jack stiffened alertly at the sudden movement.

"You came halfway across Texas to pay me compliments, Crescent? I'm truly flattered." Jack's skepticism did not faze his visitor, however.

"I heard you were hiring guns. If the pay's good, I might just sign on," Crescent offered, his face still holding the mocking smile.

Jack shook his head in admiration. The man had nerve; he had to give him credit. "I've got all the men I need," he said. "Besides, I'd feel very uncomfortable having to watch my back all the time."

Anger flared briefly in those bright blue eyes. "I never shot a man in the back, Sinclair, and you know it."

Jack nodded in agreement. "You never had to before," he pointed out mildly.

The anger flared again, this time burning brightly in stark contrast to the grimly smiling lips. "You're pretty handy with a knife, I'll give you that." Crescent unconsciously touched the hideous scar with one fingertip. "But you're no match for me with a gun, and we both know it."

"Do we?" Jack challenged blandly, as if settling the question could not have mattered less to him.

Crescent's face twisted in rage. "If you were packing, we could find out right now, couldn't we?"

Jack gave him a condescending glare. "Luckily for you, I'm not 'packing,'" he said. He had, of course, tucked a derringer into his vest pocket for insurance, but it was hardly the weapon of choice for a fast-draw contest, and so he did not mention it. "Something else we both know is that if you pulled a gun on me, you'd never get off this ranch alive, even if you did happen to beat me to the draw, a possibility I consider highly unlikely."

Black eyes watched Crescent's fingers flex. The man was

315

itching to kill him, but Jack knew that Crescent's unique code of honor would demand that it be a fair fight, and that his common sense would decree it occur in more neutral territory. Still, Jack did not relax, but continued to watch him the way he would watch a coiling snake.

Crescent finally broke the tense silence that had fallen. "I reckon the next thing you'll do is tell me to get off the place. Since that might just make me mad, I'll go ahead and leave of my own free will." He paused, his expression growing smug, and then warned, "Just remember, I'll be around."

"Like I said, I'll watch my back," Jack retorted, enjoying the fury that narrowed Crescent's eyes before he turned on his heel and left.

Out in the parlor, Maggie rushed to the front window to watch him leave. After her conversation with Consuela, she had suddenly remembered the mysterious visitor. When she had questioned the housekeeper and determined that she really did not know who the man was or what he wanted, Maggie had hastily washed and dressed, and then followed Jack to his meeting. At first she had felt like a fool for listening outside the office door, but then she had heard Crescent's threats, and fear had overcome her embarrassment.

Trembling now, she watched the stranger named Crescent descend the front stairs. From the back he did not look at all dangerous, except perhaps for the gun strapped to his hip. He was actually a fine figure of a man, a little short, perhaps, but well made. Then he reached his horse, which was tethered at the hitching rail in front of the house, and when he turned to mount, she saw his face.

She could not help her cry of horror. He could not possibly have heard her, but as if he felt her eyes on him, he lifted his head alertly and found her standing framed in the window. He studied her for a moment, savoring the revulsion in her look. It was an expression he was used to seeing on women's faces, and every time it happened, it served to remind him of the debt he owed Jack Sinclair. It was a debt he would enjoy paying off, in spades.

Maggie knew it was inexcusably rude to stare, but she could not seem to help herself. The man's deformity was fascinating, and now that he was staring back, she felt almost hypnotized, the way a small bird might feel trapped in the deadly gaze of a snake. How long she stood there like that she never knew, but finally, he doffed his hat and ducked his head in a mockery of chivalry and then turned his horse and rode away.

She watched until the horse was a small dot on the road to town, and then suddenly realized that she was no longer alone. She took an extra moment to compose herself before facing Jack, but that moment had not been long enough. He was watching her curiously, warily, and she feared that those black eyes saw much more than she wanted them to. "Who was that man?" she asked. Her voice was much too breathless for her taste, but it was too late to remedy that.

He smiled that awful blank smile. "Just a drifter looking for a job," he said, his voice pleasantly cool.

That coolness sent chills up Maggie's spine. It was the same tone that he had used on Crescent. "Don't lie to me," Maggie snapped. "I heard him threaten to kill you."

Jack clucked disapprovingly. "Listening at doors, Mrs. Sinclair? I would have thought you were above such things."

He still had not answered her question, and she would not be so easily dissuaded. Feeling the same fury that Crescent had felt in the face of Jack's calmness, she stalked over to him and said, "I'm not a child! Stop treating me like one, and tell me who that man is and why he wants to kill you!"

Coming so close had been a mistake. She could smell the Bay Rum and see where he had shaved off every whisker, and her knees grew weak at the memories that assailed her.

His dark eyes studied hers. Hers were almost completely brown now, and so huge in her little face. She was angry, but frightened, too. It was not in him to frighten her more. The

317

mustache tilted. "He's a man I used to know, a long time ago, and he doesn't like me. I doubt very much that he will really try to kill me. He simply wanted to make me sweat a little."

The cold fingers of despair closed around Maggie's heart. He was lying through his teeth, and she knew it. She recognized hate when she saw it, and hate oozed from Crescent's every pore. Had she not once felt the same way about Jack Sinclair? At this moment, she could almost hate him again.

Her eyes closed when he brought one hand up and lightly grazed the knuckles across her cheekbone. Even this simple touch affected her, warming places that would welcome him once more, and she really did hate him for his power over her.

"Tell me, little witch, would you care if he did kill me?" he whispered, his breath warming her lips.

No! Oh, no! her mind screamed. Not again. She could not let him use her again, no matter how much she might want it herself. He had to see her as a person. He had to know that she was not simply a child in a woman's body, a mindless being designed for his pleasure. "At this moment, I could kill you myself," she whispered back, startling him with her honesty.

The hand dropped away, and he stepped back. Her eyes flew open, but she was not quick enough. She had missed the flash of pain that crossed his face. "Ah, yes," he said, his calm mask back in place. "Then you would have achieved your ambition to become a rich widow."

Being a widow of any kind was the last thing Maggie wanted, but her pride would not permit her to admit it. Let him think that though, she decided. She only hoped that her lie had caused him as much pain as his had caused her.

They stood, facing each other for a long time, each still hearing the echo of the other's words, each feeling the pain that the other had inflicted, until Consuela interrupted them. "Breakfast is ready," she announced, pretending not to notice the tension roiling in the room.

Both Jack and Maggie started at her words, but both were grateful for the interruption. Jack took the opportunity to turn his back on his wife and head into the office. "Bring mine on a tray," he told the housekeeper. "I have some work to do."

Maggie knew perfectly well that he could not possibly have any work that was so pressing that he would have to eat while he did it, but still she was glad not to have to face him another moment longer. As it was, she was much too upset to eat, but she followed Consuela into the dining room and allowed her to serve breakfast just the same.

A few mouthfuls of butter bread—she would have to find out how Consuela had contrived to make butter—and a cup of coffee was about all she could stomach, and she left her untouched plate for the sanctuary of her bedroom. Trying not to notice the rumpled bed, she tore off the dress she had so hastily thrown on earlier, and dug out her riding clothes. A good, long ride was exactly what she needed just now. Alone and free, with the wind whipping her face, she would be able to think. What she would think about, however, she had no idea, since it seemed that all the important subjects were also much too painful to consider.

She halfway expected an argument when she ordered a horse saddled, but no one so much as batted an eye. She probably should have been uneasy riding out alone with that man Crescent around, but she had seen him heading toward town, and she had no intention of heading that way herself. Besides, she reasoned, it was Jack he was after and not her. If she had any fears at all, it was for Jack to go riding out alone.

While she waited impatiently for the boy to saddle her horse, Swede rode into the ranch yard. He stopped his horse a polite distance away, dismounted and ambled over. "'Morning, Miz Sinclair," he ventured, warily eyeing the way Maggie was slapping the quirt against her skirt.

Maggie still hadn't quite decided if she should forgive

Swede for his part in Jack's little scheme or not, but she thought it would probably seem juvenile to refuse to even speak to him. "Good morning," she said, her voice lacking a certain warmth.

"Heard you had a visitor up to the house this morning," he said quite matter-of-factly, but Maggie recognized his curiosity. She also recognized a possible source of information.

Squinting in the morning sunshine, she looked up into his homely face. "It was a man with a terrible scar on his face," she said, watching his reaction carefully. She was not disappointed.

The pale blue eyes widened, and she thought the normally red cheeks paled just a bit. "Did he give his name?" Swede was trying to pretend it didn't matter one way or the other whether he had or not, but he just wasn't as good at hiding his feelings as Jack was.

"I think it was Crescent," she said, her eyes never leaving his face.

Swede swore, the words slipping out before he even had time to think, and then he caught himself and started apologizing, but Maggie cut him off. "Who is he, Swede? What does he want?"

She saw the pale eyes grow wary. "He . . . he's a fellow I used to know, long time ago, that's all," he said.

Maggie was just about ready to use her quirt on a two-footed jackass. Why were all men such liars? And so unoriginal? "Who is he really?" she gritted, trying in vain to hold on to her temper.

Nervously, he backed up a step. "What did Mr. Jack say?" he hedged.

Maggie smiled with saccharine sweetness. "He told me the same miserable lies that you're telling me," she informed him.

Swede nodded agreeably. "Reckon that's all he wants you to know, then," he allowed, backing away.

"Swede!" she called, but it was too late. He was hightailing it for the house. He and Jack would put their heads together, and then she'd never learn the truth. When the boy finally led her horse out, she vented her frustration on the unfortunate animal, leaving the ranch yard in a cloud of dust.

Two black eyes watched her go. Jack was unaware of the unconscious way his fingers curled into fists as he silently swore. He had really botched it now. He had been so certain that he could win her, so sure that once he had tamed her body, he would be able to bend her will to his. Now he had fixed things so that she cringed at his very touch, and how it had happened, he had no idea. When she had come to him last night, of her own free will, he had thought . . . well, it was no use going over that. Whatever he had thought, he had been wrong. Now, by her own admission, she hated him, wanted him dead. It was a humbling experience, and humility was a new emotion to Jack Sinclair. His biggest mistake had been falling in love with her, but how could he have prevented it when he never even suspected that such a thing could happen? He had had plenty of experience with women before, women much more worldly and attractive than Maggie, and he had never succumbed. How could he have been caught by such an innocent young girl? Not that it mattered how it had happened. The fact remained that it had happened, and now he must do something about it. But what?

Common sense as well as his wounded pride told him that he should just leave her alone as he had determined to do just this morning. Give her a little time, let her see that he wasn't really as bad as she thought. The flaw in that plan, of course was that she might very well decide he was every bit as bad as she had thought, and worse. On the other hand, he could continue to take advantage of her physical attraction for him, forcing her to give in to her feelings regardless of what her opinion of his character might be. Women were much more sentimental about such things than men, and she very likely would convince herself that she was in love with him to justify what she felt in bed. He smiled grimly at the irony that, at the moment, he was feeling very sentimental himself.

"Boss?"

Jack started at the sound of Swede's voice. He had not even heard the foreman come in.

"I heard that Crescent showed up," he was saying.

Jack waited a moment until he had seen Lee Parker mount up and ride out of the ranch yard in the direction that Maggie had taken, and then he gave Swede a weary smile. "As if we don't have enough problems, eh?"

Swede swore. "You should have killed him when you had the chance."

Bowing to Swede's superior judgment, Jack agreed. "If you'll recall, I thought that I had."

"What'd he have to say?"

"He asked for a job," Jack reported with amusement.

Swede swore again, this time at length. "What in hell'd he do a thing like that for?" he finally asked.

"Well, certainly not because he wanted a job; I think that's safe to assume. Probably, he just wanted to let me know that he's in the neighborhood and more than willing to pay me back for the little present I gave him." Jack walked over to one of the stuffed chairs and lowered himself into it. "Any signs of more squatters?"

Swede shook his head. "None yet, but word is that there's some on the way. That batch we run off the other day is still camped just outside of town. Guess they're waiting for the dust to settle before they come back."

Jack's mustache stretched into a grim smile. "Then I guess it's up to us to make sure it doesn't settle."

Without really planning to, Maggie found herself riding in the direction of the Snider cabin. Today no plume of smoke guided her, and when she crested the last hill she saw nothing but a pile of charred rubble where the shack had once stood. Jack had told her that they had torn it down, but seeing it made the whole thing seem so much more final. What had happened to that poor family? Where would they have gone? Would they try to come back? Maggie knew that she shouldn't care, but she couldn't help it. Besides, worrying about those strangers made it much easier for her to forget about her own problems.

Her own problems. What on earth was she going to do about Jack? Maggie recalled with irritation all the romantic stories she had read in which the lovers got married and lived "happily ever after." Somehow, without even realizing it, she had always looked on marriage as a solution to problems instead of a major source of them. How wrong she had been! Now she was faced with the humiliating situation of being in love with a man who was practically despicable and who thought she was . . . was what? She wasn't certain, but she knew he didn't think highly of her. If he did, he would have confided in her that morning. It hurt very much knowing that he did not respect her or trust her enough to share his problems, and it hurt even more to realize that she had no idea how to go about winning that trust and respect.

Then there was the physical side of their marriage. Somehow she knew that something was not right there, either. While it was wonderful while it was happening, she knew there should be more, a more equal sharing, perhaps. Not just his making love to her, especially when she knew he didn't really love her.

Maggie twisted the small emerald ring that Jack had given her. Her eyes still rested on the ruined cabin, but she was seeing the small hotel room where Jack had placed the ring on her finger. Maybe he did care, just a little. Why else would he have brought the ring? Maybe . . . maybe if she were more warm and loving toward him, she could touch that part of him. It was worth a try, and it was certainly something she had not yet attempted. If only she could keep from losing her

323

temper. Being sweetly charming was something she had practiced at Miss Finley's, but it was not something she had ever been able to sustain for very long. Maybe if she tried it in small doses at first . . .

Unfortunately, by the time she got back to the ranch, she had realized that being nice to Jack would have to wait a few days. It was odd that she hadn't noticed the cramps earlier. Usually she had more warning, but then again, she had had a lot on her mind lately. She only hoped that she could get to her room before anyone noticed the growing stain on her riding skirt. How could she have been so careless?

The house seemed empty, but Consuela came bustling in when she heard the front door slam, and she seemed to know immediately what Maggie's problem was.

"It's my time of the month, Consuela," Maggie explained unnecessarily as Consuela escorted her to her room.

The housekeeper nodded. "I will make you some tea. Is it bad?"

"About average, I guess," Maggie allowed, "but I shouldn't have gone riding."

Consuela crooned something to her in Spanish that she did not catch, and when they were alone in her room she undressed Maggie as if she had been a child, in spite of her protests. The Spanish woman seemed totally unconcerned with Maggie's embarrassment, and she helped her with the necessary preparations and then slipped a nightdress over her head and put her to bed.

"I will make you some tea, and some soup, too, I think," she remarked before gathering up Maggie's soiled clothes and taking them away.

Maggie blinked back the tears of self-pity that stung her eyes. It simply wasn't fair, she decided, as she tried to curl herself into a comfortable position. How could her own body have betrayed her once again? When she didn't want it to surrender to Jack Sinclair, it did just that, and when she had decided that it should, it fixed thing so that it couldn't. It was all so confusing. And frustrating, too. Her only consolation was in knowing that she was not yet pregnant. Whether that pleased her or not, she wasn't certain.

Renita had easily found the office belonging to S. Kincaid. Finding it had been no more difficult than discovering the extremely interesting information that Kincaid was trying to carve up the very land that Jack had invested so much time and energy in acquiring. Renita found herself quite eager indeed to meet an adversary of Jack Sinclair's.

She had been very put out when it had been Swede who delivered the tidy sum that Jack had promised her. She had planned a nasty little speech for her parting scene with Jack and greatly resented being denied the opportunity to deliver it. Now she had calmed down enough to decide that her best revenge would be to join forces with Jack's enemy. Not that she had any desire to remain in this one-horse town for very long, but she did have an urge to see Sinclair taken down a peg or two, and if she could have a hand in it, so much the better.

The office was decidedly dingy, and the boy who greeted her, unprepossessing. "M . . . May I h . . . help you?" he stammered nervously, jumping to his feet the moment she walked in the door. He had obviously never seen anyone quite like her before.

Renita gave him a look calculated to turn his knobby knees to water, and it succeeded admirably. "Is Mr. Kincaid in?" she asked sweetly.

"Y . . . yes, ma'am, he is. I . . . I'll tell him you're here," he offered, hastening toward the rear door.

Renita watched him duck into the other office and announce to his "Uncle Sam" that there was a "lady" here to see him. She could not hear his reply, but the boy quickly reappeared and told her, "He says to come right in."

She cast him a very interested glance as she swept past him

325

into the office, and wondered if he had outgrown wet dreams yet. If not, he'd surely have one tonight.

This office was just as dingy as the other, and smelled of dust and stale tobacco. A curtainless, fly-specked window looked out on the trash-strewn alley and cast a pale square of light on the man seated behind the desk. Sam Kincaid was nothing like she had expected. A massive hulk of a man with a face as plain as dirt and manners to match. He did not even bother to rise when she entered the room, but instead simply studied her through his small, colorless eyes. Renita was used to a much more interested response to her presence, and so her voice was slightly annoyed when she said, "I am Renita McFadden."

He nodded slowly. "Billy said it was a 'lady.' I see you're not." The voice was so soft that for a moment she did not even realize that it had come from him, and it took another moment to grasp the meaning of his words. She stiffened in irritation as eyes that made her think of a pig's eyes roved over her dress in disapproval. Not that the dress was immodest. It was cut quite severely, in fact, covering her from neck to wrists to toes. It was the color that set her apart, the red that was just a shade too bright to be quite respectable. That and the fact that she wore no corset, allowing her charms to sway freely. She had come here today to barter those charms, and the last thing she had expected was to be insulted.

"I am an old friend of Jack Sinclair's," she informed him, letting him see her irritation.

The large head bobbed up and down in comprehension. "I never saw you around before," he said, that quiet voice flat and expressionless.

Renita controlled the urge to stalk out. Perhaps the man was just dull-witted. "I only arrived in town yesterday. Imagine my surprise to find that he had married." Her dark eyes widened in mock surprise, watching him for any reaction.

This time he had one. One pale blond eyebrow lifted slightly. "Does that mean you're not 'friends' anymore?"

She smiled in triumph. Perhaps he was not so dull-witted after all. "Exactly," she said.

"Sit down," he invited, motioning to a nearby chair, and she did. "Just why did you come here, ah, Rita, is it?"

"Renita," she corrected. "I thought we might just join forces, if you're interested."

Kincaid's broad face grew ever so slightly more guarded. "What you got in mind?"

She gave him a knowing smile. "I know Sinclair very well, his strengths as well as his weaknesses. I could be a lot of help to you."

"And what if I don't need your help?" he asked.

Renita let her eyelashes flutter coyly. "Then maybe we could just be 'friends.'" Kincaid was, she decided, a typical male. He did not think he needed her help, would never admit even to himself that he might depend on a woman for anything, but in the end she would control him. It always happened that way, or almost always, she corrected herself, remembering Jack Sinclair.

Kincaid was considering her proposal. He rose from his chair and made his way over to the door that Billy had left slightly ajar. "Let's see what you've got to offer," he said as he pushed it shut.

At first she didn't know what he meant, and when she figured it out, she felt a small rush of excitement. Did he plan to take her right here? Glancing around, she realized that the room didn't even have a sofa. Would he do it right on the floor? The very thought caused a flood of warmth between her thighs. "Should I undress?" she asked, her voice husky with an arousal that for once was unfeigned. The door had no lock. The boy might walk in at any moment and see them.

The large head shook ponderously. "Just take off your drawers." Still he betrayed no emotion, and Renita found that much more exciting than the slobbering eagerness most

327

men displayed.

Slowly, seductively, she stood up and lifted her skirts and petticoats. Pulling the drawstring loose with one swift movement, she let her pantalettes drop to her ankles and then stepped out of them, allowing her skirts to fall back into place again.

The sight seemed not to affect Kincaid in the slightest. He simply nodded his approval, and then stepped over to his desk and cleared a space along the edge. "Right here," he said, patting the cleared spot, and Renita realized he wanted her to sit there.

This was something new, something completely unique in her experience. Men always wanted her naked, always wanted the trappings of seduction, but this man wanted only a stark coupling. With more eagerness than she had ever felt, she went to him and hoisted herself onto the desk.

He made no move to assist her, but waited patiently until she was settled, and then watched calmly as she lifted her skirts and spread herself for him. Only then did he loosen his own clothing, drawing out his manhood and shaking it erect. With no pretense at tenderness, he rammed into her with a swiftness that made her cry out, but not in pain.

It was wonderful. Never had she had it like this and never had she known such pleasure. Clinging to his massive shoulders, she wrapped her legs around him and threw back her head in abandon. His thrusts were slow, almost methodical, his large hands gripping her hips more for support than as any kind of embrace, but she didn't care. She didn't need his affection. She didn't need anything but this.

When the small shudder shook him, he withdrew immediately, first untangling himself from her arms and legs and then tucking away his organ with as little concern as he would have tucked away a handkerchief. Renita sighed in disappointment. She didn't want it to end, but then, she knew there would be other times, many other times. At least, she hoped there would be other times. Now that she noticed, the man wasn't smiling, wasn't looking pleased, wasn't even breathing hard. What was wrong with him?

Kincaid buttoned his pants with the same methodic slowness that he did everything else, while at the same time studying her flushed face. "You'll want a place to live, I guess," he said finally.

It took Renita a full minute to realize that their bargain had been sealed. The smile she gave him was a genuine reflection of how pleased she was. "Of course," she agreed. "I can't stay at that fleabag hotel much longer, especially if you intend to visit me." She was certain that he would not be able to stay away, especially when she had had a chance to show him her many talents. This was only the beginning.

He stepped away so that she could get down from the desk. "I'll tell Billy to find you a place. It might take a couple of days." His voice still hadn't changed, and his face betrayed no hint that what had just happened had affected him in any way.

She shook out her skirts and lifted her face to him. "I'll be waiting," she assured him huskily, an unspoken promise lighting her eyes. Having accomplished what she had come for, she gave him a parting smile and left.

She was halfway to the front door when Kincaid's voice called her. "'Nita!"

Renita turned in irritation. She hated that nickname. "RE-nita," she corrected, and then grinned when she saw that he was holding up the pantalettes she had discarded earlier.

"You forgot these," he told her blandly, oblivious to the strangled sounds that Billy was making.

Renita glanced at the boy, enjoying his scarlet blush and gaping mouth before turning back to Kincaid. "Keep them as a souvenir," she suggested. "You can always buy me another pair." She thought he almost smiled.

*   *   *

329

Jack was furious when he got back to the house and Consuela told him that Maggie was sick. He'd had just about enough of her cowering in her room, and he stormed past the housekeeper, ignoring her protests, and burst into Maggie's room without bothering to knock.

"And what's wrong with you *now,* Mrs. Sinclair?" he demanded sarcastically, but when his dark eyes found her curled up on the bed looking alarmingly fragile in the delicate nightdress, he instantly regretted his hasty words.

Groggy from Consuela's mysterious tea, Maggie had been dozing, and Jack's intrusion had brought her only partially awake. She raised up on one elbow and blinked at him. "Jack?"

He knew immediately that she wasn't faking this time, that she really was sick. The sight of her little face, so pale and drawn, tore at his heart, and he felt a nameless panic sweeping over him. "Maggie! What is it! What's wrong?" Frantically, he raced to the bed, longing to take her in his arms but afraid of hurting her. He settled for sitting down beside her.

Maggie knew she must be dreaming. Why else would she be seeing Jack Sinclair sitting on her bed looking positively concerned? Because she was so certain it was a dream, she did not bother to answer. Instead, she simply stared at him, enjoying this strange Jack who didn't really exist.

When she didn't answer, his terror grew. "Are you hurt?" Then he remembered that she had been riding earlier today. "Was it a riding accident?" He mentally cursed himself. He never should have agreed to let her go riding alone, even if Lee Parker was following her. If Parker had let anything happen to her . . .

Responding to the urgency in his voice, Maggie felt compelled to reply. "No . . . I'm not hurt." She felt a little silly, answering like that when she knew he wasn't really there.

"Why do you not leave her alone? Can you not see she is

330

sick?" Consuela stood in the doorway, her arms crossed in disapproval.

"What's wrong with her? Have you called a doctor?" he demanded, placing one hand on Maggie's forehead to check for fever. He knew it must be serious. The hazel eyes that stared back at him were so dull and lifeless.

"Woman troubles, that is all," Consuela dismissed Jack's concerns.

"Woman troubles?" he repeated blankly, looking in frank puzzlement at his wife for a moment before the truth dawned on him. "Oh," he said in comprehension, and then took a closer look at those strange eyes with their unnaturally large pupils. "What did you give her?" he asked, turning to Consuela in suspicion.

The housekeeper shrugged noncommittally. "Some tea . . ."

Jack scowled. "That same stuff you gave me that time in San Antone?"

Consuela nodded reluctantly, wincing at the explosive curse that followed her admission.

Maggie was having a little trouble following this conversation. It seemed that they were talking very quickly and her mind was only picking up every other word. Jack seemed mad, though, that much was clear, and that made everything seem right. Jack usually was mad about something. She only hoped he wasn't mad at her because she was going to have a terrible time arguing back. If only they would both go away and let her sleep.

To her mild surprise, when he turned back to her, all traces of anger were gone from his face and the hand that stroked wisps of hair from her forehead was exquisitely gentle. "Are you having cramps?" he asked in a voice that matched his touch.

Maggie nodded, slumping back against the pillows, tired of the effort of supporting herself. Some deep little inhibition niggled at her consciousness, warning her that it wasn't proper to admit such a thing to a man, but she ignored it.

"I'll rub your back," he offered, and not waiting for her agreement, he turned her tenderly onto her stomach. As Consuela watched in astonishment, he began to expertly massage the small of Maggie's back, his skilled fingers drew moans of relief from the sufferer. Jack was too engrossed in his task even to notice when the housekeeper slipped discreetly from the room.

As he worked on Maggie's body, Jack thought back to the woman who had taught him this little service. Belle. Odd, he had not thought of her in years. She had been the first woman he had ever made love to. Not that she had been the first woman he had ever had sex with, of course. That had been an embarrassingly brief encounter with his mother's quadroon maid in an upstairs linen closet. That first experience had led to others, with many other women, but until Belle he had never dreamed that sex could be anything more than a quick, blissful release.

He had met her on a riverboat where he had been earning his living as a professional gambler. The life had appealed to his gypsy nature, constantly moving and every moment bringing a new risk. She was the most beautiful woman his immature eyes had ever seen, but then, he had seen her through the eyes of youthful infatuation. Her sophistication and worldly wisdom had intrigued him, and he had been thrilled when she returned his interest. She was, she told him later, on her way to New Orleans where she planned to marry a wealthy, older man, and Jack was to be her last fling.

He became much more than that, however, after their first encounter. She had been appalled at his ignorance and had undertaken to complete his education. It was to be, she told him, a form of missionary work, and Jack was an eager convert. He had quickly mastered the techniques for increasing a woman's pleasure and therefore his own. Giving up poker for the remainder of the trip made his lessons very expensive, but he did not mind.

Belle's rules had seemed strange at the time. She had insisted that they always make love in the dark, and that he leave her room well before dawn. Then he would not see her until midafternoon, when she would appear heavily veiled. Only after sundown would she bare her face. He was too naive in those days to realize that she depended on cosmetics to enhance her fading charms and did not dare show her face in the harsh light of day.

It was only on the last day of the trip when he had begged her to stay with him, to marry him, that she had lifted the veil, letting him see for himself the reason why she could not. She was still beautiful to him, of course, but he was surprised enough to give her the time she needed to get away, and although he searched for her for weeks, he never found her in the busy city of New Orleans.

It was one day during that long trip when he had broken the rules, going to her room in the afternoon when she did not appear at the usual time, that he had learned about "women's problems." He had found Belle suffering from cramps in the shadowy cabin, and she had been compelled to explain this aspect of femininity to the boy. His eagerness to help had led her to teach him just how a woman liked to have her back rubbed, and when she had felt better, she had thanked him by showing him the new French way of making love.

Jack smiled grimly as he imagined Maggie's reaction if he were even to suggest such a thing. Still, it wasn't completely out of the realm of possibility, he decided. When she was in the mood, she was remarkably responsive. Maybe someday, when the time was right, she could be coaxed. . . .

Her regular breathing told him that she was asleep. Damn that Consuela and her herbs. The poor little thing was dead drunk on that concoction. At least she wouldn't have a hangover, though. That much he remembered from his own experience with that "tea."

333

He knew he should leave her now, let her get some rest, but he couldn't resist sitting there just a little longer, studying her while she slept. With no sparks flying, either from passion or from anger, he could do what he rarely had the opportunity to do, simply look at her. She really was incredibly lovely. The russet hair, now tangled into an appealing mess, reminded him of autumn and riding full tilt to the hounds after a little fox that was the same color as that hair. Maggie was like that little fox, always trying to get away from him and fighting like a fury when he finally caught her.

It didn't have to be that way, though, he decided, running a hand over one firm buttock, tracing its shape through the thin material of her nightdress. If they could declare a truce, enjoy a brief period of peace during which they could get to know each other, maybe, just maybe . . . It was certainly something to aim for, and he decided to do just that.

She mumbled a protest when he withdrew his hands and stood up, but although he waited hopefully, she did not wake up. After a few moments, he drew the covers over her tenderly and tiptoed quietly from the room. Soon, Maggie, he promised silently. Soon.

The next day Maggie awoke feeling much better and ravenous. Before she could even think about getting up and dressed, Consuela brought her breakfast on a tray, insisting that she stay in bed for the day. Maggie had never been one to coddle herself, and she really did feel fine, but when Consuela mentioned in passing that Jack had gone out with the men early that morning and wasn't expected back until evening, she decided there really was no reason to get up until then, and so she didn't.

When Jack finally did get back, he found Maggie looking worlds better, sitting by the cold hearth in the front room reading a book. Maggie was a little surprised. She had never seen him dressed in range clothes, and they made him look different somehow, more approachable. Not that she approached him, though. She simply stood up right where

334

she was, her lips trembling into an instinctive smile of greeting, while her fingers fiddled nervously with the book she held. All day she had been trying to remember exactly what had happened when Jack had come to her room the day before. She remembered that he had been there and that something very nice had happened, but what that something was, she had no recollection.

His carefully controlled features gave her no indication, either. Jack returned her polite smile, removing the dusty Stetson he wore and hanging it on a peg by the door. "Are you feeling better?" he asked.

Maggie felt her face growing warm. She simply was not used to discussing such personal matters with a man. "Yes, much better, thank you," she replied.

She looked so fresh and sweet that he had an almost overwhelming urge to march over there and kiss her senseless, but he reminded himself of his determination to be more gentle. Besides, he was filthy, having helped work cattle all day. The thought of her reaction to being mauled by a man who reeked of sweat and horses and who badly needed a shave was enough to restrain his impulse. "That's good," he responded to her reassurance, his mind on other matters entirely. "I think I'll go take a bath before supper." With that he left the room, calling for Consuela to heat him some water.

Maggie was strangely disappointed. She must have truly imagined the gentle Jack who had come to her room last night. There was certainly no trace of him in today's Jack. Nor did she find any trace of him in the immaculate man who shared a meal with her later at the huge dining table. He made polite conversation, said all the right things at the right times, but she could see that his heart was not in it. He didn't even pick a fight with her. How could she be nice to him when he was so coldly courteous? She could not even hope for a passionate interlude during which to show him her change in attitude, at least not for a few more days.

It was early when she excused herself and went to bed, and she really was tired. Tired of enduring the ordeal of civility when what she really wanted was something far more stimulating. It was all very discouraging.

Jack was only too glad to see her go. If he had had to maintain his pose one second longer, he was afraid he might have gone stark raving mad. She had been so cool to him that he wondered if Consuela was still putting something in her tea, in spite of the fact that he had forbidden her to do so. It was so very tempting to scratch that serene exterior of hers and rediscover the real Maggie, that he had found himself weak from the strain of resisting.

Sighing with relief when he heard her bedroom door click shut, he poured himself a generous splash of brandy and downed it in one swallow. Wondering how long it would take to "gentle" her, how long he would have to maintain this pose, depressed him beyond measure, and he indulged in another splash of brandy. It was all very discouraging.

The next morning Maggie truly was fine, much too fine to waste another moment in bed, and so she got up and dressed. She was in a hurry, but not in such a hurry that she did not make certain that she looked her best before heading for the dining room after determining that Jack's room was empty.

Although it was still early, she discovered that he had already left for the day, again, and she consoled herself by helping Consuela with the housework. Thoroughly bored by afternoon, she ordered a horse saddled and took off for a ride, hoping to be able to kill the rest of the afternoon until Jack's return.

As always, she found touring the CMC to be a very therapeutic exercise, and she was able, temporarily at least, to put her problems completely out of her mind. Not wanting to dwell on the problems of the nestors, either, she chose to ride in a completely different direction from that of the Snider cabin. She headed for her old swimming hole instead. It was much too early in the spring for swimming, of

336

course, and she couldn't have indulged in her present condition in any case, but she wanted to make certain it was still there, anyway, for future reference. There was a line cabin nearby, too, where she could stop and have a cup of coffee from the supplies she knew would be stored there. The cabin would be deserted now, since all the hands had been pulled in to work the roundup.

The cabin was not deserted, however. Once again Maggie saw a plume of smoke indicating that the cabin was occupied, long before she actually could see the cabin. When she thought about it, she realized that Jack had probably left a man at the cabin because of the nestor trouble, but when the cabin came into view, she knew her theory was wrong.

The tiny one-man cabin now housed what appeared to be an army of children. They were milling around the yard like so many ants, each carrying out a specific task, but taking the time to run into each other in playful attack, as children will.

Maggie watched, fascinated, for a while until someone in the yard noticed her and yelled a warning. One of the larger ants ducked into the cabin and came out brandishing some sort of rifle. She did not think to be alarmed. Why on earth they should consider her a danger, she had no idea. What she failed to realize was that at this distance, they would not be able to tell she was a woman. She heard the thundering hooves at the same moment she saw the rifle leveled in her direction. The faint pop of the shot was lost in the hurricane of sound as she was rudely jerked from her saddle and thrown unceremoniously over a running horse.

After what seemed an interminable length of time, during which Maggie tried unsuccessfully to regain the breath that had been forced from her body, the horse stopped and a vaguely familiar voice asked anxiously, "You all right, Miz Sinclair?"

Being unable to respond, Maggie refrained from doing so. Her attacker hastily dismounted and then very carefully lifted her from where she had been slung across the horse. Once lying prone on the ground, Maggie was finally able to breathe normally again, and when the blessed air had filled her lungs and restored her to full consciousness, she opened her eyes to see just who it was who had almost cost her her life.

"Lee Parker!" she gasped. He was about the last person she would have considered capable of such an attack.

"You all right, Miz Sinclair?" he asked again, his eyes searching over her for any wounds. "That sodbuster didn't hit you, did he?"

"You're the only one who hit me," Maggie informed him indignantly, struggling up to a sitting position and gingerly feeling her ribs for any damage.

"Sorry I had to be so rough," he said, not looking a bit sorry, "but I couldn't take no chances when I saw that fella take a bead on you. I figured you was out of range, but I didn't want to take a chance."

Maggie suddenly remembered the ant with the rifle. "He actually shot at me?" she asked incredulously.

Lee nodded. "We'd better get out of here, too, in case he comes to see if he hit anything. Mr. Sinclair'll have my hide if anything happens to you."

He had already pulled her to her feet before the import of his words sank in. A sneaking suspicion crept into Maggie's brain. "Lee, how did you happen to be so close by?"

She watched his face turn slightly red and his eyes dart nervously in the direction of the cabin. "I was just riding by," he hedged.

Lee Parker was, Maggie decided, a very unaccomplished liar. "You were following me, weren't you?" she challenged.

"Don't reckon we'll be able to find your horse," he allowed. "We can ride double back to the ranch. You wanna be up front or behind?"

"I don't want to be within ten feet of you, you low-down, sneaking varmint!" Maggie informed him, noting with

338

satisfaction that he truly blushed this time and looked remarkably uncomfortable.

"Please, ma'am, we gotta get out of here," he pleaded.

Maggie treated him to one last, withering glare. "Behind," she said reluctantly. She took a minute to brush herself off while Lee mounted his horse. When he reached down a hand to her, she put her foot in the stirrup he had freed for her and swung up behind him. Out of necessity, she wrapped her arms around his waist, and he spurred the animal into motion.

The ride back to the ranch was accomplished for the most part in silence, except when Maggie asked the one question she thought would disturb Parker most. "Does Consuela know that you follow me on my rides?"

She felt him stiffen. "I never told her," he said, but from his tone, she knew that that didn't necessarily mean that she didn't know. Consuela seemed to know everything that went on at the ranch, and more than likely, she had figured this out, too. What irritated Maggie was that if the housekeeper had known, she had not told her. Maggie should have known that Jack had something up his sleeve when he had agreed so readily to allow her to ride alone.

When they arrived at the ranch, they discovered the place in an uproar, because Maggie's riderless horse had preceded them by about five minutes. The poor animal had been terrified by Lee's rescue and had hightailed it back to the safety of the barn. Fortunately, Jack had not had time to organize a search party yet. He did, however, look almost mad enough to chew nails by the time he reached up to pluck Maggie from the back of Parker's horse.

"What happened?" he inquired tersely, his eyes moving over Maggie checking for damage the same way Parker's had earlier.

Maggie opened her mouth to reply, but apparently Lee was anxious to get in the first word, and he beat her to it. "There's some squatters over at the South Creek Line Camp.

Miz Sinclair rode up to look them over, and they took a pot shot at her before I could get her out of the way."

Jack muttered something that sounded like, "Dear God," before pulling Maggie into his arms for a swift, bone-crushing embrace. She knew it was a little late, but she suddenly felt the reaction from her close call set in and her arms automatically went around Jack's waist.

The voices questioning Parker for details were only muddled sounds to her until she heard Jack's harsh command. "Swede, get rid of those people, and this time don't be too nice about it."

Swede eagerly agreed, and Maggie heard the murmured approval of the rest of the men as they went for their horses. "Jack . . ." she started to protest, but he was busy scooping her up into his arms so he could carry her back to the house.

"I don't need to be carried!" she insisted, grateful anyway for not having to make the long trek.

"Humor me," he grated, not daring even to look at her face so close to his. For those few, awful moments when he thought he had lost her, he had understood, for the first time, the despair that had driven his brother to suicide. That terror, followed so closely by the relief of discovering she was all right, had broken through the careful shell of reserve that usually protected his emotions, and he felt precariously close to disgracing himself.

Once inside the house, he deposited her on the settee and went straight for the liquor cabinet. This time, however, the brandy he poured was not for himself. He carried it back to Maggie. "Drink this," he ordered gruffly, thrusting the snifter into her hands.

Without thinking, Maggie obeyed. The awful stuff scorched its way down to her stomach, and she came up gasping and choking. "Are you trying to kill me?" she demanded between coughs, and then noticed that the hand that relieved her of the brandy glass was trembling. "Drink it yourself. You look like you need it worse than I do, anyway," she added.

He did, too. Under the touch of sunburn that he had acquired the past few days, he looked remarkably pale, and the black eyes that watched her held a sad, almost tortured look. Maggie watched, fascinated, as he did as she had commanded and downed the brandy, pausing first to turn the glass so that his lips touched the place where hers had rested.

Then, as if he had suddenly remembered himself, he slammed the glass to the table with a force that threatened to shatter it and bellowed, "What in the hell did you think you were doing, riding into a squatter's camp like that?"

Maggie blinked at the sudden mood swing, but she recovered quickly. "I didn't 'ride into' the camp at all! I was only close enough to see what they were doing, that's all. Even Lee said I was well out of rifle range." At the skepticism she saw reflected in those dark eyes, she amended, "Well, he said he *thought* I was. . . ." Loath to be on the defensive, she decided to attack. "And what do you mean by having Lee Parker follow me everywhere I go? I'm not a child!" That still rankled, and her face burned from the shame of it.

Jack made an exasperated sound. "You've got a nerve asking me that after what just happened!"

Maggie had to agree, but still . . . "You could have told me I was being escorted," she suggested sarcastically.

This time Jack blinked in surprise, and then both black eyebrows rose in amusement. "So you could give him the slip, Mrs. Sinclair?" he inquired, his mustache tilting in that way that made Maggie's hackles rise. "As I recall, I suggested that you might not be safe riding alone and should take an escort. You refused my suggestion. Since I knew perfectly well that if I forbade you to ride at all you would delight in sneaking out at every opportunity, I decided a small compromise was in order. Lee Parker was that compromise."

Maggie could only fume silently at his high-handedness,

341

especially now that there was proof his precautions were necessary. It was just so difficult to believe that she could be in any serious danger. Suddenly, she felt very weary. "I . . . I think I'll go to my room now," she said, swinging her feet to the floor, but when she rose, the whole room seemed to tip precariously. Jack caught the hand she threw out to catch herself, and in the next instant he had swept her up in his arms again and was carrying her to her room. "I don't need to be carried," she protested once again, but this time the protest was so feeble that it made Jack smile, and he didn't even bother to reply.

He set her on her bed and proceeded to pull off her riding boots, commenting to no one in particular that he'd never met anyone who could get drunk on one swallow of brandy.

"I am not drunk!" she said indignantly as he laid her back against the pillows.

"No," he agreed amiably. "It's probably just the shock setting in." He removed the hat that still hung down her back from the chin strap, and started to unbutton her shirt.

"Stop that!" she ordered, slapping his hands away. "I didn't have *that* much of a shock. I can still undress myself."

"All right," he said, standing back and crossing his arms expectantly, "go ahead."

Maggie's roar of outrage brought her upright as she reached for a pillow and flung it at his insolent face.

He ducked it easily and grinned in unabashed delight. God, he loved her. He didn't really care if they never did anything but fight for the next fifty years, as long as she was there, with him. In one swift lunge, he grasped her face in both his hands and planted a resounding kiss on her furious lips. "I'm glad you're not dead, Mrs. Sinclair," he said, and then he was gone.

Maggie stared after him for a long time before bringing trembling fingers up to touch the lips that he had kissed. She was very glad that she was not dead, too.

Chapter XII

Running off the newest bunch of nestors was a lot more exciting than running off the first bunch had been. They put up a fight, or at least the father fired off a few shots before his wife's hysterical screams had convinced him to surrender before he got himself killed.

The boys had been pretty mad about his taking a shot at Mrs. Sinclair and they roughed him up a bit until he had convinced them that he hadn't had any idea he was firing at a woman. Kincaid had warned him to be ready for trouble, and he had been, that was all there was to it.

Still, the boys had taken great pleasure in rather carelessly loading the family's meager household belongings into their wagon and hurrahing them on their way. Judging from the way the kids were howling, Swede and the others were pretty sure they'd seen the last of these folks.

By midmorning of the next day Maggie had had just about all she could stand of being treated as if she were made of spun glass. Everyone was so solicitous and kept tiptoeing around the house, until she was ready to scream. Finally, unable to stand another moment, she stormed into Jack's office where he was pretending to work when she knew perfectly well he was only hanging around to keep an eye on her.

"Do you suppose, if you sent along three or four men as an armed guard, it would be all right if I went to town to visit Abby Wheeler?" she asked sweetly.

Jack's mustache twitched suspiciously, but he managed to keep from actually smiling. "I don't see why not," he decided after a moment's thought. "The road to town is relatively safe, however, and I doubt you'll need more than one armed guard. Why don't you ask Swede to take you in the buggy?" She would never know what a concession he had just made her. He really wanted to go along himself, but felt reasonably certain that she would balk at such a proposal. Besides, he had admitted to himself grudgingly, Swede probably wanted to see Mrs. Wheeler just as much as, if not more than, Maggie did.

On the way into town, Maggie inquired about what had happened when Swede had gone to run off the nestors.

"Nothing much," he replied. "We run 'em off, that's all."

"Was there any shooting?" she asked, fearing that the men might have taken revenge on her behalf.

"He fired some shots. Didn't hit anything, though. We didn't fire back. Too many kids in the house."

Somewhat relieved, Maggie settled back to enjoy the ride.

Abby was thrilled to see them both, although she was much more subdued in her greeting to Swede than she had been with Maggie. The foreman had blushed his usual scarlet and asked if she had any jobs he could do. Maggie had stared in wonder when Abby had put him to work on a broken back step. Every cowboy she had ever known would have preferred death to such a menial task. Swede, Maggie decided, must be hopelessly in love.

Since it was almost noon, Maggie helped Abby get dinner on the table for the boarders and Swede, and when they had all eaten and gone, the two women cleared up the mess and started on the dishes.

"I feel mighty poor, asking a guest to help with the dishes," Abby lamented.

"You didn't ask, I volunteered," Maggie pointed out. "Besides, it gives us more time to visit if I help." Maggie told her all about her adventure with the nestors, fully enjoying her friend's shocked response.

"Swede run them off, you say?" Abby asked when she had finished the tale.

"Yes, he and the other men."

Abby shook her head sadly. "He hates that, I know. He can't stand putting those poor folks out of their homes, even if they got no right to be there in the first place."

Maggie had gotten the same impression from the foreman. "Why does he do it, then? He doesn't have to work for Jack Sinclair. He could go anywhere, get a job anywhere."

"He'll never leave Mr. Sinclair. Not as long as he thinks Mr. Sinclair needs him," Abby predicted.

"Why?" Maggie asked, her curiosity thoroughly aroused. She had been much too busy to consider it before, but now she began to recall the full extent of Swede's loyalty to Jack, the way he had betrayed her father to serve Sinclair, the way he had helped in her forced marriage, and now the way he stayed on, doing a dirty job that he hated.

Abby cast Maggie a thoughtful look, as if she were weighing just how much it would be safe to tell her. "He owes Mr. Sinclair a debt. Not a money debt, nothing like that. It's more a debt of honor, and he'll stay on until he thinks it's paid off."

This was getting better by the minute. "What on earth could Jack have ever done for Swede that would inspire such loyalty?" Maggie asked, truly mystified.

"That's something you'll have to ask one of them," Abby said, effectively closing the subject. "And just how are you enjoying married life?" she inquired, the teasing glint in her blue eyes betraying the fact that she already had a pretty good idea of the answer.

Maggie grimaced. "It seems like all we ever do is fight,"

she lamented, "even when I make up my mind that we won't. Does that change after you've been married a while?" Maggie's question had been innocent enough, and so she was startled to see the way Abby's friendly eyes suddenly turned cold.

"Sometimes," she mumbled before concentrating her attention back on the dishes.

Only then did Maggie recall the things that had been said about Abby's dead husband. Jack had said that he'd gotten what he deserved, but no one had ever told her what he'd done to deserve it.

"Was your marriage very bad?" she asked tentatively, hoping against hope that Abby would be willing to tell her.

At first she feared that she would not. The larger woman hunched up her shoulders defensively for just an instant before forcing herself to relax. "Not at first," she admitted. "Wheeler was a dreamer, and at first I believed all his big talk. I was young then, and didn't know any better, and anything seemed possible. It was only after our first farm failed when things started getting bad. He moved me to a new place and we started over. What I didn't know was that he'd never be a success, no matter where we moved to, and we moved to a lot of places. One day I stood up to him, told him what I thought, and he hit me. Just like that."

Maggie's little cry of anguish only stopped her narrative for a moment. "He was all sorry, promised he'd never do it again, but he did, of course. I'd fight back sometimes, but that only made it worse."

"Why didn't you leave him?" Maggie demanded, her sense of outrage thoroughly aroused.

Abby gave a mirthless little laugh. "And do what? I didn't have any family left. I could either stay with Wheeler or go to work in a saloon . . . or worse. There's not much a runaway wife can do, you know."

Maggie did know. She could recall only too clearly the choices Jack had given her when he demanded she marry

346

him. For the first time she began to realize the marvelous thing her father had done for Abby by setting her up in a respectable business. Had he known? Had he done it simply out of guilt for the fact that one of his men had killed her husband or had he also known how she had suffered at the hands of that awful man? "Did my father know about . . . how he treated you?"

"He knew," Abby said, scrubbing with unnecessary force at a pot. "I didn't have to tell him, either. When he and Swede came to tell me about Wheeler, they could see for themselves. He'd beat me up that day, before he went into town looking for more trouble. My arm was even broke, although I didn't know it then. I was packing, though, broken arm and all. I couldn't stay with him anymore, not another day," she told Maggie proudly.

Maggie nodded her understanding and admiration. Suddenly her problems with Jack seemed insignificant. "I guess you were glad when he died, then," she said.

"I hope I'm not that mean," Abby replied as she finished off the last pot and emptied the dishwater into the slop jar. "I was sorry for him but glad for me. I guess that's the only way I could feel."

How had she felt toward the man responsible, Cal Colson? And how had she felt toward the man who had done the actual killing, whoever that had been? "You never did say, which one of my father's men was it who killed your husband?" Maggie tried to guess while she waited for the answer.

Abby dried her hands on her apron, taking much longer than necessary to perform the task. When she looked up, her blue eyes held a guarded expression that Maggie had never seen. "Swede," she said.

She could not have said anything that would have shocked Maggie more. Her jaw dropped and her hazel eyes grew wide. *Swede?* Calm, silent Swede? The same man who had just fixed Abby's broken steps? "Then you don't hate him, do

347

you? You said yourself it wasn't his fault," she said, remembering their very first conversation when Abby had defended the man responsible without mentioning his name.

"No, I don't hate him," Abby assured her in a voice tight with suppressed emotion. "But now you understand why he comes here all the time and helps out around the place. He don't have any feelings for me, not the way you thought. He just feels guilty, that's all, and responsible."

Maggie knew that wasn't true. She had seen the way Swede blushed when Abby spoke to him. True, he blushed when any woman spoke to him, but with Abby it was different, somehow. And then there was the way his eyes had followed her when she had walked away. No, Maggie had not been mistaken, and if Abby's defensive manner was any indication, she had not been mistaken about her friend's feelings, either. Her small chin lifted in determination. She might not be able to set things right between herself and Jack, but she would do everything in her power to see that these two nice people got together.

Some self-protective instinct warned Abby of her intention, however, and she managed to sidetrack Maggie by asking, "You in a family way yet?"

That effectively banished all matchmaking thoughts from her brain, and for the rest of the afternoon Abby managed to keep the subject clear of dangerous territory. Only when Swede rapped on the door to tell her it was time to go did Maggie remember her intentions. Oh, well, she decided, she would go to work on Swede instead.

As the buggy jolted along, Maggie tried to think of a tactful way to broach the subject, and while she did, she recalled something else that Abby had told her about Swede. That was a subject that she had no trouble introducing. "Abby said that you and Jack are old friends," she began.

Swede cast her a wary look and nodded. That was all the encouragement she needed. "She also said that you owe him a debt, a debt of honor, she called it. Is that true?"

Swede shifted uncomfortably on the buggy seat. "Sort of," he hedged.

This was probably going to take all day, she decided. "Oh, Swede, why do you keep on working for him when you hate the things he makes you do? I know how you feel about running off those nestors, forcing all those poor little children out of their homes. Why do you do it?" She managed to sound exasperated and disappointed at the same time.

"I owe him, that's all," was Swede's stiff reply.

Maggie gave a disbelieving snort. "What could Jack Sinclair possibly have done to inspire such loyalty?" she scoffed.

Swede did not answer right away, and she could almost see the inner struggle as he tried to decide whether or not to tell her. Finally, he shrugged in defeat. "I have a sister," he began.

Suddenly, Maggie wasn't at all sure she wanted to hear the story after all, but it was too late. "She took up with this fella. He was a no-good son of a . . . sorry, Miz Sinclair. He was a no-good bum, but she was just a kid, barely sixteen and didn't know any better. She run off with him."

Maggie tried to tell herself that it couldn't have been Jack. Swede would have murdered a man who had done such a thing, not pledged blind loyalty to him. He went on, "After a few months, he left her. She was gonna have a baby, and she was too ashamed to come home or let anybody know what happened to her, so she took a job in a saloon. That's where Jack found her. He took her in."

Now Maggie knew she did not want to hear the rest of the story. Something that felt remarkably like jealousy was choking her, but she managed to mumble a tortured, "Oh."

Swede's head jerked up at the sound and he studied her face a moment in amazement. "Oh, no, ma'am. It wasn't like that," he assured her. "He just took her in, gave her a place to stay. Made her send for me to take her home." Maggie knew an incredible sense of relief, although she had a very difficult time imagining Jack in the role of saintly protector, especially when she recalled the threats he had made to force her into marriage.

"That's not all, either," Swede was saying. He had warmed to his topic and that warmth had made him uncharacteristically talkative. "He wouldn't even let me take care of the man. Did it himself. Said my sister loved him, and it'd always be between us if I did it, so he took care of it. Challenged him right to his face and called him every name in the book until he had to fight. Didn't kill him, though. He thought he had, but somehow he pulled through. Only he was left with a scar so bad no other woman would ever look at him."

Maggie knew a chilling terror as the meaning of those words sank in. "That man," she whispered. "The one with the scar who came to the house. That was him, wasn't it? What was his name? Crescent?"

Swede did not reply, but the look he gave her was full of despair, and she knew that she was right. No wonder that man hated Jack so. Those threats he had made were not idle ones, either. He would kill Jack if he got the chance, and she was fairly certain that he would make the chance. Oh, dear God, what would she do?

"Miz Sinclair?" Swede asked timidly, appalled at what he had told her without meaning to. "You won't tell Jack I told you, will you? He didn't want you to know."

No, of course not, Maggie replied mentally. That would be just like him, protecting her from the ugly truth as if she did not have the strength to face it. "I won't tell him, Swede," she promised sadly. After a long time she asked, "Whatever happened to your sister?"

"She had the baby, a little girl. She's married now, to a fine man. They got a farm back in East Texas, doing real well."

Maggie was glad to hear that, and then she remembered something else she had wanted to discuss with Swede.

Deciding it would take her mind off Crescent, she plunged right in. "You like Mrs. Wheeler a lot, don't you?"

Swede's face turned the color of beets, red but with a lot of purple thrown in. "Everybody likes Mrs. Wheeler," he muttered.

"Not everybody would fix her steps, though," Maggie pointed out. She waited in vain for a response. "Swede," she finally said in exasperation, "if you like her, you should do something about it!"

The look he gave her was so full of agony that she almost gasped. "Like what?" he rasped.

Speechless for a moment, Maggie at last found her voice. "Court her, marry her, the usual things, what else?"

"I killed her husband. You think she'd ever even *look* at me?" he asked. "Besides, what would folks say?"

"Who cares what folks say," Maggie declared, forgetting for the moment how much she usually did care. "The important thing is what Abby thinks, and you'd be mighty surprised about that!"

Swede shook his head, his lips whitening as he squeezed them together stubbornly. "I ain't gonna add to her troubles by making a fool of myself," he insisted, and although Maggie tried every argument she knew, he would not be moved.

Jack felt like a consummate fool watching the road for the sight of the buggy returning, but he could not seem to help himself. He knew that Maggie was perfectly safe with Swede along, but the effects of yesterday's panic had not yet worn off, and it would be a long time before he felt easy when she was out of his sight. When the buggy did finally appear, he breathed a sigh of relief, and resisted the urge to rush out to meet it. It was bad enough he felt the way he did; he didn't have to let the whole world know it.

Swede pulled the buggy up to the front steps to let Maggie

out, and Jack deigned to go down and help her. It only took one look at Maggie's fiery expression and Swede's set jaw to determine that something was very wrong. "Have you two been arguing?" he asked in amazement as he assisted Maggie's descent.

Swede, of course, did not reply, but Maggie lifted her chin and gave Jack a withering look, suddenly remembering Crescent and all the secrets that went with him. "Men," she huffed. "You're all a bunch of idiots!" With that she stomped up the stairs and into the house, leaving a very puzzled Jack in her wake.

When Jack turned to Swede for an explanation, all he got was a muttered, "Damn fool women," before the foreman slapped the horse into motion and drove away.

Well, Jack surmised gratefully, at least he wasn't the only one around here who was losing his mind.

At supper Jack asked Maggie if she had had a pleasant visit. She was still a little angry over his failure to confide in her, so at first her replies to his inquiries were terse, but then she remembered a tidbit of gossip that Abby had shared with her which she thought Jack might find extremely interesting. In any case, it would be educational to see his reaction to the news.

"Remember that lady we saw at the hotel, the one who came to your room that time?" she asked, proud of how casual she sounded and buttering a biscuit to show how unconcerned she was.

When she glanced up at Jack, his face was expressionless, as she had known it would be. "Yes," he agreed cautiously.

"It seems that she's settled in Bitterroot," she told him, gratified to discover that the news came as a complete shock.

"Is she rooming with Abby?" he asked, his disbelief evident.

"Oh, no!" Maggie said, properly scandalized. "You see, she isn't really a lady at all, but then, you probably knew that already." Maggie watched him, her eyes wide with innocence.

"What makes you say that?" he inquired cautiously.

"Oh, because you're a man," she said offhandedly. "Men can always tell things like that, can't they?"

"Then where *is* she staying?" he asked, trying to pretend that it did not matter in the least when he had already decided to go there at the first opportunity and murder the woman. He should have had the foresight to see her out of town after paying her off, but then, he'd had no idea that she would ever spend an unnecessary minute in a town as small as Bitterroot.

"In some awful little shack on the edge of town, according to Abby. Some man is keeping her there," she added in a shocked whisper. Maggie wished she could have known if the flush that rose up Jack's neck was caused by jealousy or by some other emotion.

He shouldn't have been surprised, he knew. A woman like Renita wouldn't be long without a protector, but who on earth had she found in Bitterroot to serve the purpose? Unless . . . an uncomfortable premonition crawled up the back of his neck. "Did Abby say who he was?"

"Well," Maggie drawled, dragging out the moment as long as possible, fully aware of its dramatic possibilities. "No one knows for sure, but they say it's . . . Kincaid."

Maggie watched one hand close tightly into a fist, the only outward manifestation of his rage. She squelched the urge to demand to know why he was so angry. He might very well tell her, and it might be something she did not want to hear. Her own hands closed into fists, but she kept them safely out of sight in her lap.

Kincaid. He should have known, should even have predicted it. It was just the sort of gesture Renita would love making, although what she saw in the hulking land swindler was anybody's guess. Maybe she didn't see anything in him.

353

Maybe she didn't have to. She was an accomplished actress and was perfectly capable of faking passion when the need arose. He could only wonder if she had ever felt any at all. Seeing Maggie's curious stare, he excused himself, not wanting her to guess how her news had affected him. He certainly did not feel like answering any embarrassing questions just now, especially since the answers would destroy any hope he had of building a relationship with his wife.

Maggie found him later, pacing in the front room and nursing a snifter of peach brandy. She had learned from Consuela that the peach brandy came from an old friend of Jack's who lived in Georgia and that it was his favorite drink. Maggie only knew that it tasted much better on Jack's lips than it did straight from the glass. She seated herself in a comfortable chair after moving a lamp to the table next to it, and took up her embroidery.

Maggie hated embroidery, and she really wasn't very good at it, but this was a project that she had determined to do regardless of her personal preferences. She needed some way to get his attention, to make peace with him, and to let him know that she was ready to start their marriage on a more normal course. Threading her needle, she pretended to ignore Jack, but she was aware of his every move, sensing his eyes on her. At last he lowered himself into the chair across from hers and lit up a cigar.

Jack was tired of looking at the back of her neck. It was just too tempting the way it curved down into her dress, and he was having a difficult time resisting the urge to plant a kiss on that vulnerable spot. "What are you working on?" he asked, no trace of the strain he felt in his voice.

Inhaling the tangy smoke from the cigar, Maggie glanced up briefly before replying, "A sampler." He really was the handsomest man she had ever laid eyes on. Now that she noticed, he would have made a perfect "rake," the type of man who was always the hero in those old novels the girls at

354

Miss Finley's had read in secret.

"Oh," he said, not really caring. He watched in fascination as her fingers pushed and pulled the needle through the cloth, the metal flashing in the lamplight. She had such lovely hands, so small and delicate. And soft. He could remember only too well just how soft they really were, and how they felt stroking over his body. He took another puff of the cigar and then nervously flicked the ash into the hearth.

"That man Crescent, what happened to his face?" she asked, her eyes never leaving her work. She did not dare look up for fear that Jack would read her concern in her eyes. The needle flashed once more as it darted in and out.

Her voice was so mild that he answered without thinking, his mind elsewhere. "He got cut in a fight," he said. Only when he saw her breasts rise and heard her sudden intake of breath did he realize what was happening.

Maggie lifted her head, her eyes large in her small face. "You did it, didn't you? You cut him with a knife?" she asked. It was part question, part accusation.

He briefly considered denying it, but then decided it was ridiculous to continue the charade. "Yes," he said, volunteering nothing more.

Her eyes closed over the vision of Jack locked in a life-and-death struggle with the knife-wielding Crescent. It was so difficult to picture the impassive Jack Sinclair in such a situation, and yet she had to admit that he had oftentimes been far less than impassive with her. Still . . . "You?" she asked incredulously, her eyes flying open again. "You in a knife fight?"

Jack took a puff of his cigar, idly swirling the brandy in the glass. "I used to be quite good, as a matter of fact," he boasted lightly. The mustache tilted in amusement at her disbelief. He had been, too, and it was no wonder. He had been taught by a master. The old mountain man with whom he had wintered one year in the wilds of Kentucky had been a cousin of Jim Bowie and had drilled him in the fine art of handling a Bowie knife. It had not been too difficult to learn, either. Years of fencing instructions had given him the timing and coordination. The old man had feared that Jack's genteel upbringing might have squelched his killer instinct, but that fear had proven groundless. The knife was not his weapon of choice, of course, but in Crescent's case it had been expedient.

Maggie let this pass, deciding she did not really want to know this side of Jack. "Were you fighting over a woman?" She held her breath, waiting for the answer. Would he tell her the sad story of Crescent's sister and how he had helped her? Would he take the opportunity to appear a hero in her eyes? She hoped so. It would make things so much easier. . . .

Jack considered his answer. He could tell her the truth, of course, make himself out to be the knight in shining armor, but would she even believe it? Probably not. She would probably think it was just a ploy to win her admiration and, he had to admit, it would be. Hell, no, he wouldn't tell her the truth. If she couldn't love him for himself, he'd be damned if he'd use any juvenile tricks to impress her. After a long pause, he said, "Yes, it was over a woman." The mustache had settled back into a straight line, all amusement gone from his face.

She waited, watching as he raised the brandy to his lips and sipped. That was all. He wasn't going to tell her any more. He was going to let her think the worst. Disappointed, she lowered her eyes to her work again, concentrating on carefully outlining the letter J in dark blue floss, the scent of cigar smoke swirling around her. Still, now that she thought about it, she realized that it just wouldn't be like him to tell her the true story. It made him look like such a hero, and somehow she knew that he would cringe at such a description. No, he would never cast himself in such a role, not even to impress her. Especially not to impress her, she corrected. A secret smile curved her lips as she started outlining the letter A.

Jack saw the smile and wondered what was going on inside that pretty little head. Taking another sip of brandy, he watched her over the rim of the glass, loving the way her hands moved so competently over the cloth, the way wisps of hair that had escaped her careful coiffure curled around her face, the way the lamplight turned that hair to molten copper.

Maggie kept on smiling. He was watching her. If he watched her long enough, he was bound to notice, and when he did . . . would he be pleased or angry? Either way, it didn't matter, so long as he touched her. She wouldn't have believed it possible to yearn so for a human touch, but she found herself weakening at the mere thought of it. He would touch her and then he would kiss her and then . . . Anticipation shivered over her, and she jammed the needle into the letter C.

In and out, in and out. He watched the needle disappear and reappear, mesmerized by its progress. Lifting his eyes, he saw the tip of her pink tongue flicker over her lips and then withdraw, and he imagined what it would be like to flick his own tongue over those lips. The thought forced up a low growl, which he covered by clearing his throat.

Maggie glanced up expectantly. Now? Had he noticed yet? No, not yet, she realized as she watched him take one last puff on his cigar and toss the butt into the hearth. Then she lowered her eyes again, waiting.

Jack swirled the brandy one last time and drained the glass. Really, he was worse than a schoolboy gawking at his first girl, he told himself as he set the shifter on a side table. If he wanted her, there was no reason on God's earth why he shouldn't take her. She was his wife, after all. Enough days had passed, or had they? He couldn't quite remember, except to know that it had been far too long. Besides, if *he* didn't mind, why should she? "Maggie . . ." he began, rising impatiently to his feet, but then he stopped. What was he going to say, anyway? That it was time to go to bed? It was still much too early unless one planned to spend the better part of the evening making love. He did plan to do that, of course, but what would she say if he proposed it to her? What if she refused? Should he force her, or seduce her, or accept her refusal?

Maggie waited patiently for him to say whatever it was that he had planned to say, enjoying the relatively rare sight of Jack Sinclair at a loss for words. What was he waiting for, anyway? Didn't he know that no matter what happened, she'd eventually give in anyway? Didn't he know that she wanted him as much as he wanted her?

Apparently not. Jack forced his eyes away from her face. She was looking up at him so expectantly, he just couldn't bring himself to order her to bed. He would try gentle persuasion instead. "Maggie," he began again, his voice more controlled, more cajoling, and then something in her lap caught his eye, something he had not noticed before. The first three letters in his name.

He'd seen it! She knew he had by the way his dark eyes narrowed. In one swift movement he crossed the narrow space between them and snatched the sampler from her. His long fingers spread the cloth in an attempt to read the letters caught in the embroidery hoop. It was not a difficult task and required only a modicum of imagination to fill in the covered letters.

Jack could hardly believe his eyes. There, right in his very hands, was a sampler bearing his and Maggie's names surrounded by a flowered border. Their wedding date was penciled in, obviously the next item to be outlined. It was a wedding sampler. He'd seen dozens of them in his lifetime, each one hanging in an honored place in the household, each one commemorating a joyous event in the life of that particular home. But what about this one? Its purpose could not possibly be the same as all those others. No, she was up to something, but what was it? "What is this?" he asked suspiciously, braced for the sarcastic answer he was certain would follow.

Maggie swallowed nervously. She had expected anything but this cold skepticism. "It's a sampler," she repeated, her voice barely a whisper. "To commemorate our wedding." There, she'd said it. His anger she could handle, but if he laughed . . . Maggie swallowed once again, hoping against hope that she would not cry.

Jack nodded, his black eyes still studying the cloth he held. It wasn't exactly the best work he had ever seen, but there was certainly a lot of it. She had spent a long time on those flowers. Could it be . . . ? He stopped himself. He wasn't ready to think about that possibility yet. Slowly, reverently, he laid the piece on the table by the lamp. Only then did he allow himself to look at her. She was frightened. God, he hated it when she was scared of him. "I can think of a better way to commemorate our marriage," he told her quietly, reaching out a hand to her.

Blinking in usrprise, she hesitated only another second before placing her hand in his. He was smiling now, a real smile and not that teasing smirk he usually gave her. He was pleased. She smiled back as he drew her to her feet and into his arms. At last.

His kiss blotted out the light, and in that swirling darkness she savored the taste of peach brandy and cigars. She parted her lips to receive him, her own tongue meeting his in a sweet, moist union. Her body molded to his as his arms tightened around her, and she knew that this, above all other places on earth, was where she most wanted to be.

Without breaking the kiss, he somehow managed to scoop her up and start for the bedroom. Wrapping her arms around his neck, she lifted her mouth just far enough from his to tease, "I don't need to be carried."

"Humor me," he taunted back, nuzzling her neck hungrily. They were in her room now, and he kicked the door shut behind them before setting her carefully on her feet.

For a long time they just stood there kissing, mouth exploring mouth, tasting, sampling, while hands stroked and caressed and bodies yearned. Then, as if by mutual consent, they began to undress each other. Each garment was discarded with progressively more impatience as eager hands fumbled with buttons and hooks and ties, until they were both almost in a frenzy. When they were at last free of restraint, they tumbled together onto the bed in a tangle of arms and legs.

Maggie arched against him, unable to get quite close enough to his warmth, and he helped by locking his arms around her in an embrace that threatened to crush her but stopped just short of it. Their breath came in ragged gasps that mingled in the tiny space that separated them, tasting of peach brandy and desire.

Jack moved, trailing kisses down her throat, but Maggie pushed him away, forcing him onto his back so that she could treat him to the tender torment he had planned for her. "Oh, God, Maggie," he moaned when he realized her intent, sinking back into the feather mattress in surrender as her sweet mouth tasted the skin of his neck and then moved on to sample his shoulder.

Hardly able to believe her boldness, Maggie accepted his surrender, glorying in her newfound power. Hoping that she could give him as much pleasure as he had given her, she imitated his techniques, using lips and teeth and tongue to play over his chest. She knew she had succeeded when she found a flat, puckered nipple buried in the mat of dark hair, and heard his groan of pleasure. Her hands, too, moved restlessly over him, tracing muscle and sinew, celebrating the differences between them.

She felt his whole body stiffen when her fingers strayed into new territory, and she knew a moment's hesitation, wishing she could see his face. But the room was too dark. Did she dare?

She dared, and when her name rumbled from his chest,

she had her reward. Tentatively, she stroked the taper of his manhood, savoring this evidence of his desire, of her power. Now, in this one moment, he was hers, completely. Impulsively, she placed a kiss on the satiny flesh.

That was all he could stand. Unable to bear another moment of her sweet torture, he forced her away, turning her until she lay beneath him. Now she was at his mercy, and he showed her none. Using every trick he knew, he worked over her body with patient expertise, until she was a molten mass of need.

The shivery anticipation she had felt earlier paled into insignificance as her heart pounded out the litany of want and need and desperation. Her breasts burned, the tender peaks scorched into shriveled nubs, but when he quenched the fire in the moist depths of his mouth, it only burned brighter still. She writhed beneath him, her blood flaming through her, carrying the heat into her innermost depths, until she was aching, throbbing for the fulfillment he alone could give.

"Jack . . . please . . ." she begged, not even caring that the power she had wielded over him had now changed hands.

"Yes, darling, yes," he replied, his rasping voice testimony to the fact that if he were in control, he did not know it.

He came to her then, joining them with an infinite tenderness that belied the passion raging between them. Maggie sighed as he filled her, experiencing the contentment that came with enfolding the man she loved. She did love him, too, more now than ever, and more wildly than ever as he began to move inside her.

All tenderness forgotten, she lifted herself to him, meeting his thrusts with total abandon. The earth fell away from them as they soared upward into the bliss of oblivion, and Maggie marveled at the galaxy of stars that blazed across her eyelids as they shot through space. There was only Jack, only him, and she clung to him while the universe spun out of control and then turned inward on itself, swallowing them both.

Ever so slowly, they drifted back to earth, cradling each other for the descent, cushioning it with whispered words that only lovers knew. The night was warm, so it was a long time before they felt the chill of passion-dampened bodies cooling in the darkness.

"Wonder where my nightdress is," Maggie said lazily. She was lying curled up in Jack's arms, and she instinctively snuggled closer, seeking his warmth.

"Don't put that thing on," Jack commanded just as lazily, drawing the edge of the quilt over them. "I'm going to make love to you again in just a minute."

Maggie smiled against his shoulder. If he felt half as languorous as she did, he'd be asleep in just a minute, just as she would. "That will be nice," she commented, settling in more comfortably.

"Mmmm," he agreed.

Renita glanced impatiently at the clock once more. Less than five minutes had passed since the last time she had checked, but it was still early yet. Kincaid would be there soon. He had told her he would come, and men simply did not stand up Renita McFadden.

She got up off of the settee and began to pace restlessly around the small room, smiling grimly when she recalled that she had once called the lovely little house Jack had provided for her a 'hovel.' How he would laugh to see where she was now.

The place didn't look too bad now, of course. She had hired a girl to clean it for her and had used some of Jack's money to buy some furnishings to fix it up. Still, nothing could change the fact that it was a shabby two-room shack. She remembered how embarrassed Billy, Kincaid's nephew, had been when he had brought her here that first time. He had apologized all over the place about how awful it was, and it *had* been absolutely awful. It was, he explained, the only place available, and since she could not stay on at the hotel . . . and on and on.

Knowing that she didn't have any choice if she wanted to stay around to watch Jack's downfall had been the deciding factor. Otherwise, she would have told Kincaid exactly what he could do with this place. It was only temporary, after all. Once Kincaid was finished with Jack, he'd take her someplace nice. He hadn't actually promised, of course, but she knew how to handle men, and she knew that he would do it if she asked him.

Drawing the silk wrapper that she wore more closely around her, she checked the time again, and then checked her reflection in the mirror that hung by the front door, smiling at what she saw. She had left her long black hair loose tonight, and underneath the wrapper she wore nothing. Tonight she had a surprise for Sam Kincaid, and tonight she would get a reaction.

With irritation she recalled the first night that he had visited her here. It had taken a few days to find this place and make it habitable, just as Kincaid had warned her, but that was fine. From their first encounter, she knew his appetite for her had only been whetted, and that when she had him alone, in an atmosphere more conducive to seduction, it would take very little effort on her part to put him in her power.

Somehow it had not worked out like that, however. He had arrived that evening, just as he had sent word that he would, but he had been almost an hour late. He had seemed almost as interested in how she had fixed the place up as he was in how she looked, and she knew that she looked gorgeous. After a quick look into the bedroom, he had lowered himself onto the settee and told her, "Take off your clothes. I want to see what I've bought."

Renita had felt a flash of anger at this, but she had forced herself to smile, knowing that his indifference was only an act. Slowly, she had stripped for him, watching the piglike eyes watching her and waiting for the reaction she knew would come. Lazily, one by one, she had released the ribbons of her camisole and then let the silky garment slide down her arms and onto the floor. Her breasts were large and full, with tiny dark nipples that pointed up, and men always loved them. It was the thing about her men found most attractive, and she had never known a man who could resist fondling them the moment she revealed them.

Kincaid, however, had simply sat, still watching her, but with his smooth, slablike face expressionless. When she had allowed the pantalettes to fall, he had not even blinked. "Turn around," he had ordered, his strange, soft voice not even sounding strained.

She had turned carefully, deliberately giving him time to see all of her, and when she faced him again, he had said, "Get me a drink."

Truly angry now, she had stomped to the sideboard and sloshed some whiskey into a glass. Then she had taken it to him, stretching out her arm full length, so that when he took the glass her body was out of reach. Not that he had even tried to touch her, though. Oh, no, he had simply taken the glass and drained it in one gulp. Then he had set it down on a side table and begun to unbutton his pants.

"Let's see what you can do," he had said, settling back against the settee.

Renita had felt the fury rising up inside her. How could he pretend like that? How could he be so cool, so calm? She had wanted to slap his placid face, to scratch his pig-eyes out, but then she had realized exactly what he was doing, and suddenly she had grown amused. So he was playing games with her, was he? Pretending that he felt nothing, just as he had in his office. It was all an act, of course. No man could look at her and feel nothing. No man, least of all a dolt like Kincaid, could resist her charms. He was afraid of her, that was it, afraid of the power she could wield over him if he allowed her to see his feelings. Well, let him pretend. She knew how to handle that.

She had smiled as she had gone to her knees in front of him. She would show him what she could do, and when she was finished, he would be begging for more. . . .

It hadn't worked out that way, though. When she had finished with him, he had calmly rebuttoned his pants, stood up, and left without so much as a goodbye. Renita still seethed at the memory. Tonight would be different, however, very much different. This time she would get him to the bed. This time . . .

She heard his foosteps on the porch. Giving her appearance one last approving glance in the mirror, she slipped off her wrapper, waiting until she heard his knock. On bare feet, she moved toward the door and opened it, being careful to stay hidden behind it until he was completely inside, and then she closed it, revealing herself to his startled glance.

It would have been difficult to say who was the more surprised, but Paul Crescent was definitely the more pleased. "Well, HELLO," he said cheerfully, letting his twinkling eyes play over her nudity.

"Who the hell are you?" Renita demanded, too furious for the moment to be concerned with her state of undress.

"Paul Crescent, ma'am, at your service," he informed her. He was still looking, taking his time about it, too. "You must be Miss McFadden. Kincaid didn't do you justice when he described you," he added admiringly.

"Where is he?" she grated, reaching for her robe and pulling it on, her irritation evident in every motion.

Watching her close the robe with undisguised disappointment, he explained, "He couldn't make it tonight. Told me to come and let you know. Reckon he'll be real put out when he hears what he missed."

Only now did Renita notice the scar. She had turned the lamp down low to set the mood, and his hat had shadowed that side of his face. It really was quite hideous. "Who are you?" she repeated, her lips curling in distaste.

He saw the grimace and his smile grew ugly. "I told you, I'm Paul Crescent."

"Do you work for Kincaid?" she asked, her skepticism evident.

"As of today I do," he said, letting his gaze drop down to where her wrapper did not quite close over her breasts. "If all my jobs for him are this pleasant, I think I'm gonna like it around here."

Renita pulled the robe closed and turned her back in disgust, stalking over to the sideboard to pour herself a drink. Only now was it beginning to sink in that Kincaid was not coming. The only thing she was not certain of was exactly why he had sent Crescent. Did he expect her to sleep with him? Did he expect her to entertain the hired help? If he did, he was in for a big surprise.

"Well, Mr. . . . Crescent, was it?" she said, turning back to face him, her untouched drink still in her hand. "It's been a pleasure meeting you. You've delivered your message, and now you may leave." That scar really was unpleasant. It spoiled a very nice face, too. A pity.

He looked disappointed. "Kincaid said we should get acquainted, said we'd have a lot in common."

"For instance?" Renita tossed her head haughtily and waited.

"Jack Sinclair." He said the name as if it were a curse, and he did not miss the ripple reaction that passed over Renita.

She studied him a long time through narrowed eyes. "That scar," she said thoughtfully. "He gave it to you, didn't he?"

Crescent nodded. He looked so odd with his face twisted up like that, as if he were smiling, but with pure murder flashing from those ridiculously blue eyes.

"Then we do have something in common," she decided. He had already taken a step toward her when she stopped him by motioning toward a chair. "Sit down. I'll get you a drink."

While she poured it, he studied her back, enjoying the way her generous curves moved beneath the thin silk. She was all woman, that one. He'd have her in the bed by now, too, if it wasn't for this damn scar. If it wasn't for Jack Sinclair.

It hadn't taken him long to learn the whole story about Colson's valley or to track down Sam Kincaid. The man made his skin crawl, but any enemy of Sinclair's was a friend of his, so they had come to terms. Kincaid hadn't been too certain of exactly how he would use Crescent, but he had told Billy to put him on the payroll just the same, commenting that Sinclair had made a passel of enemies and wondering aloud if he would have to hire them all. Later he had sent word to Crescent at the hotel to call on Renita and deliver the message that he wouldn't be able to see her tonight. Billy, who had been Kincaid's mouthpiece, had seemed very disappointed that he had not been chosen to deliver the message, and considering what had happened, he had every right to be.

Renita handed him the glass. "I have an idea for getting Sinclair," she told him, seating herself on the settee.

Crescent sipped his whiskey. She wouldn't sleep with him, not willingly anyway, at least not now. He could see the way she kept looking at the scar, as if she could not help herself. She hated it, but could not keep her eyes off of it. Maybe, just maybe . . . "What's your idea?" he asked, taking another sip. Maybe if he stuck around long enough, she might get interested. It had happened before.

"That wife of his, if you get her, you've got Sinclair by the short hairs. He'll do anything you want." The plan was so simple, she wondered that Kincaid hadn't thought of it. She could see Crescent was not impressed.

"I heard he only married her to get the valley. What makes you think he'd care if we took her?" Crescent wasn't really interested in the plan. He was only making conversation. As long as she was still looking at him, he had a chance.

"He'd care, all right. Even if he doesn't love her, she's his property. Sinclair doesn't like to lose anything that belongs to him."

The good side of Crescent's face smiled. "How did he feel when he lost you to Kincaid?"

Instantly he knew he had said the wrong thing. "Get out of here!" she commanded, jumping to her feet.

"Wait a minute," he said, rising, too, and lifting his hands in a placating gesture. "I didn't mean anything. I didn't know. . . ." His eyes took her in once more from head to bare toes and back again, lingering again on the gap in her robe. "That man's crazier than I thought if he let you get away." The compliment placated her a little, but not enough. He'd blown his chance, but maybe he could get back on her good side. "If that's true, about Sinclair's wife, tell Kincaid. Maybe we can figure something out."

Renita made a disparaging noise. "If *I* tell him, then he won't listen. He's the kind of man who thinks a woman can't have an idea." She wasn't certain how she knew that, but she did, and she could see that Crescent agreed with her, although he had the grace not to say so.

"You want me to pretend I thought of it?" he asked, only too happy to do this small service for her if it might bring him one step closer to her bed.

She shrugged noncommittally. "If the idea appeals to you," she said. "Just think of having Sinclair's wife all to yourself," she added, her voice turning low and seductive. "You could do anything you wanted . . . *anything*. Have you see her?"

Crescent nodded. He had seen her all right. He had seen the look of disgust she had given him.

"Sinclair would go crazy, knowing that you'd had her," Renita went on. "It would be fun for you, too. A man who looks like you do couldn't get much fun."

She'd struck the nerve she'd aimed for, and Crescent smashed his whiskey glass to the floor in the second before he grabbed her. His kiss was brutal, and Renita tasted blood before he was finished, but she never moved.

When he raised his face from hers, he took a moment to study her face for any reaction. He found none, and flung her away from him in disgust.

Her voice stopped him just as he was going out the door. "Think about it Crescent. She's a pretty little thing. She'd fight, too. You could tie her up. . . ."

The slamming of the door cut her off.

Chapter XIII

Maggie woke up with a smile on her face. At some time during the night, Jack had made lover to her again, slow, beautiful love that had left her feeling almost incandescent. Now she reached out to find him in the tangle of bedclothes, but she touched only cold emptiness.

"Jack?" She started upright, but the room was as empty as the bed. He was gone, and from the silence and the way the sunlight was streaming in the window giving evidence of how late she had slept, she had to assume that practically everyone else was, too.

Vastly disappointed, she sank back into the bed, pulling his pillow to her so that she could inhale his scent. Bay Rum and cigars, and when she passed her tongue over her lips, she imagined that she could taste peach brandy.

Oh, Jack, she sighed to herself, why did you leave me this morning? This was the first time they had made love without fighting either before or after. She had wanted to wake up in his arms this morning and show him that things were changing between them and for the better. She no longer held him responsible for her father's death, and if he had stolen her ranch, he had done it for a good cause. Forcing her to marry him had been awfully high-handed of him, but looking back, she knew it had been the safest thing that

370

could have happened to her. True, they had had terrible arguments, but those had been as much her fault as his, and she had goaded him into saying all those awful things to her. If they could only put the past behind them, forget the terrible hurts they had done each other, she knew they could work things out. He cared for her, she knew he did. No man could be so gentle and loving if he did not. It didn't matter, anyway. She loved him enough for both of them. All she needed was his cooperation, and remembering last night, she didn't think that would be too difficult to achieve.

Renita's heels clicked an angry tattoo on the wooden sidewalk as she made her way down the street to Sam Kincaid's office. She was getting pretty sick of sitting around in that dump of a house waiting for him to come by. Now was the time for ultimatums. If Kincaid wanted to keep her, he was going to have to change his ways.

Billy Kincaid rose instantly when she stepped through the front door. "M . . . Morning, Miss McFadden," he stammered, taking her in from head to toe and blushing furiously.

It didn't take long for Renita to realize that he was trying to imagine her naked, the way Crescent had seen her last night. Apparently the man had wasted no time in spreading the story. She wondered what Kincaid's reaction had been. Knowing Kincaid as she did, she imagined that Crescent had been wasting his time trying to shock his new employer.

Striking a sexy pose, she treated Billy to a coy smile and asked, "Is your uncle in?"

The boy nodded, turning even redder. "But he's got somebody with him," he explained.

"Who?" Renita purred.

"Mr. Crescent," the boy said.

"Perfect," she murmured as she swept past the boy, ignoring his protests, and entered the inner office without bothering to knock.

The two men were engaged in a serious conversation that ceased the moment she appeared. Crescent rose when he saw her, but Kincaid merely looked up expectantly.

No one spoke for a moment, so Crescent decided to make the first move. "Good morning, Miss McFadden," he said, his words implying that it had been a very good night.

Renita glanced at Kincaid, trying to judge his mood. It was impossible to read that set face. "I want to talk to you, Kincaid," she said, her tone brooking no argument.

The great head nodded once. "In a minute," the soft voice soothed. "Crescent has an idea. Tell 'Nita your idea, Crescent."

She had no clue from his tone whether he suspected that the idea had come from her or not, so she decided to play dumb, and turned to Crescent to await his explanation.

That ruined face was glowing with amusement at her expense, but she chose to ignore it. "I say we kidnap Mrs. Sinclair, tell Sinclair that if he doesn't pull up stakes and get out of here, he'll never see her alive again."

Renita pretended to consider this. "It's so simple, it might almost work," she decided thoughtfully.

Kincaid studied her face. "You really think losing her would bring him to his knees?" Plainly he could not conceive of such a thing.

"Definitely," Renita assured him. "He has a soft streak. He's sentimental."

This was something Kincaid understood. It was the very weakness he himself had sensed in Sinclair. "Then do it," he told Crescent.

"Just like I planned?" Crescent inquired.

"Yeah, 'Nita here'll write the note for you," Kincaid replied.

"What note?" Renita had lost the thread of conversation.

Kincaid reached into his desk and withdrew a piece of paper and slid it across to her. "A note from her friend Abby Wheeler telling her to come quick because she needs help."

Renita stared in amazement. "Who's going to deliver this note?" she asked skeptically.

"I got somebody all lined up. Somebody they won't know. Don't worry," Kincaid said. "Just write the note."

Renita pulled off her gloves with great care and reached for the pen and inkwell that sat on the corner of Kincaid's desk. When she had scribbled the note, she passed it to Kincaid, who read it and nodded his approval. He then passed it to Crescent, who also approved. "Why, Miss McFadden, seems like you've got a gift for this sort of thing," he marveled. "But then, I shouldn't be surprised. A woman of your talents . . ." He let the sentence trail off suggestively.

Renita gave him a look of profound disgust. Honestly, what did he think he was doing by hinting that he was familiar with her "talents"? Making Kincaid jealous? The idea was ridiculous.

"You can send that right out, if you want to, Crescent," Kincaid said in that soft, flat voice.

"Today?" he asked in amazement.

"Why not?" his employer returned. "The sooner, the better."

"Why not, indeed," Crescent muttered with a fatalistic shrug.

Renita stayed behind when he had gone. "I want to talk to you, Kincaid," she said, remembering her original grievance against him.

He did not reply, but simply waited patiently. "Where were you last night?" she demanded when she realized he wasn't going to speak.

"Right here," he said mildly.

"Doing what?" she snapped, her irritation growing by the second.

"Nothing."

Renita could hardly believe her ears. "Then why didn't you come?" she asked incredulously.

"I didn't feel like it," he said. Those pig-eyes never

373

even blinked.

"Well, *I* felt like it!" she shrieked, unable to control her voice any longer. She really didn't care who heard her, anyway. "I don't like to be kept waiting, and I don't like to be stood up. When a man tells me he's coming, he comes. If you don't like the rules, then you can just find someone else to play with. I don't have to stick around this dump, you know."

Kincaid had risen during her tirade, circling the desk to stand behind her. She had turned to face him, noting with fury that he seemed unmoved by her threat. "If you want it, just say so," he said quietly. "No need to scream."

The blow came so quickly that she never even saw it. It wasn't hard, either, just enough to drive the air from her lungs, and before she could get her breath, she was sprawled face down on the desk with one of Kincaid's hammy hands planted in the middle of her back.

When she felt his other hand underneath her skirt and realized his intent, she tried to struggle, but a stinging blow to her buttocks stilled her. In the next instant she heard the dull sound of tearing silk as he wrenched her pantalettes from her hips. He took her from behind in one violent lunge. Her hands flew out in reaction, and one caught the inkwell, sending it crashing to the floor.

Even as the pain tore through her, she knew a savage pleasure at his brutality, and the sounds that clawed their way out of her throat soon became moans of satisfaction.

And then it was over, too soon, too soon. She felt him step away, knew he would be adjusting his clothing, but she could not move, not yet. She lay there another moment, careless of the obscene way that she was exposed, and then gathering her strength, she heaved herself over until she was lying on her side, propped up on one elbow. Her breath still came in ragged gasps, her breasts heaving in the aftermath of the struggle, and for a while he watched her.

She would never have known from looking at him that he

had just committed rape. His face was as placid as ever, his eyes unblinking, his breath slow and even. One large hand reached out and touched her breast where a puckered nipple strained against the fine fabric. It was a touch of curiosity and nothing more. "You like it rough?" he asked. "I'll remember that."

Renita smiled then. She had gotten what she came for. Not the sex, that had been a bonus, but she had gotten a reaction from him. Tonight would be even better. "You're coming tonight?" she asked, already knowing the answer.

He did not reply, but stepped over to the door instead. Pulling it open, he called, "Billy, come in here and clean up this ink."

The boy came on the run, but Renita was quicker and had managed to scramble off the desk and adjust her skirts before he arrived. Obviously, he had heard everything that had gone on, and his avid gaze darted back and forth between the two. His uncle looked the same as always, but not the woman. She looked mussed, her hair coming loose, her dress all wrinkled, and the hands that were smoothing her clothes were shaking. And ink was everywhere.

Renita could not move until Billy was finished with his task, because her torn pantalettes were tangled around her knees. When the boy was finally gone, she pulled them off and tossed them onto Kincaid's desk. "Another souvenir," she told him lightly, her poise returned. "You're coming tonight?" she asked again.

His face twisted into what she could only guess must be a smile. "You won't be lonely tonight," he said.

Glowing with her triumph, she left him, brushing past a gaping Billy on the way out.

Maggie lifted the lid of the butter churn to check on her progress. Small golden globs were beginning to form around the dasher. It wouldn't be long now. When she was done,

375

she'd put the milk that was left in a crock and set it in the well. Jack would have cold buttermilk for supper. Consuela had told her how much he loved it. "You say he had the milk cow shipped in special?" she asked the housekeeper, who was beating up batter for cornbread.

They had been discussing the Jersey cow that Jack had bought a while back. Texas longhorns weren't much as milk cows, even if you could manage to get one tamed down enough to stand still for the process, so Jack had sent back East for a special one. *"Si,* I have had her for three years now. She has a calf every year. It keeps the milk fresh."

Maggie was delighted. No other ranch had butter and milk. "What I want to know is who milks her for you?" She grinned mischievously. Knowing cowboys as she did, she knew that not a one of them would be caught dead around the business end of a heifer, and that if he ever were, he'd never live down the humiliation.

Consuela gave her a conspiratorial grin. "Sometimes I do it myself, and sometimes . . ." she paused for effect, "sometimes, Lee Parker does it for me."

Maggie whooped with laughter. That poor man must be really smitten to do something like that for Consuela. If anyone ever found out, his reputation would be ruined. "You will not tell?" Consuela asked with some concern.

Maggie shook her head, unable to speak and holding her sides. Love certainly was a wondrous emotion. It made people do the strangest things. "His secret is safe," she promised at last, when she was back in control. "But," she warned half-seriously, "you can tell him that if I ever catch him following me again, I'll tell."

Consuela frowned. "He was only protecting you, señora. It is a good thing he did, too," she added, her cocoa-colored eyes reminding Maggie of her close call with the nestors.

"Why didn't you tell me I was being followed?" she demanded, changing the subject.

Consuela gave one of her eloquent shrugs. "It was none of

my business. Besides," she added slyly, "watching you keeps him close to the ranch all day."

Maggie rolled her eyes at her housekeeper's impeccable logic.

"Miz Sinclair?" It was Slim, the boy who took care of the horses. He was calling her from the front of the house.

"I will do that," Consuela offered, taking the churn handle from her and fitting it back into the churn. "Go see what he wants."

Maggie found the boy standing awkwardly in the front room holding a crumpled piece of paper in his hand. "A fella brung this by for you. Said to give it to you right away," he told her.

"Who was it?" she asked curiously, taking the offered note.

"A drifter, I guess. Never saw him before. He asked about work, and when I told him we weren't hiring, he rode off. Said a lady in town asked him to deliver the note."

Maggie nodded and thanked him. When he was gone, she unfolded the paper. It was a woman's handwriting, all right, and what it said alarmed her. "Dear Maggie," it read. "I need you right away. Something terrible has happened and I have to talk to someone about it. Please come as soon as you can. Your friend, Abby."

If whatever had happened had caused the independent Abby such distress, it must be terrible, indeed. A glance at the mantel clock told her she had plenty of time to make it into town before dark. It would mean missing supper here at the ranch, missing Jack, and she would probably have to stay with Abby overnight, since it would be foolish to ride back after dark. But as much as she wanted to stay here, to see Jack, Abby needed her. There would be many other nights with Jack. She went straight to her room and changed into her riding clothes.

She was halfway to the kitchen to tell Consuela her plans when a thought struck her. If she told Consuela, then Lee

377

Parker would find out and follow her. Maggie felt her hackles rise at the very thought. She was only going to town, and even Jack himself had said the road to town was safe. It hardly seemed likely that any nestors would be lying in wait for her there, either. It was broad daylight. What could possibly happen?

Neglecting to recall that her last adventure had also taken place in broad daylight, she turned on her heel and headed for Jack's office instead. Finding paper and pencil, she scribbled a quick note of explanation and propped it up in plain sight where he was bound to see it. Then she stole out of the house and across the yard.

Luck was with her. Slim was busy somewhere else, and Lee Parker was nowhere in sight. Later she would learn that he had been visiting Consuela in the kitchen. She coaxed a fairly gentle mare over to the corral fence and slipped a halter over her head. It was a simple matter of throwing a saddle over her back once she had led the animal into the privacy of the barn. After that, she walked the mare to the gate, feeling very much the fugitive. When the gate was closed behind her, she kicked the mare into a run, laughing at the ease with which she had made her escape.

She had ridden quite a ways before the consequences of her act began to occur to her. Jack would be furious. Odd that she was only now realizing that. Sneaking away had been fun, but it had also been foolish. Not that she thought anything would happen to her, of course, but it had been foolish of her to do something to make Jack angry when she had finally managed to make some peace between them.

The mare had long since slowed to a trot, and now Maggie reined her in to a walk. The slower pace matched her decreased eagerness to get to town. What was she doing? Was she really endangering her marriage? Probably not, but things were going to be mighty unpleasant when Jack got home and found her gone. On the other hand, Abby needed her. She could never remember feeling needed before. It was a difficult decision. So difficult that she did not notice the familiar whizzing sound until it was too late.

One second she was riding along and the next she was lying flat on her back in the road. The impact of the fall stunned her so that when that horrible face appeared in front of hers, she could not even cry out. The sight of that hideous grin jolted her, though, and after another minute she began to struggle, but it was too late. He had already tied her hands behind her back and was looping a rope around her ankles. "What are you doing?" she demanded breathlessly. She simply couldn't believe this was happening, and happening so quickly.

"You're being kidnapped, little lady," he informed her cheerfully.

Her mouth flew open in protest, but before she could utter a sound, he stuffed a handkerchief into it. She fought like a tigress, but he still had little trouble tying a second handkerchief around her mouth to hold the first one in place. Thoroughly silenced, she continued to thrash until she realized the futility of it and stopped.

Sobbing breath into her lungs through a nose that was rapidly filling up with tears of frustration, Maggie glared at her captor. "Better not cry, little lady," he warned her with that same fiendish grin. "If your nose stops up, you'll suffocate." He didn't seem too concerned about the possibility, but Maggie suddenly was, and she blinked furiously to clear her eyes.

How could this be happening? she asked herself frantically as he disappeared from her view for a moment. And why? What possible purpose could be served by kidnapping her? Before she could come up with an answer, he returned. With one rough jerk he freed her from the lariat that he had used to jerk her off her mare, and then he rolled her over onto a tarp that he had spread on the ground beside her. She began to struggle again, but his patience had worn thin, and this time he simply slapped her once.

379

Stunned once more, fighting off the faintness that came after the flash of stars, she allowed him to roll her up. By the time she was again capable of purposeful movement, she was hopelessly confined in the dusty-smelling tarp. Crescent picked her up and slung her over his shoulder. Maggie was aware of being carried a short distance over some rough terrain. She tried to picture exactly where she had been when the attack had taken place. She vaguely remembered some rocks and a grove of trees. From her dark cocoon, she could hear the rustle of branches as they passed through the trees. Then she was dumped onto something wooden.

It was a wagon bed. She could tell that from the sound of the wagon gate being closed, and then she could hear the horses snorting and feel the whole thing tip as Crescent climbed up into the seat. In another moment he had slapped the team into motion, and they were on their way to wherever it was that he was taking her.

The gentle sway of the wagon helped to calm her somewhat so that she was able to take stock of her situation. Fighting tears again, painfully aware of how difficult it was to breathe inside the filthy tarp with her mouth stuffed with cloth, she tentatively twisted her hands, trying the strength of the ropes that bound her.

The action sent a shooting pain up her arms. The ropes were not only secure, but agonizingly so. She could already tell that her hands were growing numb from lack of circulation. To fight the ropes would cause her discomfort, but would bring her no closer to freedom.

The bonds on her ankles were more difficult to judge. He had tied the rope around her riding boots, but since her feet seemed glued together, she could only assume that they were as tightly tied as her hands.

Her head still felt a little funny, a combination of the fall and Crescent's slap, and her cheek, where he had struck her, was starting to tingle uncomfortably as the initial numbness wore off. Still, in spite of everything, she wasn't seriously

380

injured, and as long as she was alive, she had hope of getting away. She had no way of judging the direction in which they were going, but from the motion of the wagon she judged that they were still on the road. Since it seemed unlikely that they would be heading back toward the ranch, they must be going toward town. In town her chances for escape would be good. All she would need to do was get off one good scream. Of course, that would necessitate removal of her gag, but if that happened . . . meanwhile, she would not panic. If she kept her wits about her, she had a chance. And, she reminded herself, if Jack were as angry as she suspected he would be when he discovered she had gone to town alone, he would be hot on her trail. She could only pray that he returned to the ranch early.

Crescent could hardly believe his luck. The note had worked like a charm. Not only that, but she had left the ranch alone, and no one had even followed her. Kincaid had assured him that she'd be alone, but he hadn't been so sure, and he had used field glasses to watch, just in case. Oh, he wasn't stupid enough to think he had a lot of time, of course. He would have to get off the main road soon and cover his tracks. He didn't dare ride into town until full dark, and that was several hours away, and somebody was bound to come after her, especially when her mount came back without her. He had planned to catch the mare and tie her up somewhere out of sight, but the animal had gotten away before he could do so.

Well, what was done was done. He couldn't change that, but he could get her to what Kincaid had assured him was the safest hiding place. So obvious that no one would think to look there, Kincaid had said. He had to agree, it was, too. It also happened to be the exact place he wanted to spend the night, himself, enjoying the comforts of a beautiful woman. The turnoff was just ahead. After he had brushed out his tracks, he would be home free.

Maggie had noticed the change in the road immediately,

and tried to picture just where they had been when he had turned off, but it was an impossible task and she soon gave it up. She concentrated instead on bracing herself so she would not be thrown around too violently in the back of the wagon. The ride seemed interminable, and she knew from the dryness of her throat and the urging of her bladder that many hours had passed. Whether it was dark yet or not she had no way of knowing, but she was pretty certain that it was.

Then she began to sense a change. How she knew, she would not have been able to say, but somehow she began to perceive that they were approaching the town. Why they had taken such a roundabout route she had no idea, but she would have bet her life that that was where they were. Eventually, the wagon ground to a halt. She heard Crescent climb down, walk around to the back of the wagon and lower the gate. Then she was being hoisted again, and carried. Resisting the urge to struggle until she knew exactly where she was, she literally held her breath, listening for the slightest clue.

He stopped and she heard him knocking on a door. The door opened.

"What are you doing here?" a woman's voice demanded. It was muffled from the tarp, but Maggie knew it just the same. *That woman.* How had Crescent gotten involved with *her?*

Renita was not amused to see Crescent at her door again, but before she could slam it in his face he forced his way past her. "I brought you a present," he told her, placing his burden on the floor with very little gentleness.

"Well, whatever it is, get it out of here and take yourself with it," Renita snapped. Really, she had had just about all of this man she could take.

"Maybe you'll change your mind when you see what it is," he suggested, unrolling the tarp with a flourish.

Renita gasped when Maggie's bedraggled figure came free of the material. "What in the hell did you bring her here for?"

382

she shrieked. "Don't you know this is the first place Sinclair will look?" She couldn't believe Crescent had been so stupid. She didn't like him much, but she hadn't taken him for a fool.

Crescent glared at her in disgust. "Kincaid told me to bring her here. He said Sinclair would go to him first and that he'd let it slip that I'd headed up into the hills. They'll be looking for her from now till kingdom come, and she'll be right here under their noses all the time." Obviously, he thought it an amazingly clever plan.

Renita did not. "I know Sinclair. Believe me, he'll come here first."

Maggie watched them as they argued, listening in growing apprehension. They were all in this together, Crescent, Kincaid, and the woman. They were going to use her to get to Jack somehow. That much was clear. It would work, too. Even if Jack didn't love her, he did care for her and she *was* his wife. He'd move heaven and earth to find her, even if he planned to murder her himself when he found her, a possibility Maggie found more and more likely the longer she thought about it. When Jack found out what kind of a mess she'd gotten into this time . . . she winced at the mere thought.

She wanted to tell them to please stop arguing, since they were making her head pound, but since she was still gagged, she could not. She also would have liked to request a trip to the outhouse, but figured that, too, was out of the question, as was the drink of water she would have sold her soul for just then.

"Look," Crescent was saying, "she's here now and she's going to stay here. That's what Kincaid planned, and he said he'd take care of the rest of it. He's not stupid. He must have it all worked out."

Renita was sure that he did. The only thing she wasn't sure of was whether the plan he had worked out was going to keep her and Crescent out of trouble or not. It seemed incredible that he would be working against them both, and yet some sixth sense warned her that it was entirely possible. Unfortunately, there was nothing she could do to change things now. "All right," she grudgingly allowed, "she stays here, but only for tonight. You'll have to move her in the morning. Sinclair might believe that story about you taking her to the hills, but that Swede is a good tracker. When he doesn't pick up a trail, they'll be back here looking for her."

Crescent knew a moment's apprehension about the way he had covered his tracks. He hadn't taken any great pains with the job, just rubbed out a good twenty feet of the wagon tracks and scattered some rocks and stuff over the place. The casual observer would ride right by, but somebody good at reading sign might not. Of course, it would be dark by the time anybody would have gotten to that spot. They'd miss it in the dark, but tomorrow . . . she was right. He'd have to move the girl in the morning. But not just yet. He had plans for the rest of the night.

"You're right. I'll take her out before dawn. No use tempting fate. There's no reason why we can't have a little fun with her until then, though, is there?" The good side of his face twitched suggestively, and Renita smiled.

Maggie had a hunch that what would be fun for Crescent wouldn't be fun for her, and a terror such as she had never known began to grow inside of her. Her whole body seemed to be flashing hot and cold at the same time, and she had an overwhelming urge to flee, while at the same time every muscle was frozen in fear.

"You were right, she is a pretty little thing." Crescent's voice came to her from very far away. In fact, the whole room seemed very far away, as if she were seeing it through a long, dark tunnel. "She's got a nice body, too." Maggie cringed as one of his hands cupped her breast. She could feel the bile rising in her throat, and tried to choke it down. She couldn't throw up, not with the gag still in her mouth. She'd suffocate for sure.

Then she squeezed her eyes shut as his hand slid up her leg, under her skirt. Oh, dear God, what was he going to do? And how could she bear it? And Jack, what would he say when he found out? Would he ever be able to touch her again without remembering that Crescent had defiled her? She sniffed loudly in an attempt to clear her nose of the tears of humiliation that threatened, and then cried out as his fingers mercilessly pinched her tender skin.

After careful consideration, Jack had decided that the day he had just lived through had been the longest in his life. Leaving Maggie that morning had been one of the most difficult things he had ever done, but their night together had been so perfect that he didn't dare risk awakening her to a possible argument. He wasn't certain why, but they always managed to have one just when things seemed to be going perfectly, and he had decided that it would be best to leave things as they were for the time being. Giving her the whole day to review the night before might make her less likely to pick a fight when he returned, and even if she did, they'd have all night to make up.

For a few blissful moments after the ranch came into view, he enjoyed the fantasy that all his problems were just about over. Little did he suspect that the day that had been so interminably long was just beginning.

A very agitated trio met him in the ranch yard, and they all started talking at once before he could even climb down from his horse. It was something about Maggie, but he couldn't make out just exactly what. "Whoa!" he ordered, raising one hand defensively when he finally had both feet on the ground. "One at a time."

Lee, Consuela, and Slim exchanged glances, silently appointing Consuela as spokesperson. She was, after all, the one least likely to be struck when Mr. Sinclair heard the news. "The señora, she is gone," Consuela told him, her plump hands twisting in agitation.

Jack's stomach gave a sickening lurch. "Gone? What do you mean, gone?"

"Here, I find this on your desk," she said, suddenly remembering the note she had stuck in her pocket.

Jack read the hastily scrawled message, and his heart slipped back down from his throat into a more normal position. She had only gone to Abby's for a visit. But why were these three so upset? Then he remembered. Lee was under orders not to let Maggie out of his sight. The poor fellow was probably panic-stricken that Jack would murder him, as well he might for having given him such a scare. Giving Lee a fierce scowl, he demanded, "Why aren't you with her?"

Lee made a helpless gesture with his hands. "She snuck off when none of us was looking. We thought she was in her room or something. We didn't even know she was gone until . . ." He paused, unwilling to give Jack the final damning piece of information.

"Until . . ." Jack repeated expectantly, his face a mask of cold fury. They needn't know that his fury was directed at Maggie for pulling such a stupid stunt.

Nobody spoke for a long moment. Finally, Slim swallowed loudly and offered, "Her mare come back without her."

Jack's curse caused the trio to wince. "How long ago?" he demanded, the terror he had felt moments ago returning.

"Just a few minutes. We went looking for her and found the note. I was just coming out to get my horse and go after her when you all rode up," Lee explained.

"Swede!" Jack called unnecessarily. The foreman had been right behind him and had heard most of the explanation, enough to know what had happened. "Tell the men to get fresh mounts, and we'll go after her."

Swede shook his head, climbing down from his saddle. "Let them get some grub first. You and me'll ride out and see

386

if we can find her. Maybe she just had a little accident and is setting out there real embarrassed with a twisted ankle or something."

Jack's look reminded him that Maggie never had *little* accidents.

Swede shrugged resignedly. "If it's something bad, I'll need some time to figure out the tracks anyway. Go on now, Slim, and fetch me and Mr. Sinclair some fresh horses." The boy obeyed, grateful to escape Jack's wrath.

Only then did Jack notice that the men had all gathered round. Word of Maggie's disappearance had spread swiftly through their ranks. "Can we help, Mr. Sinclair?" one asked.

Jack rubbed his neck wearily, studying their sun-blackened faces. Each was, he realized with some surprise, as concerned as he, if that were possible, and each would gladly have ridden into the jaws of hell for him. No, he mentally corrected, not for him at all. For Maggie. They were worried about Maggie. "Grab something to eat, boys, and then come after us. That will give Swede time to pick up her trail. Like Swede said, we'll probably find her limping home with a badly injured pride and nothing more." He tried a small smile that fell sadly flat.

The boys nodded soberly and hastened to the cookhouse to gulp down their supper, while Slim brought up two fresh horses. In a few moments Jack and Swede were mounted, easily retracing the mare's tracks, both those leaving and those returning to the ranch. At a point some distance from the ranch, the mare's returning tracks left the road, and the two men decided to stay on the road and follow the out-going trail, since it provided the straightest and most easily followed clues to what had become of Maggie.

"Wait here," Swede ordered suddenly. They had been moving along at a pretty fast clip, since the tracks were fresh, but Swede abruptly pulled up, and Jack followed suit, trusting his friend's instincts. The foreman climbed down and then squatted to study the ground more closely. "This is where it happened," he announced after a few minutes.

The lump of apprehension that had been sitting in Jack's stomach turned to agony as his last ounce of hope evaporated. He was not going to find a contrite Maggie limping home. Something had happened to her, and judging from Swede's grim expression, it was something pretty bad.

Jack swung down from his horse as Swede, his eyes still on the ground, rose and walked slowly off into the trees. After a few minutes, he returned. "Near as I can figure," he explained, "somebody was waiting for her up in those rocks." He pointed vaguely. "He dropped a rope on her when she come by here. This is where she fell." Swede studied the ground again, and Jack held his breath, waiting. "She couldn't have been hurt bad, not from the way she fought," he decided, and Jack allowed his breath to escape. Thank God for that, anyway. "This here's a puzzle," Swede went on, poining to the place where Crescent had laid the tarp. "Near as I can figure, he must've wrapped her up in something. A blanket, maybe. Maybe to hide her or to keep her quiet or something. Anyway, then he took her over in there. He had a wagon hid back in the brush. Looks like he pulled it out onto the road again."

"Was he a big man?" Jack asked. He could think of only one man who might profit from holding Maggie hostage.

Swede shook his head. "About average, I'd say, but then Kincaid wouldn't do his own dirty work. He'd hire it done, don't you think?"

It was a logical assumption. The next step, of course, was to follow and find out where she was being taken. Jack's impulse was to ride hell-bent to find her, but he did not trust his own judgment in this matter, recognizing that emotion would cloud it. "Should we wait for the boys to catch up?" he asked.

"We'll have to go slow. That'll give them time to catch up. They won't be more'n a few minutes behind us, anyways. Come on." The two mounted up again. "I just hope Lee has

388

the sense to bring along some lanterns," he remarked, squinting into the sun. "It'll be dark soon."

Lee did bring the lanterns, but even so they lost the trail after a while. It was impossible to track a wagon on the public road so close to town. Many vehicles had come and gone in the course of the day, blurring the tracks into obscurity.

"Maybe he turned off somewhere," Jack suggested when Swede came up from his squatting position shaking his head in exasperation.

"Maybe," Swede allowed, "but why'd he come so close to town if he wasn't gonna end up there? Seems like if he was gonna take her off somewheres to hide her, he would've put her on a horse and taken off cross country instead of hauling her in a wagon." Swede swung up into his saddle. "Anyways, if he did turn off, we'll never be able to track him until daylight."

Jack knew that to be true, and for a moment he struggled with the frustration that threatened to overwhelm him. He had never felt so helpless. Maggie, his Maggie, was in the hands of some awful person who was doing who-knew-what to her at this very moment, and there wasn't a damn thing he could do to help her. Or maybe there was. It might not help Maggie, but at least it would help relieve this awful feeling of impotence, and who knew? Maybe he might find out something. "Come on, men. Since we're so close to town, why don't we go ahead and pay Mr. Kincaid a little visit."

The rumble of approval that greeted his suggestion told him that his men were sharing his frustration, and it was a rowdy bunch who thundered into the sleeping town of Bitterroot.

The lights were still on in Kincaid's office, almost as if he had been expecting company, Jack realized with antagonism. Swede sent half the men up the outside stairs to Kincaid's living quarters, not that he really expected to find Maggie hidden up there, but more to give the men a feeling that they were doing something. The rest joined Jack and Swede as they stormed into Kincaid's office.

"Where is she, Kincaid?" Jack demanded, drawing the pearl-handled colt he had strapped to his hip before leaving the ranch and aiming it at a spot somewhere between the large man's beady eyes.

Kincaid never blinked. "Where is who?" he asked mildly, his soft voice hardly more than a whisper of sound in the crowded room.

"You know who," Jack gritted, barely able to keep from squeezing the trigger. "My wife. What have you done with her?"

The large man did blink this time, in apparent confusion. "I haven't got your wife," he explained patiently. "Only your mistress, but if you aren't particular, she's in that shack just south of town. All cats are alike in the dark, you know."

Jack roared his rage and might very well have fired, except that Swede and Lee Parker grabbed him.

"You'd better get out of here now," Kincaid warned quietly once Jack had been restrained. "You're trespassing, and I might just have to call the marshal."

"That won't be necessary," a voice from the doorway announced. It was the marshal, and from the look of it, he had been roused from a deep sleep and wasn't at all pleased about it. Being the town marshal of Bitterroot was at best a part-time job, and it certainly didn't pay well enough to justify being rousted out of bed in the middle of the night. "What in the hell is going on here, Mr. Sinclair? Your men ride into town like a bunch of wild Indians, raising enough ruckus to wake the dead. This ain't Dodge City, you know."

"This man kidnapped my wife," Jack explained as coolly as possible under the circumstances.

The marshal was obviously impressed with this information. "That true, Mr. Kincaid?" he inquired.

"No," the large man denied with infuriating mildness. "His wife must've run off, and he's got some fool notion I've got something to do with it. Just between us, marshal, one woman at a time is enough for me, and I've got my hands full right now."

Marshal Myron Davis watched in alarm as Jack once more lunged toward Kincaid, but his men again restrained him. Then the marshal scratched his bald head in puzzlement. "You got any proof your wife's been kidnapped, Mr. Sinclair?" he asked. "Ransom note or anything?"

Jack had to admit he did not. "But Swede read the sign at the spot where she disappeared. Somebody carried her off in a wagon."

"Maybe somebody was just giving her a ride," the marshal suggested. Jack now turned his wrath on the marshal, and the man backed up a step. "Now I ain't saying that she wasn't kidnapped. All I'm saying is that you can't come roaring into town and pointing guns at respectable citizens just because you *think* your wife's been kidnapped. Now we need more proof than that, Mr. Sinclair."

"Jack," Swede said in an attempt to soothe his employer. "He's right."

The marshal pressed his momentary advantage. "You keep this up, I'll have to arrest you for disturbing the peace," he warned.

"All right," Jack agreed reluctantly, shaking off the restraining hands and shoving his Colt back in its holster. "I'll get you your proof. Then you'll have to arrest this bastard."

The marshal agreed eagerly. "When you have proof that he kidnapped your wife, I'll be only too happy to do just that." He shot an apologetic look at Kincaid, and then stood aside as Jack and his men filed out.

Jack was almost to the front door when Kincaid's voice called out to him. "You're wasting your time here, Sinclair. You must have other enemies who might want to kidnap your wife for revenge."

Jack froze in midstep and turned back to face Kincaid.

391

The man's expression was as bland as usual, but Jack had the distinct impression that he was telling him something, something very important. "Crescent," he breathed, and heard Swede's gasp of response.

How Kincaid would have known about Crescent was anyone's guess, but he knew he would be wasting his time to ask. Intead he waited until they were all outside before turning to the marshal. "Marshal, have you seen any strangers around town the past day or two?"

"A few. Why? You think one of them might be responsible?" the marshal asked.

"Maybe. Have you seen a man with a big scar across his face?"

The marshal considered. "Matter of fact, I did. He's been hanging around the saloon some."

"Have you seen him with Kincaid?" Jack waited patiently for the answer, his face an expressionless mask, even though he wanted to shake the information out of the man.

The marshal thought it over for a moment. "Come to think of it, I did see him coming out of Kincaid's office just this morning. You think he's the one took your wife?"

"If he is, you'll be the first to know," Jack promised as he hurried to his horse. The rest of the men were already mounted.

The urge to do something, anything, nudged them into motion, but they were riding aimlessly, none of them having the slightest idea what the best course of action might be. Meanwhile, Jack's mind was racing. Somehow Crescent had joined forces with Kincaid. If so, then why had Kincaid given him that clue as to who Maggie's abductor might be? Why give away his accomplice? Unless . . . it was difficult to imagine, but maybe Kincaid wasn't his accomplice. Maybe Kincaid knew of the kidnapping but didn't approve of it, and this was his way of making certain the guilty party got caught. The more he thought of it, the more certain he became that Kincaid had purposely implicated Crescent, even though Jack couldn't think of a logical explanation for it. If only he had given Jack a clue as to where Crescent might have taken Maggie. And then Jack remembered something else Kincaid had said, something else he had made a point of mentioning: exactly where Renita lived.

"Come on, men," he said. "We're going to pay one more visit this evening."

The tiny shack was dark when they approached, and it took only a moment for the mounted men to surround it. Jack was instantly off his horse and pounding on the flimsy door. He was on the verge of breaking it in when he heard Renita's voice call "Just a minute," and saw that someone had struck a match and lighted a lamp.

The opened door revealed a delightfully disheveled Renita who had been hastily stuffed into a silk robe and nothing else. She smiled a greeting. "I knew you could not stay away, *querido,*" she purred just before he pushed her out of the way to enter the house.

"Where is she?" he asked, his black eyes searching the room for any traces of Maggie's presence. Swede and some of the others pushed their way in behind him and hastily searched the small dwelling. It did not take long.

After a very few minutes, the men returned from the bedroom, shaking their heads. "Nothing," one said.

"Did you lose something?" Renita asked sarcastically.

"I'm looking for my wife," he snapped, fed up with people pretending they didn't know perfectly well where she was.

Renita's eyes grew large with surprise. "Did you think she would come to me when she ran away from you?"

"She didn't run away, she was kidnapped, as you very well know," he grated.

"Kidnapped!" she said in amazement. "Are you sure she did not just run away? She looks to be the type of woman who would soon tire of your coldness. Are any of your men missing too? Perhaps . . ."

Jack would have struck her if Swede had not pulled her

393

out of the way just in time. "Boss," he hissed in warning, but Renita was already drowning him out with her screams.

"Get out of here, you bastard!" she shrieked, pointing to the door, heedless of the way her robe gaped open when she did. "I hope you never find her! I hope whoever has her chokes the life out of her and leaves her for the buzzards!" Mercifully, in her rage, she slipped into her native Spanish, and Jack could no longer understand her taunts, but those he had heard would be enough to haunt him to the end of his days. He was barely aware of his men dragging him out of Renita's house, away from her venomous ravings.

He didn't know where they were going, and he didn't really care when Swede forced him back up into his saddle. He just wanted to keep on looking for Maggie. In fact, he'd take this whole damn town apart, board by board, until he found her. He'd just told Swede his plan when he noticed they had pulled up outside of Abby's boardinghouse.

"Not tonight, boss," Swede said. "Come on." The foreman dismounted and waited for Jack to follow.

Swede didn't know if he was doing the right thing or not, but it was all he could think of to do. Letting Jack run loose, roaming the town in the dead of night, was a good way to get them all shot or locked up, at the very least. They needed a safe place to wait until dawn, a place where Jack could have some peace, or at least as much peace as was possible under the circumstances. When he thought of peace, he thought of Abby, and it was almost instinct that had brought him here.

"Wait here, boys," Swede instructed the other men. "I'm gonna leave Mr. Sinclair here, and then we'll all go over to the livery and bed down in the loft."

Jack instantly began to protest the plan, but Swede ignored him and walked away, forcing Jack to follow him up the porch stairs and right on to Abby's front door in order to continue the argument. Jack was still arguing when Swede began to knock. He ceased only when a muffled voice demanded, "Who's there?"

"Swede and Mr. Sinclair," Swede replied, apparently oblivious to Jack's now silent fury.

The door opened immediately to reveal a very startled Abby, clad in a nightdress and robe, her blond hair hanging down her back in a long braid. Neither man was surprised to note that she held a shotgun.

"I'm very sorry about this, Mrs. Wheeler, but . . ." Jack tried to explain, but Swede cut him off.

"Somebody's kidnapped Mrs. Sinclair," he said.

Abby nodded and stepped aside. "Come in," she said. Swede did, and Jack followed reluctantly. "Do you know who did it?" she asked when the outside door was closed.

"What is it now?" a voice called from upstairs, and two bare legs sticking out of a nightshirt appeared at the top landing.

"It's nothing, Mr. Pierce. Go back to bed," Abby called back. Grumbling, Mr. Pierce did just that. Then Abby turned her attention back to her visitors.

"We think it was Kincaid or maybe someone who is working for him, but we were just at his house . . ." Jack began.

"We searched his house and that McFadden woman's place, but she wasn't there," Swede broke in. "We figure whoever has her took her off someplace, but we got no chance to track her until daylight. I thought you might let Mr. Sinclair wait here till then."

"I told him that wasn't necessary. . . ." Jack tried once more, but Abby was also ignoring him.

"Of course," she was saying to Swede. "I've got a room in the back that's empty."

"I don't need a room. I can just sit in the parlor or the kitchen," Jack was insisting, but Abby had taken his arm and was leading him down the hallway to the back of the house.

"I think you'll like this room," Abby said as she threw open the door.

Jack blinked as his eyes adjusted from the dark hallway to the dimly lit room, and it took him a minute to realize that the room was not empty. Something, no, someone was in the bed, and that someone stirred when he entered. Stirred and sat up and then cried out.

Lamplight danced on copper curls and two arms reached out to him.

"Maggie!"

Chapter XIV

Maggie had shuddered with revulsion as Crescent's hands roamed over her, tracing her feminine contours. Grinding her teeth on the sodden gag, squinching her eyes shut against the horror of it all, Maggie cried out as he pinched her fear-hardened nipple with savage pleasure. She tried not to imagine what he was going to do to her, tried not to wonder if it would hurt or how she would bear the shame. Instead she forced herself to plan. If he took her clothes off, he would have to untie her. Would he do it here, in front of that woman, or would he take her in the other room? It would be easier if they were alone. She would have more chance to get away with only one adversary to contend with, but even as she planned she became aware that his touch, as repugnant as it was, was only halfhearted. His attention was on that woman.

Crescent's hands were on Maggie, but his eyes were watching Renita. Seeing him fondle the girl was exciting her, as he had guessed it would. He hated the way Maggie flinched from his touch, the way her very flesh quivered in loathing when his other hand slipped beneath her riding skirt to caress her thigh. Some men might enjoy rape, might enjoy forcing a woman who was unwilling, but Crescent didn't, not even if that woman belonged to Jack Sinclair. He liked his women willing, eager. He didn't even like paying for it, knowing that the woman was only pretending, and he'd never had to pay for it before, not until Sinclair had marked him.

In vengeance, he pinched the silky flesh again, savoring Maggie's involuntary grunt of pain while at the same time continuing to watch Renita. Her dark eyes glittered, and she crossed her arms over nipples that had puckered betrayingly. She was wearing only a wrapper again tonight, and he could still remember exactly how she looked without it.

"You know," he mused, "I just been thinking. That Sinclair must not be playing with a full deck if he picked this bag of bones over a real woman like you."

He had said exactly the right thing. Renita felt her self-esteem, which had been battered relentlessly in the last week, restored to its full glory. Kincaid wasn't coming tonight. She knew that now, understood his cryptic statement that she wouldn't be lonely tonight. Well, he might not want her, but here was a man who did and who made no bones about it. Funny, but even that scar didn't seem so bad anymore. In fact, she was beginning to wonder what it would be like to run her fingers over it.

"I like my women to be all woman," he was saying as he rose, leaving the girl and walking toward her.

Renita's hand came up of its own volition, but she saw it just as it was about to touch his face and jerked it away. He caught it, though, and pulled it back. "Go ahead," he urged, placing her fingers on his ruined cheek. "I've got other scars, too, in some very interesting places."

She shivered in mingled horror and desire as her fingers stroked over his face, and then cried out when his hands took her breasts in fierce possession. Arching to his touch, she leaned into him, her hips brushing his, and then she lifted her face for his kiss.

"You want to do it here, in front of her?" he whispered against her lips. Plainly, it did not matter one way or the

398

other to him, and Renita considered a moment. It would be fun to shock Jack's little *puta,* maybe even teach her a thing or two, but no, it would be too distracting with her in the room. It had been awhile since a man had concentrated completely on her, and she wanted to enjoy it.

"No, let's go in the other room." She pulled reluctantly away from him and grasped his hand, drawing him after her.

"Maybe we shouldn't leave her alone," he said, experiencing one small twinge of conscience as they stepped over Maggie on their way out.

Renita made a disgusted sound. "She's tied hand and foot. What can she do?"

Maggie had to agree as she watched the door close behind them. Still, she was relieved to find herself alone. That wave of relief was followed very quickly by another of panic, however, as she realized that if he did not intend to rape her, then he would not untie her, either. While half of her mind listened in revulsion to the sounds coming from the other room, the other half wrestled frantically with the problem of escape.

How much time did she have? She had no idea, but she did know that if she was to get free, she would have to work quickly. Twisting her hands availed her nothing. They were completely numb now, and the ropes were no looser than they had been before. Screaming was out of the question, of course. If only her feet were free . . .

Maggie looked down, for the first time able to study the way her feet were bound. Crescent had tied the ropes over her boots. They were tight, but Maggie discovered that she could wiggle her toes, proof that the bonds were loose enough to allow circulation. After another moment of study, she realized that if she could pull her feet out of the boots, her legs would be completely free.

Frantically, she cast about for something against which she could brace her boots for the removal, and then she saw it. The small woodstove that stood in the corner. It was cold on this warm spring night, but its door was shut fast, the handle at the perfect height for her need. The stove itself was fastened to the floor, making it sturdy enough to provide the resistance she would need.

Awkwardly, Maggie began to scoot herself across the floor. The sound of her clothing scraping against the rough wood planks was like thunder to her ears, but she could detect nothing from the other room to indicate her captors heard anything. They were, if anything, more absorbed than before. That woman was laughing, as if something pleased her very much, and Maggie could hear the low rumble of Crescent's voice, and then his own laughter joined hers. Then there was a space of silence, followed by more laughter.

Maggie tried not to imagine what they were doing, concentrating instead on making it across the room to the stove. Thanking God that the house was so tiny, Maggie gave one final lunge that brought her as close as she needed to be to the stove. Lifting her feet and legs was an awkward business, but after only two tries, she managed to snag the rope on the crook of the handle. The angle was poor, but after a few tentative tugs, she could feel her feet begin to slip from the boots.

Ears perked to catch the slightest hint that her captors heard her, she alternately tugged and listened, tugged and listened. By the time her feet slid free, she was damp with the strain, and trembling with tension.

Pausing only a moment to be certain of her safety, she scrambled to her feet using elbows and knees for leverage. Once up, she surveyed the room once more. Odd, she had not thought beyond this point. How was she now to get away?

The door was the obvious solution, of course, and Maggie made straight for it, only to discover that even though Renita had left it unlocked, her deadened hands could not operate the door handle blindly from their position behind her back.

400

Tears of frustration stung her eyes, but she blinked them back furiously. She would not suffocate herself, no matter how desperate she became. While she stood there trying one last time to negotiate the simple maneuver that would win her freedom, a gentle breeze chilled her sweat-dampened body. Shivering, Maggie glanced up in annoyance at the open window.

An *open* window! On silent stockinged feet, Maggie raced to the window. The ground wasn't far away. The shack was built with little foundation, the board floor being only inches from the ground. Climbing out without the use of her hands would be tricky, and she might very well fall. No, she corrected, she certainly would fall, and the noise might alert the people in the other room, but that was a chance she would have to take.

With one last pause to determine that her captors were still thoroughly occupied, Maggie resolutely swung first one leg and then the other over the sill, ducking her body until she was perched on the ledge with her head and shoulders outside. Taking a deep breath and forcing her body to relax and go limp, and closing her eyes, she tipped forward, holding herself at an angle so her shoulder would take the brunt of the fall.

The impact jarred her, the noise all but deafening in the dark stillness. For a dozen heartbeats she simply lay there, smelling dust, tasting it in the back of her throat, and listening, listening. She heard nothing more than the pounding of her own heart.

Once again she got up, more slowly this time, because her shoulder ached, and so did one knee, she discovered. Knowing only that she had to get away, she began to walk. Slowly, quietly, at first, afraid of alerting anyone, she made her way away from the tiny house. Her eyes quickly became accustomed to the dark, and her pace quickened.

There were, perhaps, a dozen places she could have gone to be safe, but only one beckoned. The big gray house loomed large in the nighttime shadows, a sanctuary, a haven of refuge for a fugitive. Heedless of the stones and debris that bruised her shoeless feet, Maggie fairly flew through the murky streets, imagining pursuit, envisioning seizure at every turn. By the time she reached Abby's house, her breath was coming in rasping sobs, her heart fairly bursting from her fears and exertion.

Unable to call out, she climbed the stairs, stumbling once, but catching her balance just in time to prevent herself from tumbling down them again. Bracing herself, she began again, trudging upward with grim determination not to fall again. The porch seemed much wider than she had ever noticed its being before, but its smooth boards felt comforting beneath her abused feet.

There was a doorbell, but Maggie had no way of twisting it, so she lifted her knee, the one that did not ache, and pounded it against the sturdy door panel. She waited to see if anyone would come, and when no one did, she pounded again, harder this time, and this time she did not stop until she heard a frightened voice inquire, "Who's there?"

It was Abby, dear, sweet Abby, but Maggie could not tell her who was there, so she continued to pound until the door, at long last, flew open.

Abby could hardly believe her eyes. At first she did not even recognize the apparition that stood before her as her friend. The gag covered a good half of Maggie's face, and one of her eyes was swollen from Crescent's blow. In the dim light, the auburn hair looked almost black, but when Abby raised the lamp she held, she gasped in recognition.

"Good Lord have mercy!" she exclaimed. "What on earth happened?" Not waiting for an answer, not even realizing that Maggie could not give one in her present condition, Abby pulled her inside and shut the door. Hastily, she set the lamp on a table nearby and began to remove Maggie's gag.

The thrum of feet on the floor above distracted her for a moment. "What's going on down there, Mrs. Wheeler?" an indignant voice demanded from the top of the stairs.

Still uncertain as to what danger Maggie might be in, Abby called back, "It's nothing, Mr. Pierce. Just some kids, I reckon, banging on the door and then running away. Go back to bed."

Mr. Pierce was grumbling about the sad state of today's young people when other doors opened and other voices called out to discover what was wrong. Pierce allayed their fears, and in another moment, all above was silent.

By that time Abby had Maggie's gag out and had turned her to begin work on her hands. "What on earth happened?" she repeated, but Maggie was unable to reply.

Like her hands, her jaws and tongue were numb, and her mouth and throat were parched. "Water," she managed to croak when Abby had finally succeeded in freeing her hands.

"My lands, yes," Abby agreed, hustling her toward the kitchen, but then she changed her mind. If Maggie were in any danger, she had best be hidden first, and so they changed direction. Abby directed her to an empty bedroom at the back of the first floor. Setting her friend on the edge of the bed, she patted her hands reassuringly, and said, "I'll be right back. I'll get a lamp and some water. You stay right here. You'll be fine." With that, she had gone after the promised items, returning before Maggie could even think to be afraid.

When Maggie had gulped down the water, and made use of the chamber pot that Abby provided when they had both determined that a trip to the outhouse was inadvisable, she found that the parts of her body that had been bound were beginning to work again, and she told Abby the whole horrible story.

"They'll be after me when they find out I got away," Maggie warned, shuddering a little at the thought.

"Well, they won't get you away from me. There's four able-bodied men upstairs, and I've got a shotgun all loaded and ready, if they even try," Abby assured her. "Meantime, let's get you cleaned up a bit. You've got some nasty

403

scratches, and those rope burns don't look so nice, either."

An inventory of Maggie's hurts revealed a lot of cuts and bruises but nothing too serious. Now that the immediate danger had passed, Maggie realized that she ached in every muscle from the battering she had taken that day, beginning with the fall from her horse. Abby bathed and treated the cuts and fixed a cup of tea to soothe the aches as best she could. Then, seeing Maggie's exhaustion, Abby provided her with a nightdress and helped her into it, even going so far as to tuck her into the large bed. For a moment Maggie actually thought she might be able to fall asleep, but then someone began hammering on the front door.

"Don't you worry none," Abby soothed her. "I'll get the shotgun. Nobody's gonna get in here who don't belong."

Abby turned the lamp down low before she left, cautioning Maggie not to betray her presence. When she had gone, Maggie clutched the covers to her pounding heart, wishing suddenly that Abby had given her the shotgun. Common sense told her that even Kincaid and Crescent wouldn't dare to come into Abby's house after her, but that did not seem to convince her overwrought nerves. Straining to hear, she made out the rumble of men's voices, and then Abby's higher one. Did the voices really sound familiar, or was it just her imagination?

They were coming closer now, and that wasn't her imagination. Abby was with them, though. Maggie could hear her talking. She jumped when the door flew open, but her panic lasted only a second. Dear Lord, it was Jack!

Her cry was mingled joy and relief, and her arms reached for him even before he recognized her. She thought he called her name, but she wasn't sure, and it didn't matter. All that mattered was that he was here, now, and she was safe. Then she was in his arms, all danger forgotten.

Abby closed the door on the reunion, and grinned up into Swede's stunned face. "How'd she get here?" he asked. "We thought she'd been kidnapped!"

404

"She was," Abby informed him with a small degree of satisfaction. "She got away." Abby gave him a brief account of Maggie's adventure.

"I'll be damned," Swede murmured, forgetting for a moment that he was in the presence of a lady. "Jack was so sure she'd be at Renita's house, and Kincaid led us right there, too. Wonder what his game is?"

Abby shook her head in amazement, but before she could come up with a theory, Swede suddenly remembered the rest of the men were still waiting for him outside. "I better go tell the boys. They'll be mighty relieved," he said, turning to go.

"You'll come back here when you're done, won't you?" Abby inquired when they reached the front hallway.

Swede paused, a little taken back. "I was gonna bed down at the livery with the rest of the boys."

"Shouldn't somebody stay here to guard Mr. and Mrs. Sinclair?" Abby suggested innocently.

Swede considered. "I reckon," he hedged. "You got a place where I can stay?"

"I sure do," Abby replied. Swede shrugged his consent, and then hastened outside to tell the rest of the men that Maggie was safe.

After posting two men as outside guards in case Crescent did come looking for Maggie, Swede went back inside. Abby was waiting for him in the darkened hallway. There was a moment of awkward silence as he realized that Abby was wearing her nightclothes, that underneath those thin layers of cloth her full body would be all soft and loose. A fantasy of how she would feel in his arms skittered across his consciousness. Finally, he cleared his throat and forced himself to ask, "You said you had a place for me to stay?"

"Yes, right here," Abby replied, leading the way back down the hall toward the rear of the house. She stopped at a partially opened door and pushed it wide for him to enter.

"Good night," he muttered as he brushed by her, inhaling her scent and belatedly removing his hat.

Abby did not reply. Instead she followed him inside and shut the door behind her.

Startled, Swede glanced around the room with widened eyes. A lamp burned on the bedside table, illuminating the scene for him. "This is *your* room," he blurted.

Abby nodded, studying his reaction as she leaned back against the door. She had done a lot of thinking since her conversation with Maggie, and had decided to find out once and for all if Maggie was right about Swede. Abby watched with great interest the small battle he fought with himself. At last his pale blue eyes settled on her face. "You're sure you want me here?" he asked, his disbelief evident.

"Very sure," Abby replied, growing more certain by the second.

He growled something that sounded like, "Oh, God," as he dropped his hat on the floor and opened his arms to her. She went to him then, not really knowing if she were being wise or foolish, but not caring.

"Oh, Maggie, Maggie." Jack kept repeating her name over and over like a litany as he rocked her in the ancient gesture of comfort. When he had at last convinced himself that she was, indeed, there, safe in his arms, he pushed her gently away. What he saw drew a curse from him. "What happened to your face?" he demanded.

Automatically, Maggie's hand flew up to touch her swollen cheek, and he caught sight of her lacerated wrist. He grabbed her hand and brought it to him for closer inspection in the dim light. Capturing its mate, he studied them both in pained silence, and then lifted his dark eyes to hers. "You really were kidnapped," he concluded. For one wild moment there, when he had found her safe with Abby, he had concluded that his fears had been groundless, that she had only gone to Abby's as her note had said. Now he recalled the evidence of the returned mare and the tracks that Swede had found, and knew that if Maggie was now safe, it was due only to some miracle.

Maggie swallowed. "Yes," she said meekly. She was going to have to explain just how it had happened that she was riding off to town alone, how she had sneaked away from Lee Parker's vigilance only to ride into a trap. Jack was going to be furious, and she wouldn't blame him one bit.

"I . . . I got this note from Abby," she began, and he gave her hands a gentle squeeze of encouragement. "It wasn't really from Abby, of course, but I thought it was, so I started for town. I left you a note . . ." she began, but his nod told her he had gotten it. She swallowed again. No use going into detail at this point. "I was about halfway there when something knocked me off my horse. . . ." From there the story poured out effortlessly, the only evidence of Jack's fury being the way his hands tightened on hers until his grip was almost painful. She watched carefully for any signs of jealousy when she told the part about Crescent and the woman going into the bedroom together, but the only emotion she could detect was relief, if that was indeed the correct name for the brief flicker she saw in those black eyes. "When I got out the window, I ran straight here, and Abby let me in," she concluded.

Jack's eyes closed once over the picture of Maggie, bound and gagged, running through the streets in the dead of night. Someone would pay for this, and pay dearly. "You're a very brave girl," he told her, reaching up to give her shoulders a reassuring squeeze.

She wanted to inform him that she was not a girl, she was a woman, but his touch brought a cry of pain to her lips instead.

"What is it?" he asked, concern evident in every line of his face.

Maggie gave a self-conscious laugh as she reached up to massage her sore shoulder. "I forgot to mention that I fell out the window."

His swift, sure hands disposed of the buttons of the voluminous nightdress and gently uncovered Maggie's injury. An ugly-looking bruise was turning various shades of black and purple. "My poor darling," he murmured, lowering his head instinctively to touch his lips to the mark.

Memories stirred, memories of their first meeting when he had kissed her burned finger. As gentle as his kiss was, it seemed to sear her flesh. "Jack?" she whispered, her body melting to his touch.

"Mmmmm?" he replied, tenderly laying her back against the pillow.

"My face hurts, too."

Instantly, his lips were on her swollen cheek in a feathering caress.

"And my wrists," she murmured, holding them up for him.

With elaborate care he encircled each slim wrist with a string of tiny kisses, and then pressed his lips into the palm of each hand. When he lifted his face to hers again, his mustache was slightly slanted. "Do you have any other wounds, my little witch?" he asked.

"Well," she hesitated impishly, all her previous fears evaporating now that Jack was here with her, "my feet . . ."

Before she could even complete her sentence, he threw back the covers. She hadn't really intended for him to kiss her feet. It had only been a joke, and she instinctively tried to curl them up out of sight, and Jack was too quick for her. Capturing one trim ankle, he lifted it, pressing a kiss on her instep much as a gentleman might kiss a lady's hand.

"Jack!" she protested breathlessly, but he was not to be deterred. He inspected the sole of her foot, and then anointed each cut and scrape. His mustache tickled and his warm breath sent chills skittering up her leg. She tried to pull away, but it was only reaction and not because she really wanted to, especially when his lips found the curve of her ankle and his tongue slipped out to caress the sensitive hollow.

Somehow her other foot had crawled out from its hiding place and made its way up to rest upon his chest. She could feel his heart pounding, betraying his arousal in spite of his amused expression. Then he carefully placed her treated foot back on the mattress and took possession of the one resting against his chest. Maggie was moaning softly by the time he had finished ministering to that one, the chills having long since warmed and then blazed into tongues of fire that licked into the most delightful places.

"Anything else?" he growled, no longer able to feign amusement.

"My knee," she breathed, pulling Abby's nightdress up much farther than necessary to expose her knee. Her eyes, now emerald green, watched his glitter as they took in the shapely expanse of her legs before his head lowered to nuzzle first the delicate bend of her leg before addressing the abraded cap.

Questing fingers skimmed up under the hem of the nightdress, and Maggie flinched involuntarily as he grazed the spot where Crescent had pinched her. Rooting instinctively, he found the spot with his lips, and soothed it, too.

"Where else?" His voice was no more than a gasp, his breath stirring the tiny hairs on her inner thighs and sweeping upward in molten waves into the part of her that throbbed for him.

Maggie shifted restlessly, encouragingly, but he misinterpreted her gesture and made to move away from her. Sensing his withdrawal, she captured his hand. "He pinched me here," she whispered, drawing his hand inside the nightdress to touch the puckered tip of her breast.

His growl was part outrage and part lust, and she thought the muffled words he uttered were a curse on Crescent. In the next second she did not care, however. When he took the pebbled peak in his mouth, her thoughts scattered, and she arched against him, burying her fingers in his thick, black hair and forcing him to her. Laving her with his tongue, he cleansed her of violation, washing from her mind all thoughts of anyone and anything but him.

She writhed against him, impatient with the clothes that separated them, pleading with him with tiny, inarticulate sounds to take her. Her hands pushed against his shoulders, tugging at his coat, and this time he did pull away, collapsing in a heap on the bed beside her.

"I'm sorry," he rasped, his breath coming in great, gasping gulps.

"Sorry?" Maggie echoed, her own breath painfully ragged.

"You're such a tempting little witch, I got carried away," Jack apologized. Good God, she must think him an animal, taking advantage of her in her condition. He'd best get out of this room and fast or even his honor would no longer protect her. The only question was whether he would be able to walk when—and if—he managed to get up off the bed.

It took several seconds, but Maggie's foggy brain finally grasped the fact that he was not going to make love to her. "But I want you to get carried away," she assured him breathlessly, curling against him and capturing one of his legs with hers.

Jack had to grit his teeth to hold his throbbing body in check. "You're in no condition . . . you've had a shock. . . ." he protested feebly, knowing he was right, but hardly able to control the more primitive instincts that urged him on. "I might hurt you. . . ." That was logical. Surely she would be convinced and let him go. If he *could* go . . .

"You won't hurt me," she assured him, running a hand down his shirtfront, past his belt buckle, and into very dangerous territory.

With a gasp and a lunge, he changed their positions, pinning her to the mattress with his weight, sealing the promise of their desire with a kiss that robbed them both of what little breath they had left and of almost all their sanity.

"You're a trifle overdressed for what I have planned," she complained when he lifted his lips from hers for a moment.

He stared down at her for a moment, dumbfounded. How could she be so playful after all that she had just been through? He had no idea, but if it helped her forget, to block out the horror, he could play along. "So are you," he replied, sitting up swiftly to wrestle out of his clothes. Clumsy in his haste, he had Maggie giggling at his fumbles and curses and at the dire threats of revenge he was making her.

"What if Crescent comes back to kidnap me again?" she asked in mock concern as Jack whipped Abby's nightdress off over her head. It was odd how such an event seemed impossible enough to joke about when Jack was near.

"He'll just have to wait until I'm finished with you," Jack muttered into the sweet curve of her neck as he eased her into the down-filled mattress. "You'll tell me if I hurt you?"

"Yes," she lied, drawing his hands up to cover her breasts. She really didn't care whether he hurt her or not. What was a little discomfort compared to ecstasy?

Still, he was careful. Almost too careful for Maggie's taste. His hands moved over her body almost worshipfully, exploring every swell and hollow with a thoroughness that drove her to the brink of insanity. If she had wanted him before—and she had, with every fiber of her being—then she would have died for him now. The flames that his curative kisses had ignited now raged into an inferno, and her sobbing voice pleaded with him to join her on the pyre.

No longer able to refuse her, he came to her, uniting their bodies with caution, lest the explosion come too soon. When her searing flesh closed around him, he breathed her name and knew a moment's wonder at the tears that started in his eyes. The agony of the past few hours added a new dimension to their lovemaking, and for a few seconds he could separate himself from the shear pleasure of it and marvel at the act itself, at his ability to join himself body and soul to the woman he loved. Even if this were all he ever had of her, he knew it would be worth suffering the pains of hell, and he surrendered to that knowledge.

411

Maggie surrendered with him, spiraling out and out, closer and yet farther away and then closer still, until they teetered on the edge. Teasing and prodding, they dangled over the precipice for eons of seconds, tiny sparkles of time that lasted forever yet were gone in an instant, and then they fell. Down and down and down into the depths of life itself, into each other, until they were truly one.

It was a long time later that Jack could finally think rationally again. Maggie slept peacefully in his arms, as safe as love and his strength could make her, and at last he understood. Life had a way of teaching a man the things he least wanted to know, and Jack had just learned the hardest lesson of his life. Years ago he had condemned a man for the very feelings he was having at that moment. Not just any man, either, but his own brother. Poor Roger. He had been obsessed with the golden Lydia, so obsessed that even marriage had not been a close enough bond. How Jack had laughed at such excess of emotion, and it was that, in the end, that had provided his excuse for leaving home. How could he be expected to witness such devotion on a daily basis and remain sane? Sanity, of course, had no part in it, as he later learned.

Reckless Lydia, how little she had understood of the power she held. Perhaps if she had, she would have taken more care of her precious self, would not have jumped that impossible fence, would not have squandered her life in pursuit of a worthless fox. But she hadn't understood, and so she had taken the fence, or tried to. When Roger had finally gotten to her, she was already dead, her lovely neck snapped in two. Inconsolable, Roger had become a wild man, and rather than see her put, cold and still, into the unforgiving earth, he had taken his own life.

It had all seemed like such a waste to Jack when he had heard the story years later. Had he known, had he even suspected, he might never have left. Leaving had seemed so easy at the time. He had just finished his second year of

412

college and returned home to find his mother dying. It was only for her that he had stayed as long as he had, and with her gone, he was free of the last obligatory tie. His father was in robust health and would live for years. When he did go, there were Roger and all the children he and Lydia were bound to have to take over the Sinclair property. He need feel no guilt at going off to sow his wild oats.

He wrote from time to time, but never stayed in one place long enough to receive any mail, and so it had taken several years for them to track him down. When they did, his father was dying, broken from the dual tragedy, and he lived only long enough to see his surviving son one last time.

Maggie moaned softly in her sleep, and Jack drew her closer. During the long hours when he had not known her fate, when he had suspected that he might never see her alive again, he had begun to understand the black despair that had driven Roger over the edge. Not that Jack would have taken his own life, but he damn sure would have taken someone else's. That wouldn't have brought Maggie back, though, and the thought of life without her was so bleak that he shuddered at the mere thought.

It was foolishness, no, it was insanity to let this thing with Kincaid go on any longer. He would have to go on the offensive. He would try the law first, but if the law didn't work—and he had a sneaking suspicion that Kincaid had himself covered there—then Jack would simply have to go around the law. It wouldn't be the first time.

Too keyed up to really sleep, Jack dozed for a while, until the sounds in the house told him that it was late enough to rise. Maggie muttered in her sleep when he left her, but he soothed her and tucked the covers around her, and she quieted. Then he dressed as silently and as quickly as he could. His clothes were quite a bit the worse for wear, since he had worn them the day before to work in and most of the night searching for Maggie. Having lain on the floor all night had done them no good at all, and his disreputable appearance did not improve his mood. He was out for blood this morning, and someone was going to serve some up.

He stole almost silently from the room, closing the door behind him without so much as a click, and when he turned, he saw Abby emerging from her bedroom already dressed for the day. "Good morning, Mrs. Wheeler. Do you by any chance know where I can find Swede?" he asked in a whisper.

Abby colored slightly, but maintained her dignity. "He's getting dressed. He'll be out in a minute."

Jack gave her a blank look until he heard the scuffling sounds coming from the room she had just left. Then the door opened, and a very flustered Swede appeared, hastily buckling on his gunbelt. "Did you want me, boss?" he asked. He was trying to sound nonchalant, but his face was scarlet and his hands were unusually awkward with the buckle.

Jack glanced from Swede to Abby's flushed cheeks and back to Swede again. Who would have believed it? Sanguine Swede and the buxom widow. He struggled to keep his amazement—and amusement—out of his voice. "I have some business with Kincaid this morning," he told his foreman. "I want you to stay here and guard Maggie. I don't expect any trouble, but you can't be too careful with a man like Kincaid."

Swede nodded. "I put two men outside last night, too," he said.

"Good," Jack remarked absently, letting his gaze drift over to the widow again.

Now she was starting to look flustered, too. "I'll go start breakfast," she offered and hurried away.

Jack brought his eyes back to Swede, who had gone from painfully embarrassed to angry in a very brief time. "We're getting married," Swede announced defensively.

"Congratulations," Jack said quite sincerely. At Swede's skeptical look, he added, "I really mean it. She's a fine woman, and I'm glad you're getting married. Misery loves company."

Swede softened at Jack's self-mocking smirk and grinned back, taking Jack's outstretched hand and pumping it vigorously. "You ain't always miserable," Swede pointed out.

"No, not always," Jack conceded, recalling what had happened in Abby's back bedroom not long ago. "Tell Mrs. Wheeler that I'll be back for my breakfast later," he instructed, suddenly remembering his earlier intent. "I've got some business to take care of."

Renita had not waited until daylight to take care of her business. When Jack and his men had left her house, she had hurriedly dressed and headed for Sam Kincaid's office.

The downstairs was dark, but a light was burning in the living quarters upstairs, and Renita stormed up the outside steps, determined to get an explanation for Kincaid's shoddy planning of the kidnapping. She could not accept the idea that he had sent Crescent to her house out of stupidity, and she was going to let Kincaid know exactly what she thought of his attempt to involve her in the mess.

She had to knock twice before the door opened. Kincaid was still dressed and had obviously not been to bed that night. He also did not seem particularly surprised to see her. Stepping back to allow her to enter, he called out to someone in the other room, "It's all right. It's only 'Nita." To her surprise, Crescent came in from the other room.

When they had discovered Maggie's escape earlier, Crescent had thrown on his clothes and set out after her, but Renita had been fairly certain that he would be much too late. Her house was very close to town and a dozen places where Mrs. Sinclair could have gone for refuge. Renita had an idea that Mrs. Sinclair had not wasted any time in getting to one of them. Crescent's presence here at Kincaid's proved that she had been correct. Her only worry was what excuse Crescent had given for allowing the woman to escape in the first place.

The three stood in awkward silence for a time, and then Kincaid's soft voice broke in. "Crescent says you let the girl get away."

Renita felt her hackles rise at his choice of words, but she had to agree he was correct. "She got away, yes," Renita said, her dark eyes watching Crescent for a clue as to what story he had given. It simply would not do to admit to the man who was keeping her that she had been in bed with another man while his captive escaped.

"He said you put her in the other room, and she got out the window. That right?" Kincaid prodded. His broad face gave no hint as to what he was thinking.

"That's right," she said, still watching Crescent, who would not meet her eyes.

"He said you had her in the bedroom. That right?" Kincaid was probing again, and she realized that Crescent had switched the truth to protect them.

"Yes, we put her in the bedroom to keep her out of sight in case anyone came to the door," she explained.

"And she got out the window?" Kincaid's voice was dull, his repetition of the facts making him sound slow-witted.

"Yes, that's right," Renita snapped, irritated at being forced to lie again.

"The bedroom only has one window, and it's five feet off the ground. How'd she climb out of it with her hands tied?" The question was so mild that at first Renita did not recognize it for the accusation that it was, and when she did, she could only marvel at Kincaid's powers of observation. He had only been in her bedroom once, for a few seconds.

"I don't know," she hedged, glancing at Crescent for help. She received none.

"Fact is, she was in the front room and the two of you were in the bedroom. Ain't that right?" No one replied, but then, no one had to. Kincaid knew he was correct. "I guess I don't need to ask what you were doing, either," he remarked to no

416

one in particular.

He did not seem angry or even annoyed. His face betrayed no emotion at all. Renita struggled between relief and irritation. She had expected him to be at least a little possessive of her, but he seemed not even to care that she had betrayed him with one of his own hired men.

Crescent shifted uneasily. "Can I go now?" he asked. He was still carefully avoiding looking at Renita.

"Sure," Kincaid said amiably. "You hook up with those fellows I told you about. Tell them I said you was to help them. They'll fill you in on the plan."

Crescent nodded his assent, and then headed for the door. Renita was blocking his way, and there was an awkward moment when she refused to move until he looked her straight in the eye and acknowledged her presence. He had the grace to look extremely uncomfortable until she stepped haughtily out of his way. She waited until the sound of his boots on the stairs and the sidewalk below had died away before turning to Kincaid.

"You knew Sinclair would come straight to my house looking for the girl, didn't you?" she accused.

She had half expected him to deny it, but instead, his face twisted into that parody of a smile. "Yeah, I figured he would. Just to make sure, I gave him a hint when he came here first." He ignored Renita's gasp of outrage. "I figured it would be a good way to get rid of both of you at once. I'm a little tired of taking in Sinclair's leavings."

Renita would have slapped him, but his blow came first. His fist colliding with her head had the force of a sledgehammer, and it knocked her to the floor. Fighting the ringing in her ears, the unconsciousness that threatened, she heard him say, "I don't take anybody else's leavings, either. When you're mine, you sleep with me and nobody else."

She struggled to her knees, some instinct warning her that she had to get away, but Kincaid's booted foot pushed her

417

down again, her face to the floor. In the next second, his hammy hand grasped the neckline of her dress and yanked. The material resisted for one awful moment when Renita thought he would choke her, but then it gave with a savage tearing sound. She struggled feebly, fighting him, but he used his fist again until she lay limp and unresisting while he ripped the rest of the clothing from her body.

She watched him then from where she lay, a naked, crumpled heap at his feet. She saw him unbuckle his belt and slip it from its loops, but only when he doubled it and raised it did she guess his intent. Barely conscious, still she found the strength to protest, raising her arms in an instinctively protective gesture and uttering a faint cry of alarm, but still the leather struck her, and her next cry was one of agony as his arm raised and came crashing down again. And again. And again.

Marshal Davis scratched his bald head. "From what you say, Mr. Sinclair, the man Crescent had lots of reasons to hate you, and if your wife says that he's the man who kidnapped her, then it makes sense. It even makes sense that the woman would want to help him. What don't make sense is why Mr. Kincaid would be in on it."

Jack made an impatient noise and wondered if coming to the law had been such a good idea after all. He should have taken justice into his own hands. He was just too civilized, he decided, not for the first time. "I told you, Kincaid is trying to take over the CMC land. If he had my wife, he could dictate any terms he liked and I would have had to agree to them."

"Still, he would have had to give your wife back, sooner or later, or else killed her. Sorry, Mr. Sinclair," Davis added, when Jack's face tightened dangerously. "Either way, all hell would have busted loose then, and Kincaid never would have gotten out of the country in one piece. No man takes a

418

woman by force and lives to tell about it. You know that as well as I do."

What the marshal was saying was true, yet Jack knew from what Maggie had overheard Renita and Crescent saying that Kincaid had planned the whole thing. "Let's question the parties involved and find out what they have to say about it, shall we?" Jack suggested as patiently as he could. Plainly, the marshal was going to be difficult to convince.

A trip to Renita's house proved wasted when they found the place empty. Jack was not too surprised. He only hoped that she had not skipped town before he had a chance to pay her back for her treachery. Kincaid's office was open, but the boy Billy informed them that his uncle was still upstairs in his rooms, so the two men went up to find him.

The marshal led the way, and Kincaid answered on the first knock. "Sorry to bother you, Mr. Kincaid, but we'd like to ask you a few questions about Mrs. Sinclair's kidnapping. Can we come in?"

Kincaid stepped back and allowed the two men to enter. Jack looked around the sparsely furnished room. It was almost as barren and comfortless as the office downstairs, but it suited the man who occupied it. A closed door obviously led to another room, probably a bedroom.

"Maybe you heard, Mrs. Sinclair was kidnapped last night. A man name of Crescent was who done it. He took her to Miss McFadden's house. From what Mrs. Sinclair heard, she got the idea that you knew something about it." The marshal waited respectfully for Kincaid's reply.

To the surprise of both Jack and the marshal, Kincaid nodded. "I knew about it," he said, and raised his hand to stop the flood of rage from Jack. "Crescent came to me with some crazy idea of kidnapping the woman. I told him to forget it, but I guess he decided to go ahead and do it on his own."

Jack knew he was lying, or at least he was pretty sure, but

before he could accuse him of it, the marshal asked, "Why didn't you say anything about this last night?"

Kincaid blinked once, his only reaction. "I forgot."

Unable to restrain himself any longer, Jack demanded, "Where's Renita? She was in on it, too, and you know it."

"Let's ask her," Kincaid replied. "'Nita, come in here," he called, looking toward the closed door to the other room.

Startled, both Jack and the marshal looked toward the door expectantly. Only the faintest sounds of movement hinted that Kincaid's order was being obeyed, and after what seemed a long time, the knob turned and the door opened slightly.

"Come on out and tell the marshal what happened, 'Nita," Kincaid urged calmly.

The door inched open a little more until the figure behind it was visible, and both Jack and the marshal gasped in horror. Jack barely recognized her. Her beautiful face was swollen grotesquely, both eyes blackened and her lovely lips split and caked with dried blood. Her dark hair hung in wild disarray about her stooped shoulders. She was wearing what was clearly a man's robe. It hung past her hands and dragged the floor around her feet. She held it together in the front. It had no other fastening.

"Come on," Kincaid urged again. "Don't be afraid. They won't hurt you." Jack thought he heard a hint of irony in Kincaid's soft voice, but he couldn't be certain.

Renita came forward then, but slowly, moving as if she had suddenly grown very old and fragile. Jack knew instinctively, from the careful way she moved, that she was in pain. She stopped when she was a few feet inside the room.

"'Nita came to me this morning," Kincaid explained. "She told me that Crescent forced his way into her house last night with Mrs. Sinclair. He told her that he'd kill her if she didn't let him keep the woman there. She didn't want to, of course, so he took her into the other room and beat her up. While he was busy, Mrs. Sinclair got away. Ain't that the way it

420

happened, 'Nita?"

Renita's haunted eyes had stared at Kincaid through his whole recitation. She never even blinked. On cue, she nodded once.

"That's a lie," Jack insisted. "Marshal, I was at her house last night with my men, *after* Maggie escaped, and she didn't have a mark on her then."

Plainly, the marshal did not know who to believe.

"Show them what he did to you, 'Nita," Kincaid said. When she hesitated, he said, more sharply, "Show them."

Before anyone could stop her, Renita opened the robe and let it slip from her shoulders and fall in a heap at her bare feet. Jack heard the marshal's gasp as if from a great distance. The sight before him was so awful that for a moment he could think of nothing except the outrage of Renita's beautiful body having been desecrated in such a horrible way. Then her eyes lifted to him, and he saw in them her pain and her shame, and pity moved him to rush to her. Lifting the robe, he placed it gently around her shoulders and drew it together in the front.

My God, he thought, she had been beaten, whipped unmercifully, and were those *teeth marks?* He didn't want to know, didn't even want to think about it. In that moment, he felt her pain, her humiliation, and all thoughts of revenge against her soured, leaving a bitter taste in his mouth.

She looked up as if only just now recognizing him. "He hurt me, Jack," she whispered.

The marshal at last found his voice. "Have you sent for the doctor?" he blustered. "She could be bad hurt."

"Nothing but some cuts and bruises," Kincaid assured him. "She'll be fine in a couple of days. Won't you, 'Nita?"

Jack cringed, knowing how she hated the nickname and seeing the meek way in which she nodded her agreement. Whatever her sins, she had paid for them, Jack decided, looking down into her vacant eyes. All the life, the spirit of the woman he had known had been snuffed out. Whoever had beaten her, and Jack would have bet his life it had not been Crescent, had beaten the life out of her. Even though her body still lived, the real Renita had been killed just as surely as if she had been stabbed through the heart.

The marshal cleared his throat nervously, unwilling to break the uneasy silence that had fallen, but anxious to get away. "Reckon we'd better go, Mr. Sinclair. Seems like we got no evidence against these folks, and Miss McFadden ought not to be up in her condition."

Reluctantly, Jack agreed. With Kincaid acknowledging that he knew about the kidnapping but had nothing to do with it, it was his word against Maggie's, and Maggie really had no proof that he had been involved. Kincaid could argue that she had been hysterical and had misunderstood what Renita and Crescent had said about his involvement. Renita would swear to his lies, and he would get off scott free. No, Jack's initial impression had been correct. He was wasting his time with the law.

Jack narrowed his gaze at Kincaid, studying the man for any signs of remorse. He found none. "You win this round, Kincaid," he said, "but the fight's not over yet, and this time you won't be fighting a woman."

Kincaid blinked once. "We'll see."

When Jack got back to Abby's, he found Maggie enjoying breakfast in bed. The smile she gave him made his heart lurch, and a sudden vision of Renita's broken body caused him to shudder. How easily that could have been Maggie.

Maggie's smile quickly became a pout when she recalled her irritation at waking up alone for the second morning in a row. For a moment she had thought perhaps the whole thing had been a bad dream, but then she had realized that she was, indeed, in Abby's house, sleeping naked in a badly rumped bed beside a pillow that bore the indentation of a head and smelled of Jack Sinclair. No, all of it had really

422

happened, and she was extremely lucky to be free this morning.

Abby had heard her moving around and had come in with a breakfast tray and informed her that Jack had gone after Kincaid with the marshal. That had been only a short time ago, and judging from Jack's bleak expression, he hadn't gotten the revenge he had gone after.

"Where have you been?" she demanded, with just the right amount of martyrdom.

The mustache tilted. "Out cutting a hickory switch," he informed her, crossing the room in a few quick strides and standing over her forbiddingly.

Maggie stared up at him in bewilderment. "A hickory switch? Whatever for?"

"Didn't your father ever use a hickory switch on you?" he asked in mock exasperation, planting his hands on his narrow hips. "No, of course not," he answered himself. "That probably explains why you're so disobedient to this very day."

Maggie swallowed the sudden lump in her throat. Last night she had gotten off easy because he had been so glad that she was all right, but now he was going to let her have it for getting into such a mess in the first place. Sinking down into the bedclothes, she looked up at him through her lashes and decided that the best way to defuse the situation was to admit her guilt outright. "I know I shouldn't have gone off like that alone. I'm sorry, Jack," she said meekly.

Jack's eyes grew large with amazement and then narrowed skeptically. "Oh, no you don't, you little witch," he said, reaching for her breakfast tray and setting it safely on the floor and out of the way. "You aren't getting off that easily."

Seeing the determined look in his eye, Maggie made a desperate attempt to scramble off the opposite side of the bed, but she got tangled in the bedclothes. Jack looped an arm around her waist and pulled her back, seating himself on the bed as he did so. Maggie fought like a wildcat, her aches and bruises momentarily forgotten, but she was no match for him. After a furious but brief battle, he succeeded in dragging her across his lap and applying one very restrained smack to her backside before releasing her.

Maggie struggled free, rising up on her knees, her face the picture of outrage. "How dare you!" she cried before she could catch herself.

Amusement flickered in his eyes, but he kept a straight face. "It's a lot less than you deserve," he pointed out. "That didn't even hurt."

"You . . . you BEAST! It most certainly did hurt!" she lied, rubbing her wounded derriere.

This time he could not hold back the deliciously wicked grin that split his face. "Would you like me to kiss it and make it better?" he inquired.

Maggie's jaw had barely had time to drop before he lunged for her, and the squeal that escaped her just before he pounced was as unplanned as it was loud. They were a tumbling mass of arms and legs when the door flew open, banging into the wall with a crash that brought them both upright in an instant.

Swede crouched in the doorway, gun drawn, ready to do battle. His pale eyes scanned the room for intruders, and finding none, settled on the couple on the bed. For a long moment everyone simply stared at everyone else, and then Swede visibly relaxed and lowered his gun. "This fella bothering you, Mrs. Sinclair?" he deadpanned.

Maggie choked back a giggle at the flush crawling up Jack's neck, and when he angrily jerked down her nightdress to cover a rather beguiling expanse of leg, she couldn't hold it back any more. Collapsing onto the pillows, she dissolved into gales of laughter. Caught between her giggles and Swede's knowing grin, Jack found himself grinning back.

"I'll be outside if you need any help," Swede smirked as he pulled the door shut behind him.

"You see . . . how . . . ir . . . irritating it . . . is to . . . have a . . . guard," Maggie gasped, holding her side.

Jack grumbled something unintelligible before leaning over to give her a resounding kiss. "Get your clothes on, Mrs. Sinclair. I'm taking you back to the ranch where you won't have anybody to rescue you. Then you'll be sorry."

Maggie doubted that very much.

Chapter XV

Maggie dozed on Jack's shoulder in the rented buggy all the way back to the ranch. Unfortunately—or at least Maggie thought it was unfortunate—Jack did not feel that that constituted enough rest for her and ordered her straight to bed as soon as they arrived. That would have been fine with Maggie, except that she soon realized he had no intention of joining her. Instead, he sent Consuela in with a cup of her notorious tea.

At first Maggie refused to drink it, so Consuela left it sitting on her bedside table, but after a fruitless half-hour of tossing and turning, which only served to aggravate her many bumps and bruises, Maggie gave in. The drink was stone cold, but that did not seem to affect its potency any, she noted as she almost immediately drifted off to sleep.

When she awoke, she could tell by the shadows on the wall that it was almost suppertime, and she was famished. Quickly, she rose and dressed, choosing one of her favorite floral print gowns. She left her hair loose and tied it back with a ribbon. Pinching her cheeks and biting her lips for the color that seemed to have fled permanently from her face, she smiled back at her reflection, hoping that Jack would be as pleased with her appearance as she was.

She found him sound asleep in one of the huge chairs in

the parlor, one foot propped up on a neighboring chair, the other stretched out in front of him. It was just like him, she decided, to be too proud to take a nap even though he had been up all night, too. He had not shaved, and his growth of beard gave him a rather sinister air, which was enhanced by the scowl that even sleep had not had the power to erase. She knew instinctively that he had been thinking about Kincaid and Crescent and what they had done to her, and in a rush of tenderness, she bent to kiss the frown lines from his forehead.

Jack's reaction was the result of years of essential wariness. He came instantly awake, but even before his eyes opened, he had grabbed his attacker. Angry black eyes stared into startled hazel ones for a moment before he realized that it was Maggie whom he held, and his ferocity immediately melted into gentleness as he eased her into his lap.

Maggie blinked in surprise at the sudden change, but allowed her body to relax from its self-defensive reaction into surrender. "I'll have to remember never to sneak up on you again," she remarked, slipping her arms around his neck. How wonderful it felt to be close to him again, so safe, as if nothing and no one could ever hurt her again.

"Uh-huh," he murmured, not really listening to what she said, only enjoying the way her lovely lips moved and the way her sweet breath fanned his face when she spoke, savoring this one delicious moment of anticipation before he kissed her.

She knew he was going to kiss her, could see it in his eyes, and she sucked in her breath at the intensity she saw in those dark depths, inhaling the scent of cigars and Bay Rum and Jack Sinclair. Her love for him was a pleasant ache somewhere in the region of her heart, and when his lips touched hers, so gently at first, she thought for a moment that she might die from the joy of it.

Their mutual need deepened the kiss almost immediately,

427

mouth opening against mouth, tongue seeking out tongue in a moist duel that had no loser. Jack's arms tightened around her, drawing her close and closer still, as if he would pull her into his very soul, a place she would have willingly gone.

"Boss!"

Swede's voice calling from the office startled them apart, and while they were still gazing at each other in the fog of passion, he called again, his booted steps carrying him into the room they occupied. "Boss? Oh, excuse me," he stammered, flushing crimson at the sight of Maggie still curled in Jack's lap.

"This had better be important," Jack growled as he reluctantly released Maggie's pliant body and assisted her to her feet.

Maggie was quite irritated herself, but her sense of humor overcame her irritation as she noted Swede's agonized embarrassment. It was the second time today he had caught them in a compromising position, and plainly it bothered him a lot more than it bothered them. She coughed to cover a laugh, but almost lost control completely when she glanced at Jack and caught his thunderous look. Plainly, he was not amused.

"Well?" Jack inquired expectantly of the discomfited foreman.

"More nestors," Swede choked out.

Jack swore under his breath and ran a weary hand over his face. Well, he had wanted to go on the offensive. Here was the perfect opportunity. "How many?"

"Just a man and wife, from what Harvey saw. He was making the rounds, like you ordered. They're at the old Peters' place. He only got close enough to count heads and then he come hightailin' it back to tell us."

"Do you think the boys are up to a fight today?" Jack inquired casually.

Swede's homely face lit up. "They're spoilin' for one," he assured Jack.

428

"Oh, no," Maggie protested, alarmed by the gleam she saw in both men's eyes. "You aren't going to . . ."

"We certainly are," Jack replied, rising purposefully from the chair. "Excuse us, please, Mrs. Sinclair. We have some plans to make."

Maggie had no intention of excusing them, and she told them so, but as usual, Jack paid her no attention, rudely slamming the office door in her face after he and Swede had entered it. Muttering a curse at the closed door, Maggie resisted an urge to kick it and stomped off to the kitchen where she hoped she would get some sympathy from Consuela.

Jack took supper with the men, and the meal was a hurried affair when they heard what was planned for the evening. Innocent bystanders or not, this batch of nestors would pay for their temerity, and in doing so, would carry a clear message back to Kincaid.

Maggie watched with a heavy heart as Jack emptied her father's gun rack, issuing a Winchester to each man who, in turn, checked the gun and the loads before stepping aside to make way for the next in line. One by one, they filed past her on their way out the door, their eyes meeting hers for a fleeting instant. It took a while before Maggie sensed that they were telling her something, sending her a silent message, and even longer before she realized what it was. When she did, she was not certain she was pleased.

They were doing this for her; that was the message. Not for pay, not because they rode for the brand, not even for Jack, although each man owed his loyalty first and foremost to Jack Sinclair, but for her and her alone. Only now did she sense the rage they had felt when that nestor had taken a pot shot at her and the impotence they had experienced when she had turned up missing and they had not been able to find her. She had known and understood that Jack had felt that way. She was, after all, his wife, and she belonged to him. What she had not known was that, in a very real sense, she also belonged to these men, or they belonged to her. She wasn't certain which way it was, and she didn't think it really mattered. What bound them together was the land, of course, the CMC, but it was more than that, just as human relationships are more than material ones. In their own rough, crude way, these men loved her, loved her as they could never love another man, and they welcomed the opportunity to serve her. Tears of gratitude stung her eyes, and she blinked them back. She would not let them think she despised their loyalty. Instead she forced a small smile to her lips, an acknowledgment of their fealty, and made herself forget the poor, defenseless nestors they were going to attack.

Jack was the last to leave. He paused before her for a long moment and read the understanding in her eyes. His mustache tilted in self-mockery. After all he had gone through to take possession of her and the CMC, in the end they both possessed him, and here he was, riding out to defend them both.

This time Maggie did not bother to hide her tears. "Be careful," she whispered.

"I hadn't planned on being anything else," he quipped. For one heartbeat neither moved, and then they were in each other's arms, their kiss savage with suppressed longing. After a long time, he pulled away, setting her firmly from him. "And when I get back, I'll expect you to be properly grateful," he said hoarsely, and then he was gone.

If she had only known what was going to happen, she could have saved herself a lot of useless worry, and worried, instead, over something that needed worrying over.

The nestor and his wife turned out to be two men, one wearing a skirt to make him look like a woman from a distance, and they weren't alone by any stretch of the imagination. The cabin they occupied sat on the bank of a creek and was flanked by a grove of cottonwoods that effectively concealed their reinforcements.

Only the fact that Jack and the men rode in with guns drawn, expecting to provoke a fight, saved them. That and the fact that someone in the cabin couldn't wait and fired off a shot before they were too close to find cover. It didn't take the CMC men long to figure out that shots were coming from the woods as well as from the cabin and from far more than two guns, although exactly how many adversaries they were actually facing was impossible to tell in the twilight shadows.

"Kincaid set us up," Swede commented during a lull in the firing. He and Jack were crouched behind a rock that was inadequate cover for one man, much less two.

"He almost had us, too," Jack replied, taking careful aim and putting a rifle bullet through one window of the cabin. A shrill cry of pain marked his accuracy. "One more minute and they would have had us in the crossfire between the cabin and the woods."

Swede grunted his assent.

"We're wasting our time here," Jack decided after another shot ricocheted off the rock in front of them. "It'll be dark soon, and they'll be able to slip away. We might get the two in the cabin, but not the rest of them. I've got a much better idea. Signal the men. We're pulling out."

Swede's piercing whistle caused the men to fall back. Some of the horses had gotten away in the melee, so some of the men had to ride double. When they were out of range, Jack sent two men to stand sentry and report back if someone rode into town to report to Kincaid. The rest of the men headed back to the ranch.

Maggie was a little surprised to hear them returning so quickly. They had hardly had time to pack up the nestors, and even if they'd killed them—Maggie shuddered at the thought—they had not had time to bury them, either. Still, she stood on the porch, hands twisting nervously in her skirt, until she had identified Jack in the group.

Only then did she notice that the group was much smaller than the one that had ridden out, and she heard Consuela's surprised gasp when she realized the same thing.

"Some are riding double, señora," the housekeeper observed after a moment.

Some, yes, Maggie agreed mentally, but not all. Some were still missing, and the fact that some horses were missing was another indication that there had been a fight.

Time seemed to stand still as Maggie waited for Jack to unsaddle his horse and make his way up to the house. Swede and Lee Parker were with him. Maggie's two friends could rest easy, at least for the time being, she thought to herself.

"There was a fight," Maggie said when Jack had finally reached the porch.

"Yes," he agreed, mounting the stairs, his dark eyes devouring her. She knew he wanted to take her in his arms but was restraining himself because of the others.

Having no such compunction, she ran to him, holding him close, burying her face in his chest, thankful beyond words that whatever else had happened, he was all right. She felt a shudder go through him and knew he was as glad as she.

"Kincaid had an ambush waiting for us," he told her, pushing her gently away. "My guess is that this batch of 'nestors' is nothing more than a bunch of hired guns."

"Was anybody hurt?" she asked, remembering the missing men.

"Al got a crease on his shoulder, that's all. We were very lucky."

"What about the men who didn't come back?" she asked again, certain that he was, once again, sheltering her from the awful truth.

"They're guarding the road to town to see if anybody goes to make a report to Kincaid. We want to be sure he gets word of what happened . . . or rather, what didn't happen tonight. He's going to have to come up with a new plan, and we'll be

432

ready for him when he does. Come on in the office, boys," Jack invited to Swede and Lee. "You go on to bed, now, honey," he ordered her when the men had gone inside.

"Jack!" she protested, but he was already shaking his head.

"There's nothing you can do, Mrs. Sinclair, and you could use a good night's sleep, without interruptions," he said, his mustache tilting in a very provocative way.

"I've already had a good *day's* sleep, and I'm not tired!" Maggie informed him, but in spite of her fury at being so summarily dismissed, she knew her arguments were useless. If necessary, he was perfectly capable of carrying her to her room and chaining her there if he thought he had to in order to get her out of the way.

"Maggie," he warned, the steel in his voice meant to frighten her into obedience.

It had the desired effect, even though she wasn't the least bit afraid of him. Standing on the front porch arguing wasn't going to convince him that she was a mature, capable woman, and would, in fact, do the reverse. Besides, if he thought she was being meekly obedient, she would have a better chance of finding out exactly what he was planning to do about Kincaid. "Yes, dear," she replied through gritted teeth. No use in being too agreeable. He would only get suspicious.

"That's a good girl," he praised her sarcastically, obviously amused by her reluctance. Planting one very chaste kiss on her forehead, he brushed past her and followed Swede and Lee into the office.

When the door closed, Maggie allowed herself one brief curse, which caused Consuela, who was still lingering in the shadows, to giggle.

"Quit snickering and fetch my shawl," Maggie snapped.

"Your shawl?" Consuela echoed, puzzled.

"Yes, my shawl. If I have to stand outside to eavesdrop, I'm not going to catch pneumonia."

It wasn't really all that cold outside, but after she had stood underneath the window, barely breathing for fear of being discovered, for over an hour, Maggie was thoroughly chilled, shawl or no shawl. By then she knew all there was to know about Jack's plan, and she had to agree, it sounded masterful. If only it would work. The whole thing depended on how little respect Kincaid had for Jack's intelligence, but Jack seemed to think he had very little and that that would not be a problem. When she heard Jack offer the others a drink to toast their success, she knew that their meeting would break up soon, and she slipped silently back into the house and to her bedroom. Swiftly she changed into her nightdress and crawled into bed.

Still, it was a long time until she heard Jack's footsteps in the hall. She waited expectantly for them to turn toward her door, but to her disappointment, he went instead into his own. It was only natural, of course. Gentleman Jack would never think of disturbing her, especially after the ordeal she had been through the night before. He hadn't even wanted to make love to her this morning, even when she had practically thrown herself at him. She consoled herself with the knowledge that *he* needed a good night's sleep before carrying out the plans he had for tomorrow.

Maggie, however, was finding it impossible to fall asleep after her long nap. The mantel clock in the parlor struck the hour and then the half-hour, and still she lay wide-eyed, listening to the sounds from the room across the hall. No matter how much Maggie might reason that Jack needed sleep, he apparently was finding it as difficult to achieve as Maggie was herself. Even worse, he wasn't even trying, if the sounds of his pacing back and forth and the drifting scent of cigar smoke were any indication. Was he worried about tomorrow? Or excited perhaps, the anticipation of battle making him too keyed up to sleep?

Maggie had no way of knowing, but she did know that she had the power to remedy whatever it was that kept him from

434

his bed. Smiling slightly, her body tingling with an anticipation of her own, she slipped from the bed and padded silently across the floor, out her own door and over to Jack's. A moment of listening assured her that she had not been mistaken. Light still shone from the crack under the door, and the click of heels on the bare plank floor testified to Jack's restlessness. ▪

She lifted her hand to knock, but then lowered it. After all, he never knocked when he came into her room, did he? Taking one last breath for courage, she twisted the knob, opened the door, and stepped inside.

She saw his hand automatically go to his hip for the gun he was no longer wearing, an action that told her things about him she had never suspected. Then he relaxed, letting surprise replace his instinctive alarm. "Maggie," he said. "Is something wrong?"

As she watched, his face grew guarded, that blank mask slipping back into place. Yes, she admitted silently, something was very wrong. Closing the door behind her, she leaned back against it, her hands clutching the knob for support. This was not exactly the reception she had expected. She had thought he would at least be happy to see her, but instead he looked almost wary. Was it possible he did not know why she had come?

"Is something wrong?" he asked again when she did not reply.

Her glance darted around the room, perversely looking for some means of escape from what was rapidly becoming an embarrassing situation, when all the time the only escape was conveniently at her back and she knew she would not take it.

The room was different than she remembered it from when her father was alive. All his things were gone—of course, she had gotten rid of them herself—and Jack's were in their place. The room smelled of Bay Rum and the air was practically blue with cigar smoke. "The . . . the smell of cigar smoke was keeping me awake," she said lamely. It was partly true, at least.

Jack stared at her for an instant as if he did not quite comprehend what she had said and then he looked down at the burning cigar butt he held between his fingers as if he had never seen it before. Suddenly, he understood. "Oh, excuse me," he apologized, taking her at her word. He stubbed the cigar out on a dish that already held the remains of several others, and then snatched up a section of newspaper that he had carelessly discarded at some past time and began fanning the air, moving quickly over to a partially opened window and raising it further.

Maggie rolled her eyes in exasperation. What did she have to do, anyway? She was standing in his bedroom wearing only a flimsy nightdress. Couldn't he take a hint?

The fanning was having very little effect on the smoke, so Jack gave it up after a few more swipes, turning back to Maggie. She was still standing there by the door, poised as if for instant flight, her hair a fiery copper cloud around her head in the lamplight. Then the breeze from the opened window caught her, molding the thin fabric of her nightdress to her naked body. Jack's breath snagged in his chest and he felt a familiar tightening in his loins. God, she was beautiful. "Was there something else?" he ground out. Didn't she know how tempting she was, standing there like that? She shouldn't have come in here, unless . . .

Casting about frantically for something, anything, to say except what she really wanted to say, she decided the best thing to do was probably to make him mad. "I know what you're planning for tomorrow," she blurted.

So that was it. He lifted one eyebrow, and his mustache tilted in amusement. "Have you been listening at keyholes again, Mrs. Sinclair?"

In spite of the blush she could not control, Maggie lifted her chin defiantly. "No, at windows," she informed him.

"And do you approve of the plan?" he asked. Plainly her

approval meant little to him, or else he was not letting her see that he cared.

Maggie considered. "It's dangerous," she hedged, "but I think it might work."

Jack knew something else that was even more dangerous and that was Maggie's being here if she did not know the invitation she was issuing by her presence.

"Maggie, why did you come in here?" he asked, only a slight huskiness betraying him. That, and the way his fist was crumpling the newspaper he still held.

Maggie glared at him. Was he so simple-minded that he hadn't figured it out yet? No, of course not, she reasoned. He knew. He was going to make her ask for it. Maybe even beg. He was the most infuriating man alive. "I don't ask you embarrassing questions when you come to my room at night!" she snapped, ready to storm out of the room completely if he so much as smirked.

It took a moment for her words to register. She had come to him, of her own free will, because she wanted him. Her name was a strangled sound that came from deep in his throat. He was not even aware that he had dropped the newspaper and started toward her.

She met him more than halfway, the sound of her name and the look on his face enough to propel her from her position of safety straight into his grateful arms.

His kiss was urgent and his embrace lifted her off the ground, nearly cracking her ribs in the process. She didn't mind the pain, though, not as long as he was holding her, not as long as he was as desperate as she was.

And he was desperate. His hands roamed over her, feeling the warmth of her flesh through the fragile fabric. He would never get enough of her, not if he lived to be a hundred, he decided as he delved into the honeyed cavern of her mouth.

Maggie clung to him with hands and feet and arms and legs, wrapping herself around him, glorying in his strength and solidity. Her mouth opened beneath his as if she would

437

drink him in, even as her very flesh sought to absorb his essence by the force of physical contact.

Muttering something unintelligible, Jack struggled with her over to the bed, hoping to reach it before his legs gave out from the sheer urgency of his need for her. They tumbled down together in a tangle of arms and legs and clothing half-removed. Maggie tried to help Jack shed his clothes, but found her hands far more concerned with stroking the heated flesh he exposed, glorying in the groans her explorations elicited.

"Witch," he murmured when the last of his clothing was gone. He rolled over on her then, pinning her to the soft feather mattress with his weight while he began leisurely to undo the buttons of her nightdress. She squirmed with impatience, but he ignored her, very carefully avoiding touching the satiny skin he uncovered.

When the buttons were all freed, he peeled the nightdress off first one shoulder and then the other, baring each straining breast with tantalizing slowness while at the same time imprisoning her arms in a tangle of cloth. She struggled to release herself, but he tightened his hold.

"No, wait," he rasped. "Just let me look at you for a minute."

Maggie stilled, watching him watching her. His dark gaze moved over her with a sort of possessive wonder, and she marvelled that the heat from those dark eyes did not scorch the flesh from her bones. As it was, her whole body seemed to be on fire, and her heart's frantic beating only served to fan the flames, sending them raging outward to singe her fingers and toes and then back again to settle in the depths of her femininity. His breath was warm across the creamy mounds of her breasts, tautening the rosy nipples almost painfully with the need to be touched, caressed.

He answered her inarticulate cries of need, and she sighed rapturously when his head lowered. He took one tender peak into his mouth and suckled gently, causing ripples of reaction into the more sensitive, hidden reaches of her and bringing a moan of pleasure to her lips.

By the time Jack had moved to her other breast to treat it to more of the same tender torment, Maggie had freed her arms and wrapped them around him, drawing him closer and lifting herself, demanding that he take more of her into his devouring mouth. He happily obliged, feasting on her delicate flesh as one starving, drowning in the fragrance of lilacs mingled with the musky scent of woman.

Maggie writhed beneath him, the warm satin of his mouth contrasting with the rasp of his whiskers across her sensitive skin to drive her close to madness. Her hands moved restlessly across the sinewy muscles of his back in silent plea, while her lips mouthed his name over and over in supplication.

Somehow, without her knowing or caring, her nightdress disappeared completely, and he pressed against her, no barriers blocking the delicious contact of flesh with flesh, want with need, man with woman. Her eager hands guided him to her, helped him find the only refuge from the storm that raged between them, and together they rode out that storm, clasped heart-to-heart and soul-to-soul. Clinging together, they neither knew nor cared where one ended and the other began, their mutual compulsion uniting them into one striving entity.

The end came with cataclysmic finality, release quaking through her with such force that she thought her very bones must shatter. Even so, she heard Jack's simultaneous outcry, so agonized she imagined it might also have come from pain, and the breath he drew just before sliding his weight from her might even have been a sob.

"Jack?" she whispered. Their passion-dewed bodies still clung, without conscious effort, almost of their own accord, as if unwilling to break the contact.

"Hmmm?" he replied, contentment oozing from every pore as he idly stroked her silky hip.

"Nothing," she sighed, snuggling closer and placing a kiss on his damp shoulder. "Just 'Jack.'"

In a few minutes they would have to get up and pull down the covers and put out the lamp, but for now he drew the edge of the quilt over them as he had once before. He still could not believe that she had come to him. He had almost ruined it, almost driven her away. The look on her face when she had accused him of asking embarrassing questions had been priceless. Adorable. Yes, that's what she was, adorable, and he adored her.

And all that talk about cigar smoke and eavesdropping on him to learn his plan . . . Jack's passion-warmed body suddenly went cold as he remembered that she had overheard his plan. She was right, it was dangerous, although it was no more dangerous than waiting around for Kincaid to make his next move, but would it seem to Maggie that he was risking his life to save her ranch? The more he considered, the more he was convinced that it would. His motives were selfish, based on his pride's refusal to accept any more defeats from Kincaid, but they would seem unselfish to Maggie, sweet, idealistic Maggie. She would credit him with a nobility he did not possess, and she would be grateful.

Gratitude made people do strange things, things they might never do otherwise. Jack's eyes narrowed suspiciously as he gazed down at the auburn head nestled against him. Could it bring rebellious little Maggie voluntarily to his bed?

"Maggie," he said, shaking her a little to wake her out of her languor. When she lifted bleary eyes to his, he asked gently, "You're grateful, aren't you? About tomorrow, I mean?"

She wrinkled her forehead in puzzlement and then it cleared as she comprehended his question. "Yes, of course," she replied with a sleepy smile. Grateful, and so much more, too. If she had had more energy, she would have told him exactly how much more, but for now he would have to be satisfied that she had shown him instead.

440

"I thought so," was all he said, and Maggie thought his voice sounded funny, almost as if he were angry, but that wasn't possible, and so she snuggled back down against him and fell asleep.

Jack slept, too, but much later. His thoughts kept him awake for a long time. Guilt helped, too, guilt over knowing that he never should have accepted what Maggie had offered him tonight. From the start he had taken things from her that he had no right to take, her ranch, her home, her friends, her freedom, and then her virginity. Once he had prided himself on being a man of honor, and once he would have killed a man who treated a woman the way he had treated Maggie. It was humorous now to recall that he had once thought to win her affection and even her love with his high-handed tactics. All he had succeeded in doing was arousing her passions, using the physical attraction he had known existed between them. Why, then, should he be surprised that she came to his bed to reward him for what she must see as his heroic actions? It was a natural reaction when he realized that she must think that was the only way she could please him.

Sickened by the thought, appalled at the knowledge that he had only himself to blame for her misconceptions, he lay in an agony of self-discovery. Even as he held her close, he understood that if he truly loved her, if he truly wanted her happiness as he had deluded himself into believing that he did, he would offer her her freedom, offer to return to her all the things he had taken, or at least those things it was within his power to return. A man of honor would do so. Jack simply wasn't certain he was still a man of honor.

For the third morning in a row, Maggie awoke to an empty bed. Her gasp of outrage died in her throat, however, when she heard the sounds from the ranch yard and knew that the men had not left yet. Scrambling from the bed, she darted across to the still open window and looked out, being careful not to show herself at the same time. She had been correct. The men were just beginning to saddle up, and if she hurried she could catch Jack before he left.

Not bothering to wonder why on earth he had sneaked away this morning without waking her, or taking the time to hunt for her discarded nightdress, she snatched the quilt from the bed, wrapped it around her naked body, and made a mad dash across the hall to her own room. There she hastily threw on a dress without bothering with the requisite underwear or even with shoes. Raking her fingers through the tangle of her hair as she went, she raced for the front door and out onto the porch.

"Jack!" It took her only a moment to pick out his black-clad figure from among those in the ranchyard. It was a long way, and he very well might not have heard her above the noise the men were making, but he did, his head turning instantly as if he had sensed, as much as heard her call.

Standing on the porch with the morning wind plastering her skirts to her bare legs and whipping her russet curls into a copper halo around her head, she looked every bit as wild and wanton as she had been in his bed last night. He fought down the fresh wave of desire that washed over him, knowing a twinge of jealousy that she should show herself in such a manner in front of the rest of the men. Holding on to the anger that that jealousy produced, he marched across the yard and up the porch steps to where she awaited him.

Her first words defused that anger. "Weren't you even going to say good-bye?" she asked, obviously stricken.

Her pain at his thoughtlessness only served to strengthen his conviction that he had treated her abominably. He had thought he was doing her a favor by leaving without saying good-bye, without reminding her of the wrongs he had done her. Now he realized he was only being selfish, trying to spare himself the ordeal of facing her, knowing what he now knew about himself.

"I thought you needed to rest, after last night," he

442

explained, his face and voice revealing nothing of the emotions roiling within him.

"Jack!" she protested, the frustration she felt at once again being treated like a child making her voice sharp. They simply had to get a few things straightened out, and she was just about to tell him so when he lifted his hand to stop her.

"Let's not air our dirty linen in public, Mrs. Sinclair," he warned, repeating an admonition he had made once before. "The Virginia Sinclairs simply do not behave in such a manner."

He was right, of course. Texas Colsons did not behave in such a manner, either, arguing on the front porch in full view of the hired help. Still, she could not help the tears of frustration that stung her eyes. How could he expect her to let him go like this, with so much unsettled, when he might very well not come back?

The thought instantly dried her tears and turned her whole body numb with shock. "Jack," she whispered, barely able to speak around the lump that had suddenly formed in her throat. "You'll be careful, won't you?"

His mustache tipped in that way that she had come to adore. "I am rarely anything else," he said. "Now go inside. I want the men to be thinking about Kincaid, and I'm afraid you're providing too much of a distraction." His black eyes skimmed over her inadequately clothed figure with a combination of admiration and disapproval.

He had made no move even to touch her, much less to give her the good-bye kiss she wanted so very much. Stung, she stared at him for a moment, unable to comprehend his coldness. Did he not want to kiss her in front of the men? How ridiculous! She threw her arms around him, holding him close for one last second, and then lifted her face to him in invitation.

She felt the tremor of desire shudder through him, but the lips that touched hers were coolly impersonal, and the kiss was disappointingly brief.

443

Steeling himself against the weakness that threatened, Jack put her away from him. "This may take several days, so don't expect us back for a while. I'm leaving two men to guard the ranch, so you'll be safe, just in case Kincaid doesn't do what he's supposed to do. I'll send word on how things are going." He took a deep breath and forced out the words his honor dictated he must say. "When this is all over, if you want, I'll give you your freedom."

Maggie knew she must have heard wrong. "My freedom?" she echoed stupidly.

"Yes, I'll give you a divorce. The CMC will be all yours, the way it should have been." He was proud of the way his voice sounded, cool and detached.

A divorce? Maggie had hardly ever even heard the word spoken, but still she knew what it meant. "I don't want a divorce," she insisted. "I don't even believe in it." She didn't, either, at least not if it meant she would no longer be married to Jack.

Jack appreciated her loyalty. It was just what he had come to expect from her. She had grown into a fine woman. The thought startled him momentarily. He had never thought of her as a woman before, at least, not outside of bed.

"Boss? Harvey's ready to leave," Swede called from the corral.

Grateful for the interruption, Jack nodded in the foreman's direction, and turned his gaze back to Maggie one last time. "We'll discuss it when I get back," he said, and then he turned on his heel and left her standing there, alone and bereft.

She resisted the urge to call him back, or even worse, to run after him. How he would hate it, hate her, if she made a scene, but after what he had just said to her, it took all her will power not to do just that. Curling her fists with the effort that it took to restrain her impulse, she backed up a few steps into the shadow of the porch where she would not be as visible to the men but from where she could watch them as they mounted up and left.

Instinctively, her eyes searched for Harvey. He was talking with Jack, and she could tell from the way the cowboy was shifting his weight from one foot to the other that he was anxious to be on his way. He had an important mission in town, a mission Maggie knew was pivotal to the whole operation.

She stood there in the shadows, shivering in the early morning chill, until they all rode out, Harvey in one direction and the others in the opposite. They were going to fake a cattle drive in the hopes that Kincaid's hired guns would attack them. It was only then that she realized that Jack had worn a suit, hardly the proper attire for working cattle, but just the thing if he wanted to set himself apart from the others, to make himself a target. Cold fingers of fear clutched at Maggie's heart even as she unconsciously admired the figure of the man she loved riding away into the distance. That couldn't have been what he intended, she reasoned. He had promised to be careful. She could only pray that he meant it.

Harvey permitted himself one tiny smile of satisfaction as he paused outside the marshal's office. His interview with the town's law officer had gone exactly as planned. Jack had chosen Harvey precisely for his ability to get excited, and he had had a pretty easy time of it with Marshal Davis. Harvey had reported to Davis exactly what had happened out at the phony squatters' camp, and then had gone on to inform the marshal that Mr. Sinclair was scared that Kincaid's men were planning to steal the cattle that had been gathered for the spring drive.

The marshal had insisted, as Jack had known he would, that such things were beyond his jurisdiction as town marshal, and that if Sinclair wanted protection from the law, he would have to contact the county sheriff or the Texas

Rangers. That was when Harvey had gotten mad and started yelling, knowing that his voice would carry through the open door into the street, where it would be overheard. It had really galled Harvey to have to pretend that Mr. Sinclair was scared to death of Kincaid's hired guns, but Jack had impressed him with the importance of doing so, so he poured it on thick. The marshal had been adamant in his refusal to get involved in what he viewed as a personal feud, though, and Harvey had stormed out in a self-satisfied huff.

Forcing his face into an expression of outrage, he marched across the street to the saloon where he knew someone was bound to question him about his argument with the marshal. The way gossip spread in this town, it wouldn't be any time at all before Kincaid got the word that Sinclair had all his men working to move that herd of cattle before Kincaid could steal it. Men on a cattle drive were sitting ducks for an ambush, and once Kincaid figured that out, he was bound to take this perfect opportunity.

The only hitch would be if Kincaid saw through the plan. Personally, Harvey couldn't see how he could miss. Knowing Mr. Sinclair as he did, Harvey found it difficult to believe that Kincaid thought Sinclair to be weak and cowardly, but Mr. Sinclair had insisted that he did. Harvey could only hope that he was right. Otherwise they were wasting their time and running a lot of fat off those cows for nothing.

"Whiskey," Harvey demanded of the bartender. "Make it a double.

"What was you and the marshal jawing about, anyways?" the bartender asked as he pulled down a glass. It was all Harvey could do to keep from smiling.

Jack had promised he would send word, but he apparently didn't feel it was necessary to do so the first day. Or even the second. Maggie reckoned that the ranchhouse had never

446

been so mercilessly clean in its entire history, and of course she was right. Never had the house been at the mercy of two women who were worried out of their minds about their men and unable to do a thing to help them. She and Consuela had attacked every nook and cranny, washing, sweeping, scrubbing, and scouring, until not one speck of dirt remained anywhere in the entire structure.

Now they sat in the front room, not daring to meet each other's eyes lest they remind themselves of the subject neither dared to mention. Maggie looked down at her hands and thought with some humor of how appalled Miss Finley would be if she could see how Maggie had ruined them with the lye soap. She would have to remmber to put some lard on them tonight before she went to bed. If she even went to bed. Last night had been awful. She had hardly slept, and when she had finally drifted off, she had been tortured with dreams of Jack's being shot by a fiendish devil with a very familiar-looking scar. Even the thought of lying down in a dark room made her cringe.

They should be starting to think about supper, she knew. The men Jack had left at the ranch would be hungry even if she and Consuela weren't. If only Jack would send someone to let them know what was happening.

It was then that she heard the horse. Or thought she did. At first she wasn't sure, thinking she might have wished so hard that she was imagining it, but then she saw Consuela's head lift. She had heard it, too.

Together they raced to the door and out onto the porch. Squinting into the afternoon sun, they could make out the lone rider. He was coming fast, much too fast just to be bringing a progress report. Something had happened.

"It's Swede," Consuela said after what seemed an endless agony of waiting. Maggie had identified him at almost the same instant. They did not move, feeling sure that he would come straight to the house with his news, but instead he made for the barn, jumping from his horse before it had even

447

stopped running. He was shouting something, and the men came racing from their stations. Swede was giving them orders. She could tell because they were listening and nodding, and when he was finished, they disappeared into the barn to do his bidding.

Unable to wait a moment longer, Maggie was halfway across the yard when Swede finally turned to make his way up to the house. He hurried to meet her.

The news was bad, that much she could guess from the ashen look of Swede's face. "What is it?" Maggie gasped, her breath coming quickly both from her run across the yard and from the apprehension that was twisting her insides.

Swede swallowed once. "We got 'em. Kincaid's dead, got caught in the stampede. Crescent's dead, too. The rest are either dead or run off."

This was not the news she had expected to hear. It did not tally with the expression of doom on Swede's face. That could only mean one thing. "Where's Jack?"

She saw the pain flicker across Swede's face, and knew a moment of abject terror. "He got hit," the foreman said, his big hands reaching instinctively to catch her when the cry of agony tore from her throat.

"He's not . . . ?" She couldn't bring herself to say the word, but Swede was shaking his head.

"He's still alive, but he's hit bad, Miz Sinclair." His strong hands tightened their grip on her shoulders.

"How bad?" she whispered, even as her mind shrieked out a denial. This could not be happening.

"He's gut-shot."

Maggie sagged for just an instant as the horror of it washed over her. Gut-shot. She had always thought that was such a horrible expression, and now it had passed beyond horror in her mind, into the realm of unspeakable darkness. Frantically, she tried to remember ever hearing of someone who had survived such a wound. She failed. Heedless of the tears that had begun to course down her cheeks, she lifted her chin in defiance of despair and said, "Take me to him."

Swede nodded. "I told the boys to hitch up the spring wagon. If he's still . . . we'll bring him back to the ranch."

Of course, they would. Maggie felt the strength returning to her limbs. She straightened in Swede's grasp. "Yes, tell them to fill the wagon bed with hay, lots of it." Looking around, she was surprised to find Consuela standing right beside her. "Consuela, we'll get the feather tick off my bed and put it on the wagon, too." The tears had stopped, still unnoticed. "You stay here and fix up Jack's room. Get everything ready. I'll need to take some bandages and . . ." she stopped to think, hardly aware that Swede's hands had dropped from her shoulders, and he was staring at her in some amazement. "And some whiskey to clean the wound, and . . . was anyone else hurt?" The question had come more from a desire to know how many supplies to take than from true concern, but when she glanced at Consuela's face, she remembered that other people had had loved ones in the fight.

"A couple of the boys got scratched, but Jack is the only one hurt bad. Lee's fine," he assured Consuela. It was a very small comfort to see the relief on Consuela's face, knowing that Jack was lying out there. . . .

"Did you send anyone for the doctor?"

Swede's expression told her what she already knew. The nearest doctor was over a day's ride from there, and by the time he got there . . .

"Send someone, right away," she ordered. "And tell the men to hurry," she added over her shoulder as she began to run back to the house. The preparations passed in a frenzied blur as Maggie helped throw together a bundle of everything they would need to care for Jack. All the time Maggie's mind was repeating the desperate prayer that he would live, at least long enough for her to see him one last time. She couldn't let him die without knowing what she had always been too proud to tell him before, what she should have told him last night, but hadn't.

Finally, everything was ready, and she was riding away with Swede in the wagon. "How far?" she asked, eyes fixed on the horizon as if she might somehow catch a glimpse of him.

"About an hour, I guess, in the wagon," Swede said.

Maggie watched his capable hands work the reins for a while until she got up the courage to ask, "What happened?"

For once, to Maggie's great relief, Swede seemed inclined to talk without much prompting. "Everything went just like we planned. Even better, come to that," he began, pausing as if to picture the action in his mind before telling her the story. "Harvey went to town, spread the word about the cattle drive. Jack said you knew the plan?" he asked, casting her an inquiring look. She nodded sadly.

He continued. "We knew Kincaid would send his men word, but what we never hoped for was that he'd come himself. He even rode along with them. Guess it was just like Jack figured—Kincaid thought Jack was afraid and wanted to be on the ki . . . the end," he corrected, seeing Maggie cringe. "We moved the cattle along real slow, making a cloud of dust you could see for a hundred miles. They saw it, all right, but what they didn't know was that we had Lee posted up in that big old cottonwood out on Four Mile Creek. That boy's part Injun, and he spotted 'em before they got within a mile of us, so we were ready.

"Just like Jack figured, they tried to set up an ambush there where the trail narrows down, but we turned the herd, so that before they even got close to cover, we had a clear field, and then we stampeded the whole sheebang right into them." Swede stopped to rest after such a long speech, and Maggie waited apprehensively for the rest of the story, the part that would tell her how it had happened that Jack had gotten shot.

"That's when Kincaid got it. Guess his horse couldn't carry him, and it fell trying to get away. Just about the whole herd ran over him. He never had a chance. Some of the others tried to keep up a running gunfight, but most of them just hightailed it out of there. One of the ones who fought was Crescent."

Swede stopped to shake his head. Maggie was beginning to wonder now how Jack could have possibly been wounded in such a paltry fight. She had the irrational conviction that if Swede would just hurry up and finish the story, they would both discover that he hadn't really been hurt at all, that it was just not possible. "Swede?" she prompted.

"When the shooting stopped," he went on obediently, "we found Crescent hunkered down behind a rock. He must've had three bullets in him, and his right arm was just about blowed off. He was done for, and he knew it, but it didn't stop him from cussing us up and down. Jack tried to tell him to calm down, that we'd tie up his wounds and get him to a doctor, but he just started laughing, saying all kinds of ugly things about . . . about things." Maggie knew the dying man must have taunted Jack about kidnapping her, but she did not dare stop Swede to inquire. "Nobody even noticed when he slipped his left hand inside his coat." Swede's voice trailed off into the same despair that washed over Maggie. Her fantasy was just that. This story did not have a happy ending. "The gun was such a little bitty thing, we didn't even see it until after he fired, and then it was too late."

Maggie could picture the scene. Jack would have been standing over the wounded man, trying to talk sense to him, not paying any attention to his own safety. The shot would have been point blank, so close that even someone who was already more than half-dead couldn't miss. "Crescent?"

Swede sighed. "When we heard the shot, we all fired back at him. Even Jack," he added with awe. "It was the funniest thing. He drew and fired, just like the rest of us. It was a long time before anybody even noticed he was hit, we were all so busy watching Crescent, making sure he was really dead. I don't guess Jack even knew himself, at first. Then he must have felt something. He made this noise, kind of like he does if he gets a spot of mud on his good suit, you know? Like he was irritated about something, and when I looked at him, I saw the blood."

Maggie saw the blood, too, in her mind's eye, Jack's blood, and before she knew what was happening, she was sobbing. Swede stopped the wagon instantly, making an awkward attempt to comfort her, but she pushed him away. "Don't worry about me! Just keep going. I have to get there before . . ." Her sentence ended in a strangled sob, but Swede understood, and he slapped the team into motion again. After awhile, he offered her a slightly soiled bandana as a handkerchief, which she gratefully accepted.

When the deluge of tears had slowed to a trickle, Swede cleared his throat, and Maggie's senses snapped immediately to attention. Swede was going to say something important. "You really care about him, don't you?" he asked. Maggie nodded, too miserable to trust herself to reply to such a volatile question. "Then maybe you aren't too mad at me anymore?" he ventured.

Quite truthfully, Maggie had forgotten that she ever had been, but now she recalled his role in her hasty marriage, and his supposed betrayal of her father's trust. "Some of the things you and Jack did were a little questionable," she chastised, wiping the last of the moisture from her cheeks.

"I knew your pa was gonna lose the valley, Miz Sinclair," he began, his homely face twisted into an expression so earnest, it touched her heart. "I saw it coming, and a lot of others did, too. That's why I sent word to Jack. He was looking for a place to settle, and I figured the two of them together . . ." Maggie nodded her understanding. Now that she knew the whole story, now that she knew Jack, it was difficult to imagine that she had ever thought him capable of stealing the valley from her father.

"When your pa's men started quitting," Swede was saying, "I hired men Jack sent me. We had to be sure the men working at the CMC weren't gonna betray your pa."

Maggie nodded again. She understood it all, every bit of it. It might have seemed like treachery, but that had not been the intention. Of course there was still the matter of the cavalier way Jack had treated *her,* but then she hadn't been exactly kind to him, either, and hadn't she planned an even worse revenge?

"You gotta believe me, Miz Sinclair, I never would've let him marry you if I didn't think he really loved you, down deep inside. I knew he'd never hurt you, not really. He wanted you to be safe is all."

Fresh tears flowed as Maggie took in this new bit of information. Could Swede be right? Frantically, Maggie ransacked her memory for evidence. They had fought, oh, how they had fought, right up until their wedding, and she had been so afraid that night. There hadn't been anything to be afraid of, though. Jack had been so gentle, so . . . yes, so loving, and then he had even said the words. "I love you, little witch." She could hear them even now, as clearly as when he had first spoken them.

She hadn't believed him, though, had thrown his words of love right back in his face, had accused him of unspeakable things, had driven him away. Even if the words had been true then, could they still be true after all she had done? It seemed impossible, and yet he had not been able to stay away from her, even though he had sworn to. That was proof; that, and the fact that each time they made love was more wonderful than the last. Then there was the evidence of their last night together. She had been so certain that there was hope for them then, right up until that morning when he had behaved so strangely, offering to divorce her, of all things, when divorce was the very last thing she wanted from him. It was all so confusing, and she had so little time to figure it out.

Swede's voice broke into her racing thoughts. "We're almost there."

Instantly Maggie's attention snapped back to the present,

her eyes eagerly searching for the first glimpse of the men. A shouted greeting was the first evidence that Swede's statement was true, and then Maggie saw them. Some of the men were putting the finishing touches on what she knew must be a grave, and that same litany she had repeated over and over at the house began again in her mind. Please let him be alive. *Please.*

She saw him then. He was lying on a saddle blanket in the shade of a scrub oak tree. Someone had covered him with his coat, and he almost looked as if he might just be taking a nap. Almost, except for the deathlike stillness that seemed to surround him, and the deathlike pallor of his face.

She couldn't be too late, she simply couldn't, and with her brain screaming in denial, she scrambled down from the still moving wagon, her lips crying his name as she ran, stumbling, over the rough ground to where he lay.

Chapter XVI

Common sense told her that he couldn't be dead. If he were dead, they would have covered his face. If he were dead, Lee Parker wouldn't have been sitting there fanning the flies away. Later she would credit that common sense with keeping her sane until she was able to reach his side and find out for herself.

"Jack?" Her voice was no more than a whisper as she knelt beside him. At first he did not move, and she thought her heart would break, so great was the pain. He looked so pale, so white, as if all the blood had been drained from his body, leaving only an empty shell, and when she touched his hand, the skin was cool. But not cold, not the way her father's hand had been, thank God.

"Jack?" she said again, louder this time. She lifted his limp hand to her cheek, her eyes never leaving his face.

Ever so slowly, as if it took a great deal of effort, his eyelids lifted. Only the faintest glimmer remained in those dark eyes. "Maggie? Are you really here?" The thin thread of sound was a parody of the voice she knew.

"Yes, yes, I'm really here," she assured him, placing a fervent kiss on the back of his hand. She longed to take him in her arms, to cradle that dear body against hers, but she knew she dared not touch him, not if it would cause him further hurt.

That mustache tilted. "Out without a hat, Mrs. Sinclair? You'll freckle if you're not careful."

Maggie stared. Could she have heard right? What a ridiculous thing to say at a time like this! Protecting her complexion from the ravages of the sun was the last thing she had been thinking of when she had left the ranch. How on earth could it become the very first thing a dying man thought to mention? Unless . . .

Was it possible? Would . . . *could* a dying man take the time, the energy, to tease her? It never occurred to her that he might be trying to make things easier for her. Instead she came to the wrong conclusion entirely. With no more evidence than this one remark, and with every evidence to the contrary, Maggie decided at that moment that Jack might live. It wasn't a conscious decision, and she would realize later that all she had had at that particular instant was the tiniest shred of hope, but it was enough.

Jack Sinclair would not die, not if Maggie Colson Sinclair had anything to say in the matter. His image blurred diamond bright for just a second while she blinked the tears away, and then she smiled at him. "And what about you, Mr. Sinclair? Didn't anyone ever teach you to duck? You said you were going to be careful."

"The Virginia Sinclairs do not duck. It isn't dignified," he managed to rasp out.

Maggie could have laughed for joy. It didn't matter how badly he was hurt. It didn't matter that no one ever survived an injury such as this. Jack would live. She would force him to. She squeezed the hand she held more tightly against her cheek, resisting the almost overwhelming impulse to shower his face with kisses. She mustn't jar him, mustn't cause him any unnecessary pain. There was already enough necessary pain. "Jack, I brought some things to bandage your wound," she explained very slowly.

Glancing up, she was amazed to discover that Lee Parker

had slipped away and Swede had taken his place. The foreman clutched the bundle that she and Consuela had prepared back at the ranch. At her nod, he knelt and began to untie it.

"I don't want to hurt you, but it's important to make sure the wound is clean so that it can heal properly," she said, reluctantly loosening her grip on his hand and laying it back by his side.

"Don't bother," he whispered, but she ignored him.

"This won't take long, but you tell me if you get cold, and I'll cover you up again," she rattled on, carefully lifting the coat someone had thoughtfully placed over his prone body.

She almost lost her nerve then. The sight of the bloodstained bandages staggered her for a moment, but only for a moment. Steeling herself against the wave of nausea that tried to overwhelm her, she reached for the scissors that Swede was holding out to her.

The men had torn Jack's white shirt into strips and used it to bind up his wound, but the shirt had been far from clean, and now was sodden with blood. With a few careful snips, Maggie cut through the fabric and peeled it away to reveal the deceptively small bullet hole. It looked almost harmless, like a second navel located a bit above and off center from the true one. The bleeding had almost stopped.

Swede handed her the bottle of brandy, and she carefully worked the cork loose, not allowing herself to think about what she had to do next.

"I hope you thought to bring a glass."

Once again Maggie stared at Jack in shock. "A glass?"

"For the brandy," he replied, each word an effort, but still his mustache tipped rakishly.

Maggie glanced at the bottle and then back at him. "I didn't bring this for you to drink," she explained patiently, forcing herself to keep her tone light. "I brought it to clean your wound."

His grimace was almost comically tragic. "You could

have used your father's rot-gut for that."

She choked back the sob that threatened. He was so weak, but he was still Jack, still the irreverent, darling man she loved. She forced her face into an indulgent smile. "Only the best for the Virginia Sinclairs," she informed him.

"Better give him some to drink first," Swede cautioned her quietly. "He'll need it."

Her face frozen into that parody of a smile, she leaned down and slipped a hand beneath his head. "But if you promise to behave yourself, I'll let you drink some, too," she said. Swede helped her lift his head, and she held the bottle to his lips. He took two long swallows and then shuddered slightly and turned his head away. They laid him back down carefully. His wound had started to bleed again, and she knew they had better hurry.

"I'm going to do it now. Are you ready?" Hating the false cheerfulness of her voice, she kept her smile securely pinned in place, thanking God for all the training Miss Finley had given her in being pleasant even during unfortunate circumstances. Things didn't get much more unfortunate than this, she decided.

Jack closed his eyes and curled his hands into fists. "Ready," he said through clenched teeth.

The hand that held the brandy bottle shook ever so slightly, but Maggie took one last, steadying breath and poured.

Jack never made a sound, but his whole body shook with the most awful tremor and then went limp. For a moment Maggie thought . . .

"Jack? JACK?" she cried, her panic rising with each second of silence.

"He's just passed out, I reckon." It was Swede, calm, quiet Swede, reassuring her. "It must've hurt awful bad."

Maggie nodded stupidly, her eyes never leaving Jack. Awful bad. She could imagine. The pain that tore her own stomach was agonizing, and no bullet had ripped through

458

her insides. After a moment she saw that he was still breathing. It was labored, but it was breath. The sweat that had beaded on his forehead ran in rivulets down his temples. This small movement somehow gave her the reassurance she needed.

"We'd best finish up while he's still out," Swede was saying. His voice seemed to come to her from a great distance.

"Maggie?" He was closer now, and she forced herself to look at him. "The bullet came out in the back. It's a lot worse there. I'll do it if you can't."

She shook her head. "No, I'll do it. Help me turn him."

Swede was right, it was worse, much worse. The exiting bullet had torn out a chunk of flesh the size of her fist, so this time she allowed Swede to pour on the brandy because her hands were shaking too badly even to hold the bottle. Then he helped her tear the sheet she had brought into strips and pads.

They were just tying the last knot when Jack stirred. "Maggie?"

"I'm here, darling. I'm here," she assured him, taking possession of his hand while Swede went to bring the wagon up closer.

"There's something I have to tell you," he said. His voice sounded stronger, as if he were drawing on his last reserves.

"Not now," she cautioned. "Save your strength. There'll be plenty of time later. I have some things to tell you, too."

"This can't wait," he rasped, but it was too late. The men had come to lift him into the wagon bed. When Maggie scrambled in beside him, he had lost consciousness again. She breathed a prayer of thanks that he would be spared the agony of the trip home, and contented herself with tucking the blanket more tightly around him.

The trip that she and Swede had accomplished alone in less than an hour took almost two going back, because Swede was taking great care not to jar his passenger. Still, an occasional lurch brought an involuntary groan from Jack and an answering one from Maggie, who felt his pain even if he could not.

Jack was still out when they laid him in the bed that Consuela had so carefully prepared. She and Maggie undressed him and tucked him in, and Consuela left to fetch the poultice she had prepared. Maggie drew up a chair and sat down beside the bed, taking Jack's hand in hers. She watched him breathe with a fascination born of her conviction that he would not die, willing his very chest to rise and fall as if she could preserve his life with the force of her own will.

After a while, his eyelids flickered open. "Maggie?"

"I'm here," she said, moving closer so that he could see her without moving his head.

"You'll be free now," he said. "A rich widow, just like you wanted."

A small cry escaped her lips. Is that what he thought, that she wanted him to die? "I don't want to be a widow, Jack," she told him frantically. "I don't want a divorce, either. I only want to be your wife. *I don't want you to die!*"

His mustache tilted. "Thank you for that," he whispered.

Maggie looked down at him in horror. He thought she was lying, lying to make his last moments easier. "It's true!" she insisted. "I don't want you to die! Damn you, Jack Sinclair, don't you dare die! I'm not finished with you yet!"

Jack thought she had never looked lovelier. Her hair was a tangled mess from the wind and her nose was red from the sun and her eyes were bright green, glittering with unshed tears that he could almost imagine were for him.

Somebody came into the room, and from the corner of his eye he could see it was Consuela. She was carrying a pot of some foul-smelling concoction that he knew must be one of her poultices. Now they would go to work on him again. He wished they would just leave him alone, let him die in peace. He almost didn't mind, not if he could just lie here and look at Maggie. She was so pretty and he loved her so much. If she would just stay here and pretend she loved him back, he almost felt like he might just try, just a little, not to die, not to leave her. It would be hard work, though. Right now, he didn't even dare to blink for fear that once his eyes closed, he wouldn't have the strength to open them again, and he wanted to look at her for as long as he had left.

There was something else, too, something he had wanted to tell her, something he had to tell her before it was too late. The memory niggled around the edges of his consciousness, teasing and tormenting him while he concentrated all his energy on keeping his eyes on her.

"You must help me, señora," Consuela was saying. "We will have to take off the bandages again."

That was when he remembered what it was. "I love you, little witch," he said. Or maybe he only thought it.

Consuela had put a cot in the room for Maggie, but she hardly had a chance to lie down on it that night or during the nights that followed. The fever started not long after Consuela had applied the poultices, and Jack raged, delirious, all night and most of the next day. The two women took turns sponging him off and spooning broth into his mouth when he begged for water. He would only lie quietly if Maggie was beside him where his fever-glazed eyes could see her, and so she sat, holding his hand, for hours on end.

Sometimes he would talk, calling her name until she had reassured him that she was, indeed, there, and then rambling on in disjointed sentences that only occasionally made sense. When he was quiet, Maggie spoke to him. "Don't die, Jack. Please, don't die," she begged him over and over. She had no idea if he even heard.

The doctor arrived at noon on the third day. He was a little the worse for wear and quite disgruntled that he had been compelled to come such a long way for what everyone knew was a hopeless cause, but the fact that Jack was still alive pacified him somewhat. He turned up his nose at Consuela's poultices but that was only because the smell was so awful. "They seem to be working, drawing out the infection," he commented, but seeing the light of hope in Maggie's eyes, he added, "That doesn't mean he'll live, though."

"But there is a chance," Maggie insisted.

The grizzled old doctor shook his head. He'd seen too many such wounds to be optimistic. "I'll grant you that he should be dead by now, but that doesn't mean he won't be in another day or two. You have to understand, Mrs. Sinclair, there's half a dozen vital organs right in there where that bullet passed through. He's real lucky that it went through at an angle and missed his spine, but the chances that it missed everything else in there are one in a million. The fact is that it probably hit three or four important things, any one of which could kill him. If the infection doesn't get him, that will."

"But what if you're wrong?" Maggie asked. "What if Jack is that one in a million and what if he survives the fever?"

Awed by such faith, the doctor could only wag his head again. "Even if he does survive, and that's a mighty big if, he might never be the man he was. He might be weak and sickly the rest of his life, maybe even an invalid. Not the man you knew at all."

A weak and sickly Jack was better than no Jack at all, Maggie decided. What did doctors know? Consuela and her remedies had probably helped more than this old pill pusher ever could have, anyway.

"Then if he survives the fever, there's a good chance he'll live?" Maggie demanded.

Sighing, the doctor shrugged. "A chance, a small one," he agreed.

That was all Maggie needed to hear. They let the doctor leave the next morning. He had left some laudanum in case Jack needed it, but Consuela's tea had served up until now to keep him sedated.

The days and nights settled into a monotonous routine. Jack alternately slept and raved, and Maggie alternately dozed and comforted him. She rarely even left the room, and then only to summon Consuela or one of the men to help her move him. Consuela kept busy in the kitchen, stewing up poultices and making nourishing broths of beef and bone marrow. Everyone urged Maggie to take a few hours off, to get some much-needed sleep, but they all knew that only she had the power to calm his delirium, and so when she refused, they did not press her.

It was the morning of the seventh day after he had been shot. Maggie was asleep on the cot, and it was only when she heard Jack call her name that she realized she had been asleep for most of the night. As one well trained, she responded to his call, rising instantly, answering him even before she was fully awake. Automatically, she took his hand in one of hers and placed her other on his forehead to check for fever. The shock of cool skin beneath her palm brought her fully awake. The fever had broken!

The eyes staring up at her were really seeing her for the first time in a week. The overbright fever glaze was gone.

"Water," he croaked.

It took Maggie a minute to respond to his request. She was too busy touching him, testing his cheeks, his throat, his chest, verifying that his temperature was normal. It was true! All she could think of was the doctor's promise that if the fever broke, there was a chance, however slim, that he would live.

"Water," he said again, more loudly this time, and Maggie hastened to supply it from the pitcher sitting by the bed. Half of it sloshed onto the table top and down to the floor, but she managed to fill the glass somehow, and when she lifted his head and put it to his lips, he drained it eagerly.

Jack lay back with a contented sigh. More than anything, he wanted to go back to sleep. Amazingly, the simple act of drinking the water had sapped what little strength he had, but he knew that he must not sleep, not now. He had something to tell Maggie, something she had to know before it was too late.

"Maggie, there's something I have to tell you," he said. With great effort, he made his voice a little stronger.

"I know," she soothed, smiling down at him, smoothing the tousled hair back from his forehead. "You can tell me later. Just rest now."

His mustache tilted at this. "There won't be a 'later' and we both know it," he said, amazed that she could be so kind.

"Of course, there will," she assured him, joy bubbling up in her heart. If he had the strength to argue, he would have the strength to live. She just knew it.

Jack studied that smile in wonder, grateful beyond words that she would smile and lie like that to ease his passing. "Maggie, I love you."

"I love you, too, Jack." The words came easily to her lips now; she had spoken them so many times without knowing whether he could even hear them.

He barely heard them now, noticing them only to marvel at the extent of her loyalty. "I never meant to hurt you, Maggie, not even in the beginning. I only wanted you to be safe."

"I know," she said. His words were not new. He'd told her this many times during the past week, though perhaps never quite so coherently.

"When I made you marry me, I told myself it was only to keep you from causing trouble, but that wasn't the truth. The truth was that I loved you and wanted you all to myself."

She wanted to stop him, to beg him to rest now, to tell him that it wasn't necessary, but he wasn't listening to her. His words were coming quickly, like those of a man who knows he hasn't much time left, so she listened, unable to keep the tears of joy from streaming down her face.

"I knew you didn't love me, but I didn't think that

mattered. Women have always liked me, and I thought that after a time you'd fall victim to my charm." His face contorted into a grimace of self-mockery.

"I did fall victim to your charm," she said, but he wasn't listening. He couldn't listen. He needed all his energy simply to talk.

"I admit that I did want the valley, but I didn't steal it, not the way you thought, and I didn't kill your father, either."

"I know," she assured him. "Swede told me everything. I never really thought that, anyway, not really."

"I'm sorry, Maggie. For everything."

His eyes closed and Maggie almost gasped. Plainly this was his dying speech, the one he had repeated over and over to her in rambling fragments during the time he had been out of his head. She had heard it all before, every bit of it, but never had it seemed so final.

"Jack? Jack! Wake up!" It was cruel, but she couldn't let him sleep now, now when he thought he was dying. His eyelids lifted with obvious effort. "Jack, listen to me! You aren't going to die. You're going to get well, and when you do, you'll have plenty of time to show me just how sorry you really are."

His smile was infinitely sad. "There's no need to pretend anymore, darling. I know where I'm hit. I know I can't last more than a day or two."

Was it possible? Could he truly not have any idea? "But you can! You did! Don't you know? It's been a week since you were shot. You've been very sick, but the doctor was here, and he said that if you survived the fever then you'd live." It was a small lie, but an important one.

Clearly he did not believe her, but something in her face made him want to. Ever so carefully, his dark gaze studied her, and he began to notice things he had been too intent to notice earlier. Her hair, that beautiful auburn mass, hung in limp, unbrushed strands. Lines of strain showed in her unusually pale face where none had ever been before, and purple smudges shadowed her eyes. Loath to look away from her, he forced himself nevertheless to turn his head, to look around the room. It was then that he saw the cot for the first time, and the accumulation of sickroom supplies on the bedside table. From the looks of the room and from the look of Maggie, a lot of time had certainly passed since the day of the fight.

"A week?" he asked, still unable quite to believe it. No one survived a stomach wound for longer than a few days. It was a fact of life, and he had seen more than this share of proof if he had needed convincing. That he really had such a wound was indisputable. Even if he had not been able to remember the incident with such crystal clarity, he still had the omnipresent ache in his vitals that had tortured him even in the depths of insensibility. The pain had become such a constant companion that he no longer even remembered being without it.

Maggie was nodding, her cheerful smile making a mockery of the tears that still dropped occasionally from her eyes. "Yes, a week, and now the fever's broken, and you're going to be fine."

A week, and Maggie had taken care of him all that time. It was obvious, so obvious he didn't even bother to inquire. He felt the twinge of a new pain, this one closer to his heart. It was imaginary, he knew, yet it rivaled the true one in intensity. How could she have done such a thing for him after all that he had done to her? She hated him, *must* hate him for all the things he had robbed her of, and still she had kept him alive, staying with him day and night. His pride rankled at such a sacrifice. "Where's Consuela?" he asked.

Maggie stared at him a moment. It was such a strange question. "She's right here. Shall I call her?"

"Yes," he whispered. He was getting weaker by the minute. Soon he would be asleep whether he wanted to be or not, and right now, he didn't want to be. He had something to take care of first. He prayed Consuela would hurry.

She did. At Maggie's call, the housekeeper came rushing into the room, her look of concern quickly changing to joy when she saw that Jack was finally conscious.

"Madre de Dios," she murmured, crossing herself. "You are awake at last."

Jack took one painfully deep breath. "Mrs. Sinclair is tired. Please see that she goes to her room and gets some sleep," he ordered.

Consuela was startled, but Maggie was furious. How could he dismiss her, just like that? His voice was no more than a hint of sound, and yet the steel thread of command was unmistakable. "I'm not tired," she began to protest, but a familiar glint in those dark eyes stopped her.

"I don't want you here, Maggie," he said.

Maggie stared at him in horror. He didn't want her there, didn't want her caring for him, after all she had done. . . .

"Señora, come. Please, come with me. Señor Jack is right. You are tired. Later, when you have rested, you will come back," Consuela urged, leading a resisting Maggie from the room.

Maggie didn't want to leave, not now, especially not now that she knew he was going to be all right, but when she tried to protest again, Jack closed his eyes.

"You see, he is already alseep. He will sleep for hours now," Consuela said. "You should sleep, too. You have not slept for days."

"I couldn't possibly sleep, not now," Maggie argued. "I'm too excited, too . . ." She had almost said happy. She *had* been happy, too, until Jack had sent her away.

"I will make you some tea. You will sleep. He will need you later, and it will not help if you are sick yourself."

This was an indisputable argument, and so Maggie allowed herself to be put to bed in her old room and dosed with one of Consuela's potions. She almost slept the clock around.

Jack was not so fortunate. He awoke again a few hours

467

later. Automatically, he called for Maggie, but it was Consuela who answered him. "She is not here. It is just as you wanted."

He did not miss the note of censure in her voice. "Some water, please," he requested.

Consuela was not as emotional about the process as Maggie had been, and she quickly poured him a glassful. Holding it to his lips, she said, "You should be ashamed. You owe her your life."

Jack pretended not to know what she was talking about, but he saw that she suspected there had been more to his sending Maggie away than simple concern for her welfare.

"She stayed with you every minute. She did everything for you. Everything. Things you do not even want to know, and then you send her away. You hurt her very much."

Jack winced under Consuela's scowl, but he refused to reply. Maggie had kept him alive, and he was properly grateful, but he had already taken enough from her. As long as he was able, he would refuse to take any more. "From now on, you can take care of me. I'm not helpless now, so it will be easier."

Consuela made a rude noise, telling him she knew exactly what he was doing and disapproved heartily. It was useless to argue, though. She knew him well enough to know that. "Are you hungry?" she asked. At his nod, she left the room to fetch the meal she had prepared earlier. If he could eat the soft food, then he would regain his strength, and then he would be able to tolerate the red meat he would need to get completely well again. The señora's wish would come true. For all the good it would do her. Stubborn man.

When she awoke, Maggie's first wish was to see Jack, but Consuela forestalled her, saying he was asleep and hinting that she might want to get cleaned up before letting him see her. For the first time in over a week, Maggie gave some thought to her appearance and decided to take Consuela's advice.

After bathing and washing her hair, she went to the kitchen to dry her hair before the kitchen fire and watch Consuela prepare a tray for Jack. "Will he eat all that?" she asked, amazed at the amount of food on the tray.

"I hope so," the housekeeper replied. "Mostly he just drinks and drinks. He is thirsty from losing so much blood, but he eats, too, and that is good."

"He *is* better, then?" Maggie asked, hardly daring to hope.

"*Si,* he is better. Each time he wakes up, he seems stronger." Consuela did not pause in her preparations, bustling about the kitchen so she would not have to meet Maggie's eyes.

"Consuela?"

The housekeeper froze in midmovement, knowing instinctively that the time had come to answer the questions she was hoping would not come.

"Why did he send me away? Why did he say he didn't want me there?" It hurt bitterly even to remember his harsh words, and it hurt even more to probe into the reasons for them.

Consuela feigned nonchalance and shrugged one shoulder. "He was worried about you. He knew you would not leave him unless he forced you to." It was silly, she knew, to prolong it. She should tell her the truth right now, that Jack would no longer permit Maggie to care for him, no matter how many arguments Consuela had presented, but she just couldn't bring herself to do it.

"You're lying, Consuela." Maggie surprised even herself with the words. How shocked Miss Finley would be to hear her say such a thing. The time for worrying over such trifles was past, however. Now was the time for truth. There had been far too little of that in her life lately.

Slowly, Consuela turned to face her, drying her hands on her apron with unnecessary care. "The señor, he is a proud man. He does not like for his woman to see him so . . . so weak, so helpless, like a baby."

"As if that made any difference to me!" Maggie raged,

jumping to her feet, her brush clattering unheeded to the floor. Men could be so stupid! It was absolutely incredible.

"It makes a difference to him," Consuela pointed out. "Do you know what he wanted first? After he ate?" Maggie shook her head, hoping he had wanted to see her. "He wanted a shave. He made me call Swede in to shave him."

Maggie had to admit that seven days' worth of beard growth had made him look rather disreputable, but she never would have guessed a man could be that vain. "But I'll have to see him if I'm taking care of him," she pointed out.

Here it was, the moment Consuela had been dreading. "He doesn't want you to take care of him anymore," she said, finding it very difficult to look Maggie in the face as she said it.

"What?" Maggie gasped, at first unable and then unwilling to believe what Consuela was telling her. "Did he say that? Did he say *exactly* that?" she demanded, certain that Consuela had misunderstood.

"*Si,* exactly that. Please, señora," Consuela begged, seeing Maggie's expression of combined fury and hurt, "try to understand. He is ashamed for the way he treated you. You shamed him when you saved his life and he did not deserve it."

"But he did deserve it, and I love him!" Maggie argued. "The whole thing is ridiculous!"

Consuela shrugged eloquently. "Men are ridiculous, señora. Who can understand them?"

Who, indeed? Maggie wondered, slumping back into her chair.

"It is good, in a way," Consuela ventured, hoping to ease Maggie's misery. "He will work hard to get well so he will no longer be a burden to you. That is good, no?"

Maggie wasn't certain, but she nodded dully. She rather liked having Jack as a burden. At least she knew he wasn't going to walk out on her, wasn't going to start talking about getting a divorce. She wondered vaguely if he could divorce her without her consent. Just let him try, she vowed. She'd give him such a fight. . . .

Consuela smiled at the way Maggie had unconsciously squared her shoulders and lifted her chin. The housekeeper had no idea what was going on in the señora's mind, but she was comforted by the gleam that had returned to her eye. The little *gringa* would fight for her man.

By silent agreement, Maggie and Consuela exchanged tasks, although now that Jack was no longer delirious, Consuela's sickroom duties became much lighter than Maggie's had been. Maggie cooked and washed sheets and boiled bandages and brewed poultices, while Consuela served the food and changed the sheets and changed the bandages and applied the poultices.

Not trusting anyone's judgment but her own, Maggie made it a point to see Jack every day, even though her first visit was less than pleasant.

"What are you doing here?" he demanded of her that first day when she brought him a tray of food.

Maggie could have wept, so happy was she to see him groomed and propped up on some pillows and so angry was she to see that all too familiar bland mask of an expression on his face. "I just wanted to see for myself how you were doing," she replied with equal blandness. She set the tray down on the bedside table and automatically reached to touch his face to test her fever.

He dodged her hand with surprising agility for one so weak. "I don't have a fever," he informed her through gritted teeth. "Send Consuela in to help me eat."

Maggie sighed dramatically. "'How sharper than a serpent's tooth it is to have an ungrateful child,'" she quoted, noting with satisfaction the flush that rose on his neck. At least he had the grace to be embarrassed over his rudeness to her.

"I am not ungrateful," Jack explained with an effort. "In fact, I want to thank you for all you did. . . ."

"There's no need to thank me," Maggie replied lightly. "consider it my wifely duty to keep you alive, however little you might appreciate it."

Jack managed to keep from groaning aloud. There were times, of course, when he had not appreciated it, and this was one of them. More than anything, he wanted to pull her into his arms and kiss the impudent pout off those lovely lips, but the mere fantasy left him feeling weak. Oh, he knew that if he asked, she would come to him, and even kiss him, if he asked, but he would not, could not ask. A man who couldn't even kiss his own wife was no man at all, and until he could, he didn't even want her in the same room with him, reminding him that he was less, far less, a man than she deserved.

"Will you please ask Consuela to come in," he repeated the strain of keeping his emotions in check draining what little color there was from his cheeks.

Determined not to be offended, Maggie meekly complied It would do no good to argue with him, Consuela had convinced her of that much, at least, and she didn't like the way he looked. "All right," she agreed reluctantly. "But I'm warning you, if you don't do everything Consuela tells you to, I'm taking over again."

Leaving in a swish of skirts, she had no way of knowing how Jack's gaze followed her, or how in subsequent days he had strained simply to catch a glimpse of her as she passed his door or to hear a single word spoken by her voice.

He felt like a fool to lust so greedily after the sight and sound of her when he himself had forbidden her to come into his room, but he could not help himself. He did not know that when he slept, she indulged a greed of her own by sitting at his bedside and simply watching him breathe. Maggie took great comfort from the fact that she could see improvement in him every day, could see the color returning to his gaunt cheeks, and then see the flesh returning to his wasted body.

Consuela kept her informed of how well his wounds were

healing, and soon the poultices were no longer needed. Before too many more days had passed, Jack was able to sit up with Swede's help and feed himself. It was only a matter of time before he would be up and walking, and then . . .

That day came much sooner than she would have wished. One day Consuela did not come back from taking Jack his noon meal, and after awhile, Maggie became concerned. A quick search of all the other rooms proved fruitless, but when Maggie started down the hall toward the bedrooms, she heard the housekeeper's voice coming from Jack's room.

"It is too soon. You are not strong enough yet. A few more days . . ."

"I don't need any lectures, Consuela," Jack's angry voice interrupted her. "Just make sure you haven't forgotten anything before you call Swede to get the buggy."

Alarmed, Maggie pushed open the unlatched door, and the scene that met her eyes alarmed her even more. Jack was up and dressed, the first time she had seen him so since the day of the fight. He was seated in a chair, glaring at Consuela, who was glaring back, hands on hips. Lying on the freshly made-up bed was a carpetbag that someone, probably Consuela, had been in the process of packing.

"What's going on here?" she demanded, sickeningly certain that she already knew.

Instinctively, Jack started to rise, his inherent training overcoming his common sense for an instant before he realized his folly and sank back into the chair again. A little breathless from the effort, he did not immediately reply.

Consuela took up the slack. "He is leaving," she informed Maggie, disapproval radiating from her plump body.

"Leaving?" she repeated incredulously. "Where on earth are you going?"

His mustache tilted in a sad parody of his usual jauntiness. "Home," he said. Seeing her puzzled expression, he added, "Home to the house I lived in before . . . before I came here. The old Simpson place, remember?"

Maggie was too stunned to reply immediately. How could he even consider going back there? The place had been little more than a shack to begin with, and even though Consuela had told her that he had improved it considerably, no one had lived there for months now. It would be filthy and . . . "Who's going with you?" she asked suspiciously.

"I don't need a keeper," he informed her. "I can take care of myself now."

Pride. Stupid, idiotic pride. The man couldn't even stand up without help, and he thought he could take care of himself. "Don't be ridiculous," Maggie snapped, thoroughly irritated. "You're as weak as a kitten." She knew immediately she had used the wrong approach.

Jack lunged to his feet, his face crimson from the exertion, one hand clutching the wall for support. "I'm not going to stay here another day," he declared with rather pathetic dignity. "I've been a burden to you long enough, and I'm tired of having women clucking over me like so many mother hens. I should think you'd be glad to get rid of me."

Maggie's jaw dropped at that. What had she ever done to give him that impression? She was only too glad to have him around, in any condition, and she certainly hadn't been allowed to "cluck" over him at all, lately.

"I would appreciate the use of your buggy," he was saying, straining to maintain his poise. "If you refuse, I will be forced to ride my stallion. Failing that, I will walk, if necessary, but I am leaving here today."

The picture of Jack, as weak and gaunt as he was, staggering down the road in an effort to escape her was so appalling that she could only stare in mute horror.

Consuela, who had been listening to this exchange with only half an ear, broke the uneasy silence that had fallen. "Señora, we must do as he asks," she said.

"What?" Maggie could not believe her friend would betray her, but before she could say so, Consuela had taken her by the arm and begun to hustle her from the room.

"Come, señora, I will explain," she murmured, dragging Maggie unwillingly into the hallway.

"Sit down before you fall down," Maggie ordered Jack just as she made her unseemly exit.

Jack would have liked to remain standing just to spite her, but found that his body was not being too cooperative, and he sank back gratefully into the chair. With a sigh, he leaned his head back and closed his eyes in an attempt to blot out the vision of Maggie's face. She was magnificent when she was angry, and it was certainly gratifying to know that she cared enough about him to protest his departure, but he also knew that if he didn't get away from here soon he would go stark, raving mad.

Having Maggie so near, loving her and wanting her as he still did, and yet knowing he had succeeded only in winning her undying loyalty as well as a great deal of her sympathy was almost more than he could bear. Added to the fact that at present, at least, he was little less than half a man, it all became too much. Maybe when he had had a chance to sort things out alone, when he was completely recovered physically so that he could face her standing erect on two strong legs, maybe then he would be able to deal with the situation.

It was that "maybe," however, that haunted him, that small, niggling little doubt. He tried not to consider it, but it was there, all the same, the prospect that he might *never* be able to face Maggie that way, might never be able to stand erect on two strong legs again. What chance would he have then of winning her love? Unable to answer that question, he forced himself to concentrate on the whispered conversation he could hear taking place in the hallway. He couldn't make out the words, but he could distinguish Maggie's voice, and he contented himself with listening to it.

"Are you crazy?" Maggie had demanded as soon as the two women were alone. "We can't let him go off alone. He'll die!"

But Consuela knew that. "*Si,* señora, but we cannot keep him here, either. You hear what he says about walking away. He is determined."

No more determined than she was to keep him here, Maggie thought angrily. If she had only been angry, it would have been all right, though. It was the hurt with which she was having a difficult time dealing. In one breath he said he loved her and in the next he ordered her out of his room, out of his life, and now, with his last ounce of strength, he was running away from her. It made her want to cry and scream at the same time.

"Señora?" Consuela interrupted her musings. "You must let him go. You must let him save his pride. If you keep him a prisoner, he will grow to hate you."

Maggie almost groaned aloud. "I'd rather that he was alive and hating me than free and dead!" she raged.

"There is another choice," Consuela suggested. "We will send him to your friend, Mrs. Wheeler."

Maggie considered this. It was a difficult process, since she was still fuming over Jack's insane bid for independence. Once she had turned the idea over in her mind a few times, though, it began to sound almost sensible, as if it might be the answer to all their problems, assuming, of course, that Consuela was right and she really didn't have any choice but to let Jack go.

"He could rent a room from her. . . ." she said thoughtfully, remembering the unoccupied room where Abby had given her refuge and where Jack had found her. It wouldn't be a bad idea for him to stay there, either. The room held pleasant memories.

"She would take care of him, too, if you ask her," Consuela pointed out. "She would cook for him, be sure he eats well, everything that you would do yourself."

Everything except love him, Maggie corrected silently, but she was nodding her approval of the plan. If Jack was bound and determined to get away from her, if she had to let him go, then this was the perfect solution. "He'll never agree, though," Maggie predicted, recognizing the only flaw in the plan.

Consuela smiled conspiratorially. "Then we do not tell him. We will tell Swede to drive him there instead of to his old home," she explained, seeing Maggie's bewilderment. "He is weak. He will sleep most of the way and will not know where they are going until they are there. By then he will be too tired to argue anymore. I think by the time he is strong enough to move again, he will see the wisdom in staying at Mrs. Wheeler's boardinghouse."

Maggie felt an involuntary smile curve her mouth. It just might work, at that. Not only was it a wonderful idea, but it was a chance to beat Jack at his own stubborn game.

Consuela was smiling back. "I do not think Swede would mind staying there, too. He could keep an eye on Señor Jack, and send you word."

Maggie nodded her agreement, and then remembered something else. "Maybe he might even get together with Abby, after all," she said.

Consuela's grin widened. "You do not know? They are betrothed."

"Since when?" Maggie gasped in total surprise.

"Since the night you were kidnapped. I guess no one thought to tell you in all the excitement." Consuela shrugged apologetically.

"I guess not," Maggie murmured, but her mind was on other things. It was perfect. Jack would be properly cared for and also exposed to Swede's and Abby's burgeoning love affair. How long until he remembered that when he had confessed his love to her, she had replied in kind? How long until the memories of the night they had shared in Abby's back bedroom began to haunt him? How long until they drove him back into her arms? Her mind made up, she began issuing orders. "Go ahead and finish packing his clothes. Then go find Swede and explain everything to him. I'll write

Abby a note. We can send a man on ahead with it so Abby will be expecting them."

Consuela nodded her approval and turned to go back into Jack's room. "Consuela," Maggie cautioned, "wipe that grin off your face or else he'll know we're up to something."

Maggie's note to Abby began: "Dear Abby: Once you told me that you owed me a debt. Now I am asking you to repay it. . . ."

Consuela's prediction had been correct. By the time Swede and Jack had arrived at Abby's house in town, Jack was too exhausted even to execute the front stairs, much less put up a fight about having his orders disobeyed.

In spite of his protests, Abby waited on him much the same way Consuela and Maggie had for the next few days while he recovered from his exertions. It was only when Abby assured him that it wasn't any extra bother, especially now that she had Swede around to help with the heavy work, that he realized his foreman had stayed with him.

Jack and Swede had an argument over that in which Jack told Swede he didn't need a guardian, and Swede told Jack to mind his own business, that he was only using Jack as an excuse to stay at Abby's house. Unable to think of a suitable reply for that, Jack let the matter drop, especially when Swede casually mentioned that Abby had set up a cot for him in the storeroom but that he didn't sleep on it very often. Jack already felt guilty, because he had a sneaking suspicion that Swede and the widow would have been married by now if he hadn't gotten himself shot up, so he decided not to press it, and grudgingly let his foreman stay without further protest.

At the ranch Maggie tried to fill the long, empty days by taking a renewed interest in the running of the ranch. To her surprise, she discovered that instead of resenting that, the men seemed to welcome her management. Lee Parker was acting as foreman in Swede's absence, and he filled her in on what had been done. Together, they arranged to drive the cattle that Jack and the men had used to trap Kincaid to the railhead for shipment. Soon the ranch would be back in the black again. Maggie wasn't sure if that were good or bad, realizing that she might have pleaded poverty in luring Jack home. Only her pride kept her from doing so.

Shortly after the cattle had been shipped, Lee broke some rather unpleasant news to her. "Mr. Sinclair, he had some cattle that he'd picked up when he bought out your neighbors," he explained. "We branded them with the new CMC brand, too, and threw 'em together with yours." Maggie could tell by the way he was shifting in his chair that he was going to tell her something he would rather not. She waited patiently. "Swede sent us word yesterday that Mr. Sinclair wants us to cut out the cattle that used to be his and run them back over onto his range."

His range? As if his range and her range were different, Maggie fumed.

"Should we do it?" he asked uncertainty in his voice.

"Of course not," she told him. "At least not until . . . no, don't do it." She had almost said, "until I know whether he's coming back to me or not," but she had caught herself just in time. That was something she had refused to let herself consider. He would come back. He just had to.

Abby sent almost daily reports on Jack's progress, and he seemed to be making a remarkable recovery. After a slight setback caused by his move, he had quickly regained his strength, and Consuela had been right in guessing that he would see the wisdom in living at Abby's. As soon as he was able, he had begun to spend most of the day seated in a rocker on Abby's wide front porch. Gradually, he had begun to take short walks and then longer ones, until he became a familiar sight to the people in town.

What those people in town were saying about Jack's

479

having left his hearth and home to stay in a boardinghouse when he had still had one foot in the grave, Maggie shuddered to think, but she tried not to dwell on it. She and Jack had already given the good folks of Bitterroot so much to talk about that one more scandal couldn't possibly make that much difference.

That the doctor had paid Jack a visit Maggie knew, because he had first called at the ranch, expecting to find his patient still there. He had been nearby on another call and had decided to find out if the rumors that said Jack had survived were true. Maggie would have sold her soul to learn what he had thought of Jack's condition, but of course the doctor didn't bother to return to inform her. His expression had clearly told her his opinion of a woman who would let her husband go off in that condition, and it wasn't very high. Maggie tried not to dwell on that, either.

Jack had been at Abby's more than a month when, one afternoon, Swede came hurrying down the street and up the boardinghouse steps to where Jack was sitting, reading the weekly paper. "Boss, I think you'd better come down to the saloon."

Jack scowled at his foreman. "What on earth for?"

Swede swore briefly as his complexion deepened several shades to crimson. "Billy Kincaid's in there, and I think you'd better hear what he's saying about Renita."

Renita. The memory came to him from some distant place, so far distant that it took him a moment even to recall how he knew the person called Renita. Odd, but since that day he had seen her at Kincaid's, he hadn't thought of her again. He guessed he had supposed that she had left town when Kincaid died.

Jack rose from his comfortable chair, completely aware that this was the first purposeful move he had made in many weeks. "Better take your gun," Swede advised, and Jack felt something stir within him, something vital and alive.

As the two men made their way down the nearly deserted

street, Jack could actually sense the change in himself. For weeks he had been simply drifting, from room to room, from place to place, with no direction, no goal in mind except to get well. For the first time, he began to believe that he might actually have reached that goal. By the time they arrived at the saloon, he was certain of it.

Billy Kincaid was seated at one of the tables, his back to the door so that he did not see them come in. He was engaged in conversation with two strangers.

"You say she's a real looker?" one of the men was asking.

"Prettiest woman you ever laid eyes on," Billy assured him. "Only two dollars. She's upstairs, in the rooms over my office. Only thing, you gotta tell her Kincaid sent you. You tell her Kincaid sent you, and she'll be real nice."

"And we give you the money?" the other man asked doubtfully.

Jack listened to this exchange in mingled horror and disbelief. He couldn't see the boy's face, but he could tell from his voice that Billy Kincaid had come into his own since his uncle's death. *His* office, indeed. Jack cast an incredulous look at Swede.

The blond man nodded gravely. "He's pimping for her, but it's even worse than that. Somebody who'd been up there told me that she's out of her head. She thinks Kincaid is still alive, and that he's coming back for her. She's really bad off, Jack."

Guilt was becoming entirely too familiar to Jack, but he experienced it once again. Here was another person whom he had wronged and who was suffering now because of his selfishness. His body surged with a vitality he had thought lost forever as he considered how best to right this wrong.

He strode purposefully over to where Billy Kincaid sat and very deliberately kicked the chair out from under him. The boy went sprawling and came up trailing a stream of outraged curses. They ceased when he came face-to-face with Jack Sinclair.

Jack raised one eyebrow disdainfully, but Billy was not intimidated. His young face had grown impudent, and he smirked up at Jack. "If you want to see your lady friend again, you're gonna have to pay *me,* now," he gloated.

A gentleman never fought with his fists, so Jack simply gave the boy the back of his hand, the slap coming so suddenly that Billy never even saw it.

"You damned . . ." he bellowed, reaching for the gun he wore strapped to his hip and dragging it from the holster. The unmistakable click of a sixgun cocking stopped him, and he stared in amazement down the barrel of Jack's pearl-handled Colt. He hadn't even seen the man move, much less draw the gun!

Jack's voice was surprisingly cool when he finally spoke. "The only reason I don't simply shoot you where you stand is because scum like you isn't even worth the price of the bullet it would take to put you out of your misery." For a second, the only sound in the room was the gulp when Billy swallowed nervously. "However," Jack continued, "if I ever see your face in this town again, I will make the sacrifice. Do you understand me?"

He might almost have been discussing the prevailing cattle prices, so calm was his voice, but his dark eyes glittered dangerously, and Billy nodded. "You have five minutes to saddle a horse," Jack informed him, holstering the Colt.

Turning on his heel, Jack started back toward the door. Good God, he thought, I'm *alive.* Really alive. His shirt was damp beneath his coat and the blood was singing in his veins, and he hardly even noticed the ever-present ache in his belly.

"JACK!"

Swede's warning came almost too late. Coward that he was, Billy Kincaid had drawn his gun at last, taking his aim at Jack's retreating back. Instinct took over, and Jack drew even as he turned, firing almost blindly at the spot where he had last seen Kincaid standing.

The two shots rang out almost simultaneously, and for a

moment the cloud of gunsmoke fogged the room so that it was impossible to see exactly what had happened. Then a gun clattered to the floor, and Billy Kincaid cried out in anguish, clutching desperately at the blood that had begun to gush from his chest.

Jack waited, knowing how the pain would come, knowing that in another heartbeat he would realize where he had been hit, but heartbeats passed, and he felt nothing.

"Jack? Are you all right?" It was Swede, and it was Swede's hands who turned him, Swede's eyes that examined him from head to foot. "You're all right," he concluded with a relieved sigh, then added very gently, "You can put the gun away now."

Jack looked down at the gun in his hand as if he had never seen it before and then stuffed it quickly back into its holster. He couldn't believe it. Once again he had cheated death. It must just not be his time to go.

Swede grinned crookedly, the only evidence of the fear he had felt in the slight paling of his cheeks. "You'll have to get a new hat, though," he pointed out.

When Jack removed the Stetson and examined it, he discovered a rather large nick in the brim.

"Damn you, Sinclair." Billy's voice was alarmingly weak, but still he found the strength to curse his killer.

Jack looked down at the boy who now lay stretched out on the dirty barroom floor. Someone had tried to staunch the flow of blood with a bandana, but it was useless. The bullet had lodged too close to his heart, and each beat sent out a fresh flow.

Jack and Swede and the bartender and the two strangers Billy had been talking to all stood around and watched him die. There was no doctor to call and nothing else to be done as they watched his life's blood drain away.

Jack had killed men before, better men than Billy Kincaid, surely, and yet none had ever caused him more regret. The tragic waste of a life thrown away so carelessly impressed him as nothing ever had before. He guessed he was getting sentimental in his old age, or perhaps coming so close to death himself had given him a new appreciation for living.

Whatever the cause, Jack found himself impatient with the marshal's questions during the necessary investigation. He was restless, eager to get on with it, without even knowing what "it" was.

Swede sensed this in him, and as the two men left the saloon and began the short walk back through town, he noticed that the gloomy air of lethargy that had hung over Jack since his injury had at last lifted. "You've got some things to do, you know," he suggested tentatively, hoping Jack would take the hint and get on with his life.

His suggestion was unnecessary. "I know," Jack replied. And he did.

Chapter XVII

Before he could consider the future, Jack decided he had to clear up a few things from the past. The most unpleasant of those "things," of course, was Renita.

It was a little later the same day that Jack finally found himself in front of Kincaid's office. He paused on the wooden sidewalk for a long time, simply staring up at the dingy upstairs windows, wondering if what Swede had said were true. He had some difficulty imagining Renita as anything except the proud beauty he had known, even when he remembered the blankness of her eyes the last time he had seen her.

Reluctantly, he at last forced himself to climb the outside staircase. No one answered his first knock, and so he opened the door and went on in. The front room was empty. "Renita?" he called, almost hoping she would not be there to answer.

Faint rustling sounds of movement came from the bedroom, and then the door to that room opened. At first he thought there must be some mistake. This woman could not be Renita, and when she spoke, he was certain of it.

"Kincaid? Is that you?" she asked. The voice was small and whining, almost apologetic. When he did not reply, the figure moved farther into the room, head cocked curiously.

"Jack? What are you doing here?"

It *was* Renita, and the knowledge left him sick and weak. Renita, yes, but she was now no more than a frail shadow of the woman he had known. The luxuriant black hair that had once been her greatest vanity hung in greasy, uncombed tangles down her back. Her dark eyes glittered vacantly up at him, and seemed too large for the frail face that had practically shriveled from its former beauty. She was still wearing that same man's robe that she had been wearing the last time he had seen her, but now it was filthy, and from the clawlike hands that clutched it shut and her sunken cheeks and shadowed eyes, he concluded that she was virtually starving. Whether Billy had neglected to feed her or whether she was simply not interested in eating, Jack had no way of knowing, but he felt a righteous fury, nonetheless.

"You shouldn't be here, Jack. Kincaid won't like it," she said in that odd little voice that didn't sound like hers at all.

"Billy's dead. He won't bother you anymore," Jack assured her gently.

She stared blankly back at him. "Billy? That's too bad," she said vaguely. "Kincaid will be back soon. You'd better go," she urged.

Jack blinked in surprise. Swede had heard right: She did think Kincaid was still alive and that he was coming back. "Renita, Sam Kincaid is dead, too. He's not coming back anymore," he told her, speaking as one would to a small child.

Something flickered in those blank eyes and then was gone. She smiled slightly. "You're teasing me, Jack. Kincaid's not dead. He's coming back. He told me."

She said it with such childlike conviction that he almost hated to disillusion her. "No, he's not, Renita." He reached out a hand to touch her reassuringly, but she dodged it like a wild thing and darted quickly across the room where she cringed in a corner.

"You're lying!" She was upset now, her large eyes,

486

accusing. "He'll come back, and then you'll be sorry! I won't go to bed with you, either," she announced triumphantly, but then she faltered, becoming confused. "Unless he said it was all right . . . sometimes he sends men here and I have to go to bed with them. Billy told me. . . ."

Jack could have wept for her. The proud, vibrant woman he had known might have bartered her charms for a life of ease, but she had never sold herself like a common prostitute. The Kincaids, between them, had destroyed her, grinding her down until she spread her legs in placid obedience for every man who walked up those stairs, and all because she had made the mistake of thinking that she could use Kincaid to get even with Jack. Renita might have made some poor choices in her life, but that one had been tragic. And it was all his fault.

"Kincaid told me that I was to get you dressed and take you over to the hotel. I'm going to buy you supper and get you a room over there. You're supposed to stay over there from now on," he explained slowly, watching her carefully for any reaction.

Her confusion increased. "I . . . I don't have any clothes here," she said uncertainly. "Kincaid tore them. . . ."

Jack suppressed a shudder of revulsion at the pictures that flashed across his imagination, and managed a small smile. "I'll go over to your house and get some for you, then," he offered. "I'll bring someone back to help you, too. You'll wait right here until I come back?" he added. She nodded, and he turned to go, but then remembered something else. "Kincaid also said you aren't to have any more men up here, so if anyone comes but me, don't let them in. Do you understand?" She nodded again, and he turned slowly, hating to leave her alone, but knowing it was necessary.

Swede was waiting for him at the bottom of the stairs. "It's even worse than you heard," Jack told him grimly. "I want to take her over to the hotel and get her something to eat, but she doesn't even have any clothes up there. I'm going over to her place to get some."

Swede fell into step beside him as they walked the short distance to Renita's shack. "Swede, she needs a woman to help her get cleaned up. Do you think Abby . . ." Jack let the sentence trail off. He knew how difficult it would be to get a decent woman up there to help Renita. She had been a pariah even when she had been a semirespectable mistress. Now that she was a common whore, he'd be lucky to find anyone even to spit on her. He could sense Swede's reluctance, but the foreman shrugged.

"We can ask her," Swede mumbled.

In the end, Abby did come, and so did the marshal. Abby had pointed out that if Renita was as bad off as Jack said, she would need someone to take care of her, someplace where she would be safe and where no one could take advantage of her as Billy Kincaid had done. That meant an institution, and that meant getting the law involved.

When Jack thought about it, he recalled just such an institution, a private one where the conditions were good and where she might even get well, given time. It took a while to make the arrangements, and in the meantime, Jack made sure that Renita was protected. He got her a room at the hotel, ignoring the disapproving looks Festus gave him, and made certain that she got three square meals a day in the hotel dining room. He even managed to hire a woman to accompany her to her destination when the time came to send her.

Swede and Abby watched all this with an odd combination of approval and disapproval. It wasn't proper, not at all, for a married man to take such an active interest in the welfare of his former mistress. On the other hand, it was so wonderful to see him taking an interest in anything, that they could not complain. Swede was more than delighted to carry out Jack's instructions in the matter, thankful beyond words that Jack was finally giving him some.

Abby simply neglected to mention the role that Jack was

playing in Renita's situation in her reports to Maggie, judging, correctly, that Maggie might not be as pleased as she and Swede were. Abby did tell her, however, that Jack's mental attitude was improving daily, hinting broadly that soon, very soon indeed, he would be completely himself again.

Maggie wasn't certain exactly what that might mean for her, and she was afraid even to guess. With every day that passed she grew more restless, more concerned that Jack might never return to her. She wrestled with the impulse to go to him, arguing almost daily with Consuela on the subject, while all the time she knew that the housekeeper was right and that she would have to wait until Jack had shown some indication that he was ready and willing to discuss their marriage.

At night she slept in Jack's big bed, hating the huge emptiness of it, but comforting herself with the memories of their last night together.

Jack's nights, too, were haunted by memories. He never entered Abby's back bedroom without remembering how he had found Maggie huddled there in the bed. When he tried to sleep, he imagined Maggie's body next to his, her face alight with desire, her sweet mouth curved into a tempting smile.

The doctor had warned him that he might never recover fully, might never again be the man he was. He had even suggested, however obliquely, that Jack might encounter some sexual difficulties. Jack thought of that often when he awakened in a cold sweat from some erotic dream of Maggie, his manhood swollen and throbbing with an ache that matched the one caused by Crescent's bullet. He was encountering sexual difficulties all right, but they were all of his own making.

Something had to be done, and soon. That much he knew. What he did not know, however, was what that something was. A lot depended on Maggie and how she felt, of course— if she would be willing to remain married to him, if she could possibly ever forgive him, and then, somehow, learn to love him. The fact that she hadn't come to visit him, or even come to visit Abby, was not encouraging. Of course, when he was being rational, he realized that he had made it perfectly clear he didn't want to see her, and what could he expect, anyway? Unfortunately, he wasn't always completely rational when he was thinking about Maggie, and so, each day, he managed to find another excuse for not riding out to the ranch to see her.

At first, it was easy. He couldn't ride and didn't relish being driven by someone else. Then Swede brought a docile mount from the ranch, and shamed him into mounting up. After that, he had ridden a little farther each day until he had built up his stamina. Now he knew that he had no legitimate excuse, so he made up phony ones: The sun was too hot, he was expecting a telegram, and on and on.

Swede pressed his lips together in a tight line and let him get away with it for a time. Then one day he sauntered up to where Jack sat sunning himself on Abby's porch and remarked, "There's something over to town I think you ought to see."

By now Jack was used to Swede's cryptic temptations and recognized them for what they were: tricks to get him up off his posterior and back out into the world. Seeing no reason to refuse, Jack rose lazily. "Shall I bring my gun?" he asked, only a trace of irony in his voice.

Swede never even blinked. "Not unless you plan to shoot yourself," he replied, clumping back down the porch steps.

Jack shrugged and followed. He didn't pay much attention to where they were going, and Swede seemed even less talkative than usual, so they walked in silence until they reached the far side of the livery stable where the corrals were situated.

"There she is," Swede said, pointing toward the nearest corral.

At first Jack saw only a lovely little mare trotting restlessly

490

around the enclosure. It took a moment for the significance of that sight to dawn on him. "My God," he breathed, stepping forward to get a closer look. "When did she arrive?"

"She got to the railhead about a week ago. I sent Harvey to fetch her. He just got back a little while ago." Swede paused to roll a cigarette so he could lower his head. He didn't want Jack to see the look of triumph he knew must be on his face. If this didn't do it, nothing would.

Curious now, the mare trotted over to where the two men stood, and whinnied a greeting. A slow smile spread across Jack's face as he reached a hand out to her. Cautiously, she approached, encouraged by the friendly sounds he was making. Her delicate nostrils flared to catch his scent, and pleased with what she learned about him, she allowed him to pat her slender neck.

As Jack stroked the velvet hide, he marveled at the familiarity of the color. It was the same as Maggie's hair. How well they would go together. The mare had Maggie's playfulness, and her spirit, too. He could see it in the fine, wide-set eyes, and in the way the mare was nuzzling him now, searching for a treat.

This was it, then, the excuse for which he had been looking. With sudden clarity, he realized the reason for his hesitancy to return to the ranch. He had not really been hunting for excuses to stay away, but rather for a legitimate excuse to go, one that would justify him if he discovered that Maggie was waiting with a shotgun to send him on his way, an excuse to hide behind if he needed to salvage his pride.

Just to be on the safe side, though, he wouldn't tell Swede he was going. If things didn't work out, he didn't want to have to come back and explain to Swede why they hadn't. He'd wait until afternoon.

All day Maggie had had the funniest feeling. She couldn't exactly put her finger on it. She wasn't even sure if it was a good feeling or a bad feeling. All she knew was that it somehow concerned Jack, and she wasn't going to let another day go by without seeing for herself how he was doing.

When she had announced her plans to Consuela, however, all hell had broken loose, and the two women had had a terrible quarrel.

"*He* left *you*," Consuela had ruthlessly pointed out. "You cannot return to him. It is his place to come to you. Have you no pride?"

Maggie had angrily replied that she didn't give a damn for her pride, that she couldn't talk to it, or sleep with it, or make love to it, so what good was it? They had gone on like that for quite a while, until finally Consuela had realized that Maggie was near hysteria. In an attempt to pacify her, the housekeeper had promised to go into town herself that very afternoon and find out exactly what was happening with Jack. She would even, she promised faithfully, drop some very large hints that Jack would be quite welcome out at the CMC. Mollified, if not quite happy, Maggie had agreed to the plan.

That was how she came to be seated on the front porch all alone when Jack rode into the ranch yard. At first Maggie had not allowed herself to believe that it was Jack, even though she knew that no other man alive sat a horse the way he did. From the instant she had spotted the two horses in the distance, she had sensed that it was he, but even when he was near enough for her to be certain, she could not quite admit it for fear that it was only her own longing that had identified him.

She had been vaguely aware that he had another horse on a lead rope, but had paid no attention, being unwilling to take her eyes off his beloved figure for even an instant. He rode with the same ease and arrogance that he always had, and from his seat, she would never have guessed that he had so recently suffered such a severe wound.

He wasn't riding the stallion, of course. That would be a little too much, even for Jack, but still he was in complete control of the animal. He pulled up in front of the barn, pausing a moment to look around before dismounting.

The place looked exactly as he remembered it, although why he should have expected otherwise, he had no idea. Perhaps it was because he himself felt so changed.

Maggie was there, on the porch, he knew. He had seen the bright flash of her dress almost as soon as the ranchhouse had come into view, but he did not dare ride up there, at least not yet. He needed a little time simply to get used to being there again. It was odd the way he felt riding into the yard, as if he had come home at last. He knew he had no right whatsoever to think of the CMC as home, and yet he could not help the sensation of peace that had come over him. It was, he supposed, a place that got into your blood, whether your roots lay halfway across the country, as his did, or were buried deep in the Texas soil, the way Maggie's were.

He was a little tired from the long ride, but the anticipation of seeing Maggie had quickened his blood, helping him forget the mild fatigue and the aching of long-unused muscles. Taking a determined breath, he swung down from his saddle and began tending to the little mare who had followed him from town.

If Maggie had had any doubts about Jack's recovery, they were put to rest when she saw the ease with which he dismounted. A man suffering great pain would never move with such grace, and she let out the breath she had been unconsciously holding. She still stood on the porch, having risen from her chair to see him better, and then having walked over to the edge of the porch, drawn by the force of his presence. She watched him walk over to the horse he had been leading. She could see now that it was a mare, and a beauty at that. With gentle hands he led the animal to the corral gate, and after slipping off the hackamore that bound her, he turned her loose into the empty enclosure.

Maggie watched, transfixed, as he observed the little mare skip away, exploring the limits of her new environment. It was then that Maggie realized he had not yet made any move to come to her. She remembered vividly what Consuela had said about waiting for him to come to her, but damn it, he had come all the way from town. Couldn't she go the last two hundred feet? Without bothering to dispute the matter with herself any further, she started down the stairs and across the yard, concerned only that she not impulsively break into a run in her eagerness.

It was the longest walk she had ever taken. Her instinctive smile of gladness soon felt frozen on her face as she worried over why he made no move to meet her, but simply stood there by the corral, watching the little mare. She tried to read his expression, but he had been careful to mask whatever feelings he was having at this moment, so that she could only guess at what they might be. Taking comfort in the fact that he was standing tall and straight, as she had once feared he never would again, she concentrated in placing one foot in front of the other in a dignified manner until she stood within arm's length of him.

"Hello, Jack," she said, proud that she sounded almost normal in spite of the way her heart was trying to hammer its way out of her rib cage and her lungs seemed no longer capable of supplying her body with quite as much air as she needed.

Ever so slowly, Jack turned to face her. He had not dared to watch her approach for fear his resolve would break and he would do something totally foolish, like running to her and falling at her feet. Allowing himself a full minute in which to simply look at her, he did not speak at first. Instead his hungry eyes feasted on the sight of her, devouring the vision of the auburn curls that tossed freely in the Texas breeze, the eyes that were an uncertain shade of brown at the moment, the sweet mouth that was fixed into a polite little smile, the hands that twisted nervously into the fabric of her

494

skirt. She was wearing one of those flowered dresses that made her look so young and innocent yet hugged the curves he remembered only too well, proving that she was not quite so young or innocent as he wanted to believe. "Hello, Maggie."

She was different, somehow, and at first he could not decide quite what had changed. She might have been thinner than he remembered, but it was more than that. And then he knew. It was the same thing that he had noticed that last morning when he had left her standing on the porch and ridden out with the men: She had grown up. When he put it into words, it sounded almost trite. Had he expected her to remain the silly child he had first encountered? Could he have fallen so hopelessly in love with that silly child? Of course not. Somewhere along the line she had become a woman, without his even having noticed, although he must somehow have been aware of it on an unconscious level.

For the first time, he knew a spark of hope. Perhaps this new Maggie could understand. Perhaps she could forgive him. Perhaps . . .

"You're looking well." Maggie had been casting about helplessly for something to say. She didn't want to ask him how he was. Except for the fact that he was still too thin, he looked wonderful, but that might only have been because she was so very happy to see him. His color was good, though, and she could still see the way he had swung so effortlessly down from his saddle, even though he must surely be stiff from such a long ride.

"So are you," he replied, wondering what she would say if he told her exactly how good she looked to him.

Another uneasy silence fell as they continued to stare at each other, each wondering how to say the things they knew must be said. The mare watched them expectantly, and when they did not pay her the attention she felt she deserved, she whinnied, startling them both.

"That's a beautiful mare," Maggie remarked, feeling that it was a ridiculous thing to say, but unable to think of anything else.

Jack glanced at the mare, a little surprised because he had completely forgotten her in the thrill of seeing Maggie again, and feeling more than a little stupid since the horse was his main excuse for being here. "She's yours," he said, enjoying the play of emotions that swept across Maggie's expressive face.

Surprise and then pleasure brought a bloom of color to her cheeks, and then puzzlement wrinkled her brow. "Where . . . ?" she started to ask, but before she could speak the question she knew the answer. The horse had come from Virginia, from the Virginia Sinclairs, and he must have sent for it especially for her.

Unaware that she had already figured it out, Jack explained, "I sent to my cousin for her. I told him to choose the best. She was to be . . . your wedding present."

She realized then that he had ordered the horse months ago, probably quite soon after they had married. Had he hoped to please her? Had he *wanted* to please her even then? She recalled quite clearly what Swede had told her about how Jack had loved her right from the start. Was this beautiful filly proof of that? "She's Arabian, isn't she?" Maggie asked, not really caring. The animal might have had two heads for all that it mattered. The important thing was that Jack had been thinking of her even then.

"Yes," he replied, as by mutual consent they both stepped over to the corral fence. He pointed out the "Jibbahs," the slight protrusions over the eyes that indicated intelligence, and the distinctive "dished" face and arched neck.

Maggie listened with half an ear, wondering if Jack had mentioned to his cousin that his bride had auburn hair or if it were merely a coincidence that the mare matched her perfectly. Maggie reached out a hand, coaxing the filly over with her voice.

The mare trotted over, her fine nostrils flaring, but she

took one whiff of Maggie and snorted, dancing away. Then, as if to tease, she trotted back, ignoring Maggie's outstretched palm, and reached out to nuzzle Jack.

Maggie laughed delightedly while he backed off, a bit embarrassed, yet pleased beyond belief to hear that musical sound. "She needs to learn some manners," he commented.

"And so do I," Maggie decided, suddenly inspired. "I haven't even thanked you for my gift." Impulsively, she went to him, and rising quickly on tiptoe, she placed a quick kiss on his mouth.

Jack stood perfectly still, all color drained momentarily from his face, and Maggie thought he might almost have been carved from marble. She had no way of knowing the effort that it took for him to stand that way, or how very much will it took for him not to touch her, not to kiss her back. If he had, well, he probably would have ended up dragging her into the barn and tumbling her right there on the hay. Instead, he managed to say, very hoarsely, "Maggie, we need to talk."

Irritated, relieved and even a little frightened, Maggie could only nod her consent. "Shall we go up to the house?" she asked after a moment.

He made a small gesture with his hand indicating that she should precede him, and so she did, wondering every step of the way what he was thinking, what he would say, and how she would get her way if he were unwilling to resume their marriage.

Once before when he had come to talk with her, she had chosen to meet with him in the office. This time, without hesitation, she entered the door to the front room. They would definitely not be discussing business at this particular meeting.

"Would you like to sit down?" she asked automatically, knowing full well she could not have remained seated under the circumstances.

Jack did not even seem to have heard her. Instead, he was

looking around the room in much the same way he had looked around the ranch yard when he had first arrived. He was experiencing that same sensation of having come home again. To cover his uneasiness, he strode to the fireplace, as if fascinated with the items on the broad mantel, and then reached up and moved one pewter candlestick infinitesimally, as if making that slight adjustment had been the sole reason for his visit.

Maggie waited patiently, eager to know what he would say, but dreading it nevertheless, in case he said the wrong thing.

At last he spoke. "I told you once that if you wanted it, I would give you a divorce." He did not seem to hear the small sound of protest that involuntarily escaped her. "I've spoken to Judge Harris about it, and he said it would be difficult and expensive, but that it could very likely be done, if that's what you want." His fingers reached up and moved the candlestick again, as if he were completely unconcerned with her reply, as if his blood were not thundering in his ears so loudly he had begun to wonder whether he would even hear that reply, and as if his very life did not depend on her answer.

Maggie fought her way out of the daze of pain his words had caused, forcing herself to remember that he had placed the burden of choice on her. "Is it what *you* want, Jack?" she asked, her voice thick with the tears that she refused to shed until she knew for certain.

He looked at her then, straightening to his full height with all the dignity bred into him for generations. His face had been wiped clean of all expression, but his dark eyes seemed almost to glow with the intensity of the feelings he was trying so hard to hide. "I want you to be happy, Maggie," he said simply.

She waited. She would have liked for him to say that he loved her, that he wanted to come back to her, but she supposed that was too much to ask. The Virginia Sinclairs would never beg. The very fact that he was here at all was somewhat of a miracle, and she would have to content herself with that. The Texas Colsons didn't beg, either, but they weren't above issuing orders.

"Then I suppose we'll have to stay married," she concluded, amazing even herself with the steadiness of her voice. She waited as the shock of understanding spread across his face, before adding, "And I think it's time we started living together as man and wife again, too."

Something very close to pain flickered across his face. "Are you sure?"

She smiled at the trace of humility in the question. "Very sure," she assured him.

A long moment passed, and just when Maggie began to fear he would not come, he came, scooping her into a bone-crushing embrace, which she returned in kind. He held her that way for almost an eternity before he finally bent to take the kiss she offered. His lips were surprisingly gentle, almost tentative at first, as if he were testing her response, until she drew away just a bit and whispered, "I love you."

He responded with the force of an avalanche, overwhelming her with a sensory onslaught. Hands and lips and arms and tongues touched and explored, seeking out remembered delights and questing for new ones. Just when Maggie thought she might faint from sheer joy, he drew away, but before she could even object, he had scooped her up into his arms.

"Jack!" she squealed, "you'll hurt yourself!"

He had noticed a slight twinge as healing tissues objected to the strain, but he ignored it. They weren't going far. He grinned down into her lovely little face. "You'd better be worried that I might hurt *you*," he warned.

Her eyes widened in surprise, but he noticed that they were very green, and then she grinned back at him. He almost stumbled at the message in that smile, and quickened his pace. Maggie buried her face in the curve of his neck, inhaling the musky scent of him before stretching up to catch his earlobe between her teeth. Encouraged by his groan of response, she traced the shell of his ear with her tongue, completely oblivious of the fact that they had arrived at their destination until he set her on her feet.

The slam of the door when he kicked it shut startled her into noticing that they were in the bedroom, Jack's bedroom, *their* bedroom. Maggie glanced around, allowing her gaze to linger for a long moment on the oversized bed. Forcing her face into a mask of shock, she protested, quite convincingly, "Jack! It's broad daylight!" As an added touch, she placed a hand over her heart, and then fanned herself slightly, as if she might be coming down with a case of the vapors.

Jack's mustache tilted as he watched her performance appreciatively. "I don't believe it is against the law to . . . ah . . . enjoy ourselves in the daylight," he remarked, and then his face grew suddenly serious. "I don't think I'll ever be able to believe you've really forgiven me until you let me love you again."

Maggie thought her heart might burst with mingled joy and pain, but she did not want to mar the happiness of the moment with any solemnity. Instead of weeping the tears that clamored to be released, she drew herself up and gave a martyred sigh. "Well, then, I suppose I'll have to make the sacrifice."

Even before Jack had caught the betraying glint in her eye, she had her bodice unbuttoned, but before she could slip it off her shoulders, he was on to her game.

"You little witch," he growled, picking her up again and tossing her onto the bed.

The next few minutes passed in wild frenzy as clothing was removed without much regard for fastenings or even comfort. "Ouch!" Maggie complained at one point. "This would be a lot easier if we were standing up, you know."

"I don't think I could stand up now," Jack replied,

running a hand across the silky plane of her abdomen until his fingers tangled into the curls below.

"Neither could I," Maggie gasped, experiencing the familiar flutter of desire that turned her bones to jelly.

"Although we might try it that way sometime," Jack murmured.

Maggie's shocked reply was lost in a strangled cry as Jack's mouth closed over one swollen nipple.

They came together in an explosion of passion, all reason for tenderness forgotten in their mutual need. Abstinence proved to be a powerful aphrodisiac, eliminating the need for technique or seduction.

Maggie welcomed him home, offering him the haven of her body as a resting place where he could finally find the peace he craved. He entered that haven with a relief that far surpassed any physical release he had ever known, and he left within her a living part of himself, a promise of forever.

Their blissful union was over much too quickly to satisfy their desire for renewal, but they had no choice except to rest until their bodies were again able to enact their love. In the meantime, they simply clung to each other.

"Tell me again why you married me," she asked. She was stretched out beside him, her body half covering his, enjoying the solid feel of him beneath her and the idle play of his hands over her skin.

Jack scowled down at her in mock irritation. "I married you because I wanted to steal your ranch, and I was afraid that if I turned you loose, you'd cause me no end of trouble. Little did I know that marrying you would only make things worse."

Maggie giggled delightedly. "You were right, you know. I *was* going to make trouble for you." His scowl turned to skepticism. "It's true," she insisted. "I was going to take the money you paid me for the ranch and marry a rich man, and he was going to help me get the CMC back."

Jack's features settled into the cool, expressionless mask

she had hoped never to see again. "Anyone I know?" he asked with apparent unconcern.

It took her a minute to figure out what he was talking about, and then she realized with a start that he was *jealous* of this anonymous "rich man." "Of course not, silly," she assured him. "It wasn't anyone I know, either. It was just a ridiculous idea that I had when I was young and foolish." Now that she thought of it, she could hardly believe that it had been such a short time ago that she had been hatching her plots for revenge on Jack Sinclair.

"Then, when you made me marry you," she went on, raking her fingers lightly through the mat of raven hair on his chest, "I decided to make your life miserable."

"You succeeded there," he commented with exaggerated lightness.

"You weren't exactly fun to live with yourself," she reminded him with a pout that made him smile.

The smile she returned to him held a promise that those days were gone for good, but then a small scowl creased her forehead. "Why did you leave me?" she asked.

Jack winced at the pain he saw in her eyes, and only then did he realize how much she really did love him, and how much he had hurt her. "I had this ridiculous idea that I couldn't make you love me unless I was well and strong, and I was afraid I might never be again. I couldn't stand having you pity me."

"Oh, Jack," she sighed, the sweet smile on her lips belying the tears that glistened in her eyes, "I guess we were both young and foolish, weren't we?"

"That's over now," he told her, placing a small kiss on her nose.

Maggie was smiling up into his face, all her love shining in her eyes, when suddenly, she heard him gasp and felt his whole body stiffen. When she looked down, she saw that her wandering hand had touched his scar. In their earlier haste, she had had no time or opportunity to examine his body, and his wound had been the farthest thing from her mind. Now she did examine it, cringing at the angry red blotch that marred his perfection.

"Did I hurt you?" she asked in genuine concern, withdrawing her fingers from the spot.

"No, no," he said, forcing himself to relax again beneath her touch. "It doesn't hurt, at least, not exactly. It's just . . . when you touched it . . ." He could not find the words to explain how her touching the scar had somehow triggered all his guilt feelings about the way he had treated her. "It does hurt sometimes, of course," he explained, hoping to divert her attention. "The doctor said it will probably always bother me from time to time." He gave her a rueful grin. "It will remind me never to treat you badly again."

Maggie uttered a tiny cry of protest, and this time she did not bother to hide the tears that sprang to her eyes. In Maggie's opinion, they had both suffered far too much already, and the last thing she wanted was for Jack to bear any additional burdens of guilt. "I don't want you to hurt anymore," she told him.

He watched, fascinated, as one tiny tear spilled from her eye and glistened on her cheek in the afternoon sunlight like a small, very precious jewel. Then, rising up, she lowered her head and pressed a gentle kiss onto his scar. As he had once done for her, she sought to soothe away his hurts with her love, and when she lifted her head, his own eyes were suspiciously moist.

"I love you, little witch," he rasped. "I love you so very much."

His kiss was infinitely sweet, and it went on and on, drugging them both until all thoughts of anything except their own passions vanished. Jack's hands on her were amazingly gentle, almost worshipful, and he made love to her with a care bordering on reverence. Their first urgency now sated, they could afford to linger, and linger they did,

503

over every sensitive spot, over every little pleasure.

The heat built slowly, slowly, kindled with delicate touches and feather-light kisses that teased and tormented. The radiance of their union seemed to illuminate the room with a golden glory that bathed their flesh and then melded them into one.

Maggie thought she must surely be glowing as she held Jack to her heart and listened to his whispered declaration of love and devotion. He bared his heart to her the way he had moments earlier bared his soul in the nakedness of his physical need of her.

The depths of her own feelings went beyond words, and even beyond tears, and so she simply cradled him to her, telling him with her body how very much she adored him. Sometime later they fell asleep, bodies still entwined in the twilight of their passion.

"Señora! Señora!"

The summons came to Maggie through the heavy veil of sleep, but she answered its urgency instinctively. "In here, Consuela," she called, only really awakening when she felt the vibration of Jack's surprised start rumble through her own body.

"What the . . ." he muttered, half rising in alarm.

Before either of them could get their bearings, the door flew open. "Señora! Señor Jack, he . . ." Consuela had burst into the room in a flurry of skirts and flailing hands, but she stopped dead at the sight of the couple on the bed.

The bedclothes were in a hopeless tangle and had been pushed halfway onto the floor, but Jack managed with one frantic jerk to free enough of one blanket to cover them both fairly adequately, mumbling curses as he did so.

"Madre de Dios," Consuela murmured as her sharp eyes took in the scene. Clothes were scattered quite literally everywhere. One of Jack's socks had caught on a bedpost

nd Maggie's pantalettes were hanging from a picture on the
ther side of the room. Everything else had landed either on
he floor or on various pieces of furniture in what could only
e described as a scandalous manner.

By the time Consuela had made a mental note of every
etail, she had managed to puff herself up to the extremes of
isapproval. Crossing her arms over her rather ample
osom, she glared down at the couple. "Are you all right,
eñora?" she asked with some asperity.

Jack opened his mouth to demand to know why she
houldn't be, but Maggie's stifled giggle stopped him. "I've
ever been better, Consuela," she gleefully informed the
ousekeeper.

Startled, Jack glanced down at his wife, taking in her
npish grin. To his horror, he felt himself flush. Whether it
as from embarrassment or pleasure, he did not take the
me to decide. Instead, he turned back to Consuela with
enewed outrage at her intrusion. "Was there something you
anted?" he inquired through gritted teeth.

Consuela nodded solemnly, desperately trying to conceal
knowing smile. "Si, we go to town to see you today, and
eñor Swede, he say you are disappeared. No one can find
ou. He think maybe you have gone to see the señora, but we
id not see you on the road." She paused, a look of
ccusation on her round face.

Jack did blush at that. "I . . . I took a shortcut," he
ammered in uncharacteristic chagrin. He was loath to
dmit that he had come cross country because he hadn't
anted to meet anyone he knew on the road and have to
xplain where he was going. Consequently, he had missed
ee and Consuela.

Plainly, Consuela did not accept this statement, but his
lare of defiance dared her to question him. It was a dare she
ecided to forego. "We were very worried," she chastened,
lancing around the room again with a look that said he had
ome nerve, enjoying himself like that when people were

505

combing the countryside looking for him.

Maggie stifled another giggle. "You'd better send someone to town to tell Swede that Jack's all right, then," Maggie advised with a smile. "You can tell him that Jack is just exactly where he should be."

Consuela didn't bother to hide her knowing smile. *"Sí señora,"* she said. With one last, telling look around the room, she started for the door, pausing just before closing it to ask, "Should I bring your supper on a tray?"

Jack's sense of propriety dictated that he say no, but Maggie overruled him. "Yes, that would be an excellent idea," she decided, giving Jack a provocative look that quenched all thoughts of propriety.

"And Consuela," he added as the housekeeper was closing the door behind herself. "This time, *knock* before you come in."

Author's Note

The battle between the cowman and the "nestor" was long
and often bloody. For a time it looked as if the cowman
would win by default, for even the forces of nature, or rather
the vagaries of nature, had conspired against the farmer,
making it impossible for him to raise his crops in the arid
southwest. Progress, however, in the form of improved
methods of irrigation, suddenly changed the odds in the
farmer's favor. That progress, combined with the invention
of the windmill, which could pump water into places where
water had never been before, and the barbed wire fence,
which would even allow the farmer and cowman to live side
by side in relative peace, ended the age-old struggle once and
for all.

There are two schools of thought on the origin of the word
"nestor." In *Western Words* (University of Oklahoma Press,
1981), Ramon F. Adams says, "The term was applied with
contempt by the cattleman of the Southwest to any early
homesteader who began tilling the soil in the range country.
Viewed from a ridge, the early nester's [sic] home, with its
little patch of brush cleared and stacked in a circular form to
protect his first feed patch from range cattle, looked like a
gigantic bird's nest." On the other hand, in *The Look of the
Old West* (Bonanza Books, 1960), Foster-Harris says,

507

"'Nestors' . . . were probably given this name ironically after the old Greek counselor named Nestor in *The Iliad,* meaning 'wiseacres,' and not because of any connection with nests." I have arbitrarily chosen the more literary spelling. Please forgive me if I erred.

As some of you may already have noticed, Jack Sinclair bears a striking resemblance to Jason Vance, the villain of my first book, *Texas Treasure.* Several people have mentioned to me how much they liked Vance, and I must admit I share their admiration. Jack Sinclair is the man Vance might have been if he had set his sights a little higher.

I love to hear from my readers, and always try to answer every letter personally.

Regards

Victoria "Vicki" Thompson

P. O. Box 1374
Hightstown, NJ 08520

If you enjoyed this book we have a special offer for you. Become a charter member of the ZEBRA HISTORICAL ROMANCE HOME SUBSCRIPTION SERVICE and...

Get a
FREE
Zebra Historical Romance
(A $3.95 value) No Obligation

Now that you have read a Zebra Historical Romance we're sure you'll want more of the passion and sensuality, the desire and dreams and fascinating historical settings that make these novels the favorites of so many women. So we have made arrangements for you to receive a *FREE* book ($3.95 value) and preview 4 brand new Zebra Historical Romances each month.

Join the Zebra
Home Subscription Service—
Free Home Delivery

By joining our Home Subscription Service you'll never have to worry about missing a title. You'll automatically get the romance, the allure, the attraction, that make Zebra Historical Romances so special.

Each month you'll receive 4 brand new Zebra Historical Romance novels as soon as they are published. Look them over *Free* for 10 days. If you're not delighted simply return them and owe nothing. But if you enjoy them as much as we think you will, you'll pay *only* $3.50 each and save 45¢ over the cover price. (You save a total of $1.80 each month.) *There is no shipping and handling charge or other hidden charges.*

—— *Fill Out the Coupon* ——

Start your subscription now and start saving. Fill out the coupon and mail it *today*. You'll get your FREE book along with your first month's books to preview.